Tom Robbins' New National Bestseller
JITTERBUG PERFUME

"*Jitterbug* is a crazy, jazzed-up jambalaya of gems, trifles, tidbits and practical jokes. Our language wasn't meant to do the things Robbins persuades it to, but it is the better for it. This wild comic rip through eternity and beyond shows some of the most disarming wit and original writing around. *Jitterbug* should make you dance—maybe not jitterbug, but shimmy at least—with joy."—*Detroit News*

"Robbins again celebrates the joy of individual expression and self-reliance. He lays before us the time honored warts and hairs of the world's philosophies—problems with religion, war, politics, family, marriage and sex—and leaves no twist or turn unstoned."—*Saturday Review*

"*Jitterbug Perfume* has a large and exotic cast of characters, all of whom are interested in immortality and/or perfume . . . Lovingly plotted, with every conceivable loose end nailed down tight . . . But I've forgotten the *beets*! It would be hard to find any other book that even mentions beets, yet this intricate book, about perfume and immortality, has beets on nearly every page. Why? Go see for yourself; you'll have a good time."—*Washington Post Book World*

"Robbins is still in top form, still mixing the lunatic and the thoughtful—or rather, doing a literary watusi up every page and jitterbugging back down. . . . The season's most outlandish and uproarious book."—*Publishers Weekly*

JITTERBUG
PERFUME

TOM
ROBBINS

BANTAM BOOKS
NEW YORK · TORONTO · LONDON · SYDNEY · AUCKLAND

FOR DONNA AND THE WATER MUSIC

*for those whose letters I still
haven't answered*

JITTERBUG PERFUME
Bantam hardcover edition / December 1984
Bantam paperback edition / November 1985
6 printings through March 1989

ISBN 0-553-26844-9

Published simultaneously in the United States and Canada

*Bantam Books are published by Bantam Books, a division of Bantam
Doubleday Dell Publishing Group, Inc. Its trademark, consisting of
the words ''Bantam Books'' and the portrayal of a rooster, is Registered
in U.S. Patent and Trademark Office and in other countries. Marca
Registrada. Bantam Books, 666 Fifth Avenue, New York, New York 10103.*

PRINTED IN THE UNITED STATES OF AMERICA

KR   15   14   13   12   11   10   9   8   7

The author is grateful to his agent and friend, Phoebe Larmore; to his intrepid editor, Alan Rinzler; to Laren Elizabeth Stover, who passed him fragrance-industry secrets in lipsticked envelopes; and to Jessica Maxwell, whose ancestor once owned a perfume shop in New Orleans, and who traded him that shop for a flying conch shell.

The distinctive human problem from time immemorial has been the need to spiritualize human life, to lift it onto a special immortal plane, beyond the cycles of life and death that characterize all other organisms.

—ERNEST BECKER

The history of civilization is the story of man's emancipation from a lot that was harsh, brutish, and short. Every step of that upward climb to a sophisticated way of life has been paralleled by a corresponding advance in the art of perfumery.

—ERIC MAPLE

Rage, rage against the dying of the light.

—DYLAN THOMAS

(And) always smell as nice as possible.

—LYNDA BARRY

TODAY'S SPECIAL

THE BEET IS THE MOST INTENSE of vegetables. The radish, admittedly, is more feverish, but the fire of the radish is a cold fire, the fire of discontent not of passion. Tomatoes are lusty enough, yet there runs through tomatoes an undercurrent of frivolity. Beets are deadly serious.

Slavic peoples get their physical characteristics from potatoes, their smoldering inquietude from radishes, their seriousness from beets.

The beet is the melancholy vegetable, the one most willing to suffer. You can't squeeze blood out of a *turnip* . . .

The beet is the murderer returned to the scene of the crime. The beet is what happens when the cherry finishes with the carrot. The beet is the ancient ancestor of the autumn moon, bearded, buried, all but fossilized; the dark green sails of the grounded moon-boat stitched with veins of primordial plasma; the kite string that once connected the moon to the Earth now a muddy whisker drilling desperately for rubies.

The beet was Rasputin's favorite vegetable. You could see it in his eyes.

In Europe there is grown widely a large beet they call the *mangel-wurzel*. Perhaps it is *mangel-wurzel* that we see in Rasputin. Certainly there is *mangel-wurzel* in the music of Wagner, although it is another composer whose name begins, B-e-e-t——.

Of course, there are white beets, beets that ooze sugar water instead of blood, but it is the red beet with which we are concerned; the variety that blushes and swells like a hemorrhoid, a hemorrhoid for which there is no cure. (Actually, there is one remedy: commission a potter to make you a ceramic asshole—and when you aren't sitting on it, you can use it as a bowl for borscht.)

An old Ukrainian proverb warns, "A tale that begins with a beet will end with the devil."

That is a risk we have to take.

SEATTLE

PRISCILLA LIVED IN A STUDIO APARTMENT. It was called a "studio" apartment because art is supposed to be glamorous and landlords have a vested interest in making us believe that artists prefer to sleep in their workrooms. Real artists almost never live in studio apartments. There isn't enough space, and the light is all wrong. Clerks live in studio apartments. File clerks, shop clerks, law clerks, community college students, elderly widows, and unmarried waitresses such as Priscilla.

The building in which this particular studio apartment donned its false beret was built during the Great Depression. In Seattle there are many such buildings, anointing their bricks in the rain on densely populated hillsides between Lake Washington and Elliott Bay. Architecturally, its plain facade and straight lines echoed the gown Eleanor Roosevelt wore to the inaugural ball, while its interior walls still reproduced faithfully the hues of the split pea mush dished up in hundreds of soup kitchens. Over the years, the building had been so lived in that it had acquired a life of its own. Every toilet bowl gurgled like an Italian tenor with a mouthful of Lavoris, and the refrigerators made noises at night like buffalo grazing.

Most older studio apartments—the ones in those buildings of New Deal brick—harbored odors as definitive as their colors and sounds, odors arrived at through generations of

salmon cakes frying and broccoli boiling, but here was where
Priscilla's apartment differed. It smelled of chemicals—less
mephitic than sweet—and it was that *smell* that leaped to
greet her, like a cooped-up pooch, when she let herself in on
a weary midnight.

The first thing she did after switching on the overhead light
was to kick off her low-heeled waitress shoes. The second
thing she did was to stub a toe on a table leg. The table, at
which innumerable widows had sat down to canasta, shuddered paroxysmally, causing beakers of chemicals to rattle
and sway. Fortunately, merely a few drops of their contents
were lost.

Priscilla flopped on the couch that was also her bed and
massaged her feet, devoting special attention to the affronted
toe. "Goddamnit," she said. "I'm such a klutz. I don't deserve to live in this world. I ought to be sent to one of those
planets where there isn't any gravity."

Earlier that evening, at the restaurant, she'd dropped a
whole tray of cocktails.

Inside her hose, her feet were as red as newborn mice.
Steam seemed to rise from them. Mouse gas. She rubbed her
feet until they felt comforted, then she rubbed her eyes.
With a sleepy sigh, she let herself topple over on the couch,
only to be startled by a shower of silver coins. The evening's
tips had cascaded from her pockets and scattered about her
head and body, the couch and floor. She watched a dime roll
across the worn carpet as if heading for the exit. "Is this what
they mean by runaway inflation?" she asked. "Come back
here, you coward!"

Sighing again, she arose and gathered the money. The few
crumpled bills she stuffed in her purse, the coins she trickled
into a dusty fishbowl on the dresser. The bowl was full to
overflowing. "Tomorrow I'll open a bank account," she vowed.
She had made that vow before.

She removed her uniform—a blue sailor dress with piping
of white and red—and tossed it in a corner. At the bathroom
sink in her panty hose and bra, she washed her hair. She felt
too tired to wash her hair, but it so reeked of cook grease and
cigarette smoke that it competed with the resident smell of
the apartment, and that would never do. There was no cap

for the shampoo bottle. In fact, she couldn't remember when it—or the toothpaste—had last had a cap. "I could have sworn there was a cap on it when I bought it," she said.

A number of short, curly hairs were stuck to the cake of soap. They made her wince. The hairs reminded her of an incident at work. She and Ricki usually took their breaks together. They would lock themselves in the employees' washroom and smoke a joint or blow a line of coke. Anything to lighten the load of the trays. Inevitably, Ricki made lewd suggestions. Sometimes, she'd casually lay her hands on Priscilla's body. Priscilla was not really offended. Ricki was one of the few people on the restaurant staff who could read something more intellectually demanding than a menu. Moreover, she was pretty, in a dank, faintly mustachioed way. Perhaps Priscilla was obliquely titillated by Ricki's advances. Usually, she brushed them off in a manner that made them both laugh. On this night, however, when, on the pretext of leveling a molehill that allegedly had bunched up in Priscilla's panty hose, Ricki administered to the back of her upper thigh with lengthy and ever-widening caresses, Priscilla had snapped at her and punched her hard on the arm. At the end of the shift, Priscilla apologized. "I'm just tired," she told Ricki. "I'm truly goddamned exhausted." Ricki said that it was okay, but said it in a tone that intimated damage below the waterline of their friendship. Priscilla brooded over this as she plucked several pubes from the soap.

The secondary function of a bathroom mirror is to measure murmurs in mental mud. Priscilla glanced at her "seismograph" and disliked the reading. She was as pallid as a Q-tip and as ready to unravel. Dropping the soap in the sink, she imposed a smile on her reflection. With a sudsy finger she pushed at the triangular tip of her crisp little corn chip of a nose. She winked each eye. Her eyes were equally enormous, equally violet, but the left eye winked smoothly while the right required effort and a scrunching of flesh. She tugged at her wet autumn-colored hair as if she were stopping a trolley. "You're still cute as a button," she told herself. "Of course, I've never seen a cute button, but who am I to argue with the wisdom of the ages?" She puckered her bubble gum mouth until its exaggerated sensuality drew attention away from the blood-blue crescents beneath her eyes. "My bags may be packed, but I haven't left town. No wonder Ricki finds me irresistible. She's only human."

Leaning her forehead against the scummy rim of the sink, Priscilla suddenly wept. She continued weeping until the heat of her tear water, the sheer velocity of its flow, finally obscured the already vague circumstances of its origins. Then, as memory after memory relinquished its sharp focus, and even fatigue and loneliness proved water soluble, she shut her tear ducts with an almost audible resolve. She blew her nose on a washcloth (she had been out of toilet tissue for a week), tossed her clammy hair, pulled on a lab coat over her underwear, and stepped into the living room cum bedroom cum laboratory where, over an assortment of burners, beakers, and bubbling glass tubing, she would toil with uncharacteristic fastidiousness until dawn.

In the life of Priscilla, the genius waitress, this night was fairly routine. It differed significantly from every other night of her year in but one respect: at what she reckoned to be about five in the morning—her clock had run down and she hadn't gotten around to winding it—there was a soft rapping at her door. Since her neighborhood, Capitol Hill, was a high-crime district and since she had no wish to be interrupted by Ricki or some man she'd once slept with out of need and then forgotten, she'd chosen not to answer. At sunup, however, just prior to retiring for her customary and inadequate six hours of rest, she cracked the door to see whether her caller had left a note. She was puzzled to find on her doorsill a solitary lump of something, which, after cautious examination, she identified as a beet.

NEW ORLEANS

"WHAT IS THE HOUR, V'LU?"

"Dee *whut*?"

"The hour. What is the hour?"

"Why, ma'am, dee hour is whut is on dee clock. 'Tween dee numbers."

"V'lu!" said Madame Devalier. When Madame Devalier raised her voice, it was like Diamond Jim raising a poker pot. Even the termites in the foundation paid attention. "What time is it?"

"It three o'clock, ma'am."

Madame Devalier clasped the overbite of her bosom in disbelief. "Three o'clock in the morning!"

"Three o'clock in dee night, ma'am. You knows dat in New Orleans it not morning 'til dee sun come up." V'lu laughed. Her laughter resembled the tinkle of a toy xylophone. "Sometime, when dee hurricane drops be passing 'round, it not git morning all day."

"You are correct, as usual, chérie. But let us not be speaking of hurricane drops. Nothing goes out of this shop but perfume. And what perfume! Three o'clock in the morn—in the night! This boof has made me so dizzy I have lost all sense of time." She peeked into a vat of percolating petals. Inside the vat the scene resembled an Esther Williams water ballet filmed in the lagoons of hell. "This is the strongest jasmine I have ever smelled. It makes my head spin, V'lu. We must buy from that Jamaican again."

The Hershey-skinned maid nodded. "Dat island nigger dee talk of dee Quarter, ma'am. He be selling flowers, he be singing songs, and all de time dose honey bees buzzing 'round he head. . . ."

"That *is* most unusual," Madame Devalier agreed. "Sometimes they circle him like a halo, and other times it's as if they form *horns*. He wears those bees like a crown, a living crown."

"You think he wear dem bees to bed at night?"

Madame Devalier wagged a finger at the young woman. The finger was plump, wrinkled, ringed, and tipped with a crimson nail. "If you know what's good for you, you won't be concerning your pretty self with his habits in bed. Now fetch me some more alcohol, cher. We must dilute this boof before it starts a chain reaction and blows New Orleans into the Gulf. We have a jasmine Nagasaki cooking here!"

Indeed, a solitary wino weaving down Royal Street was aroused into momentary sobriety by the olfactory force of the aroma that seeped through the closed shutters of the small shop. The man, a longtime resident of the area, stared at the faded sign—Parfumerie Devalier—and crossed himself before continuing on his way.

For forty years, Madame Lily Devalier had kept the shop. Her father had kept it for fifty years before her. In its day, allegedly, some odd business had passed through its arched doorway. Moon medicine and jazz powders. Lucky root and come-together potent. Mojo cream and loa lotion. Hurricane drops, kill-me-not juice, coonass courting pomade and a special "oil of midnight" that had nothing to do with overtime at the office. Among fashionable folk in the French Quarter, Madame D. was known as the Queen of the Good Smells. There was a time when certain people in the Quarter pronounced it "Spells." Nowadays, however, with much of the Quarter gone to seed—the shop along with it—Madame was trying to reattract some of the clientele she had lost to the large international fragrance houses, so she dealt in perfume and nothing but perfume. Or so she claimed.

Under her mistress's watchful eye, V'lu poured molasses-distilled alcohol into a crock. The crock had been collecting the essential oil as it dripped through a filter tube attached to the steeping vat. The Jamaican jasmine was so pungent, however, that the diluting agent barely dulled its edge.

"Ooh-la-la!" exclaimed Madame Devalier. She plopped down her pumpkin patch, her Spanish ballroom, her pagan idol of a body on a lime velvet love seat. "This boof may cause me to faint."

"Ah gitting a sinful headache," V'lu complained.

Out on Royal, following in the footsteps of the departed wino, a tall, lean black man in a greenish yellow skullcap paused before the shutters of the Parfumerie Devalier. He sniffed the air like a stag. He sniffed again. He clapped his hands in delight and cackled aloud. And shifting a bit on his head, emitting a sleepy whisper, his skullcap stirred its many little wings.

Since there were no witnesses, it is impossible to say whether that man was responsible for the single garden-variety beet that V'lu discovered on her cot—tossed in through the open second-story window, perhaps—when she went to lay herself down that night (and thanks to some medication strongly resembling hurricane drops with which her employer had treated her headache, it *was* still night, wasn't it, V'lu?).

PARIS

IN THE CENTER OF A MARBLE-TOP DESK, DIrectly under a crystal chandelier, sitting alone on a silver tray, was a large, raw beet. The beet must have been out of the ground a week or more, for it had the ashen exterior of a cancer victim. Yet, when struck at a particular angle by a flicker of candlelight from the chandelier, its heart of wine-drenched velvet shone through.

The desk was in an office, the office in a skyscraper. The skyscraper was like any other, a slender tower of steel and glass, totally without embellishment or dash. Even its height—a mere twenty-three stories—was unremarkable. Its lone distinguishing feature was the neighborhood from whose midst it rose. Across the street from its entrance was a monastery and a cathedral, the limestone steps of which had been worn as radiant as blue serge trousers by centuries of pious comings and goings. To the right of the building was a block of bicycle shops and cafés; to the left a slate-roofed hotel where, a few decades past, artists *had* slept and worked within the same four walls, never dreaming that their miserable circumstances might be romanticized in the "studio apartment" market of the future. Above the building, the sky recalled passages from *Les Miserables*, threadbare and gray. Below it (everything sits on something else), were the ruins of a brewery that once had been operated by monks from across the street. In the 1200s, Crusaders returning from Palestine introduced perfume to France, and after it achieved popularity there, the monks had made perfume as well as beer. Vestiges of the ancient perfumery could be explored in the basement of the skyscraper. In fact, the LeFever family, which built the skyscraper, had purchased the perfume business from the monastery in the seventeenth century and was still in the trade.

On this day, already described as meteorologically evocative of Victor Hugo at his most dire, Claude LeFever had barged into the office of Marcel LeFever unannounced. Why not? They were blood relatives and both vice-presidents of the firm. Surely, formalities were unnecessary. Yet Marcel seemed annoyed. Perhaps it was because he was wearing his whale mask.

Claude put his hands on his hips and stared at his cousin. "Thar she blows!" he yelled.

"Kiss my ass," said Marcel, from inside the mask.

"Forgive me but I would not quite know where to look for the ass of a fish."

"A whale is not a fish, you fool."

"Oh, yes."

(Claude and Marcel LeFever were speaking in French. This simultaneous English translation is being beamed to the reader via literary satellite.)

Holding degrees in both accounting and law, Claude made the financial decisions for the LeFever family. Marcel, who had grown up in the perfume labs, learning to think with his nose, was in charge of "creativity," a term that Claude did not completely comprehend, but which, to his credit, he recognized to be essential. If creativity was enhanced by pacing the executive suites in a papier-mâché mask, it was all right with Claude, no matter how it frightened the secretaries. It was Marcel's habit of making large cash donations to ecology commandos intent upon sabotaging the whaling industry that bothered the frugal Claude. Claude was well aware of the previous importance to the perfume industry of ambergris, a substance secreted by temporarily infirm whales, but he was convinced that petrochemical and coal tar fixatives were completely adequate substitutes. "Fish puke is a thing of the past," he'd tell Marcel.

"A whale is a mammal, you idiot."

"Oh, yes."

In Marcel's office, as in Claude's next door, there was a floor-to-ceiling window from which one could look down on the cathedral spire. "We are closer to heaven than the monks," Claude was fond of saying. On this day, however, the sky, layered with thin altostratus clouds and smog, appeared to reflect human suffering and failed to awaken in Claude visions of paradise. It did, in its grim emaciation, remind him that he had skipped breakfast in order to be punctual at a board meeting that Marcel, it was probably just as well, had not attended. "Why don't you take that stupid thing off and let's go to lunch," Claude suggested.

Through the eyeholes of the mask, Marcel continued to stare out the window. "Something rather interesting arrived in the morning mail," he said.

"What was that?"

"What else but a beet?" Marcel shifted his gaze from the window to the centerpiece of his desk.

"Oh, yes. I wasn't going to mention the beet. In my years as your cousin and business associate, I have learned that it is frequently best to let sleeping dogs lie. Now that you've broached the subject, I must admit there is a beet on your desk, rather prominently displayed. Arrived in the mail, you say?"

Without a trace of self-consciousness, Marcel lifted off the mask and placed it on the floor beside his chair, revealing an imposing Gallic nose, a gray-streaked spade of a beard, wet brown eyes, and black hair slicked back to resemble patent leather. Were it not that Claude's eyes were less moody, his hair more lightly greased, the cousins were identical, even to the cut of their pin-striped suits. Business competitors often referred to them as the LeFever twins.

"It hadn't actually been posted, if that's what you mean. Nor was it wrapped. It arrived in its corporeal envelope, which is to say, its own body of beet flesh. It was merely sitting atop the basket of morning mail when I came in."

"A token from an admirer. Some woman—or man—in the building. A beet is not entirely devoid of phallic connotations."

"Claude, this is the third time since I've returned from America that there has been a beet with the morning mail."

"You see? Someone's got it bad, you handsome devil, you. Or else it's a joke."

"The receptionist claims that on all three occasions there was a strong, unpleasant odor in the foyer just before the beet was mysteriously delivered. . . ."

"A joke, as I said. An unpleasant odor in the LeFever Building? A *practical* joke."

"Yes. And a trace of the odor still clings to the beet. It is something I've smelled before. Musk, but more intense. Claude, I encountered such a scent in the United States, but I can't seem to remember where and it is driving me coocoo. You know how it is with my nose."

"Indeed I do," said Claude. "I would never have allowed LeFever to insure your nose with Lloyd's of London for a million francs were I not convinced of its infallibility. All the more reason to be unconcerned. Your snout will solve the puzzle even if your intellect should not. Meanwhile, this silly talk of beets is whetting my appetite. Let's get to a restaurant before the noon rush." He buttoned his jacket. After a short hesitation, Marcel rose and buttoned his. There was something about that morose sky scraped by the LeFever Building that indicated that protection against elements might be wise. "By the way," Claude added, "speaking of the United States, what do you hear from V'lu?"

At the mention of V'lu, Marcel unbuttoned his jacket. He sat back down. He pulled the mask over his head and moaned as a whale might moan were it about to upchuck some ambergris.

PART
I

THE
HAIR
AND
THE
BEAN

THE CITADEL WAS DARK, and the heroes were sleeping. When they breathed, it sounded as if they were testing the air for dragon smoke.

On their sofas of spice and feathers, the concubines also slept fretfully. In those days the Earth was still flat, and people dreamed often of falling over edges.

Blacksmiths hammered the Edge Serpent on the anvils of their closed eyelids. Wheelwrights rolled it, tail in mouth, down the cart roads of *their* slumber. Cooks roasted it in dream pits, seamstresses sewed it to the badger hides that covered them, the court necromancer traced its contours in the constellation of straw on which he tossed. Only the babes in the nursery lay peacefully, passive even to the fleas that supped on their tenderness.

King Alobar did not sleep at all. He was as awake as the guards at the gate. More awake, actually, for the guards mused dreamily about mead, boiled beets, and captive women as their eyes patroled the forested horizon, while the king was as conscious as an unsheathed knife; coldly conscious and warmly troubled.

Beside him, inside the ermine blankets, his great hound, Mik, and his wife, Alma, snoozed the night away, oblivious to their lord's distress. Well, let them snore, for neither the dog's tongue nor the wife's could lap the furrows from his brow, although he had sent for Alma that evening mainly

because of her tongue. Alma's mouth, freshly outlined with
beet paint, was capable of locking him in a carnal embrace
that while it endured forbade any thought of the coils beyond
the brink. Alas, it could endure but for so long, and no
sooner was Alma hiccupping the mushroom scent of his spurt
than he was regretting his choice. He should have summoned
Wren, his favorite wife, for though Wren lacked Alma's special sexual skills, she knew his heart. He could confide in
Wren without fear that his disclosures would be woven into
common gossip on the concubines' looms.

Alobar's castle, which in fact was a simple fort of stone and
wood surrounded by a fence of tree trunks, contained trea-
sures, not the least of which was a slab of polished glass that
had come all the way from Egypt to show the king his face.
The concubines adored this magic glass, and Alobar, whose
face was so obscured by whiskers that its reflection offered a
minimum of contemplative reward, was content to leave it in
their quarters, where they would spend hours each day gazing at the wonders that it reproduced. Once, a very young
concubine named Frol had dropped the mirror, breaking off a
corner of it. The council had wanted to banish her into the
forest, where wolves or warriors from a neighboring domain
might suck her bones, but Alobar had intervened, limiting
her punishment to thirty lashes. Later, when her wounds had
healed, she bore him fine twin sons. From that time on,
however, the king visited the harem each new moon to make
certain that the looking glass had not lost its abilities.

Now, on this day, the new moon of the calendar part we
know as September, when Alobar conducted his routine in-
spection, he looked into the mirror longer, more intently
than usual. Something in the secrets and shadows of the
imperfectly polished surface had caught his eye. He stared,
and as he stared his pulse began to run away with itself. He
carried the glass to an open window, where refracting sparks
of sunshine enlivened its ground but refused to alter its
message. "So soon?" he whispered, as he tilted the mirror.
Another angle, the same result. *Perhaps the glass is tricking
me*, he thought. *Magic things are fond of deceptions*.

Although the day was rather balmy, he pulled up the hood
of his rough linen cloak and, blushing like blood's rich uncle,

thrust the mirror into the hands of the nearest concubine, who happened to be Frol. The other women gasped. They rushed to relieve her of the precious object. Alobar left the room.

With some difficulty, for others tried to insist on accompanying him, the king excused himself from court and took the giant dog Mik for a romp outside the citadel gate. Circuitously, he made his way into the woods to a spring he knew. There, he fell to his knees and bent close to the water, as if to drink. Smothered under a swirl of cloudy mixtures, his reflection only spasmodically came into focus. Yet, among the bubbles, twigs, and jumbled particles of light and color, he saw it once more: a hair as white as the snow that a swan has flown over. It spiraled from his right temple.

Undirected—and unencumbered—by thought, King Alobar's hand shot out as if to ward off an enemy's blow. He yanked the hair from its mooring, examined it as one might examine a killed snake, and, after glancing over his shoulder to assure that none save Mik was his witness, flicked it into the spring, in whose waters it twisted and twirled for a long while before sinking out of sight.

Alma gnashed her semen-greased teeth in her sleep. Each distant owl note caused Mik to twitch. Between them, Alobar lay wide-eyed, his war-marked hands caressing the fur covers for comfort. *It is with shame and fear that I rest tonight,* thought the king. *The way bewilderment lies upon me, I have no need of blanket.*

In Alobar's kingdom, a minute city-state, a tribe, if you will, it was the custom to put the king to death at the first sign of old age. Kings were permitted to rule only so long as they retained their strength and vigor. Regarding its rulers as semidivine—god-men upon whom the course of nature depended—the clan believed widespread catastrophes would result from the gradual enfeeblement of the ruler and the final extinction of his powers in death. The only way to avert those calamities was to kill the king as soon as he showed symptoms of decay, so that his soul might be transferred to a vigorous young successor before it had been impaired. One of the fatal signals of fading power was the king's incapacity to satisfy the sexual passions of his wives. Another was the debut of wrinkles or gray hairs, with their indiscreet announcement of decline.

Heretofore, Alobar had not considered this tradition unfair. After all, were the king allowed to grow senile and ill, would not his weakness infect his domain, interfering with the multiplication of cattle, causing beet crops to rot in the fields, disabling the men in battle, and generally perpetuating disease, delirium, and infertility among those whom he ruled? And did not all intelligent peoples (which left out the Romans) hold this to be true? Why, in some nearby kingdoms, a slight blemish on the royal body such as the loss of a tooth was enough to bring about the death sentence. In Alobar's city, the execution was a ceremony of much dignity and aesthetic weight, the king's Number One wife bearing the responsibility for delivering to her husband's lips the poisoned egg. Among less civilized peoples in the region, the ruler was dispatched by the crude, though perfectly sufficient, process of being knocked on the head.

Heretofore, the ritual of putting the king to death had seemed to Alobar natural, inevitable, and just. But tonight . . . tonight he cursed that cruelly traitorous strand, that hoary banderole of mortality that waved so thoughtlessly from an otherwise dark temple; that skinny, silver scroll upon which was written in letters bold enough for all of nature to read, an invitation to the burial mound. O most unwelcome hair!

From the lemony southern islands to the mountainous haunts of trolls, there was no honest person who could call King Alobar a coward. Numerous times he had risked his life in combat, exhilarant the cry of his charge. And why not, what was there in death to fear? Death was this world's tribute and the other world's bequest. To shun it was to cheat both sides. In yanking out the gray hair, he felt that he had betrayed his people, his gods—and himself. Himself? Self? What did *that* mean? Alobar pounded the pillow with his head, causing Mik to growl softly and Alma to flail both arms, although she did not surface from that sea without fish.

At first light, ere a rooster had reached the doodle part of his cock-a-doodle-doo, Alobar shook Alma awake, ordering her back to the harem and requesting that she send Wren in her stead.

"What are you grinning at?"

"My lord, I am merely happy to notice that you have regained your appetites."

"What are you insinuating, woman?"

"Nothing, my lord."

"*What?*" He seized her by her yellow braids.

"Don't be angry, sire. It is just that some of your wives grumble among themselves that you have neglected them of late."

The king released her. Automatically, he raised his fist to the temple where the white hair had sprouted. Were another about to emerge, he would squash it in its follicle.

"Have they . . . have they spoken of this to the council?"

"Oh, no, my lord! It has not come to that. To tell the truth, I think they are merely peevish because you spend your best seed in that clumsy little cunt, Frol."

In the depths of his tangled beard, Alobar managed half a smile. Young Frol was pregnant again, and from the size of her belly, there developed therein a second set of twins.

Kissing had yet to be discovered in Europe, alas, so Alobar rubbed Alma's nose with his own. "My balls are so heavy I cannot leave the bed. Quickly, now. Fetch me Wren!"

As soon as she had gone, he arose and forced open the massive oak window. While Mik licked his feet, he uttered a succession of prayers to the rapidly diminishing sparkle of the morning star.

Those whom Alobar governed were a blond race, of such recent northern origin that snow-trolls and mystical red toadstools still figured in the tales the elders told around the fires, although the king himself, save for that morbid filament he had drowned in the spring, was on the dusky side. Wren, the daughter of a southern chieftain slain in battle by Alobar's predecessor, was even duskier. "The only dark meat in the king's larder," some of the warriors joked. Her coloration was one reason he favored her. More importantly, however, he loved her good sense, although in that place in that time, "good sense" was considered no more a virtue in a wife than "love" in a king.

Alma's advance advertising must have been effective, for Wren arrived in the royal chamber already nude and lathered, wine in her cheeks. Thus, she was surprised to find her husband fully clothed, sitting with his hound on the great bear rug at the foot of his bed.

"I—I—I am sorry, my lord," she stammered. The vintner in her veins pressed a more ruddy grape. "I was informed that you had summoned me."

"That I did, dear Wren. Please come sit at my side."

"Well, all right, of course. But first let me fetch my robe. I've left it in the anteroom."

Smiling at her decorum, Alobar started to detain her. Even in his agitated mood, he could admire this walking flower of intelligent pink, this industry of honey and brine. But the image of the hair cast its shadow, and he allowed her to dress. He petted the dog.

"So, you plucked it," she said, after he had related the events of the previous day.

"Yes, I did."

"Plucked it?"

"Yes."

"But why?"

"I hoped that you could help me answer that."

Wren shook her head of skunk-black curls. She appeared puzzled. "No, my lord, I think not. I have never met nor heard story of one who so resisted fate."

"Surely I am not the first," said Alobar. "If so, I must be madman as well as coward."

"Oh, neither, my Alobar."

"Then what?" He watched dispassionately while Mik got up, yawned, stretched, and lumbered to a far corner of the room to relieve himself. "Tell me, Wren, what do you believe awaits you after you die?"

"Awaits *me*? Me, Wren? I have never pondered what death might hold for this one person, born Wrenna of Pindus, now

Wren, wife of Alobar. Death is not a personal matter, is it? It is the business of the clan. Our clan is responsible for maintaining the continuity of our race against the terrible whims of heavens and earth, and since the clan is weakened by the loss of one of its members, any death can be an ordeal for the whole."

The king nodded. No gray hair nodded with him, though not having viewed himself that morning he could not be certain of that. "Which explains why our people hold such elaborate and energetic funerals. We entertain the immortals in order that they might be persuaded to help us recover the strength and unity stolen from us by death. However—and this occurred to me only last night as I lay abed undreaming— the clan usually succeeds in closing that breach death tore in its defenses, but what of the one who died? In some regions, they believe that he will pop up again in springtime like a crocus, but never have I observed such a blooming. In the past, I have thought: I shall entrust myself to whoever is more powerful in the next world, the gods or the demons. Yet now, my own speedy demise a rising possibility, I do not willingly submit to playing the part of prize in an other-worldly tug-of-war."

"Is this blasphemy, my lord?"

"I think not. Those who crafted me, be they gods or demons, crafted this mind that shapes my resistance to their schemes. Surely they were wise enough, at the wheel where I was thrown, to anticipate future resistance in the heart they were abuilding." Alobar looked at her hopefully. "Can you not agree?"

Wren placed her own soft hand upon Mik's coat. At her touch, the huge hound seemed almost to purr. "I can neither agree nor disagree. I came here this dawn a quarter asleep, expecting to have my furrow plowed, only to have you sow in my mind such strange ideas." She gave her fingers to Mik so that he might affectionately wet them.

"Perhaps," said Alobar, "I ought to turn to the necromancer for advice."

"No, no, Alobar. Do not. Please do not."

"Indeed, why?"

"This is hard for me to express, my lord, but I shall try.

The kings of your ancestors have been celebrated around many a bonfire. But celebrated for cunning and for brawn. Wisdom, true knowledge, has been the province of the necromancer alone. You have changed all that, and Noog does not like it. You must forgive what I am about to say, for it is fact. There are men inside these city walls more powerfully built than you, Alobar; more adept with the spear. Men who can run faster, hurl a stone farther, face an awesome enemy with an equal absence of trembling, and pacify a harem with as sturdy a shaft. But you, well, while I cannot imagine how you acquired it, you have a brain. Time and time again, you have demonstrated your unusual ability to see inside of men and to interpret the silent pleas they aim at the stars. In the past, many kings have *ruled* this people. You have *governed* them."

"Governed?"

"It is a Hellenic word—"

"Hellenic." Alobar closed his eyes and thought of what he had heard of the Hellenic city-states far to the southeast, near the edge of the earth. How glorious they were rumored to have been, how wealthy and learned and proud of their arts. Long ago northern tribes, not unlike his ancestors, had sacked them. What good was righteous governing if rough people could come along at will and chop you up?

"—a Hellenic word, meaning to exercise a directing influence. That you have done. The heroics of past rulers only kept your kingdom in a state of agitation. You have calmed it. And Noog resents you for that, because as a result of your reasonable leadership, the necromancer is less necessary and less admired."

"I am not surprised. There is a limit to the admiration we may hold for a man who spends his waking hours poking the contents of chickens with a stick."

"Divination has its worth."

"Yes, and so, perhaps, does the elimination of time-trapped kings. Yet, rebellion stirs within me this daybreak. I appreciate your warning about Noog. Were I to tell him what I am about to tell you, dear Wren, I would be dining on bitter egg ere the moon is ripe. I have seen kings bite that egg, watched them turn green as ivy leaves and flap about the yard like

freshly beheaded fowl. And all the while the populace on-
looking as if it were at a bear-and-dog match. Now, in the
eyes of the stars, men may be no more exalted than beasts,
and kingly men no worthier than the wretched. Well, forgive
me, perhaps the sap of that silver hair has made me drunk
from inside my skull, but I am seized with desire to be
something *more*. Something whose echo can drown out the
rattle of death."

As Wren blinked her bituminous lashes at his queer behavior, Alobar stood, disrobed, and turned slowly around and
around before her like prime merchandise at a slave market.
Save for the occasional phosphorus mark where some blade
had stung him, his body was smooth and tan, braided with
muscle, supple, quick; neither as massive nor as hairy as
many warriors who had marched behind him. His chestnut
mane was chopped an inch below the ears, his beard was
shaggy and full. Less prominent than her own southern model
(maybe there is simply more to whiff in tropic climes), his
nose was banded at the bridge with a ribbon of scar tissue.
His eyes, bright as torches in an ice cave, were so blue they
seemed on certain days to bleed into the sky. Alobar's mouth,
what could be glimpsed of it through the whiskers, was
thinner than the meaty mouths of his fellows, and at the same
time less crude; it reminded Wren of her late father's mouth,
and she admired it most of all. On several occasions in his
company, she had come within a pucker of discovering kissing.

When he had completed his exhibition, he planted a palm
against each of his jowls and said in a voice both defiant and
shaky, "This man before you is part of the community, the
race, and the species, yet is somehow separate from them.
That notion shocks you, I can see. But, Wren, I cannot
tolerate the passive obliteration of all that I am to myself. My
deeds have not been so small that they will never be recalled
around the fires, yet that fails to satisfy my longing. My life is
not merely a public phenomenon, it is a solitary adventure as
well." He slapped his thighs. "It is with difficulty that I
imagine this familiar body gone cold. These limbs, this trunk,
the heart that drums, they urge me, against all my training,
to prevail over submission to the collective destiny."

Wren's mouth opened as tentatively as a mollusk shell.

"Vanity?" she asked. A wife, even in shock, she made certain that it was less an accusation than a query. "Vanity?"

"Vanity? I am unsure. It *feels* different from vanity. If I be but vain, then the demons will kick my ghost from pit to pit. In my defense, I can say only this: I have fought for my people and would fight for them again, let them name the foe. But I am not ready to have them place the crown on another's noggin, though his be as yellow as sulfur and mine whiter than any winter's drift."

For a long while, Wren sat quietly, poised as if she were a blood-drop on the point of a dagger. Then she said, "You seem to value my opinion, my lord. This then I say to you: It would be painful for me to pass you the poison. I would ache should I find your body still and icy, even though it meant that our clan might easier endure. Your words puzzle me no end. But I trust you as I have trusted no other, save my father. If survival through deception be your wish, then I shall endeavor to support the deceit. Most assuredly, I shall refrain from any mention of it."

"It is no major deceit. Unless my parents lied, I have lived through but thirty-seven Feasts of Feasts. I remain young and able, no matter what that treacherous hair did shout." Again he slapped his thighs. Then, all at once, the bluster drained out of him. "Ah, but, Wren, you may not have long to guard our secret. I have observed the habits of hairs, and before many mornings there will arrive another as colorless as that last. And another and another, like doves at a roost. Every single day I would have to regard my head in the looking glass, yet I cannot retrieve the glass from the concubines without raising suspicion. You are more than loyal, but there is little use. . . ." He slumped down on the fur beside her.

"I will be your mirror," said Wren.

He understood and, in gratitude, embraced her until at length he felt his humor return. A slow smile bent back his foliage.

"I've a mind to lay you down and split you like a rack of mutton. What would you say to that?"

"You know very well what I would say. I would say those half-formed, half-crazed words the she-panther speaks when in the delirium of her seasonal heat she is mounted by her mate."

Alobar moved to shut the window against the beginning buzz and bustle of the city day. Then he thought better of it and left it wide. It would be to his advantage, he reasoned, should the populace overhear she-panther yowls emanating from his chamber.

Days grew shorter. The citadel was hidden by morning fogs. Beets, resembling the hearts of gnomes, were piled in the storage cellars. Ducks lined up to buy their tickets to southern swamps. Mead was jugged. Blades and leathers oiled. Wolves made clouds when they sang at night. Maybe that was where the fogs came from. Everywhere there were sounds of husks cracking, virgins dancing, the rush of bees on last-minute shopping sprees, the roar of altars ablaze with some sacrifice.

King Alobar was likewise undergoing a season change. True to her word, Wren was his mirror, and approximately once a week she discovered a white settler aspiring to colonize the shady hirsute shores. She drove it promptly out of the neighborhood.

More pensive than ever, Alobar shared his thoughts with her. "I think that I am seeking something," he confessed once as they stood alone in the western watchtower, overseeing, from a bloodless distance, the butchering of skinny beef. "What I seek is neither spoils nor territory, new wives nor new glory, nor, for that matter, merely a lengthened life. What I seek never was, not on land or sea."

What he sought was to become something singular out of his singular experience—and labor as she might, Wren could not understand. If the notion of an individual resisting death for his own sake was foreign to her (as indeed, it would have been to anyone in that milieu), the concept of the uniqueness of a single human life was alien to the point of babble. Preferring the chaos down in the cattle pens to her husband's god-offending nonsense, she shut it out entirely and yelled encouragement to the butchers.

Yet, Wren served Alobar in ways beyond the call of duty. In an attempt to prove his stamina, the king set upon his harem like a starving rat let loose in a peach barrel. Night after night, he rooted, rolled, and reamed. He climbed delicately upon Frol's swollen belly. He left Juun and Helga complaining of soreness in their nether regions. He generated funky auroras around the bodies of Ruba and Mag. He gave Alma a taste of her own medicine. Each night, when he had done with one or the other of them, he would rub their noses, tug their blond braids, and send them back to their quarters to fetch Wren. While Alobar, exhausted, lay beside her panting and making imprudent comments, such as "Wives are wonderful, but why did I have to accumulate so *many*?", Wren would fake her lioness cries. Mornings, while he dreamed of the relative tranquillity of war, she would fake them again. In time, the subterfuge shamed them both so deeply they could scarcely bear to look at each other. It was actually a relief when it was brought to an end.

Noog the necromancer paid close attention to the king's activities. He had done so for years. He had chronicled Alobar's gradually declining sexual enthusiasm, so the desperation implicit in the sudden reversal was not lost on him. When he read verification of his suspicions in the intestinal texts of several hens, he decided to see for himself.

It so happened that on the morning that Noog stole up to the royal window, after bribing a guard with a glass bead, Alobar and Wren were actually making love. Her phony demonstrations had excited him that dawn. After all, he cared for her above any other. So he had touched her stomach with uncommon tenderness, and soon her groans were being uttered in earnest. Disappointed, Noog was about to turn away when the magpie that rode upon his shoulder abruptly took flight and swooped into the king's chamber. Undetected as yet by the copulating couple, a long, curly hair as bright as an icicle had unfurled during the night in Alobar's beard. The magpie flew directly to the hair, pulled it free with its beak, and delivered it into the gizzard-stained hands of the magician.

Following a full day of chanting, singing, and frenzied dancing by painted figures in animal suits, the execution took place at twilight.

Awaiting his mortal exit, Alobar sat on a bronze throne wearing for the last time a thick crown of hammered gold. In his lap, he held the sacred turtle shell. The shell and crown rivaled the Egyptian looking glass in the hierarchy of the city's treasure trove. At precisely the moment that the sun's eye winked behind the western hills, Wren stepped from a tiny hut of pine boughs, constructed for the occasion, carrying on an ermine pillow the smoking egg. Without missing a cue, as if she had rehearsed for days, she dance-stepped thrice around the bonfire, then up to the throne. Supposedly, the egg had been laid by a viper, although Alobar suspected it was the product of Noog's magpie.

In any case, Wren lifted it gracefully to Alobar's mouth, and as the singers fell silent and the dancers froze, he gulped it down. Presently he commenced to writhe. His face turned the color of the pine boughs. He toppled over and, green tongue lolling, thrashed about in the mud. Noog approached, recovered the crown that had spilled, and placed it upon the head of the young hero who had taken Alobar's place on the throne. Alobar kicked with both boots, then lay still.

The new king flicked a dab of green foam off the throne. He raised his spear and smiled. Cheering broke out in the city, but it was shortlived because Mik lunged for the bronze chair and would have chewed off the occupant's leg had he not been restrained. No sooner was the hound muzzled than a new snarling began. This time it came from Frol, the fourteen-year-old concubine, who horrified the crowd by pulling the magic mirror from inside her maternity gown and smashing it against the logs of the bonfire.

The burial mound was outside the city walls, in a field dotted with cow pies and large stones. The stones had been arranged geometrically in patterns that were supposed to mean something to the gods. Presumably, the cow pies had fallen at random, ·although then, as now, the division between what is random in nature and what is purposeful is extremely difficult to determine.

Warriors carried Alobar's body to the mound's summit, where a shallow indentation had been dug. After the body was laid in the hole, the councilmen covered it with dirt. They sprinkled mead on the grave. They chanted an incantation half as ancient as the stones in the field; words arranged, like the stones, in sensuous patterns; words that saber-toothed tigers may once have overheard. There were no tears, except the ones that Frol had shed back in the citadel yard. Death was not a weeping matter. The indentation in the mound-top represented the navel in the Great Belly. Alobar was back where he had begun. Birth and death were easy. It was life that was hard.

Alobar was back where he had begun. But not for long. As soon as the funeral procession had wound, imitating the undulations of the Serpent, back through the gates of the city, Wren ran from the shadow of an upright stone and started frantically to dig him out. Only two feet of earth lay over him, so he was soon uncovered. She had a vessel of mead concealed in her cloak, part of which she used to clean dirt out of his mouth and nostrils. The remainder she poured down his throat. A potent beverage, the mead gradually counteracted the effects of the nightshade belladonna that she had placed in the egg. Since belladonna, in small amounts, will slow heartbeat, it had helped Alobar feign death. Wren also had stuffed the egg with algae that she had scooped off the surface of a stagnant pond. It was the algae that had given the green cast to his skin.

There had been no fatal poison in the egg Alobar devoured. Following a plan they had devised in the week between Noog's discovery and the execution ritual, Wren had secreted Noog's death egg in her bodice while she waited in the hut, substituting an egg filled with the algae and a nonlethal dose of nightshade belladonna.

Alobar was considerably dazed, but as soon as he demonstrated to Wren's satisfaction that his breathing was of sufficient velocity to billow the sails of his soul, she left him. "I must return ere I am missed. I have to prepare myself to receive my new husband." The last she said matter-of-factly, but she rubbed his nose poignantly before fleeing.

As dazed as he was, Alobar had the presence of mind to let his body roll down the slope of the burial mound, which was starting to be illuminated by a rising moon. He came to rest in shadow. He also came to rest in a more or less fresh cow pie—but he uttered no oath. *I may be mad,* he thought, *but I prefer the shit of this world to whatever sweet ambrosias the next might offer.*

East was good enough for the morning star, it would be good enough for Alobar. He should not travel westward, for the Romans, with whom his people had traditionally skirmished, controlled the westlands, and for a long time now the Romans had been increasingly under the spell of some borrowed god who sounded like particularly bad news. Modern Romans insisted that there was only one god, a notion that struck Alobar as comically simplistic. Worse, this Semitic deity was reputed to be jealous (who was there to be jealous of if there were no other gods?), vindictive, and altogether foul-tempered. If you didn't serve the nasty fellow, the Romans would burn your house down. If you did serve him, you were called a Christian and got to burn other people's houses down. There was a long list of enjoyable things Christians could *not* do, however, including keeping more than one wife. "Come to think of it," mused Alobar, "that might not be such a bad idea."

Ah, but Christians were meddlers, and a man on the run from death, duty, and who knew what else? was a man who didn't need meddling with. It was possible that he had insulted quite a few deities of his own acquaintance, so he didn't relish some aggressive foreign hothead getting in the act. Christians populated the south as well as the west, while up north the pebbles lay with their faces already in snow, and Alobar had neither furs nor spear. It was settled. He would

journey into that east whose pinchers had so recently released October's buoyant moon.

When the last spasm of nausea had subsided, when all
traces of dirt and drug had washed away and his blood flowed
melodious and clear, he stood, stretched, gathered his burial
wraps about him, and set off at a trot toward the east—and
the multiplying unknown.

As he trotted, he could hear in the distance the drunken
din of the city, where his people simultaneously lamented the
broken mirror and celebrated their rescue from feebleness
and decay. Then he turned upwind, and the night was suddenly quiet. He paused to look back. The red glow of torches
and bonfires caused the city to resemble a miniature sun
a-setting. *Let it set*, he thought. *A fresh one will rise in the
east*. Nevertheless, there were pangs in his heart. Mixed in
that caldron of sound that had just faded might have been the
feline wails of Wren, who, no doubt, lay with the new ruler
beneath his ermine covers. Did Mik snore at the foot of the
bed? he wondered. All of Alobar's wives belonged to his
successor, if he wanted them, but Mik was eternally Alobar's
and would have been buried with him had he not demanded,
prior to his "execution," that the hound be spared. "I would
vow to retrieve you, Mik," whispered the former king, "but
as sorely as I miss you, I will not be back. Not one companion
from my reign will I ever see again."

He was quickly to be proven wrong.

He was now at the threshold of the dark forest. Unarmed,
he dare not venture deep inside lest enterprising beasts
process his flesh into sausage cakes and brew their winter's
ale from his blood. Therefore, his plan was to lie down just
inside the tree line and sleep until daybreak. At earliest light
he would strike out, attempting to transverse the wood before it again grew black. Having a terrible thirst, however, a
need to rinse his mouth of the accumulated residue of mead,
mud and egg surprise, he decided to first go in as far as the
spring and drink. Then he would retire to a resting place less
convenient to the wolf kitchens.

The spring bubbled in a little glade, a clearing lit like an altar by the ever-ceremonious moon. So bright was the glade that Alobar could watch his shadow slide along the promenade of moss and kneel with him to drink. "Me and my shadow," he said wistfully, anticipating the popular song by a thousand years. "Me and my—" What was that? His shadow had attracted a second, a companion, shadow, slightly smaller than itself though nonetheless human in shape. If his shadow was no longer alone, did that mean that he, too, enjoyed companionship? And if his shadow's shadow friend aimed a shadow spear, could Alobar conclude that a spear was pointed at him, as well?

Still on his knees, Alobar whirled and lunged at the place where the shadow had led him to expect he would find legs. Yes, those were legs he grabbed! He yanked them hard, hoping to upset the body they supported before it could shove a blade through one rack of his rib cage and out the other. He felt the spear point graze first his cheek and then his shoulder, as the being who wielded it crashed down on top of him. Alobar no longer knew how the shadows were behaving, but as for himself, there was an attacker straddling his head. Disgust mingled with fear as he labored to withdraw his face from his adversary's crotch. In the struggle, some part of him, most likely his nose, fired a message to his brain. The message contained a single word: female!

Alobar pulled himself free with such force that he fell backward into the spring. When he surfaced, spewing and sputtering, dead leaves and the addresses of a dozen hibernating frogs strewn throughout his beard, he found himself contemplating a spear tip again. This time, however, he could see the face of his assailant, and while he was no longer surprised that it was a woman, he was astonished that the woman was Frol.

Alobar's amazement was mild compared to Frol's. When she realized that she had tried to puncture her recently executed lord and husband, her young mind reeled at the potential redundancy, and she fainted straight away. Alobar revived her with water that he wrung from his clothing, and they spent a largely incoherent hour sorting things out.

Following her destruction of the prized mirror, only the

intervention of the new king had prevented the clan from ripping Frol to shreds. It seemed the king desired to honor Alobar's precedence, desired to govern rather than merely rule (Alobar detected the influence of Wren), so he urged compassion, as he believed Alobar would have done, and reduced Frol's sentence to banishment. Moreover, as Frol was driven from the city in a blizzard of curses, his highness handed her his own spear, with which she might at least delay the dinner of the bears (Alobar could picture Wren whispering instructions in the freshly royal ear).

Five minutes or less was required by Frol to explain her presence in the forest. The remainder of the hour was taken up by Alobar's protests that he was not a specter. Slow to be convinced, Frol accepted Alobar's concreteness only after he produced the terminus of his urinary network and arced a stream in front of her. "Everyone knows that ghosts don't piss!" he exclaimed, and although she was unacquainted with that particular wisdom, it sounded too logical to be denied.

Upon those travelers who make their way without maps or guides, there breaks a wave of exhilaration with each unexpected change of plans. This exhilaration is not a whore who can be bought with money nor a neighborhood beauty who may be wooed. She (to persist in personifying the sensation as female) is a wild and sea-eyed undine, the darling daughter of adventure, the sister of risk, and it is for her rare and always ephemeral embrace, the temporary pressure she exerts on the membrane of ecstasy, that many men leave home. Alobar was presently in her arms, having made a sudden shift in direction due to Frol's heavy load—she was timed to give birth on the next full moon—and was now bearing west, after all, seeking a nearby haven where Frol might deliver, rather than the distant edge where he might test fate. On the surface, it seemed a less adventurous choice, yet the prospect of raising a family in Christiandom was far more challenging to Alobar than any potential combat with man or monster, and the very spontaneity of the decision inflated his humor. Thus, even though his back now was turned to the allure of the morning star, even though a stout breeze flattened his beard against his Adam's apple, even though his damp clothing clung to him like frost, he whistled from stump to rock as if he were a teakettle leading the pack in the annual pot-and-pan cross-country marathon.

Three days later, still whistling, pulling a stumble-footed Frol along, he entered the village of Aelfric. Abruptly the whistling stopped.

Aelfric was a huddle of hovels, an ugly little settlement of thatch and mud in which dwelt the peasants who farmed the manor of Lord Aelfric, whose imposing manor house loomed over the village, although it stood a quarter-mile away. Alobar's blue eyes scrutinized the rude peasant houses and the peasants themselves, bent and beat from a crowded calendar of toil; he examined the granite turrets of the manor house, surveyed the surrounding fields and woods. His toes curled nervously in his boots, but just when they were about to uncoil and propel him toward a scenic bypass of downtown Aelfric, his gaze settled on Frol's belly. He calmed his toes. He took Frol's hand. "Here we shall build our muddy nest," he said.

The peasants received them warmly. Naturally, they were suspicious, but newly baptized, they were sensitive to the responsibilities of Christian charity. Recognizing in Alobar the mien of a warrior, they suggested that his proper employment would be as a vassal in the military service of Lord Aelfric. They were both amazed and gladdened when the stranger insisted on remaining among them. They could always use another strong back in the pitiless acres of Aelfric.

For his part, Alobar knew all too well how life would be in the manor house. He had been a mighty warrior, he had been an exalted king. Now it amused him to see what kind of serf he would make. Besides, for some reason—perhaps it was connected to the trauma of the white hair—he had grown tired of violence. "I sense that there are different sorts of battles to be fought," he told Frol, "and I shall fight them for myself, not Lord Aelfric."

Despite his reputation, Alobar had little fear of recognition. Aelfric was a mere forty miles west of his former castle, but there was not a single serf who had traveled more than ten miles from his or her birthplace. Once his beard was shaved, his hands callused, his body stooped to the processing of the harvest, not even the most cosmopolitan of the lord's knights would be able to identify him. Moreover, he was "dead." "Long live death," whistled Alobar as he winnowed grain from chaff.

To Frol, Aelfric presented a more difficult challenge. Pregnancy afforded a peasant woman no relief from work, not even in its final hours. Softened by the sables and scented pillows of the harem, Frol fainted two days in a row while pounding flax with heavy scrutchers. Thereafter, she was dispatched each dawn to the manor house, where she waited upon ladies. Ever spunky, Frol served without complaint, and the ladies soon learned not to trust her with breakables.

One night in bed, Alobar removed Frol's hands from his waist and lifted them temporarily above the rough blankets. Examining her stubby fingers, he said, "Here is where glassware comes to die."

They fell asleep smiling. It is to erase the fixed smiles of sleeping couples that Satan trained roosters to crow at five in the morning.

Among the observations made by Alobar during his first few weeks as a citizen of Aelfric were these:

(1) "Here the people bury their dead not in communal mounds but in individual graves. Now that I have come to regard death as a private challenge rather than as a social phenomenon to be exploited—once it has occurred—for the common good, as my clan regards it, I wonder if Christianity may not have something in its favor, after all."

(2) "The priest of the manor reminds me to no end of Noog. He is absorbed with his position on the estate and manipulates everyone, lord, lady, and serf, alike, to better his station and to tighten the Church's grip on the society. There resides, however, in a hut of sticks beyond the fringe of the village, another kind of priest, a wise old man called a shaman. The shaman lives outside the social system, refusing to have any part of it. Yet, he seems to connect the populace

to the heavens and the earth far more directly than the priest. Perhaps that is why the priest despises him."

(3) "The main vegetable consumed in Aelfric is the turnip. With my clan it was the beet. Could that explain why these people are so docile and mine so fierce?"

More than once during his first year in Aelfric did ex-king Alobar reconsider applying for a vassalic position with the lord of the manor. The life of the peasants was brutally hard. In return for the lord's protection, they had to work for a prescribed number of days a week on his lands. In the few remaining hours, they plowed, seeded, and harvested their own meager holdings and performed an endless succession of chores, such as chopping wood, butchering game, shearing sheep, digging ditches, drawing water, mending roads, carting manure, and building carts in which to cart still more. In the quiet ache of evening, Alobar listened to his calluses grow, a sound that merged in his ear with the echo of the switch on the ox's hide.

By then, gray had overtaken one of every four hairs on his head, and some nights he would pluck those pale hairs as if they were petals, saying to Frol, "If I wasn't elderly when our clan decreed I was, I soon will be. Harsh labor pierces the rosy membrane of youth and lets the shriveling brine seep in."

Nevertheless, the work-worn months held satisfactions. The novelty of one wife continued to fascinate Alobar. Frol remained as devoted as when he was her sovereign, and she showed signs of maturing into a woman as sexually adept as Alma and only slightly less intelligent than Wren. With her company he was content, and when she issued twins, one of each gender, that first November, a new dimension was added to his life. Back in his home city, his offspring had been raised communally in a nursery adjoining the harem. The nursery was a female province, as foreign to his bootsteps as the serpent-seared cliffs of the edge. Now he discovered children, and the discovery blew blasts of sugar into every chamber of his heart.

When Alobar had enough energy, he cataloged his experiences and observations and tried to profit from them, to what end he could not say. Because Christianity emphasized the value of the individual, in the Roman scheme every person had his or her place. In the frame of mind in which he'd been since first he was violated by the hair, this concept appealed to him, providing food for mental mastication.

The peasants were a dull lot, by and large, but they had exhibited extraordinary kindness in helping the strangers set up housekeeping in a flea-bitten cottage with a dirt floor. Their friendliness increased after first Frol (out of conviction) and then Alobar (as a strategic maneuver) agreed to be baptized in the name of their exclusive god. However, certain activities were conducted in the village from which Alobar and his family were barred. These activities seemed to be social in nature, generally merry, and coincided with seasonal observances.

The traditional winter festival, which among Alobar's folk as well as many other Europeans was celebrated during the twelve days that separated the end of the lunar year (353 days long) from the end of the longer solar year (365 days), and whose purpose it was to equalize the two different celestial years, had been appropriated by the Christians and transformed into a religious holiday called "Christmas." As far as Alobar could determine, Christmas was the same winter festival of yore, except that the profound emotionalism annually precipitated by moon/sun influences the priest here attributed to the natal anniversary of "Christ," a Semitic man-god whose exact relationship to the One God Alobar could never quite get straight.

On their first Christmas Day in Aelfric, Frol and Alobar were obliged to spend the entire morning in church, listening to sermons and hymns in a language they could barely understand. Later in the day, they tramped through the snow to the manor house, where the lord served up a mammoth meal for all his serfs. At dusk, Frol and Alobar returned to their cottage to sleep off the food and drink, but long after their candles had been extinguished, lights flickered in the homes of others, as well as in the community lodge, from which laughter and song poured most of the night. The songs that

Alobar overheard were most unlike hymns, and the whoops
and guffaws that mixed in the clear, frosty air were most
unlike prayers, although for his part, Alobar deemed them
every bit as godly. The revelry continued nightly until the
sixth day of January, the termination of the twelve-day "lost"
or supplementary month.

Since there were similar goings-on at the time of the old
spring fertility festival—the priest called it "Easter"—and
during the feast of the dead in late October—"All Saint's
Day," according to the Christians; since he and Frol, as
newcomers, were never invited; and since the priest steered
clear of the merrymaking while the shaman, in a horny mask,
occasionally dropped by, Alobar was to conclude that for all
their pious Christian convictions the peasants still clung to
the pagan customs that were their archaic heritage.

His conclusion was correct, although a night was fast
a-coming when he would wish he was mistaken.

His lips curled over the rim of a cider mug, Alobar sat
before the hearth. Outdoors the snow was piled halfway to
the Big Dipper, and the earth lay as passive as an eyeless
potato. More snow was falling, and Alobar praised each and
every flake. Onward, snow! The subdued landscape awaits
your crystal victory! Although the peasant women busied
themselves at the cookpot, the spinning wheel, and the loom,
weather had curtailed their husbands' labors, and for this
respite Alobar thanked the new god, the old gods, the morning star, and the snow itself, for the snow seemed energized
and awake in a universe that slumbered like a cadaver.

In front of the crackling fire, Alobar dandled his babies on
his knees and at last gave full attention to his lot. How he
welcomed this opportunity for uninterrupted thought! Externally and internally, his life had changed dramatically since
that silver hair had flagged him down, and though the next
day was Christmas, it was not upon the pigs roasting in Lord
Aelfric's ovens nor the epiphanies marinating in the prayer
book of the priest that he dwelled, but upon his path from

kingship to peasantry and upon what future twists that road might take. A life in progress. A thing to behold.

So lost in reverie was he that when there came a loud banging at the door, he let both his mug and his infants drop to the hearth. The mug rolled into the flames, but the twins, having slightly less rounded contours, stayed where they fell.

Frol unlatched the door, and out of the dark trooped a snow-dusted band of their neighbors, faces scarlet from cold and strong drink. The villagers embraced them both, not a little lasciviously, and placed wreaths of holly and cedar about their necks. They bade Alobar and Frol accompany them to the community lodge.

Frol was unnerved by the boisterousness of the peasants, normally so sober and staid, but Alobar whispered, "Let us join them. More than a year has passed. This is our second Christmas in Aelfric, and finally we've been judged trustworthy to participate in their seasonal fun. By the tone of it, we are about to be included in ceremonies more ancient, more unrestrained, and, I suspect, more heartfelt than any we will share on the morrow."

The entrance to the hall was decorated to resemble the face of a beast, eyes bulging and burning (lanterns inside goat skins), teeth of thin wooden slats. They entered through the mouth of the creature, walking over blood-drenched hides that represented the great animal's tongue—and constituted, perhaps, the original red carpet. Inside, the low rafter beams were luxuriously festooned with coniferous boughs, holly, and running cedar, although damp logs smoldering in the fireplace had smoked up the place to the extent that details of the greenery were barely discernible. It didn't matter, for there could be no mistaking the kegs of cider that rose majestically in the smoke. Frol and Alobar let their cups be filled repeatedly, though in fact most of the liquid was speedily sloshed out by the jostling of fellow citizens as they coaxed the newcomers to join with them in bawdy songs. Frol strained to learn each lyrical indecency, but Alobar simply sang over and over again the only song he knew or had ever known, an epic about battles that were fought long, long ago, back before the morning star impregnated the She-Bear who gave birth to beets.

String and wind instruments were being played inexpertly. Soon, dancing commenced. Assisted by the chemistry of the cider, Alobar and Frol relaxed and slipped into the noisy spirit of things. Frol danced with every clodhopper who asked, while Alobar munched sausages and black puddings and played at dice and cards.

Shortly before midnight, as if by signal, the singing, dancing, and games suddenly stopped. Thinking the party over, Alobar and Frol made to gather their wraps and sleeping babies and go home, but they were told that if they left they would miss the highlight of the season. At that moment, two peasant women, decked out in their finest embroidery, emerged from the greenery that was piled behind the cider kegs. They were carrying a board upon which was balanced a many-layered cake. A table had been moved into the center of the lodge, and upon it the cake was set. The way the men moved in to surround the cake you would have thought a naked maiden was about to jump out of it, but that particular advancement in the baker's art was nine or ten centuries away.

One of the women took a knife from her fancy apron and began to slice the confection. When it was divided to her satisfaction, the other wife served. One piece at a time was passed out, to men only. When all the males, including Alobar, had been served, they began to eat their slices, chewing very slowly, watching carefully all the while the chew motions of their companions; the slow, muscular rise and fall of jaws. Except for the soft chewing, the hall had grown as silent as the gills of a fossil.

The cake was so moist and sweet that Alobar would have been inclined to compliment the chefs, would not the faintest tribute have resounded in the still of the lodge like a falling tree. When he bit into something small and hard, a something that sent a shock of pure hot pain vibrating along the length of a neural wire, he dared not cry out, because if a compliment must be suppressed, then doubly so a complaint. Not wishing to hurt the feelings of the bakers, Alobar removed the object from his mouth as inconspicuously as possible, a gesture doomed to failure, for every smoke-reddened eye in the room was upon him.

Upon examination, the object proved to be easily identifiable, and for all the temporary distress it caused his molar, rather unobjectionable. Since everyone was looking anyway, Alobar, somewhat colored by embarrassment, held it aloft for them to see. "Just a bean," he said shyly. Before the word was fully spoken, a huge roar went up in the lodge. "The bean! The bean! The bean! The bean!" they cried, men and women together, and the villagers advanced on him, slapping his back, mussing his hair, hugging him, and squeezing his private parts. A wooden chair, a rickety imitation of a throne, was fetched and placed beneath a rack of antlers recently nailed to the wall. Alobar was led to the throne and made to sit on it, whereupon, amidst a deafening cacophony of whoops and hollers, belly laughs and sniggers, purposeful belches and equally intentional farts, a lopsided crown of mistletoe was laid atop his head.

When the crowd began addressing him as "king," Alobar gasped. His heart swung off its pendulum, and his blue eyes stiffened like the ponds of December in a bowel-loosening, knee-locking, cider-evaporating attack of déjà vu.

"Viva Fabarum Rex!" he seemed to hear them shout, as if through curtains of snow and cake. "Viva Fabarum Rex! Long live the King of the Bean!"

According to custom, the King of the Bean had absolute license. For twelve days following his chance selection, he reigned supreme, ordering his fellows about and indulging his passions. He was allowed to wallow in every pleasure, however sinful. No door nor bed was barred to him. At any hour, he might enter another's house to eat and drink his fill. If he wanted a neighbor's wife, she was his; likewise any daughter. Obscene behavior, such as urinating on the altar of the church, not only was permitted, it was encouraged. Wherever he went, whatever he did, the Bean King was attended by a rowdy entourage, adjusting his mock crown (so that it always sat askew), pulling at his mock robes (so that they revealed his buttocks), plying him with song and cider, cheering him, jeering him, egging him on.

When this was explained to Alobar, he thought, *Well, if they desire a king, how fitting it be me. This kingship comes to me by sheer fortune, but I daresay none other is more experienced in the role. True, I had planned to give up these wintry days to contemplation, but it is festival time, and I could use some fun. Frol has satisfied me plenty, but I confess that there be three or four skirts hereabout I would not mind lifting. They wish a monarch, do they? Little do they realize that their bean, in its vegetable wisdom, has selected the one man suited for the job. Haw haw.*

Then the peasants explained to him the rest of the custom. At the end of his twelve-day rule, on the Day of the Epiphany, the usual restraints of law and morality were abruptly restored. Still wearing his crooked crown, the King of the Bean was led to a certain meadow outside the village, where his throat was cut.

"Who's there?"

"Alobar. From the village. I must speak with you. Let me in."

"Go away."

"No! I cannot go away. I am the King of the Bean."

Inside the hut there was a laugh, or the ancient animal ancestor of a laugh; a cackle wound like prickly yarn around the wild spindle in the throat of a fox. "You have strayed from your kingdom, Your Majesty. I am not subject to your authority. In fact, go frig yourself."

Alobar leaned against the shaman's door. Never had he been so near to weeping. If only he had his beard back so that it might sop up the tears. "You don't understand. I am not playing games. I am not one of the peasants. I am a king."

"So you informed me. King of the Bean. Go swill another cup of cider, Your Highness. And don't forget to ask the priest for forgiveness when you kneel in church on the morrow."

Alobar bashed the door down with one furious lunge. He careened inside, sending broken sticks flying, and lifted the shaman from his mattress. Without a painted deer skull over his head, the old man did not seem so formidable. Alobar shook him until his various necklaces of various teeth chattered like a flock of enamel jays.

"All right, all right," said the shaman. "What are you seeking, information or wisdom?"

"Er . . . why . . . uh . . . *wisdom*!"

"In that case, you're out of luck. Wisdom takes a long time, and you're going to be dead in twelve days."

Alobar threw the shaman onto his tick. "No, I am not!" he screamed, stamping his feet. "No, I am not!"

"Oh? You're not? But you are 'king' and thus condemned." The shaman grinned like a weasel running errands for the moon.

"I am *twice* king and *twice* condemned—and I am sick and tired of it. First a hair and then a bean. If death wants me, let him ride up on a pale mount, ashes in his mouth, ice in his testicles; let him swing a scythe and make horrible noises, let him come for me in person, not send some hair, some fucking little black bean baked in a goody by mutton-butt peasant wives. Even then I might not go. Frankly, I do not like the way death does business."

A glimmer of interest showed in the shaman's eyes. He raised himself on his knobby hips. He glanced at the snow that was sifting over the contents of his hut. "Do you feel a bit of a draft? Here, help me hang this skin over the door. Then I'll brew us some mushroom tea, and we can discuss your problem."

While his host hunkered over the diminutive adobe hearth, Alobar sniffed at the various braids of dried vegetable matter that hung against the walls, each broadcasting a different version of internal conditions within the plant kingdom, and he fingered the bones, fangs, and snail shells that, like chimes to be rung by the shaman's heavy breathing, dangled from the ceiling. Each fragment of flora and fauna had been removed from its original context and juxtaposed incongruously, yet each seemed perfectly in place. The party in Alobar's head, which agitation and anxiety were throwing, now was crashed by a notion: *existence can be rearranged*. Torn between showing this thought to the door or seating it in a place of honor, Alobar was relieved of the dilemma by a steaming teacup, shoved into his grasp.

The shaman sipped ritualistically. Alobar told his whole story. When only the dregs were left of the one's tea and the other's tale, the shaman took several short pieces of string from his pocket and began to knot them together, mumbling all the while. "In my net," he mumbled, "I bind the sobs of the dark ice cracking. In my net I bind the ax's response to the pinecone. I bind the larva's curved belly. I bind the hole in the sky where the comets escape. I bind the roots of the rainbow and the flight of the alder." He went on and on in that manner—"My net binds the hornet's deaf grandmother" —until Alobar was ready to grab him and give him another shaking.

Just as Alobar reached the end of his patience, the shaman unclasped his hands, revealing the pieces of string, which in the knotting, had turned into a delicate violet, its petals the color of love bites on a collarbone. Alobar reached for the flower, but it burst into flame and was consumed in the shaman's fingers without burning them. It was Alobar's turn to mumble. "In the future I shall be more careful about whose door I knock down," he said, mopping up with his sleeve the tea he had spilled in his astonishment.

The shaman laughed. "Don't pay any attention to that old magic," he said. "It used to be powerful, but now it is only the pastime of a few crazy old farts who remember how to talk with weeds." Alobar sought to protest, but the shaman interrupted. "Man is turning away from the plants and animals," he said. "Slowly he is breaking his bond with them. Someday he will have to reestablish contact, if the universe is to survive. For now, however, it is probably best that he set out on his own in his new direction."

"How so?"

"A salamander can be only a salamander, an elk an elk, and a bush a bush. True, a bush is complete in its bushness, yet its limits, while not nearly so severe as some foolish men would believe, are fairly obvious. The peasants of Aelfric are like bushes, like salamanders. They were born one thing and will die one thing. But you . . . you have already been a warrior, a king, and a serf, and from the looks of it, you aren't through yet. Thus, you have learned the secret of the new direction. That is: a man can be many things. Maybe *anything*.

"In the past, there was little separation between the lives of plants and animals and the lives of men. Nowadays, there are men who practice separation, not only from the creatures but from other men. The Romans with their Christianity have promoted the idea of the human individual. But you are neither Roman nor Christian, and you are no less smitten, so perhaps the spirit is in the air. The Romans encourage individualism, but they maintain rigid controls. Sooner or later, men will come along whose belief in the supremacy of the exceptional, extraordinary, isolated individual will cause them to declare themselves *exempt* from controls. In their uniqueness, they will not hesitate to defy accepted standards. Oh, these men will give Rome—and the Romes that shall follow Rome—a very large headache. You, Alobar, I suspect, are among the first of such men.

"No, no, do not object. I can tell that my words both delight and excite you."

It was true. And in his delightment and excitement, Alobar had let his tea grow cold, so the shaman warmed his cup.

"Were you an ordinary peasant, I would dazzle you with another trick or two; I'd berate you and comfort you and send you back to Aelfric to face your death without alarm. Most of the peasants are content to die. For them, death means the cessation of toil. At last they can drop their soiled and battered bodies and enter the dimension of pure spirit. Plants and animals are even more comfortable with death. It is the natural end. But man by his nature is an unnatural animal. If any creature stands a chance of defeating death, it is man.

"If you were an ordinary serf, I would send you back to Aelfric to assist your neighbors in the public purification they undergo at the end of the old year and the beginning of the new, to help them mock the things they love best in order that they might revere them the more. I'd send you back to wear the sacred mistletoe, to be King of the Bean, to be sacrificed to the good old goddess of agriculture. Instead, I encourage you to ride this strange wind that is blowing through you; to ride it to wherever it will carry you."

"But which way shall I go?"

"That is between you and the wind. You seem to be searching for a kind of immortality. With that I cannot help you. In the realms that I inhabit, death is a companion. One does not quarrel with one's friend. If you desire to meet masters with power over death, I suggest you travel to the distant east."

"As far as Hellas?"

"Far, far beyond Hellas."

"To Egypt, then?" In Alobar's mind, Egypt, with its confounding mirrors, was the end of the trolley line.

"As far as Egypt is, you must go three times that far."

"Three times farther than Egypt? Are you trying to trick me? I would fall over the edge of the earth!"

The shaman snorted with laughter. "Alobar. The earth does not have an edge."

It was Alobar's turn to laugh. He thought he might be in the company of a crazy old fart, after all. "What utter nonsense," he declared.

"You are a free and special man, Alobar. Therefore I'm going to let you in on a little secret. Listen. I converse regularly with the birds and the fish. And the birds and the fish have assured me many times that there isn't any edge. We live on a ball, Alobar. We do. Keep this quiet: the world is round."

So heady was the idea that Alobar felt faint. He gulped his tea and gazed into the shaman's eyes—eyes as shiny and black as the bean in the cake—to ascertain that he was not being joshed. When he was convinced of the shaman's sincerity, he stood and gathered his hides about him. "I suppose I should be off then."

"I suppose you should."

"I surmise that several Feasts of Feasts will be consumed ere I am returned. However, I should be pleased to build you a strong new door when next I pass this way."

"You plan to return, then?"

"If the world be round, I can scarcely help it." He chuckled. "Someday, I should like to mingle with my clan again, even if I must disguise myself to do so."

The shaman shook his head. "I have it on good authority that Lord Aelfric's men are going to attack your old citadel as soon as the roads are dry in spring. They will kill all who resist and baptize the remainder. Long before you return—if you return—the independent city you once ruled will be but another Roman outpost on the frontiers of the Holy Empire."

Alobar smacked his palm with his fist. "Then I must warn the clan! I'll organize a defense! Maybe we'll attack first! By the golden whiskers of the morning star, we'll show those turnip eaters what battle's about! They'll need more than one god to save their asses ere I and my boys are through, blah blah blah . . ."

"Too late, Alobar, too late." As if to somehow illustrate his point, the shaman tore a badger mask from the wall and tossed it into the fire. "The foe is not merely Lord Aelfric but the whole of the empire. It is too large, too entrenched, has too much momentum. The world is changing, Alobar." He gestured at the burning mask. "Don't waste your life trying to hold back the tides of history. History begot Rome, and history someday will bury it. In the meantime, you've other fish to fry. Have you forgotten? Are you to be an individual, a trespasser in territory none else has had the wit or nerve to explore, or just another troublesome mosquito to be swatted by the authorities? You're no longer king or warrior, remember, but something new. It will do your clansmen no good for you to be slain alongside them, but who can guess what benefits may result from a new life wholly led?"

"You are correct," said Alobar. He sighed. "The clan, its lusty women and its noble hounds, lies behind me. It is forward I must go."

After embracing the old man, he marched out into the snow. He aimed his boots at the east and forced his heels to follow his toes. Quickly, the little hut of the shaman was out of view. Out of sight, too, was the village and the manor.

Frol must suspect that I am taking swift advantage of my beanship, straddling another's thighs at this late hour, he thought. He sensed that he was causing her some pain, and that, in turn, hurt him. He would miss Frol and the babies, perhaps more intensely than he missed Wren and Mik. But there was a strange wind blowing through him, was there not? Was it not blowing him away?

The sky was a velvety black paw pressing on the white

landscape with a feline delicacy, stars flying like sparks from its fur. The cry of an owl, brooding over its ruby appetites, cut through the frigid air like a vibrating pin. Then, all was silent except for the soft crunch, like ants chewing wax, of his boots upon the snow. His steps quickened. They took up a gay rhythm. He was very nearly dancing across the frozen fields.

"The world is round," he sang, in tune with his footfalls.

"Existence can be rearranged. A man can be many things.

"I am special and free.

"And the world is round round round."

A few weeks later, Alobar was awakened by a hot sun in his face and a hot stench in his nostrils. He sat up in the grass and rubbed his eyes. Don't ask where the rest of that dream went, Alobar. All dreams continue in the beyond.

The warm sunlight gave him a lazy, comfortable, lie-around-all-morning-and-scratch-your-armpits feeling, but inside his nose the cilia were waving, the turbinates were knocking, and the sphenoethmoidal recess was on red alert: by Woden's honey pots, what a scent!

Nearby, a flock was grazing, and Alobar guessed the aroma must be its fault, but fie on wool and a pox on mutton if sheep were so rude to the proboscis. *Perhaps in warm climates, sheep take on the odor of their cousins*, thought Alobar, for surely it was the essence of goat that permeated his nasal passages, and rutting goat at that.

With a flock so close, there must be a shepherd in the vicinity. Maybe I can talk him out of a few crumbs of breakfast ere I get me to a prettier-smelling place. Alobar went to rise but something snagged his cloak and pulled him back down. Again he tried to stand, again he was yanked to the sod. He reached behind him to free himself from the branch or vine that held him, but he touched nothing. Scooting forward a few feet on his rump, he made another attempt at rising, and another and another, each with the same result. Angry and a little frightened, he drew his knife and, still sitting, whirled around. There was no one behind him. With all of the elastic in his leg muscles, he snapped himself upward. Thud! Down he went like a sack of meteorites addressed special delivery to gravity.

This time he just sat there, fingering his blade, giving every sheep on the hillside a good look at his expression of frustration, bewilderment, and humiliation. Nearly a quarter of an hour passed before, very slowly, centimeter by centimeter, sinew by sinew, he commenced cautiously to draw himself upright. And he made it! He was standing! He stretched, expelled a sigh of relief that fluttered the lashes of a ewe twenty yards away, and strode off, only in midstride to fall flat on his new growth of beard.

An outburst of wild, magnificent laughter resounded over the hillside and echoed from the crags in the distance; wild laughter because its notes were outside the range of the normal human voice and so uninhibited as to make the shaman's cackle seem fettered; magnificent laughter because it seemed huge in scope and rare in distribution; laughter that was simultaneously strange and familiar and that instilled in Alobar the fear of the unknown and the joy of self-recognition. It was laughter that might have been squeezed from the tubes of his own darkest heart, then amplified fifty times through the bellows of a loon's ass.

The laughter evidently affected the sheep, for all at once they began to bleat and kick, the oldest rams in the flock cavorting as if they were lambs. A breeze suddenly raked the landscape, drawing from the grasses a dark murmuring, and setting the thistle bushes to chattering like thin teeth. Bees abandoned the gorse to fly in crazy circles a few feet above ground, while the birdsong that previously had gladdened the hillside lowered appreciably in volume, its capricious trills and whistles replaced by a consistent melodic line, almost reverent in tone. The unease that Alobar experienced was as piercing as a thorn, yet there was a pleasant tightening in his groin, and his limbs felt ticklish and kinetic, inspired beyond his control to join the flock in its awkward dance. The way he found himself moving horizontally through the grass made him wonder if he had not been seized by the Serpent Power, if there were not an edge, after all, and if he were not dangerously close to it.

"Hey!" a voice called out. "Why doth thy crawl about on thy belly? Art thou a man or a worm?"

Compelled by the voice, which was both dreadful and jolly, threatening and seductive, Alobar forgot his recent failures and scrambled to his feet. "Where are you?" he asked in a shaky falsetto. "Why are you laughing?"

"I am everywhere," the voice boomed. "And why shouldn't a god laugh at the puny endeavors of man?"

It was then that Alobar's battle-trained vision focused on the leer in the leaves. At first, the leer was all that he could see, but then he caught sight of a shaggy tail and realized that it was connected to the leer. (The tail bone frequently is connected to the leer bone, although today that connection is illegal in seventeen states and the District of Columbia.) In a moment, the bushes parted and into the pasture pranced an unbelievable creature, all woolly and goatlike from its waist down to its hooves; human and masculine above. Or, to be precise, human above save for a pair of stubby horns thrusting like bronze-tipped beet-diggers in the bright mountain air.

"You—you are the—the Horned One," stammered Alobar.

The creature gamboled closer, dispelling any doubts about the origin of the stench. "In some places they know me as that. Herebouts, they call me Pan." He paused. "Those who still honor me, that is." He paused again. "And who might thou be? And what is thy mission?"

"Alobar, once king, once serf, now individual—have you heard of individuals?—free and hungry, at your service. My mission? Well, frankly, I am running away from death."

Pan's hooves, which had been pawing the turf in an almost drunken little fandango, became gradually immobile, and the leer slowly slid off his face as if some weak but persistent hand had shoved it. His thick lips dipped downward in a solemn arc, and in his goatish eyes woe replaced mischief. "I, too," he said.

"What's that?" asked Alobar.

"Art thou so famished that thou cannot hear? I said that I, too, am running from death."

"But that couldn't be! You are a god. Are not the gods immortal?"

"Not quite. True, we art immune to the chills and accidents that swallow up humanity, but gods *can* die. We live only so long as people believe in us."

"Hmmm. I never thought of that," said Alobar. "But certainly for the likes of you there is no shortage of believers." Despite Pan's bedraggled curls and matted wool, despite the drool in the goatee and the manure on his hooves, he was by far the most impressive being Alobar had ever met.

"Ha! Where hath thou spent thy life, Alobar? In a pumpkin? Did thou just fall off a turnip cart?"

"I am an eater of *beets*," proclaimed Alobar proudly.

"How could such an ignoramus ever hath been a king? Doth thy people reside so far back in the sticks that they never heard the famous voice crying out over the wine-dark sea, 'Great Pan is dead, Great Pan is dead'? Of course, that was nearly a millennium ago and as even a lout such as thou can see, I am still kicking. Nevertheless, with the birth of Christ, belief in me dwindled, and I have been scrambling for my life ever since."

"Yes, now that you mention it, the priest in our church did often refer to you as one of the false deities. In fact, the way he described the devil—the silly man believes there is but one god and one demon—he could be your twin."

"Thou art *Christian*?" Pan pronounced the word with such contempt that the flock stopped dancing and glared at Alobar, the bees buzzed angrily at him, and a passing butterfly shat upon him with remarkable accuracy.

"Oh, no, no," said Alobar hurriedly, wiping the green butterfly poop from the corner of his eye. "Not really. I merely played along with my neighbors to assuage their suspicions. This fellow Christ is a bit namby-pamby for my taste. And now that I hear what he's done to you, why, I like him the less, even if he did favor individualism."

"Thou ninny."

"Sir, I will not have you calling me a nanny!"

"Ninny, not nanny! Doth thou think I would call thee after one of the things I love best?" Pan's heavy lids drooped momentarily as his thoughts strayed to other pastures on other days, days when the petal-pink genitals of the she-goats drew him down from the crags.

"Just the same . . ." Alobar's fist was about his knife.

"If thou wouldst outdistance death, don't blow thy slender lead by challenging a god, neither Christ, who is not here to defend himself, nor I, who art much closer than I need be to smite a prideful gnat such as thee." With a disagreeable thump, Alobar landed on his chin again. Pan had not moved a muscle. "Namby-pamby, huh? Christ said that illumination is found only by putting everything one has in jeopardy. Thou, of all humans, should understand the courage that is required to reject the secure blessings of society in order to woo the unpredictable ecstasies of the solitary soul. It is true that Christ had little enthusiasm for dance or copulation, that he took 'right' and 'wrong' too seriously and set himself apart from the natural world, but for all his shortcomings, he was much superior to thou mortals who hath embraced him to further thine own ends."

Although Alobar was no more fond of criticism than of being flung to the ground like a peach pit, he had learned from the shaman that the path to the marvelous is sometimes cleared by a sharp tongue, and when Pan began to move away, intimating that their conversation was done, Alobar hastened to draw him back. "Tell me, Horned One," he called, "why do you defend Christ if he is threatening your hide?"

The god paused, assuming a haunchy stance, like a woman in high heels. Instead of replying, however, he produced reed pipes and blew through them in a manner that caused the sheep to skip again and the little clouds to wiggle in the sky. The music was high-pitched and playful, a frail, tremulous, silvery sound that unfurled in lazy spirals without a care in the world. So immense was the contrast between this lighthearted piping and Pan's demeanor, his crude, simian features, and great sad eyes, that Alobar was moved in spite of himself, and when at last the music ceased, he knocked away a tear with his knuckles and said, "For you, sir, may the jaws of death have cotton teeth."

"For thee, as well," answered Pan. "But how can we toast without strong wine to lift? And thou did announce thy hunger so emphatically that even the deaf roots took note. I'll wager thou be horny, into the bargain. Come with me,

Alobar, for while we must go forever in despair, let us also go forever in the enjoyment of the world."

In a flash, Pan was across the pasture, Alobar at his heels, scaling the rugged rocks, oblivious to the thickets of violent thistles. Alobar was physically fit, hardened by his peasant labor and recent travels, but he could not keep pace with the god, and soon Pan was out of sight. That was no real problem, however, for Alobar simply followed the scent, that effluvium of goat glands that hung in the air like a salty mist and drew him ever higher up the craggy vertebrae. The higher Alobar climbed, the more piercing his unease, until he was in a literal state of panic. Just when this thrilling anxiety was at its zenith, tempting him with irrational impulses to throw himself from the cliffs, he heard girlish voices and the sound of splashing water. The panic completely vaporized as the Pan odor led him into a grotto, a ferny recess in the middle of which was a pellucid pool.

Enjoying the liquid pleasures of the pool were seven or eight unusual human females: short in stature, though full in contour, their bones packed into loaves of ivory and petunia; their tangled hair hanging like ropes of seaweed, nearly to their heels; their perfect nipples as red as guinea pig eyes, their squeals the kind that leave a glow in the dark; and not one of them older than the teenage Frol he'd left in Aelfric. Sweet genital sparks flew when they looked at Alobar, and he sensed himself in company most benevolent.

Directly across the pool, in the mouth of a shallow cave, hunkered Pan, a wineskin in one fist, an erection in the other. In a rough clay bowl at his feet, dangerously close to the sizzling bulb of his member, were olives, figs, and feta cheese. With a jerk of his head, the god beckoned. Alobar was famished, but in order to reach the food and drink, he had to wade through nymph-infested waters. Summoning his nerve, he plunged in. Brunch time in Arkadia.

The remainder of the day was spent in a luxurious, pastel stupor against which Alobar's northern temperament rebelled in vain. He had expected the nymphs to be quite wild in their demonstrations, imagined them biters, scratchers, and screamers, yet neither as king nor serf had he known such delicacy, and the softness in which the pleasures of the after-

noon were couched made the hero in him a bit embarrassed.
When he glanced about him in the pale twilight, however, he
saw everywhere evidence of his participation: dried semen
frosted the thighs of napping nymphs, clots of it floated in the
shadowy waters like weavings wrenched loose from the looms
of the trout, and upon the tips of bracken there glistened
drops too milky to be dew. It couldn't have been Pan's output
alone because Alobar's testicles were as flat and juiceless as
trampled grapes. Besides, after an hour's eventful splash in
the pool, Pan had crawled into the cave and fallen into a
lengthy snooze from which the purring ecstasies of the nymphs
were much too low to wake him.

"Pan is not well," the nymphs confided.

"I watched him scale the rocks, I watched him set four of
you to coming in a row," said Alobar. "He seems fit enough
to me."

The nymphs released a chorus of dreamy sighs. "You should
have seen him when he was in his prime. He's like a sick
dove, nowadays, compared to the goat he used to be."

"Is it Christ who is making him weak?"

"Not Christ but Christians. With every advance of Christianity, his powers recede," said one nymph.

"It started long before Christ," said a second.

"Yes, it did," agreed the first. "It began with the rise of the
cities. There simply was no place in the refined temples of
Attica and Sparta for a mountain goat like Pan."

A third nymph, who, with a wad of leaves, was scrubbing
herself clean of caked secretions, joined in. "It was man's
jealousy of woman that started it," she said. "They wanted to
drive the goddesses out of Olympus and replace them with
male gods."

"Is not Pan a male god?" asked Alobar.

"True, he is, but he is associated with female values. To
diminish the worth of women, men had to diminish the worth
of the moon. They had to drive a wedge between human
beings and the trees and the beasts and the waters, because
trees and beasts and waters are as loyal to the moon as to the
sun. They had to drive a wedge between thought and feeling,
between the lamplight by which they count the day's earn-
ings and the dark to which our Pan is ever connected. At first

they used Apollo as the wedge, and the abstract logic of Apollo made a mighty wedge, indeed, but Apollo the artist maintained a love for women, not the open, unrestrained lust that Pan has, but a controlled longing that undermined the patriarchal ambition. When Christ came along, Christ, who slept with no female, neither two-legged nor four, Christ, who played no musical instrument, recited no poetry, and never kicked up his heels by moonlight, this Christ was the perfect wedge. Christianity is merely a system for turning priestesses into handmaidens, queens into concubines, and goddesses into muses."

"And who can guess into what it will turn us nymphs?"

Alobar felt a surge of beet-red temper. Violently, he shook his head. "The world is changing," he said, "but there will always be a place in it for you. And for Pan."

"Perhaps. Certainly, we wish the moderns no harm, though Pan plays roughly with them at times. And thou? Will thou escape the fate thy feareth?"

"You misunderstand me. I do not *fear* death. I *resent* it. Everything must die, apparently, and I am no exception. But I want to be consulted. You know what I mean? Death is impatient and thoughtless. It barges into your room when you are right in the middle of something, and it doesn't bother to wipe its boots. I have a new passion, my darlings, a passion for being myself, and for being more than previously has been manifested for a single lifetime. I am determined to die at my own convenience. Therefore, I journey to the east, where, I have been told, there are men who have taught death some manners."

"We suspect thou art as foolish as brave, Alobar. In fact, bravery may be naught but foolishness. Fear, like love, is a call into the wild—into the deep, shadowy grotto. Fear is a finer thing than resentment. Resentment, an affliction of the mind, will leave thee complaining in Christ's well-lighted halls, but fear, a wisdom of the body, will lead thee back to Pan."

While Alobar was thinking that over, Pan awoke, stretched, and scampered into the thistles. When with the sun's setting he did not return, Alobar gave the nymphs a last squeeze and began his long, laborious descent, during which he several times heard thunderous laughter ring round about him and once thought he saw a moonbeam strike, high up in the crags, a fleeting horn.

Alone, with not so much as a sperm left to accompany him, Alobar again directed his steps toward the east. His was the gait of expectation, a pace set more by intuition than by reason, a clip fueled more by vague hints of wonderment than by steady assessments of purpose.

He was to continue in that fashion for an inappropriately long stretch of literary time, passing through more landscapes than there are keys on a typewriter, having more adventures than there are nibs for pens. Not once during or following a perilous escapade did it occur to him that the unpredictability of the moment of one's death might provide life with its necessary tension. But ever mindful of the kin of Pan, whose memory no encounter, however dramatic, could obscure, he allowed himself to resent death less and fear it more. And as he passed through one exotic environment after another, learning languages, wearing out boots, he sang his little song:

> "I love the ground-o, ground-o
> A ball beneath my feet
> The world is round-o, round-o
> Just like a frigging beet."

No, he would not be remembered as bard—nor, for that matter, as warrior or king. Life is fair, however, and in the fragrance industry, his name would one day become an accepted part of the nomenclature. According to Priscilla, the genius waitress, an *alobar* is a unit of measurement that describes the rate at which *Old Spice* after-shave lotion is absorbed by the lace on crotchless underpants, although at other times she has defined it as the time it takes *Chanel No. 5* to evaporate from the wing tips of a wild duck flying backward.

SEATTLE

IT SEEMED LIKE THE WHOLE TOWN was at odds over the solar eclipse. A lot of people were of the opinion that since in Seattle one seldom saw the sun anyhow, there was nothing very special about not seeing it again. Monday morning would be only a shade darker than usual, they reasoned. The difference, according to others, perhaps the majority, was that Monday was forecast to be clear. With the absence of the cloud cover that normally caused the sky over Seattle to resemble cottage cheese that had been dragged nine miles behind a cement truck, the city, for the first time in memory, would have an unobstructed view of one of nature's most mystical spectacles.

"Did you walk up to Volunteer Park to watch the eclipse?" was the first thing Ricki said to Priscilla when she came by her apartment Monday noon.

"Nope. Didn't make it outdoors," said Priscilla, yawning.

"You watched it on TV then?"

"No, I didn't."

"You didn't see it *at all*?"

"I listened to it," said Priscilla. "I listened to it on the radio. It sounded like bacon frying."

"Shit, woman. Sometimes I don't believe you're for real." Ricki looked about the room for a place to sit. The couch and the chair, the most logical contenders, were piled high with dirty clothes, clean clothes, clothes in transition, books, un-

opened mail, and laboratory equipment. There were also a
couple of beets. Ricki elected to stand. "You'd better shift
into your hurry-up offense," she said. "The meeting starts in
thirty minutes."

"I can shower on first down, make up on second, and dress
on third. If I haven't put it over by then, I can always kick a
field goal."

"Unless you fumble."

Priscilla slammed the bathroom door. Ricki had to steady a
beaker of liquid to prevent a major spill.

The football repartee was the result of Ricki having talked
Priscilla into spending the previous afternoon at the Kingdome,
an outing that revealed to Priscilla what Ricki really liked
about the Seahawks. It was the Seagals. "Fashions come and
go, come and go," said Ricki, "but the length of the cheer-
leader skirt remains constant, and it is upon that abbreviated
standard that I base my currency of joy."

Today (they each had Sundays and Mondays off), Ricki was
taking Priscilla to a meeting of the Daughters of the Daily
Special, an organization of waitresses with university degrees.
At least in the beginning all the members had had university
degrees. The group had some time ago lowered its standards
to accept waitresses with only two years of college. That was
when Ricki was admitted, back when it was still called *Sisters*
of the Daily Special. "Sisters" had come to sound too political. It suggested a feminine solidarity that the waitresses, in
their honesty, considered not just inaccurate but inappropriate. "We're out to grab us some gusto, not cut anybody's nuts
off," was the way Ricki put it.

In Seattle, as in most other large cities, there were a fair
number of women who had studied art, literature, philosophy, history, etc., only to find that their education and a
dollar would buy them a glass of Perrier. True, they hadn't
entered their respective fields with the idea of getting rich,
but neither had they expected that a summa cum laude
would take them about as far from campus as the nearest dry
water hole. Unable to support themselves in the work of their
choice, they turned to waitressing, for there they could earn
the most money for the least investment. If it wasn't possible
for them to do something meaningful and fulfilling, at least

they could be well compensated for a minimum of moral compromise and an even barer minimum of vocational commitment.

The Daughters of the Daily Special, once they learned that they had too many individual differences to call themselves "Sisters," had adopted a very clean and simple raison d'être: they planned to liberate each other, one at a time. They paid relatively stiff weekly dues, and they raised additional funds with such tried and true schemes as bikini car washes. Once or twice a year, depending upon how much was in their treasury, they awarded a grant that allowed a deserving member to lay down her tray and devote some time to her true calling. For example, they got Trixie Melodian out of the Salmon House and into the dance studio, where she choreographed her ballet based on the eruptions of Mount St. Helens; they bought Ellen Cherry Charles six months at her easel, where she completed a series of landscapes that was later hung in a restaurant ("I escaped, my paintings didn't," she commented); and Sheila Gomez was able to quit totaling bar tabs at La Buznik and finish writing her master's thesis in mathematics, "some kind of Puerto Rican trigonometry," according to Ricki.

Ricki was an unlikely candidate for a Daily Special grant, since she had majored in physical education so that she could take lots of showers with the other coeds, but she was sure Priscilla could land one, and that was why she was sponsoring Priscilla for membership. At first, Priscilla was reluctant. She was just not a joiner. "The only organization I ever joined in my life was the Columbia Record Club," she declared, "and I had to get out of that because it was too disciplined." The more Ricki talked about those big fat juicy grants, however, the better they sounded. She felt that she was close to a breakthrough in her experiments, but she was almost too tired to continue. If the Daughters could buy her a few uninterrupted months in her lab, she'd not only sign their roster, she'd kiss their behinds. "Starting with mine," chirped Ricki.

Priscilla came out of the bathroom wearing tight jeans and a cable-knit, iguana-green pullover sweater that accentuated the red in her reddish-brown hair. For a change, she'd pinked her Cupid's bow mouth—tiny in comparison to Ricki's full Latino lips—and brushed on enough purple eye shadow to make Bela Lugosi look like a lifeguard. "Wow!" exclaimed Ricki. "You're the second most impressive thing I've seen today, the first being a total eclipse of the sun."

"One would have thought a solar eclipse would have made a noise like the Mormon Tabernacle Choir," said Priscilla, "but it really did sound like bacon frying."

"You slept through it, you asshole."

They drove downtown in Ricki's rusted-out VW bug. "I'm ashamed to be seen behind the wheel of this bedpan," Ricki said. "It looks like it has a skin disease. Worse, it looks like a car *you* would drive."

"When I perfect that formula, you're gonna see me driving a BMW or a Lincoln Continental," said Priscilla. "Maybe both at the same time."

"That's why we're enlisting you in the Daughters. Gonna get you out of that smelly studio and into a penthouse. I do hope you'll keep it tidier than your present digs. Which reminds me, Pris, what were those old dry beets doing in your armchair?"

"Somebody's been leaving them outside my door. To be perfectly frank, I thought it might be you."

"Me? Why would I do an idiotic thing like that? I *hate* beets. In fact, I hate most vegetables." She paused. "I must admit, though, that vegetarians taste better than heavy meat eaters. Smokers are the worst. You wouldn't think that you could detect it, you know, *down there*. But you can." She made a face that caused the faint handlebar of hairs above her lip to bristle like the fuzz on an ostrich's cheek.

"Since I've been working at El Papa Muerta, nothing tastes good to me anymore," Priscilla said.

The holocaustal effect that serving food for a living can have on one's appetite was a subject discussed at the meeting of the Daughters of the Daily Special. "That's why it's preferable to wait cocktails," somebody said. "No, that's worse," responded Sheila Gomez. "Waiting cocktails kills your appetite for liquor."

The meeting was held in the Spotted Necktie Room at the Old Spaghetti Factory. There were about forty women present, twice as many as Priscilla had expected. After they finished complaining about appetite loss, they complained about the neutron bomb that working nights had dropped on their social lives. Then they really got steamed up over having to be nice to people they couldn't stand. It wasn't the men who infuriated them, not even bottom-pinching men (some waitresses, a minority, actually enjoyed having their bottoms pinched), it was the women. "The most unbearable aspect of this job is waiting on rich, crabby, drunk ladies," said one waitress. "Right on!" said another. "Except for the rare one who might have toted trays somewhere in her sordid past, they'll pick the tips up off the table as soon as their husbands' backs are turned."

"How true. A wife is a waitress's public enemy number one."

"Beware of blue hair and T-shirts that say 'World's Best Grandma.' They expect *you* to tip *them*."

Next they compared notes on how much their feet hurt and the psychotic states of cooks. Evidently, all restaurant cooks were psychotic, some were just less violent than others. It was all rather depressing. But, then, they began to share stories of the odd mammoth tip they'd received the previous week, the odd offer of booze, cocaine, or a big house in the South of France; the odd, interesting customer, including local celebrities, who the celebrity dined with and what they ate; and before long, drinking Chianti all the while, they got off the subject of waitressing altogether and had a fine old time exchanging reviews and critiques of the solar eclipse.

The meeting was nearly over when they got around to considering Priscilla's application for membership. As Ricki had warned it might, it met with some opposition.

"It's irrelevant that she's had only one year of college," Ricki told the assembly. "She's a genius."

"Says who?"

"Says me."

"Ha ha."

"You don't have to be a genius to recognize one. If you did, Einstein would never have gotten invited to the White House."

"Well, how about some proof."

"Go ahead," said Ricki, "test her. Ask her a question."

"What's the capital of San Salvador?" asked Trixie Melodian.

"You call that a genius question?" Doris Newton responded. "I've seen retired air force sergeants answer harder questions than that on *Tic Tac Dough*."

"Besides," said Ellen Cherry Charles, "San Salvador *is* the capital. The country is El Salvador."

"Are you positive?" asked Trixie. "Why would the city have a longer name than the country?"

"If she's such a genius, why is she working at El Papa Muerta? Everybody knows Mexican restaurants are the pits for tips."

"El Papa Muerta is about as Mexican as Juneau."

"Does El Papa Muerta mean The Dead Potato or The Dead Pope?"

"What's the difference?"

"I resent that," said Sheila Gomez, glancing at the little crucifix that dangled its gold-skinned heels above her globes.

Priscilla cleared her throat. She spoke for the first time since the meeting began. Her voice was a trifle high and squeaky. "I've worked at five Mexican restaurants in three years. I'm searching for the perfect taco."

That stopped them. Hell, maybe she *was* a genius.

Ricki stood again. "Little Priscilla here is a scientist. She's got her own laboratory. And is she onto something hot! I'm not at liberty to reveal what it is at this point in time, you understand, a slip of the lip can sink a ship, but when the moment comes . . . well, you're all gonna feel like a slow boat to China for hemming and hawing over taking her in. Let me remind you of something. None of the grants that the Daughters have awarded so far have generated a dime of income for the program. Nothing personal, Sheila, I know Third World algebra is important, but it didn't do dogshit at the box office; and, Joan, that little book of poems you printed about driftwood and your mama's melanoma was real pretty, it brought big whopping tears to my eyes is what it did, but, honestly now, the GNP was unaffected. Ditto, Trixie's harmonic tremors. I don't want to sound crass, but Priscilla here is zoned commercial. She's got a million bucks by its long green tail, and if we help her hold on and haul it in, each and every one of us is gonna soak our weary feet in Dom Perignon.

This is not the time to talk about funding her scientific research, we'll come to that a ways down the road, but this smart little goose may be prepared to lay us our first golden egg. All in favor of admitting her to the club say 'aye.' "

The ayes swept it, and out in the parking lot, Ricki looked at Priscilla and winked. "What's the capital of El Papa Muerta?" she asked. "*San Papa Muerta?*"

Priscilla grabbed Ricki and kissed her full and wet on the mouth, right in front of a great many waitresses who were pulling out of the lot in various rusted-out VW bugs. The rusted-out VW bug is the national bird of Waitressland. It was then and there that Priscilla made up her mind to go to bed with Ricki. But while her mind was convinced, her body needed encouragement, so they went to the Virginia Inn at First and Virginia and drank a gang of discount champagne. Still, Priscilla's endocrine system was lagging a few laps behind her resolve. "My pilot light has gone out and needs to be relit," she said. Ricki suggested a porno movie. She hoped that a double bill of *Starship Eros* and *Garage Girls* would turn up the thermostat. Priscilla hoped so, too.

Once in the theater, however, the Chianti and champagne began to get to Ricki. They were sitting up close, in the third row, and all of those colossal in-and-outs and up-and-downs made her queasy. It was a classic case of motion sickness. She held her tummy and moaned. Priscilla turned to the row of baldheaded men behind them. "Would you mind not smoking," she said. "This woman is having a religious experience."

"If they jiggle one more time, I'm gonna spew," said Ricki.

Priscilla helped her to her feet and led her down the aisle. A couple of the bald boys followed them. "My friend has a chronic allergy to heterosexuality," Priscilla told them. "We brought her here in an attempt to activate her body's natural immune system, but it didn't work." The men laughed kind of nervously. "Don't mock the afflicted!" Priscilla screamed at them. The Don Juans returned to their seats.

It had been a while since Priscilla had driven a car. She shifted gears jerkily. Ricki groaned. They had to make three pit stops between downtown and the Ballard district, a distance so slight that octogenarian Norwegian crones had been known to walk it, their shopping bags loaded with lutefisk. At

Ricki's duplex, Priscilla washed the victim's face and tucked her in. She appeared to have passed out, but as Priscilla was tiptoeing to the door, she called in a weak voice, "It was wonderful, Pris."

"What was, honey? The meeting? The champagne?"

"The eclipse," said Ricki. "It was probably the most real thing I've ever seen, but it was also like a dream. You know what I mean? Real and unreal, beautiful and strange, like a dream. It got me high as a kite, but it didn't last long enough. It ended too soon and left nothing behind."

"That's how it is with dreams," said Priscilla. "They're the perfect crime." She thought then of the elusive exudate, the living emerald she hunted in the forests of olfactory memory, the dream she lived in her nose. She felt her laboratory pulling her like a tide, and it taxed her strength to resist.

With effort, she drove Ricki's car to the waterfront and sipped a cup of bivalve nectar at Ivar's Clam Bar (it was a walk-up, fast-fish stand where she needn't worry about being served by a waitress who might have been at the meeting that day). Then, having resolved on her last birthday to complete every task she began, she returned to the moviehouse and watched the ending of *Starship Eros*. Everything considered, it had been the most relaxing and entertaining two days off she'd enjoyed all year. "All work and no play makes Priscilla a dull genius," she lectured herself on the way home.

It was after midnight when she arrived at her building. There was an odor in the hallway more funky than a cabbage pot, and on her doorsill there sat in certain firepluggian splendor, like a dropping from the eclipse, like a disembodied bulb that had been beamed to Earth from Starship Eros, another beet.

NEW ORLEANS

LOUISIANA IN SEPTEMBER was like an obscene phone call from nature. The air—moist, sultry, secretive, and far from fresh—felt as if it were being exhaled into one's face. Sometimes it even *sounded* like heavy breathing. Honeysuckle, swamp flowers, magnolia, and the mystery smell of the river scented the atmosphere, amplifying the intrusion of organic sleaze. It was aphrodisiac and repressive, soft and violent at the same time. In New Orleans, in the French Quarter, miles from the barking lungs of alligators, the air maintained this quality of breath, although here it acquired a tinge of metallic halitosis, due to fumes expelled by tourist buses, trucks delivering Dixie beer, and, on Decatur Street, a mass-transit motor coach named Desire.

The only way to hang up on the obscene caller was to install air conditioning. The Parfumerie Devalier never had been air-conditioned, however, and unless it lifted from its current economic slump, it probably never would be. As a consequence, both Madame Lily Devalier and her maid and assistant, V'lu Jackson, held old-fashioned lacquered paper fans, with which they stirred the humid respiration that Louisiana panted into the shop. They were sitting on the lime velvet love seat at the rear of the retail area, watching television and fanning away. On the six o'clock news there were scenes of a total eclipse of the sun as photographed from atop the Space Needle in Seattle and the Eiffel Tower in Paris (the path of an eclipse is one hundred and sixty-seven miles wide, allowing Seattle to catch the southern edge of this one and Paris the northern edge: in New Orleans, the sun had burned on as was its habit, undimmed except by a late afternoon shower).

"Whooee!" exclaimed V'lu as she watched first Seattle and then Paris go from broad daylight to supernatural darkness in a matter of seconds. "Whooee! That done beats hurricane drops all to pieces."

"I see it as an omen," said Madame Devalier.

"Say whut?"

"An omen. A sign. Paris is eclipsed, New Orleans basks in light. The perfumes of Devalier have always been as good as any in France, and now they are going to be better. Parfumerie Devalier is going to prosper, and Paris—proud, arrogant, pompous Paris—is going to play second fiddle." Madame touched the avalanche of her bosom with her fan, nodded three times, and smiled.

V'lu giggled. "Seattle, too, ma'am."

"What about Seattle?"

"Seattle e-clipsed, too. So we don't have to worry none 'bout Seattle."

"I wasn't worried in the least about Seattle. Why would I worry about Seattle, of all places?"

V'lu hesitated before replying. The young woman and the old woman stared at each other, fanning relentlessly. "*She* in Seattle, ma'am. Last anybody heard."

"So? What difference does it make where 'she' is? Not that I don't have feelings for her, but her whereabouts has nothing to do with our business."

Again V'lu hesitated. Her brown eyes opened as wide as the mouths of baby birds. "She got dee bottle," V'lu said.

"The bottle! Bah! Poof! You and that bottle. Forget that bottle, it means nothing. *Rien*. Even if it had value, what on earth could *she* do with it?" Madame's fan whirred like a sewing machine. Her fan seemed to generate static electricity. A halo of heat lightning formed around it. "Even if that bottle is all you say it is, we don't need it. We have right here in this shop the most fabulous boof of jasmine the human nose has ever tasted—"

"Bingo Pajama!"

"I beg your pardon. Is that more vulgar slang from your vulgar generation?"

"Bingo Pajama, ma'am. That he name. He be back from dee island nex week wif mo' flowers."

"And we haven't tamed the last batch yet! Tangerine seems to work okay as the top note. It aerates rather quickly, but it rides the jasmine and doesn't sink completely into it. With a middle note of the vigor of that Bingo Pajama jasmine—my Lord in heaven, girl, is that actually his name?—what we need is a base note with a floor of iron. It can't just sit there, though, it has to rise up subtly and unite the tangerine somehow with that bodacious jasmine theme. A very special base note is what you and I must find." Madame Devalier's fan fluttered wildly, and V'lu fanned hard to keep up with her.

"But let us not put the barn door before the horse."

"Ma'am?"

"We require a unique base note, and we will find one, if I have to turn my trick bag inside out to find it. Remember, I came up with hurricane drops long after the darkies said the recipe had been lost forever. Right?"

"You right."

"First, however, we have a problem with overcook. It's not rank, but it's rank enough. We are shooting the moon on this boof, cher; we have got the raw product to make half of France whistle Dixie, and we are not going to blow it because we are too poor to pump or flash. So you know how we are going to handle it? Papa's fat!"

The good Madame was up to her bouffant in the backwater of boof biz. She had selected jasmine as the theme note of her comeback scent knowing that it was a blue-chip ingredient, a botanical platinum, a tried and tested floral champion whose performance in perfumery was rivaled only by the rose, yet knowing equally well that, like any prima donna, there were conditions under which it would refuse to sing. Jasmine (known in extreme cases as *Jasminum officinale*) simply will not tolerate the heat involved in steam distillation. Even boiling water is enough to murder the aroma principal of its flowers. Jasmine oil has to be extracted, not distilled, and efficient and effective extraction is not quite as easy as tying a loose tooth to a knob.

One begins by gently percolating fresh petals in a solvent—purified hexane, to be precise. That was what Madame and V'lu did to Bingo Pajama's flowers, with fine results. But then the solvent has to be removed. No woman of grace wishes to dab about her body with industrial hexane, however pure. If the Parfumerie Devalier had owned a flash evaporator or a vacuum pump, the hexane stink would have been off that jasmine oil faster than a Japanese commuter off the bullet train. Alas, the little shop on Royal Street could no more afford that kind of equipment than a Third World spider could afford designer webs and flies cordon bleu. Thus, Lily and V'lu steeped their extract in a vat of below-boil water, forced it through a filter tube, distilled it with alcohol, and hoped for the best.

When Lily Devalier maneuvered her midget submarine of a nose along dockside of the concentration crock, oh!, a nocturnal warmth enveloped her brain, washing her in star waters, translucent cherub sperms, and the midnight blue syrups that tropical moths lick. The devouring delicacy of this jasmine swept her away, but she was not so smitten that she failed to detect a slight overcooked sensation and a faint, lingering off-note of solvent. It was then and there that she decided to resort to enfleurage, the old process, the method her Papa had used. In enfleurage, petals are laid out on trays of fat, where they are allowed to remain until the fat has absorbed most of the fragrance. When the flowers are exhausted, fresh ones are substituted. In time, the fat becomes saturated with the floral aromatic, which may then be sponged off the fat with baths of alcohol. It's all done by hand, and it's painstaking and slow; far, far too slow for the corporations of Paris and New York, but it would produce a truly superior oil, an essence worthy of the naked night creature that the Jamaican had captured for her, and worthy, too, of the rare base note that Madame had sworn to find to support it.

"It will be hard work, but we are going to go Papa's fat. Are you with me?"

"You right."

"Pardon?"

"Ah wif you, ma'am. All dee way."

The fan of Madame Devalier suddenly paused, as if her swollen, braceleted wrist had imagined it had heard the quitting whistle, then, poorer of some hopes but freer of some illusions, it resumed its hammering. "Let us have a bowl of gazpacho, cher. Then we shall nap for a couple of hours. By ten, it should be cool enough to resume our work in the lab."

"Ah sure wish you git dee upstairs air-conkditioned."

"Why, V'lu, a hardy plantation girl like you, you know you don't require air conditioning to sleep."

"Ah not talking 'bout no sleep, ma'am. Ah be talking 'bout vegables. Vegables flying in through dee winda and landing on mah bed."

"Oh, poof! Just some buck trying to attract your attention and not suave enough to send roses. Probably that crazy Jamaican."

"Oh, no, ma'am. Bingo Pajama smell *nice*."

"What do you mean, cher?"

"Nebber mind. Ah be dishing up dee cold soup now."

"*Merci*. Thank you. Let us dine down here in the shop, it might be less oppressive."

Hips swaying like mandolins on a gypsy wagon wall, V'lu climbed the narrow stairs, leaving her employer to fend off with her fan the lewd breath of Louisiana, as she awaited the seven o'clock news and yet another ominous view of the blacking out of Paris.

From the top step, V'lu called, "If Miz Priscilla not be doing nothin' wif dat bottle, how come she at dee perfumers' convention?"

There was no reply, but V'lu could tell somehow that the fanning had stopped.

PARIS

THE CARROT SYMBOLIZES financial success; a prom-
ised, often illusory reward. A carrot is a wish, a lie, a dream.
In that sense, it has something in common with perfume. A
beet, however . . . a beet is proletarian, immediate, and, in a
thoroughly unglamorous way, morbid. What is the message a
beet bears to a perfumer? That his chic, elitist ways are
doomed? That he might profit from a more natural, earthy,
straightforward approach? This beet, this ember, this miner's
bloodshot eye, this apple that an owl has pierced, is it a
warning or friendly advice?

Those were the thoughts of Marcel LeFever as he stood
staring out of his office window on the twenty-third floor.
Marcel had been standing at the window for hours. Ever
since the eclipse.

Claude LeFever, Marcel's cousin and lookalike, had watched
the eclipse from his own office window. A practical man,
Claude nevertheless had been moved. Paris is given to the
dramatic at any time, yet, as daylight began ever more quickly
to fade that morning and the great shadow rode out of the
west, the city seemed to turn into a stage set, an eerily lit
backdrop before which a drama surpassing even the talents of
the French was about to unfold. As the strange twilight
gathered, bands of alternating light and shadow began to
ripple along the facade of the cathedral across the street, and
when Claude glanced at the sky, he saw that the text of *Les*

Miserables had been painted over by Salvador Dali. The sun was so round and glossy and black that had it a figure eight on it, well, it would have validated a lot of long-standing philosophical and theological complaints, underlining once and for all just where we earthlings sit on the cosmic pool table. A silver glow, like a blaze of molten escargot tongs, erupted from behind the ebony corona, and Claude felt himself trembling with a sort of euphoria.

When, after three awe-filled minutes, a blinding diamond crust of sun emerged from the lunar umbra, Claude heard others in the building applauding, and he, too, clapped his soft, manicured hands, albeit discreetly. The sun was back on the job, but for some reason, *he* did not feel like returning directly to work, so he went next-door to discuss the celestial spectacle with Marcel. Marcel would understand his oddly euphoric state. If anyone might explain why an eclipse of the sun could arouse in him such a profound sense of derealization, Marcel might. There were those who claimed that if it didn't smell, Marcel LeFever had no interest in it, but Claude knew better. Besides, since it was Marcel's gift to detect odors too faint to register in others' snouts, well, who was to say if in his cousin's world all things did not have their characteristic aromas? Claude recalled a night on the beach when Marcel had stated that the sea smelled differently at full moon than at new. They were younger then, in their twenties, and if he wasn't mistaken, they had smoked a little hashish, so perhaps it was a joke. But if there were lunar smells, there might be solar, also. What if an eclipse emitted a particular olfactory vibration picked up by animals, say, and a few sensitive humans, and what if this signal could be analyzed, reproduced, amplified, and bottled? Talk about a heady perfume! Anyone who caught a whiff might become as giddy as he was now. Claude felt a pang in his temples, and he winced. His mind simply was not accustomed to this kind of high-flying fancy.

Marcel was standing in his window, staring out as if transfixed, and Claude elected for the moment not to infringe on his reverie. Instead, he retreated to his own office, opened the elegantly creaky door of a Louis XVI cabinet and removed a bottle of Pernod. From the executive refrigerator, his secretary procured water and ice cubes. Claude splashed himself a healthy one, noticed how the Pernod turned from clear to milky with the addition of water, and wondered if that was analogous to the way the eclipse had affected his thinking—or had it just the opposite effect? He gulped one drink, sipped another, and an hour, nearly, passed before he again called on his cousin. Marcel remained at the window, only now he was wearing his whale mask.

All afternoon Marcel stood in the window, all afternoon Claude drank. At five, when the secretaries went home, Claude took what was left of the Pernod and moved to the receptionist's desk, from where he might watch Marcel through a door left slightly ajar. Claude would have denied that he was spying. Rather, he had a protective interest in his cousin, for business as well as familial reasons. In fact, old Luc LeFever, Claude's father, Marcel's uncle, and at seventy, very much president of the firm, personally had charged Claude with the responsibility of looking out for Marcel. "He's a bedbug," Luc had said, "but you see to it that he's a safe and contented bedbug."

Claude wasn't entirely sure that Marcel was buggy, and he was less sure that he was content, but he would do whatever necessary to insure his safety. For a long time now, Marcel had been critical of the manner in which the LeFever company was evolving. Marcel was a perfumer. He *believed* in perfume. Colognes, toilet waters, and bath oils were all right with him, since they were merely diluted perfumes, and he had not objected strongly when the scents he and his assistants created had been used to enhance soaps, powders, body lotions, hand creams, and shampoos. He loathed the very word *deodorant*, however, and once at a board meeting tried to force a fellow officer of the company to eat the antiperspirant stick LeFever was about to market. He had had to be physically restrained. Yet, that was minor compared to his reaction to the news that LeFever was going to supply a scent to be used in the manufacturing of toilet paper. "Welcome to the aroma chemical industry," Claude had said. "We are now a full-fledged fragrance house." "We are a factory!" Marcel had responded, with enough contempt in his voice to wither the blubber off a bishop, and he stormed off to the Louvre, where the smell of great art calmed him down until he came upon one of those paintings by Hieronymus Bosch in which a little person is shoving a bouquet of flowers up another little person's rectum, whereupon he commenced to yell, "No used-car salesman is going to wipe his ass with my perfume!" and the museum guards threw him into the street. It wasn't long before LeFever was supplying the fragrance compounds for cleaners, disinfectants, furniture polish, textiles, stationery, rubber bands, shark repellent, and scratch-n-sniff kiddie books, and the day Claude and Luc decided to introduce "space sprays" to reodorize public buildings and subways, Marcel screamed "Muzak for the nose!" and sailed for Tahiti. In a year he was back, and they welcomed him home without question, for without their "Bunny," they were, indeed, just a factory.

It wasn't for his sexual habits that Marcel was called Bunny. Like those pious citizens who attend church every Sunday, then cheat and lie their way through the week, Marcel visited a brothel religiously on Saturday nights, then seemed to forget sex entirely for the next six days. Except for a recent encounter at a perfumers' convention in America, he had never been carnally involved with a woman who was not a professional, and then sparingly. No, his nickname came from his nose. A rabbit has been calculated to possess one-hundred-million olfactory receptors—small wonder its little schnozz is always twitching, it is trapped in an undulating blizzard of aromatic stimuli—and Marcel "Bunny" LeFever was reputed, with some exaggeration, to be the human equivalent of Peter Cottontail. In the laboratories of LeFever, there were spectrometers, gas liquid chromatographs, nuclear magnetic scanners, and other instruments, rapid and precise, with which to analyze and test aromatic substances, but since the worth of a fragrance depends upon its effect on the nose, scientific instrumentation could never hope to replace the sniffing snout of flesh as the final arbiter of fragrance value, and, by general agreement, Marcel's nose was the finest in the business. It could determine whether the balsam gum in a shipment from Peru had had too much rain, whether unscrupulous merchants in Madagascar had been adulterating the ylang-ylang oil again, or whether there was a "wobble" in the synthetic geraniol. Its greatest talent, however, was its ability to sniff out arrangements and combinations that could result in new perfumes. It functioned as a catalytic laser, oxidizing the passion that slept unaware in a violet, releasing the trade winds bottled up in orange peel; identifying by name and number the butterflies dissolved in chips of sandalwood and marrying them off, one by one, to the wealthy sons of musk.

As a manufacturer of aroma chemicals and fragrance compounds, LeFever was among the top twenty in the world. As a maker of fine perfumes, it was in the top five, and it was Marcel the Bunny who kept them there. The same Marcel who had been staring through a square foot of window glass for seven consecutive hours. Damn it, sensitive artist or no sensitive artist, pampered bedbug or no pampered bedbug, mystical eclipse or no mystical eclipse, it was time for somebody to throw a cigar at the smoke alarm.

"Pardon, Bunny, I didn't intend to startle you, but I'm afraid you're starting to get tangled up in the drapes."

"Drapes? You mean draperies. *Drape* is a verb, the noun is *drapery*. One drapes a window when one hangs draperies. It is impossible for one to become entangled in *drapes*, so I assume you were referring to *draperies*."

"Oh, yes. But *drapes* can be a convenient abbreviation when one has had too much to drink."

"If one can't say *draperies*, perhaps one shouldn't drink."

It must have been disconcerting to receive a grammar lesson through a whale mask, but, outwardly at least, Claude took it in stride. "Be that as it may," he said, "I have drunk and drunk plenty. The eclipse made me do it. Wasn't it derealizing? Didn't it give you shivers? Didn't it transport you to another plane? Didn't it make your brown eyes blue?"

The whale head nodded.

"Is that what you were thinking about here at the window?"

Marcel did not dare reveal that his thoughts, when interrupted, were of carrots and beets, for Claude, sloshed as he was, would surely find a way to connect verbally those vegetables to his nickname and coin some bad joke about bunny rabbits. So Marcel said, "No, I was thinking about perfume," which, given Marcel's perpetual obsession, wasn't a very large lie. "And I was thinking about V'lu."

"Ah-ha!" exclaimed Claude. "You know, there's not much that can be done to heal the sting of a woman. As they say in her country, it's easier to scratch your ass than your heart."

"You misunderstood me. Let me see if I can put it in words that even the inebriated might understand. For the past month I have spent most of my time down in the kitchen, perfecting the scent that we are calling *New Wave*. You are familiar with the rationale behind *New Wave*. We are predicting that for many people the fascination with nostalgia—with a past reputed to be more simple, more honest, more natural than the present—will soon subside. In the cities, there is a large, affluent, professional class that has already rejected the sweet, heavy, feminine, Oriental scents that the hippies ushered into favor in the sixties, as well as the clean, wholesome, fruity and herbal scents associated with the backpacker chic of the seventies. For this avant-garde, and for those who will flock to join it, LeFever is developing *New Wave*, a truly modern scent—sharp, hard-edged, assertive, unisexual, urbane, unromantic, nonmysterious, cool, light, elegant, and wholly synthetic—"

"I know all that, Marcel."

"Yes, but what you don't know is how boring and, ultimately, frightening I am finding this scent. I slept last night with *New Wave* on my pillowcase, and my dreams were totalitarian nightmares. The boof is not unattractive, yet when I test it, I have somehow the feeling that I am smelling the sinister vapors of fascism."

"Really, Bunny. Ha ha."

"I am not joking." Marcel removed the whale mask. His demeanor was serious, indeed. "I am not joking."

"But, surely—"

"When I smell *New Wave*, I have the sensation that I am smelling control, conformity, domination. As I have said, it has a definite appeal. . . ."

"Well, then—"

"There is a comfort in conformity, a security in control, that is appealing. There is a thrill in domination, and we are all of us secretly attracted to violence."

"A violent perfume? Ha ha. Remember that U.S. after-shave, *Hai Karate*?"

"Were I to add but a trace note of leather to *New Wave*, Claude, I would say that I had drawn on my canvas the olfactory silhouette of the Nazi."

The word jolted Claude. He shuddered. The LeFever twins had been small boys during the Nazi occupation of Paris, but they recalled it as an adult recalls the breaking of a bone in childhood: the sickening crack, the fear, the pain, the sadness, the sudden ooze of blood that shows itself like the black blush of fairy-tale witches. It was a wound upon their memory, a thud of monster boots in a distant sandbox.

"*New Wave* is an intriguing perfume," Marcel went on, "but I am growing to loathe it, and actually to fear its implications. Therefore, I have been thinking today about raw materials. The eclipse set me to wondering about those powerful and mysterious aspects of the natural world that the perfumer has not tapped yet. We moved into synthetics as natural raw materials became less available, more expensive. But there are scores, perhaps hundreds, of raw materials in different parts of the world that we haven't examined—consider the valley of the Amazon, consider the *ocean*, for God's sake—and there is history. . . . The recent love affair with the past was with a relatively recent past. Fifty years ago, a century at the most. But what of the fragrances of five thousand years ago, were they as primitive and unrefined and fundamental as we believe? History? What about the fragrances of prehistory?"

Marcel took a seat. He sighed. He was not an athletic man, and he'd been on his feet the whole strange day. "The eclipse also caused me to think of V'lu."

"Yes, back to V'lu." Claude grinned a sloppy Pernod grin. "Let me guess. This black face of the sun reminded you of her. Reminded you that her ancestors in the jungle used fragrances of which we know little—"

"Idiot. What I was reminded of, aside from things that are none of your business, was a remark she made. V'lu pointed out to me that the synthetics that predominate in perfumery today are practically all petroleum products. The price of crude oil is now subject to arbitrary decisions by the OPEC nations. V'lu suggested that since the Arabs are untrustworthy and since the future of the Mideast is uncertain, there is a strong possibility that petrochemicals will become even more scarce and expensive than natural materials. She suggested that we ought to be looking anew at the flowers."

"That is elementary and quite sound," agreed Claude. "It is an idea with some merit, I don't have to be sober to recognize that. Fuck the Arabs, anyhow. Hang them from the drapes! And the *draperies*, too; yes, Bunny? But what I can't imagine is how this shopgirl—out of the mouths of babes, uh?—communicated this to you; I mean how could you even understand her, speaking in southern Negro dialect and all?"

Marcel looked first at his cousin, then out the window again, focusing perhaps on that same invisible celestial footprint that had held his gaze all day. "I had no problem," he said. "V'lu did not express this to me in English, you see. She spoke flawless French."

Mangel-Wurzel, Mon Amour.

PART
II

LOOKING
UP
CHOMOLUNGMA'S
DRESS

AS THE AFTERNOON PROGRESSES, our shadows grow longer. At night, in the dark, we *become* our shadows. That is as true today as then. In the old days, people were aware of it, that's all. In the old days, the whole world was religious and full of interest.

Alobar had been at the lamasery twenty years when Kudra arrived, dressed as a boy. The lamas saw through her disguise immediately but put her to work moving stones. She had worked on the wall less than an hour before Alobar, too, realized she was a woman. Her shadow fell off of her with perfect discretion. Shadows do. It was her aroma that gave her away.

They took their afternoon tea by the cold river. The lama who was overseeing the construction of the wall suggested that the workers disrobe and enjoy a dip. Alobar encouraged this idea, for it had been a long time since he had seen a naked woman. He found himself trembling.

Kudra declined to swim. The lama persisted. "Come on, boy," he said. "Everybody must bathe or else the wall will fall down." In the high mountain air, there was mischief afoot.

Finally, the "boy" dashed up to Alobar, who was just wading into the water, and whispered, "Help me, please. Don't you recognize me?"

Of course, he didn't recognize her. Naked, he would not

have recognized her. She had been eight years old when he
had seen her last.

"You called me by a foreign name. Wren, little Wrenna, I
believe it was." Kudra smiled. "You haven't aged at all, you
know."

The icy water swirling around Alobar's ankles was causing
his genitals to retract. He felt ashamed and wanted to turn
his back. This mischief was a mistake.

Kudra grasped his arm. "Remember? You tried to persuade me to eat a beet."

Of our nine planets, Saturn is the one that looks like fun.
Of our trees, the palm is obviously the stand-up comedian.
Among fowl, the jester's cap is worn by the duck. Of our
fruits and vegetables, the tomato could play Falstaff, the
banana a more slapstick role. As Hamlet—or Macbeth—the
beet is cast. In largely vegetarian India, the beet is rarely
eaten because its color is suggestive of blood. Out, damned
mangel-wurzel.

Alobar was remembering. . . .

He had been put off from the moment he sighted smoke.
On a day so sultry that he moved through it the way an
inchworm might move through a mound of lye, a day so
bright that it sent his eyeballs retreating into the shade of
their own sockets, he simply could not conceive of any advantage in torches. Surely torches could have waited until after
sunset, although upon the sweltering Ganges plain it seemed
to Alobar that one's sweat poured as profusely by night as by
day. As he drew nearer to the flames, he realized that they
were borne by mourners gathering for a funeral—all the
more reason to detour to the cheerful cool of a grove. It
should come as no surprise that the traveler from the west
was, in funereal matters, slightly shy.

The road, which had seen too many monsoons and forgotten too few, passed within yards of the funeral site, alas, and
in the grassy savannas to the side of the road, Alobar had
detected the odd hiss and slither, a persuasive inducement to
stick to the well-worn path. Thus, he soon found himself in

the midst of the white-clad mourners, an unwilling witness to unappetizing customs.

Not far from the river, four tall beams had been planted in the ground to form the corners of a square. They supported four thick planks firmly held by mortises. Between the beams there lay a plexus of logs, arranged in such a manner as to leave a space in the center, into which wood chips and resin had been scattered. Around and upon the log pile, dry branches of the sort that might burn quickly and brightly lay in wait. The roof of the pyre was made of planks covered with turf. The end result was a kind of tinder shack, a cottage at which no insurance agent would ever call, a studio apartment of death.

The corpse was placed in the middle of the square, upon the pile of logs. The dead man looked comfortable enough, all things considered (it bothered Alobar, philosophically, that the dead invariably seemed more self-possessed than the living), but obviously it only would be a matter of minutes before he began to char like one of those loaves the forgetful Frol was forever leaving too long on the hearth, an image that further hastened Alobar's departure. He had progressed but a few steps, however, before his path was blocked by a procession that, with great pomp, was leading a garlanded woman to the pyre.

As the procession wound around the site, Alobar inquired of a mourner if the woman might be the widow. Hardly had the stranger nodded "yes" than the female moved slowly, but without hesitation, to the "door" of the pyre. A Brahman followed her and handed her one of the torches, with which she lit each corner of the square. Then, to Alobar's horror, she lay down beside her dead husband.

It was with calm resignation, if not dim intelligence, that she at first regarded the flames that darted among the boughs like finches from hell, but when the heat grew more intense and she felt the early bites of pain, she cried out sharply and sat upright in her intended tomb. The Brahmans poked her with the long bamboo poles that they carried to funerals in case a widow should lose her enthusiasm for suicide suttee. A full panic seized her. She brushed the poles aside and made to leap from the square of fire. Using their poles, the Brahmans brought down the roof on her head, but her overheated adrenaline lent her a flash of superhuman strength, and she managed to spring from the blazing pyre and run, her sari smoking, toward the river.

The Brahmans overtook her on the bank and wrestled her back to the pyre, which was now roaring like a furnace. While the woman struggled with the priests, the crowd screamed and yelled. To his surprise, Alobar noticed that he, alone, was cheering for the woman. Under a rash impulse to intervene, he was drawing his knife when three sturdy Brahmans pried her from the earth to which she clung and flung her into the middle of the inferno. She continued to struggle for a minute, parting the heat waves with her shrieks, but by the time Alobar reached the pyre, she was as still and silent as any log in the blaze.

Shoving jabbering mourners roughly aside, holding his nose against the cannibal recipes that were pasting themselves in the air; scattering lotus garlands, hibiscus wreaths, rice balls, and milk bowls with kicks from what little was left of his boots, he barreled from the funeral grounds with an elephant's drive, and nothing, not Brahmanic curses nor the starched curtain of heat nor the craters and clouds of red dust in the road slowed him down. He might have continued at that pace for miles had he not come alongside a small girl, who was also fleeing the scene, sobbing hysterically.

Alobar put his arm around the child and tried to comfort her. From the rags of his blanket roll, he fished a piece of honeyed coconut meat that he had been saving for his bedtime treat. The girl refused it, though her sobs subsided somewhat, and she rested her head against his side. When they reached a leafy mango tree, out of sight of hair smoke and lip ash and bowel cinders, Alobar sat her down, dried her tears, and sang for her his ditty about the world being, against all evidence, round. She took the sweet.

Between bites, the child explained that she was unrelated to the funeral party but had come upon it by chance in the course of running a family errand. Thereupon she opened her basket and revealed its contents: a dozen round and ruddy roots, caked with loam.

"Beets!" cried Alobar. "Aren't you the lucky one?" He smacked his lips. "You shall dine handsomely this night."

The girl made a face. "Nobody eats these ugly things," she said. She went on to tell how her family boiled down beets for the color that was in them. Her father had dispatched her to gather this batch so that he might dye the strips of cotton cloth in which he wrapped the aromatic cones and sticks that he made and sold. She had been born, eight years earlier, into a caste of incense makers, and since business was flourishing at the holy sites along the Ganges where pilgrims bathed, and since she had but one brother, she was frequently called away from household chores in order to help in the trade.

"Dye," grumbled Alobar. "A tragic waste of fine food." But his lament was short-lived. There was something about the girl more interesting than her beet basket. She was a miniature version of Wren! The longer Alobar looked at her, the stronger the feeling. Her eyelids, like Wren's, were as thick and languid as the peel of some pulpy fruit; she had the same chin dimple: a wormhole in a pear; the same occupied codpiece for a nose. As did Wren's, her lips parted reluctantly, like waters protecting an oyster bed, to slowly disclose the aquatic shelf of bright teeth behind them, and in the girl's eyes there fluttered illuminated parchments upon which intelligent things were written, things that Alobar could scarcely hope to read. She was two or three shades darker, and several sizes smaller, naturally, but he could not help but call her Wren, his little Wrenna, unaware that his wife had been murdered by the jealous necromancer Noog a few weeks after Alobar was carried feet-first from his citadel eight years before.

"My name is Kudra," said the child. "Kudra, not Wren, and I believe I must go now."

"Yes, you must," agreed Alobar, who was ashamed and alarmed at the way his cock was beginning to push against the folds of its tent. "I, too, must resume my trek." He pointed to the north, in whose far mountains there supposedly dwelt the teachers he had long been seeking, the masters over death. He related to Kudra only a modicum of his travel plans, but she was to remember them in times to come, just as she was to remember his parting testimony in praise of the edibility of beets and as she was to remember how he had turned and run after her, grasped her shoulders and made her promise, through a fresh outpouring of tears, that what had transpired with the widow at the pyre that day would never transpire with her. . . .

"Bones are patient. Bones never tire nor do they run away. When you come upon a man who has been dead many years, his bones will still be lying there, in place, content, patiently waiting, but his flesh will have gotten up and left him. Water is like flesh. Water will not stand still. It is always off to somewhere else; restless, talkative, and curious. Even water in a covered jar will disappear in time. Flesh is water. Stones are like bones. Satisfied. Patient. Dependable. Tell me, then, Alobar, in order to achieve immortality, should you emulate water or stone? Should you trust your flesh or your bones?"

Alobar had stared at the lama and said nothing. After several minutes, the lama had asked him why he remained silent. "Water babbles to stone," said Alobar, "but stone will not answer."

From then on, they showed him some respect.

When Kudra revealed herself to him at the river, Alobar dressed quickly and led her away. "Where are you going with that boy?" called the lama. "Come back here! We have many stones to move."

"Stones are patient," Alobar replied. "I thought you knew."

They climbed from the riverbed to a grassy outcropping, where they might find a bit of padding for their backsides and perhaps watch the mountains vying with one another to see who could be tallest. Chomolungma was winning. Chomolungma was what the world looked like when the world stood on tiptoes. Pale from the strain, blue from the lack of oxygen. The vegetation had all grown dizzy and slid down her back, snow swirled in perpetual spirals around her skull, she wore a glacier in her crotch like a sanitary napkin.

"Could it be?" asked Alobar. "You are actually the child I met by the Ganges? Yes, I can tell by your chin depression, you are the one. Or else, her brother."

Kudra removed her turban, allowing her waist-length hair to spill out. She unbuttoned her baggy phulu jacket and loosened her vest. Unbound, her breasts bubbled to the surface like jellyfish coming up to feed. She sighed with relief. Alobar sighed with appreciation. "It might be better if you remained a boy," he said.

"Why is that?"

"In this region, women are considered bad luck. They have a saying here: 'Dogs, children, and women are the roots of trouble.' "

"Oh?"

"They have another saying: 'If you pay attention to the talk of a woman, the roof of your house will soon be overgrown with weeds.' "

"Is that so? Weeds, eh?"

"They have another saying—"

"All right, all right. I get the idea."

"I am sorry. You must feel that it would be better not to be born at all than to be born a woman."

"I am sorry. I don't feel that way in the least."

"You don't? Then why are you dressed in this manner?"

Kudra produced a boar-bristle brush and laid it to her tangles. In a moment, her hair was rippling and shining. Mount Chomolungma raised a few inches higher on her toes to see where that black glow was coming from.

"I suppose I have always been pleased to be alive, female or not," she said. "These days I am more pleased about it than ever. Would you have any interest in hearing my story, or do you fear for your roof?"

Alobar decided to be intrigued. Chomolungma, on the other hand, settled back down to her customary height of twenty-nine thousand, twenty-eight feet. On that spring day, sixty-eight pairs of snow leopards and eleven pairs of yeti had mated on her slopes. What did she care about a man and a woman trying to get acquainted?

For weeks after her experience at the cremation grounds, Kudra had been troubled by nightmares. She would thrash and whimper until she would wake up the whole family. Some nights they would coo to her in soothing mantras and fetch her warm milk, other nights they snapped at her irritably. Her aunt threatened to make her sleep in the courtyard where the cow was staked, but her father objected that it would be rude to interrupt a cow at rest. While her mother was sympathetic, she could not understand the reason for the bad dreams. Suttee was a common practice, after all, and this was hardly the first time that Kudra had seen a widow join her husband's body on the pyre.

"But . . . she ran away," sobbed Kudra.

"A stupid woman," said her mother. "The life of a widow is worse than fire."

"An evil, cowardly woman," said her father. "A husband and wife are one. Eternity depends upon them being together. A suttee woman is the heroic savior of her husband's eternity. Praise Shiva." Usually, her father saved his spiritual instruction for her brother.

"Someday I will inform you about the life of a widow," said her mother.

In time, the bad dreams ceased, although one day, several months later, when Kudra's parents returned from a cremation, she was unable to prevent herself from asking, "Did the widow try to escape?" Her father slapped her face.

Nonetheless, the fiery dreams did fade, and inside rooms made of clay and painted blue, sweeter visions were nourished. At the start of monsoon season, when the great cloud ships rolled in from the sea to discharge their tanks of green rain in the rice fields and to haul away dust balls, scorpion skins, and mounds of worthless diamonds made of heat—summer's dolorous cargo—Kudra participated in the No Salt Ceremony. Each day, for five days, she dined in seclusion on unsalted food and worshipped tender seedlings that had sprouted from wheat and barley grains that she herself had planted prior to the ceremony. This ritual was to help psychologically prepare her for her designated role in life, the role of wife and mother, nurturing and sustaining her children, her husband, and the husband's relatives.

In a universe that was perceived as inherently divine,
where sacred animals munched sacred plants in groves of
sacred trees, where holy rivers spilled from the laps of mountains that were gods, to nurture life was a lovely and important thing. Kudra enjoyed taking care of babies, and the
notion of making babies excited her in some vague, itchy
way. At age eight, she already was versed in the art of baking
flat bread, and she was fast learning the secrets of the curry
pot, with its fury and perfume. Her true delight, however,
came in the hours when necessity called her out of the
kitchen and into the workshop, to assist in one way or another with the manufacture or marketing of incense. She
liked mixing gums and balsams more than she liked mixing
rice and lentils, she liked rasping sandalwood more than she
liked mending clothes. She did not consider why. As she grew
older and the incense trade grew alongside her, she began
to spend as much time in the business as in the household, and it never occurred to her that a conflict might be
sprouting, like one of the ritual barley seeds, in the moist
soil of her heart.

When Kudra was twelve, she and her brother accompanied
their father on an ambitious business trip. It was a journey of
nearly four months, during which Calcutta, Delhi, Benares,
and many smaller towns were visited in an attempt to crack
Buddhist markets, for the Buddhists had begun to use incense in greater volume than the Hindus along the Ganges.
The trip left the girl gaga, goofy, tainted, transformed, her
nose a busted hymen through which sperm of a thousand
colors swam a hootchy-kootchy stroke into her cerebral lagoon. Now, whenever she smelled the gums, the balsams,
and the special aromatics that arrived with merchants from
afar, her head reeled with images of temples, shrines, pal-
aces, fortresses, mysterious walls, tapestries, paintings, jew-
els, liquors, icons, drugs, dyes, meats, sweets, sweetmeats,
silks, bolts and bolts of cotton cloth, ores, shiny metals,
foodstuffs, spices, musical instruments, ivory daggers and
ivory dolls, masks, bells, carvings, statues (ten times as tall as
she!), lumber, leopards on leashes, peacocks, monkeys, white
elephants with tattooed ears, horses, camels, princes, maha-
rajah, conquerors, travelers (Turks with threatening mus-

taches and Greeks with skin as pale as the stranger who had befriended her at the funeral grounds), singers, fakirs, magicians, acrobats, prophets, scholars, monks, madmen, sages, saints, mystics, dreamers, prostitutes, dancers, fanatics, avatars, poets, thieves, warriors, snake charmers, pageants, parades, rituals, executions, weddings, seductions, concerts, new religions, strange philosophies, fevers, diseases, splendors and magnificences and things too fearsome to be recounted, all writhing, cascading, jumbling, mixing, splashing, and spinning; vast, complex, inexhaustible, forever.

It was then that she realized that it was the *odor* of the incense that had intrigued her all along, only now the smells filled in the fantasies that heretofore had been mere outlines, smeary contours scrawled in ghost chalk. Perhaps the most terrible (or wonderful) thing that can happen to an imaginative youth, aside from the curse (or blessing) of imagination itself, is to be exposed without preparation to the life outside his or her own sphere—the sudden revelation that there is a there out there.

The day of Kudra's fifteenth natal anniversary began like any other, with a predawn bath in the river, followed by prayers to Kali and an offering of clarified butter in the courtyard cookfire. By first light, she had served breakfast to her father, brother, and one-legged uncle and was already washing the curds that would be the principal dish at the noontide meal. She was bent over the curd jars when, from the workshop, her father called for her, just as she hoped he would.

"Honored father." She bowed to him, searching out of the corner of her eye for some fresh basket of bosmellia bark, opopanox resin, nutmeg, or patchouli, for she had heard unfamiliar voices in the shop and suspected there had been a delivery. Nothing new was in evidence, but that was all right, she'd be content just to shave some sandalwood chips as she had several days before. The coarse-grained sandalwood was so tough it made her arms ache to chip it, but with each laborious push of the rasp, it propelled a zephyr of warm,

clean, forest air past her nose, an invisible vapor that sang to
her of the pad of the tiger's paw upon dry leaves, upon fallen
parrot nests and dark Madras moss.

"Kudra," said her father, "I have good news. Praise Shiva."

Another merchandising trip, perhaps? Her imagination gal-
loped about the room astride a sandalwood broom.

"The parents of a respectable man were just here. We have
arranged for you to marry him, come the monsoons. Praise
Shiva."

The broom crashed to the hard clay floor. Kudra began to
cry. Her tears did not upset her father. He had expected
them to flow. Every Hindu girl wept and wailed about her
marriage, from its announcement through the wedding and
into the honeymoon. It was fitting that a bride-to-be weep.
Marriage meant that she must leave her father's home to live
with her husband's family, who would treat her like a servant
if she was lucky, like monkey shit if she was not. It was the
way life was. Kudra's mother had bawled. Now it was Kudra's
turn. Tradition and continuity were the flours from which the
social loaf was baked; feeding the culture, pleasing the gods.

"Father, I am not ready . . ." blubbered Kudra.

"Eh? Of course, you are ready. If you were not thinking
about catching a husband, why would you fix yourself up in
this way? Praise Shiva."

The incense merchant was referring to the crimson lac with
which she had begun to fresco her heavy eyelids, the sandalwood paste that she finger-painted over her body in sinuous
designs, the jasmine-scented unguents that these days lent
her cheeks the glow of butter lamps at dawn. How could she
make him understand that what appealed to her was the
aroma of these substances, that what she sought to catch was
not a man but the strange and wondrous images that the
aromas conjured?

Teardrops spurted. "I—I—I want to work with you, I—I
want to work here with you." Teardrops spewed.

That hit her father where he lived. The fact was, Kudra
was better help than her brother, better than her gimpy
uncle, certainly better than the lazy Sudra laborers whom he
had started to employ. She was diligent and cheerful, and she
had a feeling for the incense, not just an enthusiasm but a

rapport. It was partly on her account that his business was prospering. Still, she was a girl, and everybody knew that girls were hotter than mongooses and certain to lose their virginity at the faintest hint of an opportunity. The way this one's breasts were inflating, the way her eyes had popped when she got a look at the erotic friezes at Khujaras, it was only wise to bind her to a husband before disaster struck.

"Do not worry, my little patchouli drop. Your betrothed's family has a very fine business, praise Shiva, and is said to be shorthanded in the shop."

That proved to be the case. But her husband's family did not make incense. It made rope.

Rope. The gods have a great sense of humor, don't they? If you lack the iron and the fizz to take control of your own life, if you insist on leaving your fate to the gods, then the gods will repay your weakness by having a grin or two at your expense. Should you fail to pilot your own ship, don't be surprised at what inappropriate port you find yourself docked. The dull and prosaic will be granted adventures that will dice their central nervous systems like an onion, romantic dreamers will end up in the rope yard. You may protest that it is too much to ask of an uneducated fifteen-year-old girl that she defy her family, her society, her weighty cultural and religious heritage in order to pursue a dream that she doesn't really understand. Of course it is asking too much. The price of self-destiny is never cheap, and in certain situations it is unthinkable. But to achieve the marvelous, it is precisely the unthinkable that must be thought.

So it was rope for Kudra. Rope drab in color, rope harsh in texture, rope utilitarian in design, rope barren in smell. In late summer, she would accompany others of the caste into the steaming hills to chop the fibrous stalks of bhabar grass. The rest of the year, when she wasn't busy with household duties, she sat on the ground next to her husband, combing fiber into ribbons, spinning ribbons into yarn, twisting yarn into strands, and braiding strands into rope. Rope to keep the cow from deserting the farmer, rope to prevent the riverboat from running away to sea, rope to teach the individual stick of firewood the strategy of the bundle, rope to hold a young wife to a bedpost, an oven, a lurid panoply of gods.

In the streets of Calcutta, she had seen a fakir make a rope rear up like a cobra. Uncoiling from a basket with a dancing motion, the rope rose until its end was higher than the treetops, whereupon the fakir shinnied up it and disappeared in the sky. Now, as yard after yard, mile after mile, of rope wound through her blistered fingers, she strained to exert some influence over it, tried her best to will it skyward so that she might climb it, stopping periodically to wave good-bye to her mother-in-law, and cast her lot with the clouds.

Alas, the rope moved strictly horizontally, and then only when physically forced. Conditioned as she was, Kudra probably wouldn't have climbed the rope, anyhow, let's face it. Besides, she had established a couple of escape routes that allowed her to ascend above the world of in-laws and bhabar fiber. One was scent. Her father kept her supplied with natural aromatics, which she turned into oils and essences to lavish upon her body. Whether she was loading the rope cart, carrying out slops, or scraping cow dung from her mother-in-law's shoes, Kudra was enveloped in a portable fog of fragrance, entwined with a rope of perfume up which she could shinny and partially, at least, disappear. Since it was traditional among Hindus that one way to Shiva was through the nose, and since in India there was no such thing as too much piety, her in-laws could not object, although sometimes they fell into coughing fits when she passed by. As for Navin, her husband, he may have been publicly embarrassed by his bride's excesses, but in private he was enflamed. Navin's prurient reaction to the smells of his wife widened her second avenue of escape: sex.

Kudra took to the marriage bed the way a water buffalo takes to a mud wallow. Like any conscientious merchant-caste groom, Navin had studied the *Kama Sutra*, the Hindu love manual. Since he was thirty when they were wed, twice the age of his bride, he had had time to learn it by heart, and indeed he was well acquainted, in theory if not in practice, with the eight kinds of embrace (four mild, four hot), the four parts of the body that the handbook taught might be individ-

ually embraced, the three ways of kissing an innocent maiden,
and the four angles from which it might be accomplished; the
sixteen ways of kissing a wife (including the moderate kiss,
the pressed kiss, the soft one, the contracted one, the clasp-
ing one, and the "kiss of the hungry donkey"); the eight kinds
of love bites, the eight kinds of scratch marks that might be
left on the body (the *Kama Sutra* even described how a
lover's nails should ideally be manicured), the eight stages of
oral intercourse, the nine ways of moving the penis inside the
vagina, and the forty varieties of sound that might be uttered
the while (including thundering, weeping, cooing; words of
praise, pain, and prohibition; and the sounds of the dove, the
cuckoo, the green pigeon, the parrot, the sparrow, the flamingo, the duck, and the quail), as well as more than thirty
coital positions, with names such as "the fixing of a spike" and
"the place where four roads meet." If all that education,
aspects of which smacked of arithmetic, ornithology, carpentry, and animal husbandry, suggests that Navin was overqualified for the job of satisfying a teenage virgin, well, it must be
recorded that at no time did Kudra complain of overkill. If
she was not his equal in technique, she compensated in
fragrance and enthusiasm, and night after night they dissolved their rope burns and fatigue in the salty flux and
radiant slime of the glad-hearted fuck.

It is hardly surprising that the couple had four children in
five years. They might have had still more had not the
mother-in-law decided that the house was becoming too
crowded and introduced Kudra to pennyroyal's application as
an oral contraceptive.

Kudra loved her babies. One day, a dozen years into the
marriage, she came to love her husband, as well. It happened
on the morning after the festival of Mahashivaratri—the Great
Night of Shiva—when, weakened by fasting and loosened by
a kind of spiritual hangover, Navin revealed to Kudra that he
adored horses and that during his youth had entertained the
impossible dream of miraculously transcending Vaisya, the
merchant caste, and ascending to Kshatriya, the warrior caste,

so that he might ride. The admission of his ridiculous longing shamed him, but Kudra was touched to learn that, like her, Navin had a blasphemous desire locked away in his breast. It made them partners in a new, more intimate sense, and whenever she thought about his secret, she would reach across the rope bin to pat him tenderly. She did not share her own hidden dream because she didn't know how to articulate it. She only knew that it made her restless, that it smelled good, and that it was always there.

About a month after Navin's disclosure, a column of warriors paid a call at the rope shop to order some fancy, customized bridles, braided with bells and tassels, for their steeds. Kudra drew the leader aside and charmed him into offering Navin a ride.

"Oh, no, no, I could never," protested Navin.

"Go ahead," Kudra urged. "This is your chance. Just as far as the temple and back."

The army officer, who had his eye on Kudra's ripe hips, helped Navin aboard and gave the big horse a whack that sent it off at a gallop. Navin, terrified, leaned too far forward and sailed off into a rock pile. His head split like a milk bowl, sending forbidden ambition, mixed with blood and brain, trickling into the public light.

During the next few days, Kudra seriously considered joining Navin's corpse on the pyre. It was not because she blamed herself for his demise—guilt is a neurotic emotion that Christianity was to exploit to fullest economic and political advantage; Hinduism was healthier in that regard—but because face to face with widowhood, she learned that her mother's dire description of it was, if anything, understated.

From the moment of her mate's death, a widow was under the tutelage of her sons, even if, as in Kudra's case, the sons were mere boys. She could never remarry, and were she to engage in illicit sexual activities, the Brahmans would administer to her a whipping that would expose the white of her bones. Prohibited from returning to her parents, she must remain with her husband's family, and while she would be expected to perform household chores from dawn to dusk, she could never attend the family festivals that played so big a part in Hindu life, for a widow's gloom would bring bad luck to everyone present. For all intents and purposes, a widow was an ascetic, shaving her head, sleeping on the ground, eating only one meal a day and that without honey, wine, or salt. She could wear neither colored garments nor ornaments, she could not use perfumes.

The ban on perfumes was, for Kudra, the final straw. She found herself nodding in agreement when a delegation of village Brahmans enumerated for her the spiritual advantages of suttee. When the priests left, she ran after them to inquire how long they thought it might take for her to be reincarnated. Not wishing to interrupt their conversation, she followed them silently down the dusty road and overheard them speculating about the worth of her jewelry. Upon suttee, her personal belongings would, by law, go to the Brahmans. One priest was of the opinion that Navin, like any good merchant-class husband, had lavished gold and silver ornaments upon his wife, and that they could scarcely afford to let Kudra forgo the funeral fire.

Kudra felt her entrails turn on an axle of lead. The Sanskrit alphabet, heavy-footed and squirmy, sang itself out in her belly; a cobra's tongue swam across the waters of her eyes. As the landscape blurred before her, she could see with pristine clarity the widow in smoking sari being pulled from the riverbank and dragged, screaming, back to the pyre. And she remembered then her promise to the pale-skinned stranger that such a fate would never be hers.

That night, the eve of cremation, after the household was fast asleep, she dressed herself in her nephew's clothing. She laid out her jewelry for the Brahmans, so that they might be less inclined to pursue her. She wrapped some flat cakes, rice balls, and coins in a silk scarf. Then she undid the package and added a hairbrush and several ivory vials of perfume. Then she unknotted the scarf a second time and, without consciously thinking why, put in a small pouch of pennyroyal. As warm vanilla moonlight creamed through the windows, she knelt before her crude little personal shrine, offered a bowl of ghee to the goddess Kali and begged for forgiveness.

She knelt before Navin's casket and begged the same. She kissed each of her children in his sleep. Keeping to the shadows, she slipped from the house, stopping in the yard only long enough to kick with all of her might a flabbergasted basket of rope.

"So you ran away from death," said Alobar. He was obviously pleased. Kudra's flight brought back memories of the two times he had ducked the swipe of the Reaper's sickle. It meant that he and this woman had something in common, something revolutionary and scandalous that bound them together out on the edge of behavior where the bond is tightest and sweetest.

"No," said Kudra. "I did not run away from death. How can a person run away from death? And why would a person want to? Death is release. I did not flee death but the corruption of the Brahmans."

"Nonsense! Do you mean to tell me that had the Brahmans been interested in your eternal soul instead of your bangles, you would have dived into the flames?"

"Well . . . I have much fear of flames."

"Suppose they had wanted you to drown yourself, then. Would you have gone to water more gladly than to fire?"

"Yes. No. Oh, I do not know! Drowning is not such a good way to die."

"What is a good way to die?"

"In your sleep, I suppose. When you are old and your children are grown."

"Oh? Old and in your sleep? After a lifetime of hard work and ill treatment? And how old is old? Is it ever old enough? You could have accepted the painful life of the widow and died unappreciated in your sleep at the age of forty, you could have chosen that instead of the fire, that option was open to you, but you ran away from that, as well."

"You are shaming me. Do you bid me return?"

Alobar put his hand on her shoulder. It was the softest thing he had touched in years. The heat of her flesh, wafting through her boy's jacket, caused fish eggs of perspiration to pop out on his palm. "Not in the least," he said. "I merely want you to admit that you do not wish to die. Not even if it is Shiva's will, or Kali's will, do you wish to die. You want to live and, what is more, you want to live decently and happily, you want to live a life that you yourself have chosen. Admit that, now, and you shall be rewarded."

Kudra eyed his fingers suspiciously. They were kneading her shoulder and seemed to be of a mind to migrate south. "And what is to be my reward?"

Sensing her mistrust, he removed his hand. "The comfort and protection of a kindred spirit."

"How can you protect me? Can you not see, I am certain to be reincarnated as a spider for what I have done. A spider or a flea or a *worm*." She shuddered.

"All the more reason to live a long, enjoyable life while you are still human."

"Now I shall probably have to endure a hundred more lifetimes before I reach nirvana and gain my final release."

"What difference does it make if you live a *million* more lifetimes? At least, you can enjoy this one."

"To believe in the reality and permanence of the fleeting everyday world is foolish."

"Then why are you here and not in the ash heap at the cemetery?"

"Perhaps because I am a foolish woman."

"Good." Alobar smiled. "My own foolishness could use some company."

Kudra smiled, too. She didn't mean to smile. It just happened. The smile was an embarrassment to her, as if she had belched or broken wind. She tried to drive the smile away with thoughts of her sorrowful experiences, her disgraceful behavior, her insecure situation, but this was one smile that didn't scare easily, it hung in there like a tenant who knows his rights and refuses to be evicted. Finally, Kudra turned away, but Alobar could see her smiling through the back of her head.

"What is your name again?" Alobar moved closer to her.

"Kudra." The word swam out through her smile like a blowfish swimming through a crack in a reef.

"Mine is Alobar." He slipped his arm around her and

cupped her left breast. It was heavy and jiggled in his hand as if it were full of liquid. Melon water. Or beet juice. "The grass is soft here, Kudra."

"A mattress is softer. It is not my habit to copulate in the grass like an animal."

"Well, you had better get used to it. I mean, if you are going to be reincarnated as a bug . . ."

"Unhand me, please. I am a widow and do not even know you." The smile was gone now, although whether it had drawn back inside her head or flown off toward the ices of Chomolungma was anybody's guess.

"You know me well enough," said Alobar. Reluctantly, he dropped the satin coconut. He imagined that it gurgled when he let go. "Did not you come up into these mountains looking for me?"

"Not exactly. Back then when I was a child, you informed me that you were traveling to the Himalayas in search of masters who had power over death. When I ran away, I had no place to go, and I thought I must make my way to Calcutta to become a woman of the streets, but first I decided I would have a look for these masters myself. You were kind to me back then, and the promise you extracted from me influenced my decision not to submit to suttee. Partly because of you I took a less virtuous path. But there is a limit to how much virtue I shall allow you to talk me out of."

"If being alive is not a virtue, then there is little virtue in virtue, that is what I say."

"Disgustingly enough, I *am* finding joy in my continued presence in this world of illusions." She turned to face him. The smile came back, surprised them both, then left again abruptly without saying good-bye. "Tell me, Alobar, are these lamas you live with the masters whom you sought? And have they taught you the secret of life everlasting?"

"Um? Well, er, in some ways, I think . . . I'm not sure. Uh . . ."

"What do you mean? Are they or are they not? Have they or haven't they? They look like Buddhist monks to me, and where I come from, Buddhists die just as regularly as everybody else."

Alobar stood up and gazed at the mountains for a while.

The mountains looked like the white picket fence around the cottage of eternity, although Alobar clearly thought about them in another way entirely. Perhaps he thought of them as storehouses stocked with thunderclap hinges and earthquake parts and dusty bolts of lightning; perhaps he saw them as just another opportunity for the gods to make him seem puny and weak and mortal. In any case, he stared at the peaks for a while, and then he turned back to Kudra.

"When I crossed the border from your land into this one, I asked some herdsmen where the great teachers lived, and they answered, 'At Samye,' so I made my way here. I knocked at the gatehouse of the Samye lamasery, and some men in red robes took me in and gave me food and tea, they heated buckets of water with which I bathed myself, and they supplied me with warm clothes and boots, for my own were in tatters and falling off me. Then they asked what I wanted—I was a curious sight to them—and I replied, 'I wish to live a thousand years.' They looked at each other, and then one of them asked, 'In *this* body?' And when I said 'yes,' they shook their heads and clucked their tongues. They said they could not help in the fulfillment of my vain, misguided wish, and that after a good night's rest I must be on my way. As I was leaving the next morning, one of them, Fosco, a painter of poems, whispered to me that I might get what I was looking for from the Bandaloop doctors. He said I could find these personages in the foothills caves back down toward India. So I thanked him and off I went."

"But you didn't find them, these Bandaloopers?"

"Oh, yes, I found them, all right, although it was not easy. They had no fine stone buildings, as they have here at Samye, but lived in a honeycomb of caverns, far off the main path."

"But you found them?"

"Yes. Or, rather, they found me. I was resting in a ravine one day, thinking, 'Oh, how I wish I had something to eat,' when suddenly I was pelted with ears of corn. Hard. Very hard. Made my nose bleed and my ears ring. I drew my knife and looked up at the cliff whence the corn had come, and there were three hairy men dressed almost as motley as I, laughing at me. I shook my blade at them, and they yelled, 'Well, you *said* you were hungry.' "

"Praise Shiva. How did they hear your thought?"

"I intended to find that out. After I roasted and ate the corn, I sniffed out their trail and tracked them to a hillside riddled with caves. 'You must be the Bandaloop doctors,' I said when several of them approached. 'You must be Alobar,' one of them replied. 'How did you learn my name?' I asked. 'How did you learn ours?' he shot back. 'A Samye holy man told me,' I said. At that, they all had a hearty laugh."

"They strike me as rude."

"Rude? Yes, they were plenty of that. But, you see, a long time ago, far off in the west where I come from, I met two rude characters, one a shaman, one a god, and though each treated me disagreeably in the beginning, one gave me special courage, the other special fear, both of which I required for this journey that I am on. Those who possess wisdom cannot just ladle it out to every wantwit and jackanapes who comes along and asks for it. A person must be prepared to receive wisdom, or else it will do him more harm than good. Moreover, a lout thrashing about in the clear waters of wisdom will dirty those waters for everyone else. So, a man seeking knowledge must be first tested to determine if he is worthy. From what I have gathered, rudeness on the part of the master is the first phase of the test."

"You mean, if you allow the master to be uncivil, to treat you any old way he likes, and to insult your dignity, then he may deem you fit to hear his view of things?"

"Quite the contrary. You must defend your integrity, assuming you have integrity to defend. But you must defend it nobly, not by imitating his own low behavior. If you are gentle where he is rough, if you are polite where he is uncouth, then he will recognize you as potentially worthy. If he does not, then he is not a master, after all, and you may feel free to kick his ass."

"Interesting. Is that how it went with the Bandaloop doctors?"

Alobar shook his head. "No," he said. He took another long look at Chomolungma and the runners-up in the world's tallest mountain competition. The sun was starting to sink, and the peaks were pinned with colored clouds, like ribbons designating where each had placed in the contest. It was fairly easy to spot the winner, and numbers two and three. Miss Congeniality was a bit more difficult to identify. "No, that is not the way it went with the Bandaloop doctors. They were alternately hospitable and antagonistic. They would pour me milk to drink, then drop a turd in the cup. They would flatter me, then spit in my face. They would ignore me, then as I made to leave, they'd implore me to stay. It was damnably confusing. And there was no question of kicking ass. They invited me to strike them, but they were so quick I could not lay a hand on them. Their movements were imperceptible, yet they were always a fraction of an inch to the left or right of wherever I aimed my blow. Not one of them touched me, but I beat my own self bloody missing them and falling down."

"You were humiliated."

"My lady, that is an understatement. In my own land I had a reputation as a warrior."

"Did you leave then?"

"I was too winded to even crawl away on my knees. They gave me some oil for my scrapes and scratches and invited me into the caves. What do you think it was like in them? Sharp rocks, cold water dripping from the ceilings, bats screeching by in the darkness? Oh, no, those caves were covered with beautiful carpets and tapestries, thick and warm and opulent. Every nook and cranny glowed with butter lamps, and in little saucers powders were burning that caused the air to smell like orange groves and gardens."

"Incense!" exclaimed Kudra.

"Whatever. And there were women inside preparing spiced lamb and heating wine. Everyone drank wine until their eyes were red. They also smoked pipes of ground-up leaves from the hemp plant—"

"I know the plant. We made *rope* from it. Smoked it, you say?"

"Yes, and it seemed to make them dreamy. They would stare into the fire, laughing for no apparent reason. They offered me a pipe, they offered me wine and meat, they even offered me a woman, or two women if I chose. Of course, I refused. I thought it was a trick, a test of my purity. I fell asleep alone, splitting with desire, only to be awakened in the middle of the night by a bucket of icy water emptied upon my head. Well, *then* I got out, let me assure you. I was angry and confused—and scared. Because, Kudra, no hand held the bucket that dumped that water on me, the bucket was suspended in midair, just tipping itself on me of its own accord."

"Alobar, you were confused, all right. Or else dreaming. Or . . ." She lowered her eyelids, lids that resembled purses sewn from the skins of thick, dark grapes. "Or you are telling me a fable."

"It is all true, I swear it."

"Then I suppose I must believe you. Tell me, did they permit you to leave freely?"

"One of the company—there were perhaps a dozen of them in all, not counting the women—followed me outside to inquire about my intentions. I told him I thought I would return to the Samye lamasery. 'Good,' he said. 'You will learn much there. Then you can come back to us.' Well, that heated me up, to be sure. 'There are not enough demons in this world or the next to drag me back to this accursed place,' I yelled. I swore that I would never return. He laughed and reached into my clothes and pulled an egg from where no egg had been. He cracked the egg on the ground, and a huge dog bounded out of it—it looked exactly like Mik, my own dog from my own city that I had not seen in the span of eight Feasts of Feasts. It licked my feet in a familiar way, and then it ran into a cave and disappeared. . . ."

"Alobar!"

"I swear it to be true."

"Remarkable. And did you run after it?"

"Oh, no. I staggered off into the night and eventually did, indeed, return to Samye, where you have caught up with me. I wanted to forget the whole experience with Bandaloop. Unfortunately, it has remained alive in my mind."

"But you have never gone back?"

"I made a vow. If we mortals can better the gods in no other way, we can at least keep our promises."

"Why did you return to Samye?"

"I do not know for sure. When I arrived, I asked to see Fosco. He entered the gatehouse with his calligraphy brush in his hand, and I seized him by his robe and shook him until ink flew. 'Why did you send me to that crazed place?' I demanded. He answered me mildly. 'The Bandaloop doctors are much despised by my superiors, and I risked reproachment for directing you to them. They practice a base, orgiastic form of religion that we cannot condone. But they are powerful magicians and healers and fortune-tellers, and I thought they might assist you in your obsession with your earthly vessel. Forgive me.' Fosco was so obviously sincere that it behooved me to ask *his* forgiveness. Not only did he grant it, he persuaded the abbot to let me remain at Samye as a laborer and student. It appears that I have been here a long time."

Kudra looked him over. "Samye has agreed with you. You appear healthy and strong. I did not lie when I mentioned down at the river that you have not aged since I saw you last. Perhaps you are receiving here the knowledge you were after all along. What have the lamas taught you that would keep you in their tutelage for twenty years?"

"You really think I have not aged? We had a magic glass back at . . ." His voice trailed off, held hostage by memory. Bound, gagged, and blindfolded with a swath of ermine ripped from a concubine-stained bedspread, his voice lay in an unlit corner until memory collected its ransom or else took pity. The sun had sunk so low that it was looking up Chomolungma's dress by the time Alobar's freed voice resumed its normal life. "There are no mirrors hereabouts. The river shows me how to shave, but it shows me little in the way of skin condition or hair color. Hmm. It pleases me, what you say." He sat down, and once again he touched her shoulder. She did not pull away.

"I have found peace here. Years of one sort of turmoil or another had rubbed against my spirit until it was raw, but it has been healed by tranquillity, a calm that comes from within as well as without. The architecture, the painting, the sculpture, the music and liturgy and refined garments, but most of all, I think, the meditation, the hours each day of sitting silent and motionless, these things have smoothed my frayed edges and left me floating through life like a toad bladder in a mountain stream. The lamas have suffered endlessly from my resistance to their dogma and strict morality, but I daresay we have all benefited. I have grown serene, and they, well, many a ton of stone has been moved for them, and they have been kept on their toes. Ha ha."

"Am I to assume that they have not instructed you in the practice of long life?"

"Not openly. They speak to me occasionally on the subject, but they obtain their ideal through gradual stages of spiritual progress. And their ideal is neither immortality nor longevity, but release from the cycle of birth, death, and rebirth."

"Yes, yes. That is my people's ideal, as well. Do you fail to appreciate the perfection that lies at the heart of that goal?"

With his free hand, Alobar scratched his head, a head herringboned with equal parts chestnut and silver, like a cow pie on a frosty morning. The other hand held fast to its roost on Kudra's shoulder. "Frankly, I do *not* appreciate it as deeply as I probably should. Or, maybe it is that I long not for the perfect but for the complete, and there is something incomplete about a life that is dedicated to escape from life."

"Please, explain."

"Here they teach that much of existence amounts only to misery; that misery is caused by desire; therefore, if desire is eliminated, then misery will be eliminated. Now, that is true enough, as far as it goes. There is plenty of misery in the world, all right, but there is ample pleasure, as well. If a person forswears pleasure in order to avoid misery, what has he gained? A life with neither misery nor pleasure is an empty, neutral existence, and, indeed, it is the nothingness of the void that is the lamas' final objective. To actively seek nothingness is worse than defeat; why, Kudra, it is surrender; craven, chickenhearted, dishonorable surrender. Poor little babies are so afraid of pain that they spurn the myriad sweet wonders of life so that they might protect themselves from hurt. How can you respect that sort of weakness, how can you admire a human who consciously embraces the bland, the mediocre, and the safe rather than risk the suffering that disappointments can bring?"

Alobar was surprised by the ferocity with which he felt himself attacking the teachings of the men who had pacified him for the past two decades. Perhaps his need for Kudra was whipping long-smoldering dissatisfactions into flames. For her part, Kudra could not locate the words with which to defend her faith. Perhaps her faith had been taken from her. She looked at Alobar and said nothing. He accepted her silent gaze as encouragement to continue his diatribe—and to inch his fingers towards orbit of her coconut moons.

"If desire causes suffering, it may be because we do not desire wisely, or that we are inexpert at obtaining what we desire. Instead of hiding our heads in a prayer cloth and building walls against temptation, why not get better at fulfilling desire? Salvation is for the feeble, that's what I think. I don't want salvation, I want life, all of life, the miserable as well as the superb. If the gods would tax ecstasy, then I shall pay; however, I shall protest their taxes at each opportunity, and if Woden or Shiva or Buddha or that Christian fellow—what's his name?—cannot respect that, then I'll accept their wrath. At least I will have tasted the banquet that they have spread before me on this rich, round planet, rather than recoiling from it like a toothless bunny. I cannot believe that the most delicious things were placed here merely to test us, to tempt us, to make it the more difficult for us to capture the grand prize: the safety of the void. To fashion of life such a petty game is unworthy of both men and gods."

Alobar paused to consider what he'd said. He had not given voice, even inwardly, to such thoughts in years, although one day, watching a yak calf gambol about the rocks like a goat, he asked himself what the Great God Pan might think of the Buddhist way of life. The answer promoted a prolonged twinge of discontent.

"The lamas declare that they have no fear of death, yet is it anything less than fear that causes them to die before they die? In order to tame death, they refuse to completely enjoy life. In rejecting complete enjoyment, they are half-dead in advance—and that with no guarantee that their sacrifice will actually benefit them when all is done. They are good fellows, and I must respect their choice, but fullness, completion, not empty perfection, is this fool's goal."

"I take it that if the Bandaloop doctors were to give you another go at their provisions, you would not this time abstain?"

"There is the matter of quality, my lady. Have I implied

that a person must abandon discretion in what he enjoys, then my tongue, or your ear, has erred."

As if to correct the one or the other, he thrust his tongue into the nacreous coils of her ear, smothering all the while her breasts with his hands, lest their rocking motion somehow interfere with the process of correction. Her right ear thusly plugged, her left nevertheless clearly heard a donging back at the lamasery.

"I'm famished!" she announced, springing to her feet with such force that for a moment he feared she'd taken his tongue with her. "I do hope that is the dinner bell."

Reluctantly, he led her down from the outcropping, whose grass was destined to go unmoistened by their mingled dew. She was reassigning her hair to the turban as they walked, and frequently stumbled, on the uneven ground. She was thick-thighed, broad-hipped, and heavy-breasted, but so slender of waist that a snail with a limp could circle her beltline in two minutes flat; in short, she manifested the Indian ideal of the woman built for physical satisfaction, and while Alobar had developed slightly different standards, he could not help but watch wide-eyed as this turbulent culture of flesh fought to gain control over its barbaric frontiers (bouncing breasts, swinging buttocks) and consolidate into an integrated empire as it slipped and slid down the hillside.

Much as the departure of daylight had turned the mountains into violet silhouettes, so had the departure of inner peace silhouetted Alobar against the overcast of his frustration. He was in such a funk that when he fetched a dish of buttered barley to the rockpile outside the gatehouse, where the "boy" Kudra waited, he completely missed the significance of the pennyroyal that she sprinkled on her food.

Alobar took his simple meal with the lamas, as was his custom. After dinner, with Fosco's assistance, he found Kudra a place to sleep in the stable.

"I apologize," Alobar said, "but this is the way women are regarded around here."

"I am used to that," said Kudra. "The way *you* regard

women, however, is more of a novelty to me." She squeezed
his hand. "Come back when the moon is above the stable,"
she whispered.

Alobar went outside and walked around in the Himalayan
night, the dark at the top of the stairs. The thin, crisp air
vibrated like a hive with the chants of the lamas. White stars
pimpled the atmosphere. It was easy to imagine that the stars
were bees, that they were the source of the ubiquitous lama-
buzz. It was easy to imagine that the pale crescent moon was
the beekeeper's paddle, dipping into the hum and honey.

The nightful of chanting was soothing to him in the way
that the sound of a turning screw would one day be soothing
to men at sea. In those days, boats were only as noisy as the
winds that drove them, and there were no sailors in the
Himalayas, of course; there were not even leafy trees that
could unfurl flotillas of little sails, as green as mermaids'
curtains. Himalayan winds blew snowflakes about, and grass
seed and panda hairs and the serious, droning vowels of
lamas.

Alobar had, himself, learned a chant. The abbot had given
him the syllables personally. The chant transported him to a
place inside himself impervious to gales or breezes, a place as
unruffled as the abbot's shaved noggin, as smooth as Buddha's belly. That night, however, he felt more inclined to
sing that little ditty he had made up long ago, the one that
went: *The world is round-o, round-o. . . .* Obviously, it was
the dusky widow who was reviving in him those old sensations.

Kudra had awakened him from a long sleep. No, that was
false, he hadn't been asleep at Samye, he had been in a state
of heightened awareness, but there is a sense in which awareness can be as stagnating as sloth. His stay at the lamasery
had become a rut, a tranquil, nourishing, educational rut that
had done him little harm and much good, but a rut, nonetheless; his wheel was stuck in a ditch of light, so to speak, and
he felt an overpowering urge to steer in the direction of
darkness. If the earth needs night as well as day, wouldn't it
follow that the soul requires endarkenment to balance
enlightenment?

In any event, Alobar had lost his calm satisfaction only to
gain a kind of anxious, electric joy. Whether it was a tempo-

rary state, tied to the licentious yearning that Kudra had
reawakened in him, or whether it signaled the end of his
serene years as Samye's token pagan, he could not ascertain.
What he did know was that the lunar rooster was crowing on
the stable lintel now, and that, inside, the fugitive widow had
some need or other of him.

It is said that when a man is anticipating sexual activity, his
whiskers grow at an accelerated rate. Alobar might have to
stop and shave before we reach the end of this paragraph.
Before the last of the chanting dies out behind the high walls
and the condensed breath of a dozing yak momentarily fogs
the page.

Having finished a bath in a pony trough, Kudra was debat-
ing whether or not she should squirm back into her nephew's
clothes. There was a chill in the May night that had set her to
shivering, but the prospect of pulling those soiled, unfemi-
nine garments over her glistening brown body was less inviting than goose bumps. Besides, Alobar would only undress
her again, would he not?

She was resigned to having him mount her. She would
have preferred to postpone, if not avoid it—with so many
things to sort out in the head, the body must be regarded as a
distraction—but he was as bent on carnal embrace as a pil-
grim was bent on the Ganges. To see him again would be to
roll around with him, and she simply must see him.

He is overwhelmingly exciting, she thought. Then she added,
Not in any sexual way, of course. He excited her because he
was as damned as she was, yet had no regrets. He actually
made damnation seem attractive. She had heard of men who
rejected the gods, who professed not to believe, but here was
a *believer* who refused to grovel, a man who stood up to
Shiva, to Buddha, to the gods of his own race, whoever they
might be, who stood right up to them and demanded an
accounting for a system in which pleasure must be paid for
with pain, a system in which the only triumph over suffering
was hard-won oblivion, a system that offered its captive audi-

ence little choice in matters concerning duration of performance.

The Brahmans could explain away such complaints; she was
well acquainted with their explanations, and, furthermore,
she believed that they were right; she just wasn't in the
market for theological justifications, not anymore. She was a
sinner now, and her options were these: she could repent and
pay the certain price, or she could cast her lot with this
handsome heretic and see where it might lead. Oh, did she
call him "handsome"? She didn't mean to say that, although
he wasn't bad to look at, now that she'd mentioned it. It
didn't bother her that he was over sixty, he was fit and
youthful, and besides, Hindu women customarily were paired
with older men. Not that she had any notion of being paired
with him, you understand.

Perhaps the gods were sympathetic to Alobar's demands.
Perhaps they were considering alterations in the divine order
of things. Perhaps it was a mistake, an oversight, that human
beings had been granted short, unhappy lives, only the error
had never been corrected because no one had ever openly
complained before. No thunderbolt, in any case, had struck
Alobar down. Another thought occurred to her, then, and it
stacked goose bumps upon her goose bumps. Had Alobar
been spared out of indifference? What if the gods had not
even noticed his rebellion?

For the moment, it didn't matter. What mattered was that
she was caught up in something large and important, or so it
seemed. She felt that she had embarked on an adventure far
greater than the merchandising trip that she'd taken with her
father, that wondrous journey that had erected a towered city
on the scrubby plane of her brain and spoiled her for a life of
normal, sedentary wifehood for all time.

Pale moonlight was seeping over the stable eaves and
puddling on the surface of the pony trough. Alobar's arrival
was imminent. Good, she could inquire further about those
Bandaloopers, the magic that they practiced, and the secrets
that they knew. That was why she had invited him back, for
that and for no other reason. Let it be known.

Suddenly, he walked through the door, catching her unaware, not even dressed yet. Kudra recalled later that he had

rushed up to her, although the ponies, the moon, and the trough water remembered it another way. At any rate, there was no denying that she was in his arms, that her tongue was sliding about in his mouth, and that her hand was groping for something perpendicular—praise Kali—in the general vicinity of his groin.

Something was wrong. Instead of an elephant prod, Kudra found a braid of hemp. Was rope to be her destiny? Alobar was limp enough to knot, and even now he was pulling away from her embrace.

Bewildered and embarrassed, she grabbed a shredded old pony blanket and tried to cover her nakedness. "Is it my color?" she asked.

"What about your color?"

"A horse cannot mate with a cow. Is it possible that a fair-skinned man is incapable of intercourse with a dark-skinned woman?" Kudra had slept with only one man in her life and had experience neither with impotence nor rejection.

"No," said Alobar. The idea made him snort. "I had a reputation, in fact, as a man who relishes dark meat."

Kudra thought, *You also had a reputation as a warrior, to hear you tell it, but you did not fare too well against the Bandaloop.* She asked, "Is it my nose, then? Perhaps its size offends you."

"You are lucky to own such a fine large nose. It will serve you as a rudder and steer you through the troubled waters of life."

Was he sincere? She had never considered her proboscis in that regard. "Well, I must have been too forward: my kiss, my tongue . . ."

"A new experience for me, I do admit."

"Truly?"

"Yes, this 'kizz' as you call it is unknown in the west. A rather odd sensation, but one I would not object to repeating. I have an open mind."

You need only open your mouth not your mind, she thought. But she said, "Then why do you spurn me?" She adjusted the worn-out blanket in an attempt to protect a larger area of her body from the evening's chill and Alobar's gaze.

"To be absolutely frank, it is your smell."

"My smell?!" She was incredulous. "But I have just bathed and rubbed myself with fragrant oils. You were willing enough to take me in the grass, when I was caked with grime and sweat; I saw the bulge in your robes; yet, here on the soft, private straw, when I am clean and perfumed . . ."

"You smelled fine up there on the hill, you smelled like a woman. Right now you smell like one of those little piles of powder they burned in the caves; you smell like a—like a *fruit bush!*"

They worked it out. It was back to the trough for Kudra, to scrub the jasmine and patchouli scents from her skin, whereupon, Alobar, whose wives and concubines had known little of the science of the bath and nothing of the art of perfumery (save for the rare spices they sewed in their harem cushions), sniffed her from head to heel, pronouncing her, if not arousing, at least inoffensive. With a little help from her rope-yard-deft fingers, he commenced to wax. And wax. And wax. Until she squealed.

"Did not I explain that I was once a king?"

A king you are still, she thought, vowing never again to doubt his various reputations.

Within the hour, the molecules reaching his nose were more to his liking, although the sounds in his ears—dove, cuckoo, green pigeon, parrot, sparrow, flamingo, duck, and quail—destroyed any illusions he might harbor that he was on familiar ground.

Later, by what little moonlight that remained, she cataloged five types of scratch marks on his shoulders and back. To him, they each stung the same.

"I would like to read this *Kama Sutra*," said Alobar. "Except that I cannot read."

"Nor can I. But I can teach you those of its contents that might benefit you most. Unless you object, I will demonstrate rather than recite." She had had four orgasms and was feeling assured. "For now, however, you must tell me more of the Bandaloop doctors."

"There is nothing left to tell."

"You mean that you never heard of them again?"

"Oh, stories about them abound, but their veracity. . . . Actually, something happened once . . ."

"What happened, Alobar?"

"One spring, on the pass south of here, there was a snow slide. Travelers were buried. Some of us from Samye went to help dig them out. We removed several bodies, frozen stiff, which we laid on the side of the road. After a bit, one of them stirred. It was a female. She stood and stretched, and thanked us and walked away. Just walked away. Fosco must have noticed that I was stunned, for he put a hand on me and whispered, 'She was a Bandaloop woman.' That was all that was ever said about it. The rest of the victims behaved the way corpses ought to."

Kudra, propped on her elbows, shaking her head in amazement, said, "And she was merely one of their women."

"Yes."

"Hmmm." She lowered herself into the straw, her rump in the air. The last moonbeam of the evening was snagged in the tangle of her pubic moraine. Alobar reached in from the rear, as if to free it. Like a careless animal on the lip of a tar pit, his middle finger slipped and sank quickly from view. Kudra writhed automatically, then lay still. Her mind was off somewhere. Her body and Alobar waited patiently for its return. He fell asleep with his hand still in place. When the lamas awoke him, well after sunrise, his finger was waterlogged. But Kudra was gone.

One thing about moving out of a Tibetan Buddhist lamasery, you don't have to hire a cart. Alobar's worldly possessions—a tea bowl, a change of clothing, and a knife that in twenty years had been used only for shaving—were packed in a flash. He bid farewell solely to Fosco. Fosco put down his brush, folded his inky hands upon his belly, and regarded Alobar affectionately. The little lama did not seem surprised by the departure, but rather hurried him to the gate, where, looking into the only blue eyes the Himalayas had ever known, he said something so incomprehensible that Alobar was ready to delay his leave to get to the bottom of it. Fosco withheld any explanation, however, and soon Alobar was winding down the mountainside, pausing every few hundred yards to glance back at the placid walls of Samye. *Stone remains, water goes,* he thought. For once, at least, he knew where he was going.

In less than a day, he caught up with Kudra. She was squatting by the path relieving herself when he rounded the bend. She leapt to her feet in midstream and threw her arms about him.

"I knew you would follow me," she said, with the kind of confidence some women exude when they sense that they have made a clean capture with the vaginal net.

"You left without a word," he said. Her kiss, so wet and exotic upon his unpracticed Western lips, vented much of the steam from his accusation.

"I feared that you would talk me out of it. You have talked me out of several things already, including my widow's virtue and my obligation on the funeral pyre."

"Praise Shiva," he said mockingly.

"Praise Shiva," she repeated, after a long pause, and with more than a hint of the poignant.

She still had not pulled up her boy's trousers, and Alobar kneaded her bare, piss-damp thighs. "You made it impossible for me to remain at Samye," he said.

"Your stories of the Bandaloop made it impossible for *me* to remain there."

"So, your destination *was* the caves."

"My destination *is* the caves. And you are going with me."

Any protest he might have uttered was drowned out by the fluttering of the pages of the *Kama Sutra*, dog-eared pages with notes in their margins, which she taught Alobar to read with his one oozing eye, the *Kama Sutra* being a book that usually opens in the middle and begins at the end.

When the volume had been wiped and placed back on the shelf, they again took to the path. Irrigated by snow-melt, the recently awakened grass on the slopes glittered like spinach between the teeth of the hard earth. Far below them, in deep, narrow gorges, streams worked themselves into a lather, roaring like all the seashells in the world turned inside out; and above, great cold peaks in mineral armor were trying to smash the sky. Step by step, the path led them down and away from this terrible beauty.

"I have been considering," said Kudra, a tad out of breath, "what you said about desire."

"Ah," said Alobar. "And now you agree that the devotee's desire to be without desire is the most insidious desire of all."

"Not exactly, Alobar. Look at it this way. The word *desire* suggests that there is something we do not have. If we have everything already, then there can be no desire, for there is nothing left to want. I think that what the Buddha may have been trying to tell us is that we have it all, each of us, all the time; therefore, desire is simply unnecessary." She stopped to catch her breath. "To eliminate the agitation and disappointment of desire, we need but awaken to the fact that we have everything we want and need right now."

Alobar thought, *She is a smart one, smarter even than Wrenna, whom she resembles in odd physical ways. And her vulva is as clever as her speech. I was right to pursue her, though I must be careful that her power does not turn against me, and I must come between her and those sickening oils she likes to smear upon her flesh.*

Aloud, he asked, "Do we have everything, you and I?"

They were descending into a small valley. The valley had clouds tipping into it, and the clouds were dark, as if bruised by the jagged thrusts of the peaks. One cloud was so black that Chomolungma herself might have battered it. The wind was at their heels and beginning to bark.

"I have lost my husband, my children, my people, my faith," said Kudra. "Yet I feel that still I have everything. Everything, at least, that I deserve. Brrr. It is growing cold."

"A storm is building," said Alobar. "There is one thing we have not, and it is that thing we are obliged to desire."

"And that is?" Kudra buttoned her vest against the first blown drops of gelid rain.

"Some influence over the unknown tribunal that sentences

us to die against our wishes. A reform of that law that decrees death a certain consequence of birth."

The wind had grown so strong it practically rolled them down the path. When Kudra said, "I cannot tell if that be the one valid desire or the greatest deception," she had to yell to be heard. "Perhaps we shall have our answer from the Bandaloop."

"The what?"

"The Bandaloo-oo-p." The word sailed away on the wind, its vowels banging together and scattering, its consonants tearing the lips of the word like the bit of a runaway horse.

There proved to be no shelter in the valley, not even a boulder leaning at a protective angle, so Alobar and Kudra pressed on. Soon, they were regaining altitude. By nightfall, the rain had turned to snow, the last blizzard of the Himalayan spring. Should they continue to walk, they might topple into a gorge; should they stop, they might freeze. They walked, keeping to a pace just fast enough to promote circulation.

When dawn finally came, it was only a stain in the sky. Kudra prayed to Shiva and Kali, separately and together, and while looking for a signal from the gods that light was still on their payroll, she crashed into the trunk of a Yünnan pine that a gale had muscled into the presumed path. She had to sit in a drift until the pain subsided, Alobar draped over her like a human tent. The kneecap swelled up until it was as round as one of her breasts and as tight as a devil drum. She leaned against Alobar and, she hobbling and he shuffling, their bellies agonizing and their energy all but gone, they reentered the mainstream of the storm.

Within two hours, he was not so much supporting as dragging her. She was babbling about sandalwood groves, and marketplaces where crumbs of jasmine flower blew about the streets like music. Although his fingers were numb, he sensed them losing their grip on her.

"Please hold on. Kudra, please hold on. Please, Kudra, please, Kudra, please."

The trail was descending again, but if his calculations were correct, they were yet two days from the foothills. Three days, if the weather didn't break. An eternity, if she couldn't get back on her feet.

"Please, Kudra. It won't be long. . . ." He bit his blue lip against the falsehood. "It won't be long until we reach the caves."

She wailed. The cry was so similar to the wails of the widow on the cremation fire that a huge horror seized him, a horror shot through with adrenaline, and he picked her up in his arms and began to run with her.

The horror changed into a kind of giddiness. *This must look ridiculous*, he thought, though to *whom* it looked ridiculous he failed to name. He must have meant Death, for in a minute he conceded, "Death has trapped us, that's for sure, but he shall not take us sitting still." And, as the pageant of his life, no less ridiculous than this mad dash in the snow, flashed before him, he laughed and laughed.

Almost immediately the wind fell quiet, like a drunk who has passed out in the middle of a rage. The sun burned through and set about boiling clouds into dumplings, then into gravy.

With Kudra somewhat revived, they made the foothills in little more than a day. It was practically on their hands and knees that they covered the final mile. But nobody greeted them. The caves of the Bandaloop were empty and bare.

Alobar gathered wood and built a fire. In the process of drying their damp clothing, they slipped into unconsciousness and did not awake for hours. When his eyes did open, Alobar arose and remade the fire. He recognized some herbs not far from the caves, picked them and steeped a strong, green beverage in his bowl. After taking tea, they went to sleep again. This sequence was repeated numerous times, until upon a sunny morning, perhaps four days hence, they found themselves sitting in a cave mouth, wide awake and reasonably nourished.

Concluding his account of how he had swept her up and

run with her, Alobar ventured the opinion that they had
survived because he reached a point where he did not take
his desire to live seriously. "My desire was no less than
before, you understand, but I no longer *identified* with the
desire. Perhaps that is why desire causes men calamity. By
identifying with our desires and taking them too seriously, we
not only increase our susceptibility to disappointment, we
actually create a climate inhospitable to the free and easy
fulfillment of those desires."

"Maybe," mumbled Kudra, stretching her sun-warmed muscles until the elastic shuddered pleasurably and a mindless
animal happiness collected in a pool at the base of her skull.
Alobar is a glorious man, she thought lazily, *but this constant
prattle about the meaning of things can make a person tired*.

Mistaking her reticence for incredulity, Alobar said, "I
suppose you think I made it all up. About the Bandaloop, I
mean."

In tandem, they turned their heads to stare into the cave,
where rock was as raw as a lump in the throat and bats
orbited the dead star of a dank ether.

"I believe you."

"You do?"

"Much incense has been burned in these caves. The traces
are faint, but I can smell it."

"I cannot tell you how happy it makes me to hear you say
that. But where—"

"It no longer matters," Kudra said firmly. She retrieved a
pine bough and, favoring her sore knee, began to sweep the
entrance way. "The immortals are gone. Now we are the
immortals."

That night they made love on a bed of bhabar grass, the
twisting of her hips nearly weaving it into rope. She progressed from orgasm into dream without skipping a beat, but
Alobar did not so quickly sleep. His arms pillowing his head,
he lay beneath the echo circles of the bats and wondered
about the former occupants of the caves. In certain ways, he
was relieved that they were missing, yet in the velvet shad-

ows of his heart, he sensed that he must someday deal with them, or others equally disturbing: infinity, apparently, did not travel safe highways or join in polite company. But those strange, strange words of Fosco's, what could they possibly have meant?

Fosco, the plump little poem painter, had looked into Alobar's uncomprehending eyes and said:

"The next time you encounter Bandaloop, it will be a dance craze sweeping Argentina in 1986."

SEATTLE

HERE IT COMES, *across the stars, eating worlds, suck-ing the energy out of atoms and suns; here it comes, bullets can't kill it, dogs can't bite it, it refuses to listen to reason; here it comes, it just ate a hydrogen bomb. Oh, my Lord, here it comes, heading our way! nightmare asteroid, maniac vacuum, transcosmic pig-out; can't stop it, drunk on photons, burping pizzas of poisoned plutonium. It wants our oil, it wants our beautiful lumps of coal, it wants Air Force One, Graceland, and the wash on the line; it will slurp every erg, gnaw every volt, unless. . . . It trashed our magnetic laser net, barbed wire is useless, napalm a treat, can't evade it, can't divert it, only this little boy can stop it; big blue eyes, mustard on his T-shirt, this adorable towhead with the dis-count dirt bike and the horny mom; only Jeffrey Joshua and his fuzzy teddy bear, Mr. Bundy, stands between us and galactic oblivion; can he . . . ?*

Priscilla was watching a TV movie in the bar at El Papa Muerta. She and several other waitresses had completed the setups in the dining room and were awaiting the 5:00 P.M. opening (Seattleites dined early). Ricki was behind the bar, having been promoted recently to assistant bartender.

Priscilla was watching the movie and not watching the movie. Ricki noticed the part that was not watching and came over. "Have a hard night in the lab?"

"Matter of fact. There's gonna be nothin' but hard nights

until I can afford the stuff I need." The "stuff" Priscilla needed was high-quality jasmine oil. It came from France and cost six hundred dollars an ounce. Priscilla figured she needed a minimum of three ounces, to begin with. That would take care of the middle. Then there would still be the matter of matching the base note. What *was* that goddamned base? Sometimes she wished she had left that bottle where she found it.

"Go ahead, tell me your troubles," said Ricki. "As a novice bartender, I need the practice."

Priscilla sighed. She watched a swoosh of rocket exhaust. The TV color needed adjusting, and the rocket blast was as pink as a nursery. She could have used a jet assist herself, even a soft pastel one. "Ricki," she said, wearily, "do you ever pray?"

"Pray?"

"Yeah, pray."

"Sure I do, honey. I pray all the time."

"Well, when you talk to God, does he answer?"

"Absolutely."

"What does God say?"

Ricki glanced around her. The bar was starting to fill up with customers waiting for the dining room to open. "Have you noticed," she said, "that you and I are the only Mexicans in this place?"

"I'm Irish and you're Italian. Ricki, be serious. What does God say?"

"God says the check is in the mail," answered Ricki, moving to the waitress station where the cocktail girl stood gargling a mouthful of orders.

In a busy restaurant bar, a waitress must order from a bartender in a particular sequence: neats, rocks, waters, sodas, Sevens, tonics, collins, Cokes, miscellaneous mixes, juices, sour blended, creamy blended, beer, and wine. This was partly to aid memory, partly to facilitate arrangement of glassware, mainly to prevent the mix from one drink from tasting in the next (should a bit of 7-Up spill, in the rapid firing of the bar gun, into a collins, it wouldn't be detected, whereas Coke would definitely intrude).

"Jack/soda, tall; four 'ritas, a sunrise, a Dos Equis, and a Bud."

A bartender's beauty is in his moves. Like a lover's, like a matador's. The finished product means little: a spent orgasm, a dead bull. Satiation and stringy beef. To be sure, there are drinks of fine workmanship and drinks of poor; there are coherent ramos fizzes and incoherent; there are martinis in which the gin is autonomous and martinis where integration and harmony of ingredients prevail; bloody marys can suffer high blood pressure or low. Yet Priscilla had never heard a customer complain of a drink, unless it was to impress a companion, unless there wasn't enough booze therein, and at El Papa Muerta, at least, there was always enough booze.

A bartender's beauty is in his moves, in the way he struts his stuff, in the field of rhythms that is set up in the orchestrated hatching of a large order of drinks. A skillful barkeep no more looks at his accoutrements than a practiced typist or pianist peers at the keys, but works with both hands simultaneously, full blast, undimmed by the usual dull requirements of routine. (Even in a lull, with only one drink to mix, he will not slacken his pace nor take a glyptic approach.) When he snatches a bottle from the well, he knows, without looking, that it is grenadine and not triple sec, and if it should prove to be triple sec, too bad, dad, the drink is already mixed. Stirring and sloshing, rinsing and wiping, pouring and garnishing, with a fry cook's retention and an acrobat's timing, he virtually dances through his shift, skating, as it were, on the chunky ice he scoops with furious delicacy into each glass. The regular at El Papa Muerta was a master of bar dance, he consumed the space around his station, he had speed, presence, and finesse; his output was huge. Ricki had a lot to learn. Her style was kinky. Ugly and odd. But Priscilla sensed that Ricki would be a good one in time. To her advantage, she was impatient with small stuff and detail, and with the fussing and adjusting that the dilettante in any field tries to substitute for inspiration and thus rescue his art. She had a capacity for the grand, and it was with some faint concept of eventual grandeur that she set about to mix the first order of drinks on that autumn evening, her arms—and her mood—arched to parallel the natural curve of flowing liquid.

"Jack/rocks, C.C./water, vodka martini, five 'ritas, one grande, one strawberry; and a draft. That martini takes a twist."

It has entered our solar system. It's becoming our solar system! If that kid doesn't make contact . . . What's that? His teddybear is missing?!?!

Priscilla closed her eyes and slipped into a crack between the bar noise and the movie noise, where, under her coffee-scented breath, she prayed; asking God, in whom she only marginally believed, what to do about the formula, what to do about Ricki's lust and love. She closed, out of habit, with an "amen," not knowing for sure what "amen" really meant, but suspecting that when God finally ended the world his big boom-boom voice would not bellow "amen" but "Tha-tha-tha-tha-that's all, folks," à la Porky Pig.

Into the dining room she went, virtually limping with fatigue, screwing up her face with distaste at the diners being shown to their tables. What kind of gourmet would trust a Mexican restaurant where the entrees smelled like ketchup and the waitresses wore sailor dresses? It was a long way from the perfect taco. Five minutes later she was back in the bar, placing her first drink order.

"Two sloe gin fizzes, two fast gin fizzes; three martinis, dry, no starch; twenty-eight shots of tequila, three beers (a Bud, a Tree Frog, and a Coors lite), seven rum separators, five coffee nudges, two Scotch and waters, five vodka and buttermilks, a zombie, a zoombie, four tequila mockingbirds, thirteen glasses of cheap white wine, a mug of mulled Burgundy, nine shots of Wild Turkey (hold the stuffing on three), one Manhattan (with eight cherries), two yellow jackets, fifteen straitjackets, thirty-seven flying dragons, nine brides of Frankenstein, and a green beret made with 7-Up instead of sweet vermouth and in place of grenadine, banana liqueur. Amen."

The fraud backfired. Before Priscilla had reached the end, Ricki was in full panic, and even after Pris said, "Make that two margaritas, grande; and a Carta Blanca," Ricki just stood there, up to her elbows in glassware, looking as if she'd had the brain electricity sucked out of her by the black hole, which on the TV, had stopped eating Grand Coulee Dam and was sharing a granola bar with Jeffrey Joshua. There was at least one tear in her eye. "That was a rotten thing to do to you on your first shift alone," Priscilla apologized. Then she whispered, "Take your break at nine-thirty, if you can. I've got a special treat for us."

But, of course, Ricki wanted something more than the pinch of cocaine, and Priscilla found herself, during break, in the ladies' stall with her panty hose down around her knees.

"I'm sorry, I guess I'm pretty dry."

"That's okay," said Ricki. "I'm like a cactus. I can make maximum use of minimal amounts of moisture."

A loud rap on the restroom door caused them both to jump.

"Pris. Pris, are you in there?"

Priscilla pushed Ricki away and hurried to pull up her Danskins.

"Pris, there's a delivery for you from Federal Express."

It was with mixed emotions that Priscilla headed for the reservations desk. On the one hand, she was relieved to get out of Ricki's grasp; on the other, she was afraid of what that delivery might be. She had received mysteriously almost a dozen beets at her apartment. What if they started to show up at work?

The Federal Express envelope contained no raw vegetables, however, but a fancy, engraved invitation, requesting her presence at a dinner party honoring Wolfgang Morgenstern, the Nobel prizewinning chemist. The dinner was to be held at the Last Laugh Foundation. This was even more puzzling than the beets. Priscilla, who had completed but one year of her chemistry major, knew Dr. Morgenstern by reputation only, while, aside from the war room at Boeing Aircraft, the Last Laugh Foundation was the most exclusive turf, the most inaccessible sanctum in Seattle.

"Why me?" she asked.

"The Last Laugh Foundation," mused Ricki. "That's that immortality place."

"I know. Ricki, do you believe in immortality?"

"I'll try anything once."

The cocaine was leaning on the doorbell in Pris's tummy. She was buzzing at the same frequency as the orange auras that had begun to pulsate from the pseudo-Guadalajara wrought-iron light fixtures. Physically, at least, she was primed to return to the dinner trays, freighting what she'd sworn to one diner was "the most authentic Mexican cuisine north of Knott's Berry Farm."

"You aren't upset with me, are you?"

Ricki looked her over. "No," she said. "I realize that you're just jealous that *I* got the barkeep job. They couldn't have put you in there, Pris. You're too scatterbrained and too clumsy." She turned on her flat heel and walked away.

Priscilla made it through the shift without crying or praying, although, befuddled by the invitation and bruised by Ricki's remark, she concentrated on her duties with difficulty. So badly did she mix up orders that two tables didn't tip her. That was no way to earn three ounces of jasmine oil, let alone to earn three years of omphaloskepsis, which was what the doctor ordered (or did the doctor order the smothered burrito?).

Bicycling home at midnight, she pedaled five blocks out of her way to pass the Capitol Hill townhouse in which the Last Laugh Foundation was headquartered. It was a stately old mansion, charming of cupola, angular of gable, a university's worth of ivy clawing the ivory paint from its boards, a high, stucco wall topped with broken glass protecting its grounds. As usual, there were people at its gate, trying, in one manner or another, to get past the security guards. However, whereas a month before there might have been ten people at the gate, now—in the middle of a damp November night—they were lined up to the end of the block.

Curious, thought Priscilla, promptly pedaling over a steep curb, spilling her bike, ripping her panty hose, and scraping her leg.

By the time she reached home, attended to her wound, shampooed, and donned her dirty lab coat, she had put both the invitation and Ricki's insult pretty much out of mind. From the bathroom cabinet, she removed a Kotex box and checked under the pads to ascertain that the bottle was still hidden there. She did not remove the bottle, however. What was the use?

She needed help, but God was in a meeting whenever she rang, and the Daughters of the Daily Special had postponed her grant almost as often as she had postponed going to bed with Ricki. With Ricki, her sponsor, turning hostile, Priscilla had to assume that the grant might never come through. "Well, shit," she said. "Shit shit shit. I've got no choice but to make that call."

She shoved the Kotex box back in the cabinet, pulled on some stiff jeans, dipped a fistful of coins from the fishbowl, and ran down the hall, not even looking to see if she might have run over a beet. It was late, but she knew that her party had a habit of working into the night. Her finger was trembling, but she managed to dial.

The wall phone swallowed the quarters, Priscilla swallowed her pride.

"Hello, Stepmother," she said.

There was a pause. Then:

"Where are you?"

Madame Lily Devalier always asked "Where are you?" in a way that insinuated that there were only two places on earth one could be: New Orleans and somewhere ridiculous.

NEW ORLEANS

WHEN WE ACCEPT SMALL WONDERS, we qualify ourselves to imagine great wonders. Thus, if we admit that an oyster—radiant, limp, succulent, and serene—can egress from a shell, we are ready to imagine Aphrodite exiting from a similar address. We might, moreover, should we have that turn of mind, imagine Aphrodite *exuding* her shell, constructing her studio apartment, its valves, hinges, and whorls, of her own secretions, the way an oyster does, although the average imagination, it must be said, probably would stop someplace short of that.

"Oh, no, Miz Lily, Ah not be putting no raw oyster in *mah* mouf! Ah eats cold soup wif you, Ah eats libber spread wif you, made from goose libbers, but Ah not be eatin' no *slime*."

"Really, child! How inelegant."

Madame Devalier replaced upon its bed of rock salt and cracked ice the half-shell whose contents she had been about to slurp, and, while waiting for the word "slime" to cease its vile reverberations in her mind's ear, she poured herself another glass of champagne.

"To Papa's fat," she said.

"We done drink to fat three time," said V'lu, raising her own glass of Nehi orange soda, to which Madame Devalier had added, under protest, even though it was a celebration, a squirt of hurricane drops.

"Very well, then. To Bingo Pajama."

"To Bingo Pajama," V'lu said wistfully. "Wherever him po' soul be."

"Now, cher, you mustn't worry your pretty head about that crazy Jamaican. I am confident he can take care of himself." She sipped. She studied the circle of shellfish, each ritzy blob glistening upon the lustrous floor (or ceiling) of its own intimate architecture, the solidified geometry of its desire. The oyster was an animal worthy of New Orleans, as mysterious and private and beautiful as the city itself. If one could accept that oysters built their houses out of their lives, one could imagine the same of New Orleans, whose houses were similarly and resolutely shuttered against an outside world that could never be trusted to show proper sensitivity toward the oozing delicacies within. She sipped again. If one could accept the exaggerated fact of the oyster, one could imagine the exaggerated fact of Bingo Pajama, who had disappeared after the policeman who attempted to arrest him for selling flowers without a permit had been stung to death by bees; one could imagine that Bingo Pajama would keep his promise to bring them still more jasmine, the laborious but successful extraction of whose essence had occasioned this little celebration on Royal Street.

The telephone rang.

"I'll get it," said Madame, somewhat surprised that the dusty phone remembered how to ring. There was an odd look on her face as she pried her bulk from the depression in the love seat, much as the counterman at Acme's had pried open the oysters a half-hour before. When she returned to the rear of the shop five, maybe ten, minutes later, her expression was even more odd. She looked to be sad, but gay about it; or gay, but sad about it. Sad, gay, it was all the same to V'lu, whose immense brown eyes were becoming somnambulant, if not squamulous, a sure sign that the hurricane drops were beginning to take effect.

"Priscilla was a Mardi Gras baby," Lily said, out of the blue. "Have I mentioned that?"

"Yes, ma'am. You sho' 'nuf have mentioned that."

"A Mardi Gras baby." She drained her glass, regarding the oysters now with no appreciable indication of appetite. "Conceived one Mardi Gras, abandoned the next."

"Who she mama?"

"Pardon?"

"Ol' Wallet Lifter she daddy, who she mama?"

"Her mother." Madame sighed into her empty glass. "You know, V'lu, I no longer remember her mother's real name. She was from a good Irish Catholic family, lived in a fine house in the Garden District, I know that. But the devil will bite a young girl if she gives him a spot, and he sure took a nibble of this one. She could have watched the parade from her veranda, they lived right on St. Charles, but, no, she had to come down to the Quarter, mix with the so-called artists— she loved those artists—and that is where Wally spotted her. He seduced her on the street, under the crepe paper skirts of a float that had stalled."

"Revern' Wallet Lifter."

"That's what the cynics called him, yes. The Reverend Wally Lester was what he called himself. From the Irish Channel, poor white trash, more than likely, but he wasn't dumb. I never actually heard him preach, but he must have been fairly good, he had the looks and he had the tongue. Traveled throughout Texas; Oklahoma, too, conducting revival meetings in a circus tent; overdramatizing the word of God, turning the Scriptures into a cross between German opera and a hockey game, as only a Protestant can do. Then, every year, about a week before Mardi Gras, never fail, he'd suddenly show up in the Quarter. Oh, nobody enjoyed Mardi Gras more than Wally. He'd go on a rip that lasted well into Lent. After everybody else had wound down, he'd still be bouncing off barroom walls. Next thing you knew, though, he'd be gone; he'd go down into Mexico, some said after women, some said after gold—he obviously had more luck with the women. In any case, by Easter Sunday, he would be back to preaching, setting up his plastic pulpit on top of half the prairie-dog holes in Texas. Until Mardi Gras, when he would return to the Quarter and start the whole thing all over again. *Sacrebleu.*"

"Yo oysters be gitting warm, ma'am," V'lu announced dreamily. Ignoring her, Madame Devalier went on telling her things about the Reverend Wally Lester that she'd told a dozen times before. "Warm slime don't taste nowhere near as nice as cold slime," said V'lu. She smiled, revealing a mouthful of small, iridescent teeth. If oysters drove cars, their hood ornaments would look like V'lu's smile.

"The girl traveled with him for a season. She gave birth in his air-conditioned trailer, parked in one of those awful towns where jackrabbits hop down Main Street." Lily made a face. "I've always maintained that Priscilla got off to a bad start by not being born in New Orleans." She refilled her glass. "More champagne? Oh, I forgot. I'm sorry."

"Ah 'pose dat be Miz Priscilla on dee phone?"

"I'll never forget the day they came back. The minute they hit town, she gathered up her things and jumped on the first streetcar to the Garden District, although they managed to have *le combat* before she got away. Wally brought the baby by the shop so that I could see her, and there were claw marks on his cheek, the blood was barely dry. He rubbed the baby's bare bottom over the scratches, as if that would heal them. A few days later, he brought her by a second time and asked if I would watch her while he 'administered to those sinners who mock the true Christian meaning of Mardi Gras,' as he put it. It was a year before I saw him again. His face had healed without scarring."

"Why you?"

"Why me? Why did Wally leave her with *me*? Well, I suppose he trusted me. You see, he used to hang out at the shop—"

"He like you?"

A blush stained Madame Devalier in the way that debits color the ledgers of a failing business. "No, no, he wasn't interested in me personally. Even then I was too old and stout. I was *born* old and stout. He was interested in the 'work.' He wanted to learn the 'work,' although what an evangelist would do with it I never understood. I sold him some—some items. He was the only white man I ever sold to."

An oyster Cadillac rolled into view, V'lu Jackson incisors sparkling, leading the way. "Hee hee hee. Ol' Wallet Lifter be jazzing up Jesus wif some drops."

"Romance powders and money mojo were more in his line, but that's neither here nor there. I agreed to rear his child, because . . . well, I was convinced that I would never marry, and because I thought I could use a girl in the shop, someone to help, you see, someone to teach perfumery to. That didn't work out, of course. Priscilla always loathed the shop, and I never had the assistant I needed until—until you."

It might have been V'lu's turn to blush; whether she did or not we'll never know. She did manage a proud pursing of the lips, however, and then she asked, "Dat Miz Pris on dee line?"

"She was not a brat, you understand. In fact, she would make a sincere effort every now and again to follow in my footsteps, as it were. She was careless and messy, broke a lot of things, but she'd work hard. Then Mardi Gras would come around and, sure enough, here's Wally. He'd bring her armloads of presents: lollipops and pralines, all sorts of sweets, and dollies and stuffed animals and tricycles and, later, bikes, and the cutest clothes: little dotted-swiss dresses with ruffles and sashes. She thought her papa was rich, she believed that with all of her heart, and Wally encouraged it, the swine. When he left she'd beg him to take her with him, but he'd tell her that he had to go south of the border to attend to his gold mines and that Mexico was no place for rich little American girls. *Mon Dieu*, how it killed me to watch her fight back the tears! For months afterward she'd be moody and morose, claim that the smell of perfume made her ill."

Lily poured the last of the champagne. Briefly, she regarded the uneaten oysters, which, although beginning to look increasingly flabby, lay in perfect repose upon the remaining hemispheres of the dream houses in which they'd once enjoyed such exquisite solitude. Two strong hands and a steel blade were required to storm the privacy of the oyster's dark entrance hall. It takes a team of four horses to force the giant clam of the South Seas to yawn against its will. Every passive mollusk demonstrates the hidden vigor of introversion, the power that is contained in peace.

"About that time the shop started to lose money. I went to Paris with my formulas and was brutally rejected. LeFever showed interest, but eventually it, too, turned me down—"

At the mention of "LeFever," a blush actually did seep through V'lu's protective pigmentation, spreading upon her carob complexion like an oil slick on the muddy Mississippi, and even though her nervous system was, by hurricane drops, entertained, she flinched.

"—after stringing me along, and with not so much as a franc for my time and trouble. I should never have left New Orleans. I was depressed after that, I admit, but Priscilla was worse. At least I kept a roof over our heads, dealing in items I had rather not discuss. Priscilla wouldn't turn a hand, just talked about her papa all the time, how he was going to come and give her this and that, buy her a sports car, pay for ballet lessons, move her into a big house with a yard, until finally I had to tell her the truth about the Reverend Wallet Lifter and his Mexican fortune; I had no choice, V'lu."

V'lu was still recovering from the dent that the reference to the French fragrance house of LeFever had kicked in the fuselage of her midnight airship. She perceived that her mistress needed comforting, but "She believe you?" was the extent to which she could respond.

"No, she didn't believe me, but she never forgave me, either. Oh, I suppose deep down she may have believed me. In any case, Wally's next visit was a stormy one, and did little to improve our financial situation. Six months later, she ran off and married that accordion player."

"How old her be den?"

"Sixteen." Madame shook her head and clucked. "Sixteen."

"He hab plenny money."

"He had *some* money. Priscilla imagined that it was plenty. And money was what she wanted. I mean, he was pushing forty, not exactly your dashing Latin lover, and she was such a pretty little thing—and so smart in school! His band, it was one of those South American tango fandango bands, was fairly popular for a while. They traveled all over, from Puerto Rico to the New York state mountains, playing in resort hotels. He claimed he was going to train her to dance with his troupe. I can't fathom how either one of them could have believed that for an instant. *Mon Dieu*, the girl has two left feet!"

"Him go he home, though. Overseas."

"Yes, his band eventually folded, and he returned to Argentina alone, but I believe she had already left him by then. She left him right after Wally passed away."

"Her come watch she daddy die?" V'lu knew perfectly well that Priscilla had been at her father's deathbed, she'd heard the story more times than there were beets rotting under her cot, but she was disposed to hear it again.

"Pris was there at the end. Wally took sick in Mexico and had the decency to come back to New Orleans to expire. He was rather far gone when Pris and I got to Charity." Madame crossed herself, ringed fingers flashing like UFOs over the summits of her mountainous breasts. "The second we walked into the ward, though, he opened his eyes. His eyes were heavy and feverish, rather like yours are right now. He stared at Priscilla for quite a while before he spoke."

"Whut he say?"

"He said, 'You're startin' to turn out like your ol' daddy, darlin'. A novelty act.' That hit her like a brick."

"Then he recognized me and winked. He was only fifty, but he looked sixty-five. 'Stay in touch,' he said to me. 'Have you ever . . . ?'

"He closed his eyes and folded his arms on his chest; you could almost see the life ticking out of him. He sighed, kind of sweetly, and a contented smile softened his face. He muttered something. Then he was gone."

"Whut he mutter?"

"He said, 'The perfect taco.' That's it, those were his last words. He sighed, 'Ahhh,' and said, 'The perfect taco.' "

The two women were silent for some time, maybe meditating upon the mystery of it all—the life, the death, the goofiness—maybe, in V'lu's case, in communion with a private totem. The oysters, those tender masters of sequestrable engineering, apparently had given up the ghost, perhaps to be reborn, in distant times, in distant foams, as Aphrodites. When finally V'lu spoke, the abruptness caused Lily to accidentally jettison the last remaining bubbles of champagne.

"Whut Miz Priscilla call about?"

"Pardon? Oh. Well, Miss Priscilla is seeking help, monetary or otherwise, in obtaining some—are you prepared for this?—some premium jasmine oil."

"*Jamais!*" snapped V'lu. She caught herself. "Never," she repeated in English, catching herself once more and amending her response to: "Nebber."

"Chérie, I am surprised at you. Don't look so upset." With a yellowed linen napkin, Madame dabbed at the champagne spots on the love-seat velvet. "The Parfumerie Devalier has extracted eight ounces of the most magnificent jasmine essence the world has ever known. When we establish the proper base note, we shall own a boof that will have Paris crawling here, to *me*, on its knees. It could ruin us if our extract fell into the wrong hands, but still, Pris has some rights. It took a lot of heart for her to turn to me after I rejected her three years ago, pushed her away in favor of *you*, when she asked to come back into the shop—"

"But—"

"I am aware of what you are going to say: she refused to help me when I really needed her. Well, I refused to help her when she needed it, too."

"You hep her she whole life."

"I could have helped more."

"How?"

"I could have told her the truth about Wally. Years before I did. I could have squelched her silly fantasies." Madame paused. "But then, perfume business is fantasy business, is it not?" She draped her napkin over the shellfish platter like a shroud. "Don't fret, cher. I didn't even mention our jasmine to Priscilla, and since we have no assurance that the Jamaican will supply any more, we may not be able to afford to share with her. Yet, what harm if we did? I can't imagine how she might use it. To be frank, it would please me if her recent interest in perfumes proved sincere. But she is far from expert in the field."

V'lu sat upright, her countenance uncharacteristically grim. "Her hab dee bottle," she said firmly. "Her hab dat dadblasted bottle!"

The older woman seemed about to protest but changed her mind. The two of them just sat there, as if they were mourners sitting the night with the shrouded oysters. It was early in the week, so no bellows of alcoholic gaiety drifted in from Bourbon Street, nor any screech from a tourist having her purse snatched over on St. Ann. They might as well have been on the plantation; indeed, they could make out crickets rubbing their patent leather hooves together in some nearby courtyard. A tomcat wailed. A foghorn Mark Twained on the river. Then, directly above their heads, there was a single soft thud or plop, followed by the softer sound of something rolling across the floor.

"Hmmm," said Madame D. "Maybe our Bingo Pajama has returned."

"Yes, ma'am. Or else it be somebody else all dee time be throwin' dem beets."

That, at any rate, was what V'lu had intended to say. At precisely that moment, however, the hurricane drops hit her with full force, and, instead, she exclaimed, "Ui zeh! Ch, ch, ch, ch, ch, ch, ch."

PARIS

LATE ONE FOGGY AFTERNOON in November, just
as he was snapping shut his attaché case and calling it a day,
Claude LeFever was summoned to the offices of his father,
Luc, president of LeFever Odeurs. He arrived to find the old
man wearing a whale mask.

"Papa! What in the world . . . ? Take that off!"

Although more accustomed to giving the orders, Luc did as
he was bid. When the mask had been removed, it was easy to
see why Claude reacted as strongly as he did. There are
people in this world who can wear whale masks and people
who cannot, and the wise know to which group they belong.
A tall man, shoulders only slightly rounded by seventy years
of nagging gravity; a powerfully built man, whose torso the
blind might mistake for a home freezer; a handsome man,
nose structurally sound enough to support what might have
been the heaviest pair of horn-rimmed spectacles in Europe;
a dignified man, despite a residual patch of snow-and-rust
hair that resembled a wad of stuffing from a wino's mattress,
Luc LeFever was so staid of bearing that on those rare
occasions when he forged a smile, his body treated it as an
infection, tripling its output of interferon in a frantic attempt
to repulse the alien life form that had invaded it. This is not a
portrait of your average whale-mask man.

(Of course, Marcel LeFever was also a distinguished-looking
gentleman, sober in his selection of tailor, barber, and facial

expression, but in Marcel's eyes were telltale squadrons of milkweed seeds, eager to fly to faraway places upon the first cooperative breeze; whereas Luc's gaze was sedentary, a clump of briers that scratched with severity anything careless enough to brush against it.)

"I wished to experience, for just five minutes, what it must be like being *him*," said Luc. He smoothed his hair. He lit, with a gold-plated lighter, a Romeo y Julieta Presidente, handmade in the Dominican Republic with Cameroon wrapper: a foe of socialism, Luc had long maintained a personal boycott of Havana cigars.

"I wished to experience what it must be like to be . . . unstable." He blew a smoke ring. It was square.

Claude was more than a little surprised. "What brought this on?"

"Death."

"Pardon?"

"I was examined by physicians this morning."

"Oh, no."

"Relax. My blood pressure has escalated, but if I submit to their damned medication, it will come back down. Other than that, I have a faint heart murmur, and a slight swelling of the big toe that could herald an attack of gout. Nothing to be alarmed about, but it underscores the fact that I'm getting to be an old, old man. I mentioned this in passing to one of the doctors, and he said, 'Nobody lives forever, Monsieur LeFever.' "

"An astute observation. For once, the medical profession has issued a statement with which I can agree."

"Can you now? I suppose you haven't heard of the Last Laugh Foundation?"

"Yes, Papa, I *have* heard of the Last Laugh Foundation. What a farce. You know who operates that place? Wiggs Dannyboy, the drug addict and jailbird. Insane Irish—"

"Yes, it's true that the notorious Dr. Dannyboy founded it, but do *you* know who's cast his lot with him? Wolfgang Morgenstern. I attended the Sorbonne with Morgenstern, he was in my elementary chemistry classes, we knew one another. Splendid fellow. He went on to win two Nobel prizes. Two, mind you."

"Yes, but—"

"Morgenstern wouldn't be involved if there wasn't something to it."

"Yes, but—"

"I can tell you, Morgenstern is not the sort to join forces with a charlatan."

"Papa, are you considering having yourself admitted to the immortality clinic?" Disapproval was as thick in Claude's voice as fog was thick in the Parisian streets.

With his fingertips, Luc slowly twirled the cigar. He examined its ash. The higher the quality of the cigar, the longer the ash it will produce. Eventually, however, every ash must drop. And the drop usually is as sudden as it is final. Did Luc detect a metaphor in the cigar ash? Might he muse philosophically about the nature of the Eternal Ashtray? Might we?

"No," he said, after a puff or two. "I must confess to having experienced a twinge of temptation, knowing Morgenstern as I do. But in the end"—he sighed—"immortality is not for me. Did I make a pun, there? No? Good. In any case, dying is a tradition, and I am simply not the type of fellow who defies tradition."

"Unless there is profit in it."

"Eh?"

"You've always been willing to break with tradition if there was a profit in it. That's the secret of your success in business."

"Um. That may be. But I see no profit in struggling to live beyond one's natural limits. There's something greedy about that, and I've taught you to distinguish between the profit motive and greed. Sooner or later, the greedy lose their profits. Profiteering is honorable and healthy, greed is degrading, perverse."

"Life's not the same as money."

"Thank God! Life ebbs away, but money, properly managed, grows and continues to grow, lifetime after lifetime. Life is transitory, money is eternal. Or it could be, if the damned Americans would lower their interest rates." Luc picked up the whale mask and blew a stream of blue smoke through its eyeholes. "This small talk about death, money, and, last but not least, perversity, cannot help but bring us back to *him*."

"Christ?"

"No, you idiot, not Christ. Your cousin. Marcel."

Claude frowned. "Papa, if you're going to jump on Bunny's back again, forget it. You know how I feel about him."

"Indeed, I do, and there's something perverse about that, too. You spend more time with that bedbug than you do with your wife."

"Yes, well, Bunny is more entertaining than my wife. And he makes us more money."

"Your wife doesn't ridicule you in public. And if wearing a cardboard fish head is your idea of entertainment . . ."

"A whale is not a fish."

"So what?"

"I'm willing to accept his ridicule, and his peculiarities. And, ultimately, Papa, so are you. Without Bunny, where would this firm be?"

"That's a contingency for which I have been preparing."

"What do you mean?"

Luc propped his cigar against the rim of an alabaster ashtray. The cigar looked like some kind of vegetable, a root crop, related, perhaps, to the *mangel-wurzel*. The vegetable was on fire. Arson was suspected.

"I mean that Marcel is unstable." Luc retrieved the cigar and with it, tapped the whale mask. Ash sifted onto the jaws. The cigar burned on. Fireman, fireman, save my vegetable! "I mean that any day Marcel might up and decide to swim to Tahiti. Look at the way he's abandoned *New Wave*, attacking it as if it were some sort of dangerous political movement, rather than a highly promising perfume in which we've invested millions, and which he, himself, developed. Now he's talking about making scent from seaweed. He thinks women will pay a thousand francs an ounce to smell like low tide. I thought most women bought perfume to *avoid* smelling like the mouth of the Amazon."

"But—"

"Listen, I still trust Marcel. He's also beginning to show new interest in natural jasmines, which might be a sound idea. He's the best nose in the business, and he's been

correct too many times for me to sour on him now. Nevertheless, he *is* unpredictable, and therefore a risk. So, while
you've been taking out insurance policies on him and filling
his kitchen with assistants, not one of whom, unfortunately,
could come close to filling his shoes, I've been taking other
precautions." Luc removed a folder from a desk drawer.
"After the scare the doctors put into me today, I decided I
should go ahead and turn this over to you."

"What is it?"

"A list of agents."

"Agents?"

"Selected employees of our main competitors. France. New
York. Germany. Plus a few people situated with small perfumeries, certain promising shops off the beaten track where
something might develop that the big boys have overlooked."

"Spies?"

"If that's what you choose to call them. Let's just say that if
Marcel should go astray, we will still have access to blue-chip
recipes. And if one of the little perfumeries should strike
gold. . . . You have objections?"

A bit sheepishly Claude shook his head. "I suppose not. So
long as it's just a failsafe, a backup. You see, I'm confident
that the cuckoo is going to stay put in Bunny's clock. He
won't do anything rash." Luc shot him a disbelieving look.
"Well, nothing so rash as to endanger the firm and justify
extralegal activities. But, you know, the way he wanders
around on foggy evenings like this without a topcoat, it wouldn't
hurt to have something up our sleeves in the event that he
catches a fatal chill in his liver. I mean, those things happen."

Luc expelled such a geyser of smoke that had it come from
a derailed tank car, the authorities would have immediately
evacuated the neighborhood. Under certain conditions, Luc's
exhalation could have forced hundreds of people to spend the
night in church basements and high-school gymnasiums. "It's
not *his* liver I'm concerned about. Nor mine. I've always
been a prime physical specimen, I expected to live a century,
but the doctors have pulled the rug out from under that idea.
All right, I can accept it, I'm no sissy hippie about death.
What worries me is: what if Marcel should outlive *you*? Can
you imagine Marcel in charge?"

"Papa!"

"Jesus. This building. He'd probably rent out the top twenty-three stories and operate a little perfumerie in the basement, like the monks had seven hundred years ago, or that little Kudra shop that was next-door when our ancestors bought the business in 1666."

"Papa! How ridiculous. In the first place, I'm in better health than Bunny. In the second place, the articles of incorporation would prohibit him from doing anything like that, even if he wanted to. Third, this is the best way for a person to raise his blood pressure, worrying about things like longevity, which you have no control over."

Another column of smoke erupted from the tank car of compressed *mangel-wurzel*, delaying any hopes the neighbors might have had of returning to their homes. "But what if someone does have control?" Luc asked.

"What on earth are you talking about?"

"This. I'm talking about this. A few days ago, Marcel received an invitation to visit the Last Laugh Foundation."

"In America?"

"You idiot. Of course, in America."

"Why Marcel? Surely he isn't going?"

"His secretary says he accepted. Today."

Claude furrowed his brow. He tugged at the ax blade of his beard. "But what's this all about?"

"I wish to hell I knew. That's what I want you to find out. It may be a spinoff from that ridiculous speech he gave at the perfumers' convention, or it may be something else."

After cautioning his father to take his medication, Claude left him. On the way to the elevator, he peeked into Marcel's office. Marcel wasn't there. Everything seemed normal, except, of course, for the beet on the silver tray.

Claude rode to the ground floor. Through the plate glass windows, the foggy streets looked like Frankenstein's idea of Club Med. Claude had a hunch that before he went outside he ought to lock Luc's "agent" file in his attaché case. As he was about to put it in, he flipped rapidly through it. The name *V'lu Jackson* caught his eye.

PART
III

PROMISE
HER
ANYTHING
BUT
GIVE
HER
K23

THE HIGHEST FUNCTION OF LOVE is that it makes the loved one a unique and irreplaceable being.

The difference between love and logic is that in the eyes of a lover, a toad can be a prince, whereas in the analysis of a logistician, the lover would have to *prove* that the toad was a prince, an enterprise destined to dull the shine of many a passion.

Logic limits love, which may be why Descartes never married. Descartes, architect of the Age of Reason, fled Paris, the City of Romance, in 1628 to "escape its distractions." He settled in Holland, where, surrounded by disciples and supported by patrons, he studied and wrote about mathematics and logic. Late in the year of 1649, he was invited to visit Stockholm to instruct Queen Christina in philosophy. Descartes accepted at once. Perhaps the pay was good. There would have been a reason.

Queen Christina took her lessons lying down. Frequently she was nude. That is hardly the worst of it. The court of Sweden, like everyplace else in seventeenth-century Europe, was infested with fleas. Christina had had her craftsmen fashion for her a tiny cannon of silver and gold. As she lay about on her cushions, she fired the little cannon at the fleas on her body. That was why she was nude. It is said she was a fair to good shot.

The daily sight of Her Majesty thus amusing herself, while

he, Descartes, in dark Dutch britches, undertook to explain
the underlying perfection of an indubitable sphere of Being,
was more than his rational bias could bear. He grew rapidly
nervous and pale. On February 11, 1650, only a few months
after his arrival in Stockholm, Descartes, fifty-four, fell dead.
Christina lived thirty-nine years longer and knocked off a
good many more fleas.

In 1666—little harm love could do him then—Descartes's
body was taken to Paris for reburial. At the funeral, a disagreeable odor filled the churchyard. "It was as if a goatherd
had driven his flock through our midst," said one of Descartes's
followers. No logical explanation was offered.

The highest function of love is that it makes the loved one a
unique and irreplaceable being. Still, lovers quarrel. Frequently, they quarrel simply to recharge the air between
them, to sharpen the aliveness of their relationship. To pre-
cipitate such a quarrel, the sweaty kimono of sexual jealousy
is usually dragged out of the hamper, although almost any
excuse will do. Only rarely is the spat rooted in the beet-
deep soil of serious issue, but when it is, a special sadness
attends it, for the mind is slower to heal than the heart, and
such quarrels can doom a union, even one that has prospered
for a very long time.

The quarrel of Kudra and Alobar lasted far into the night.
Jarred by their words, things fell apart in the flat: flowerpots
tottered on the windowsills, feathers flew out of pillows, and
the teapot sang, though there was no fire beneath it and it
was not a cozy song. As if it had long fingernails, their
argument reached out into the street and scratched the cobblestones, the chestnut blossoms, the blackboard of the sky.

"A pox on squabbling lovers," muttered Pan. Pan needed
to get to sleep. He'd been in bed for hours, but instead of
dreams, what came to him were harsh voices through the
wall. Pan tossed and turned and cursed a bit, although the
irony of the situation (gods have ears for irony) was not lost on
him: Alobar and Kudra were fighting over immortality, whereas

Pan was craving sleep because he planned to get up early to attend a funeral.

Pan tossed and turned, turned and tossed. An eye at the keyhole would have been amazed. It would have spied a bed in turmoil, iron bedstead rattling, wool blankets thrashing, but not a soul in the covers.

The year was 1666 and poor Pan was completely invisible.

At seven o'clock in the morning, the door of the incense shop that had been established at 21, rue Quelle Blague opened and closed, although nobody was seen to enter or leave. A transparent mist of musk moved slowly eastward along the left bank of the Seine. At the rue St. Jacques, the acrid cloud turned to the south, insulting every snout, human or equine, by which it floated. After about eight blocks, it began traveling eastward again, creeping up the slope of a steep hill, at the top of which sat the crumbly old Gothic abbey church of Ste. Geneviève-du-Mont.

"This temple (gasp) art as tired and (wheeze) rundown as I," panted Pan, and, indeed, though the professional virgin, Geneviève, was regarded with much paradoxical affection in the City of Romance, the church would be razed in less than a century to make way for a fine new building in the neoclassic style. In 1817 the well-traveled bones of Descartes would be transferred from its yard to St. Germain-des-Pres, but on this spring morning they were to be planted in the mossy cemetery where Geneviève's own saintly remains had a thousand years been lying.

In his more vital days, Descartes had included in his philosophical treatises enough scientific fact to displease the bishops, so except for the cleric whose Latin platitudes were to be rained on his deaf skull, the Church was without representation at his interment. However, among those who were obeisant to the new religion of science, which was in its husky infancy at this time, Descartes was increasingly revered, and they attended the rite in fair number. Pan rested upon a burial vault at a far end of the yard and watched their carriages arrive.

Some of the professors and physicians were rather shabby; they were men too clothed in ideas to pay much heed to grooming. Many others, however, including the provost of the University of Paris, the president of the guilds, the designer of the Observatoire, which was about to be built, and the chairman of the mathematical society were decked out in black silks and powdered wigs. The sight of those wigs gave Pan an idea. Earlier in the century, wigs had been worn exclusively by the nobility, but now they had become popular with the bourgeoisie. If Alobar were to sport a wig, thought Pan, it might solve his current problem and put a stop to his bickering with Kudra. "No small blessing, that," he said. He rubbed his bleary eyes and yawned.

About then a small brass band struck up a dirgeful tune, and Pan, who fancied himself a musician, listened critically. "In all of Arkadia, there be not a single sheep who wouldst dance to such noise," he complained. But once the speech-making commenced, he was sorry the music had ended.

Aristotle had dealt Pan an enervating blow. Then, Jesus Christ had practically belted his horns off. Now, word was out that Descartes had applied the coup de grace. What little remained of Pan's ancient power was destined to evaporate in the Age of Reason, that's what the experts said. Pan, weary and indistinct, could not dispute them. When he learned of Descartes's funeral, some morbid (or goatish) curiosity drew him, sore of hoof, to Ste. Geneviève-du-Mont.

Like jugged bees, the funereal orations droned on. One intellectual honored Descartes's *Discourse on Method*, another convinced every moss-backed headstone in the churchyard of the departed's contribution to the theory of equations, while a third, more bombastic than the rest, rattled in its vault the untested pelvis of good Saint Geneviève with his praise of the new rationale. Just as the university provost was uncorking *his* monotone, the spring breeze suddenly shifted direction, and the funeral party found itself downwind from Pan.

The crowd grew inattentive. Out of the corner of his eye, the provost checked the environs for animal life. Those who owned handkerchiefs soon had them to their nostrils (a passerby might have assumed that they were weeping). Among those who had no handkerchiefs was the priest. "This is what the Almighty thinks of science," he mumbled, then immediately crossed himself, begging forgiveness for having attributed to God a scent that obviously was Satan's.

Of course, the group was lucky. Pan's reek was actually mild compared to what it had been in the good old days. Nevertheless, a certain waggish mathematician provoked some scorn and much stifled laughter when, in a stage whisper, he paraphrased Descartes's most famous dictum.

"I stink, therefore I am," he said, nodding toward the Swedish walnut coffin.

"Ever thus." Pan sighed. Where was the profit in invisibility if one's odor gave one away? He creaked to his feet and, on legs of wobbly wool, threaded through the crowd toward the stone gate. Halfway there, he remembered his idea about a wig and, in passing, snatched the hairpiece off a prominent man of learning. Assuming that the wind had taken it, other bewigged guests grabbed at their own adornments, anchoring them to their noggins. There the French intelligentsia stood, one hand to its hair, the other to its noses, as the god and the wig bobbed out of Saint Geneviève's decaying churchyard and down the hill to the Seine. It was the first fun Pan had had all week.

Upon reaching the riverbank, Pan stopped for a breather. He uprooted a clump of turf and hid the wig beneath it so that no passing bargeman might mistake it for a relic of an aristocratic romp in the grass. An invisible learned early that his possessions and trappings did not borrow his ability, which meant that he must go always empty-handed. Pan could not even carry his pipes.

That was a shame, because a breezy April morning such as that one was meant for a tune. On similar mornings in the old

days, the golden days, Pan's mischievous piping on the outskirts of a village would be the signal for the village men to
lock up their wives and daughters. Those who failed to secure
their women would lose them that day to the pastures, from
where they would return after dusk, tangle-haired, grass-
stained, and stinking of the rut. Pan grinned at the memory.
"Methinks I could pipe Maria Theresa right out of the palace," he mused, referring to Louis XIV's young bride.

It was encouraging that he would mention a contemporary
female, for Pan had begun to live in his memories, an unhealthy symptom in anyone, suggesting as it does that life has
peaked. Every daydream that involves the past sports in its
hatband a ticket to the grave. Yet, what did the neglected
god have to look foward to? To ambrosia, to Maria Theresa,
to a monthly pension, a flock of his own? No, only the
ministrations of Alobar and Kudra kept him going, and as
their recent quarreling intimated, the couple had other things
to worry about.

As he warmed his horns on the sunny riverbank, watching
the wind-torn chestnut blossoms drift by like melted nymph
flesh on the tide, Pan dismissed Descartes and his prideful
ambition to force nature under human control, and thought
instead of Alobar and Kudra, how they had come to Arkadia,
drunk on eternal knowledge, seeking him out and laughing. . . .

Presumably, their "eternal knowledge" was derived from
the Bandaloop, albeit indirectly. No documents, no artifacts,
no graffiti were left behind by the Bandaloop, but as Dr.
Wiggs Dannyboy of the Last Laugh Foundation has written,
"Physical immortality is primarily a matter of vibration," and
the caves certainly were resonant with the vibrations of their
former occupants.

Alobar and Kudra lived in those caves, amidst those vibrations, for seven years, during which time they learned many
of the secrets of life everlasting. Alobar believed they should
have stayed longer and learned more, and this belief kept
surfacing like a lungfish in the hot surf of their seventeenth-
century quarrels. Way back then, however, six hundred years

further back, when the cream was still thick and yellow on the magic milk and the marble egg of logic laid by the Greek philosophers had yet to hatch, Alobar was simply too happy to protest at length.

Kudra was as thrilled as he with their Bandaloop education, yet she had been yearning since childhood, since that formative merchandising trip, to go out into the wider world, and now, tingling as she was with vitality and confidence, she was impatient to plunge into far cities and countrysides. "Take me to the lands where the sun sets," she implored. "We can do our immortality work wherever we are." That was basically true, for, and here we quote Wiggs Dannyboy again, "Physical immortality is not an end result, a condition to be arrived at in the future, but an ongoing discipline, an attitude, a way of life to be practiced in the present, day by day." Nevertheless, Alobar was convinced that there were serious holes in their knowledge that could best be filled in the caves of the Bandaloop. He made a sincere effort to persuade Kudra to linger; then, having failed at that, jumped with her, lighthearted and eager, into the meandering mainstream of medieval life.

Alobar signed on as a guard with a spice caravan, and they traveled by camel to Constantinople, humpbacking out of the sandy wings of the east onto that golden stage where Emperor Basil II was directing, under the auspices of Byzantine Christianity, a long-running drama of expansion and wealth. Suspecting that immortality might be fostered more by comfort than by asceticism, but having lived hand to mouth during all of their time together, the couple elected to settle temporarily in Constantinople and sample its luxury.

Neither of them had ever resided in a large city before, and Constantinople, a major trading center, a cosmopolitan link between East and West, a mosaic-tiled hive of commercial and religious honey, woke them daily with an excited nudge from its gilt elbow. Aided by Kudra, whose understanding of raw materials was studiously passed on to him, Alobar rose rapidly from stevedore to manager of Basil's spice warehouses, a position whose salary afforded them a smart house overlooking the Bosporus, a silver tea service, and carpets thicker and more colorful than the ones that had disappeared from the caves with the Bandaloop. Upon those rugs (dyed in some cases with beet juice), they sipped mint tea, munched spinach pies and melons, made love in ways that emphasized the utra in *Kama Sutra*, and perfected the breathing techniques that apparently are indispensable to extreme longevity.

Bathing techniques also are important, and, fortunately, in Constantinople they were easy to practice. As Alobar was well aware, most of Europe's two-legged mammals thought of water as an element only slightly more suitable for external application than fire. The unpopularity of the bath was both widespread and persistent (in Louis XIV's incomparably elegant Versailles, there was not a single vessel designed for bathing, a fact that one day would lead Kudra to regard the Sun King's court a potential market for her incense; late in the *twentieth* century, there were still great numbers of Europeans who refused to wash their bodies lest they remove some quality—corporeal or incorporeal—deemed essential to their image of themselves). As a result of its constant intercourse with the Far East, Constantinople had acquired an appreciation of the protracted hot bath, for the purpose of which a network of stone aqueducts channeled water into the city from reservoirs in the nearby hills. So that they might bathe together, a practice forbidden in the sexually segregated public baths, Alobar and Kudra tapped into the aqueduct system and built a tile-roofed, waist-deep tub at the rear of their house, between the rosebushes and the pistachio tree. Kudra spoke fluent amphibian, but Alobar, conditioned by the European aversion, frequently had to be coaxed into the tub by a reminder that ritualistic bathing enhances longevity, or by a suggestion that a soak might add some unusual slippery dimension to the coital functioning of his or his companion's organs.

"Nowhere under yon setting sun will you meet water meant for bathing in," Alobar would caution Kudra whenever she grew antsy, and if that did not lull her restlessness, he would add, "No perfumes will you meet, either."

He was correct, there was no perfume west of the Bosporus. In the modern sense, there was no perfume anywhere, for the process by which a flower's fumes are extracted and

preserved using alcohol distillation was not to be discovered
for another hundred years, when Avicenna, the Arabian al-
chemist, hit upon it while trying to isolate for Islam the soul
of its holy rose. In eleventh-century Constantinople, however, aromatics were as popular as they were in Kudra's
India, and, as in India, they came mostly in the form of thick
resins and gooey gums. Each morning, a servant would bring
Basil II a small cedar box filled with resinous frankincense
and gummy myrrh, whereupon the emperor would smash the
box over his own head, allowing its contents to trickle down
his neck and beard. As time passed, Basil began to act rather
punchy from all the box breaking, and frequently his eyes
were sealed half shut from the gum. He smelled great, though,
and when he died in 1025, his successor, wishing to exude an
even larger glory, took to breaking *two* boxes over his head
every day. Perhaps it was because of their vigorous application of scent that neither of the emperors was sufficiently
alert to notice that their spice manager stayed constant in
appearance even as they aged—although others in Constantinople noticed well enough: in the court and in the church,
gossip rustled its leathery wings.

"The emperor, the bishop, the camels at the marketplace,
the olive trees on the hillsides, the ships in the harbor, every
and each grow older. This Alobar and Kudra do not."

"They are always in good humor and health, yet they never
attend devotion."

"They bathe together."

"They smile too much."

"She anoints herself with sweet unguents as though a man."

"Nobody knows whence they came."

"They are often at the act of love, as their noisy demonstrations attest, but produce not a child."

"It is whispered that they eat their children as soon as they
are born."

"Aye. Eating babies is what keeps them young."

"Dark, she is."

"Haughty is he."

"Nonbelievers."

"Supernatural."

"Agents of the Evil One."

"Our children are in peril."

Rumor by rumor, suspicion of them intensified, until—"Did you hear? A small boy disappeared yesterday at play on the Bosporus"—one night they found themselves fleeing Constantinople just ahead of a mob. Alobar bribed a Greek captain to hide them among the stacks of ivory tusks lashed to his deck, and it was from that vantage that they witnessed their home of nearly thirty years burning to the ground.

"Hold back your sobs," Alobar consoled, squeezing one of Kudra's dolphin thighs. "We have learned from this experience two important things. First of all, our Bandaloop experiment is successful; we have slowed, if not turned away, the wrinkle-carving, silver-sowing herald of death. About that we can rejoice. Second, we now are aware that a display of undue longevity creates problems in a community conditioned to age and die. In the future, we must take that cautiously into account."

He pointed to their burning house, which by then was but a glowing ember on the horizon. "We have lost a roof over our heads, a fine teapot, an overrated bath, and some carpets stained by our love. Let them go. We have aliveness, instead. And on this entire world, which I know for fact to be as round as a beet, there is no other pair like you and me."

Through her tears Kudra grinned. "I'm certain that we shall find other rugs to stain," said she. "But even you will miss our bath, wait and see. As for the teapot . . ." With a flourish, she produced it from beneath her cloak.

Gathering her to him, teapot and all, Alobar pretended to search under her wraps. "For what I know, you may have hid our bath in there, as well. Ah, I thought so! I feel something hot and wet."

"You may well wish it were a bath, before too long. Oh, what is my poor large nose going to think of a people who neither bathe nor wear perfumes?"

"Well," said Alobar, "my scheme is to condition you straightaway by introducing you to Pan. Of all who stink in the western lands, none stinks in such grand capacity as he. Pan is a god and is my friend."

"Only you, Alobar. Only you among men could claim a god

for a friend. And naturally it would be a god unwashed and smelly."

She embraced him, swabbing his beard with kisses at the same moment that the ship plunged its black, wooden tongue into the murmuring mouth of the outer waters, knocking salt teeth loose in every direction; and as the lash lines shuddered from the recoil of that ancient kiss, as the mast pole tilted its neck like a voyeur for a better view, and the mainsail, with a raucous, swift gesture, shook a skyful of stars out of its folds and creases, Kudra and Alobar were carried off to Greece— uncertain, intrepid, possibly immortal, decidedly in love. . . .

Pan remembered the breezy way they had crossed his pasture, fairly skipping as they walked, although that pasture, like all pastures in Arkadia, was weighted down with toe-stubbing rocks; and she had said, "It is so quiet out here I can hear my ears," and he had shot back, "If your nose were your ears, the noise would be deafening." Vaudeville was not dead. It wasn't born yet.

Spying on them from a bushy crag, Pan had to admit that they were as agreeable a pair of homers as he'd ever laid eyes upon ("homers" was what the surviving Greek gods secretly called mortals, a disparaging term taken from the name of the so-called bard who had spread so many lies about them). Pan admired the bounce in their step, the fun in their voice, the way they paused every fifty yards or so to fondle one another; Pan was curious about the silver pot that the female homer cradled against her round mooey breasts as if it were a babe, and Pan was amused when the male homer, when invited to inspect one of the woman's silk slippers (meant for padding about upon carpets and now ripped and frazzled by stones), had rolled it up and smoked it.

Oh, there was an air about them, all right, but it wasn't until they were directly beneath his perch that Pan, whose gaze had become fixed upon the prosperous sweep of the woman's hips—if ever a twat were a cornucopia, spilling forth meat puddings, hot wines, and sweets of every description: unending (shellfish) inexhaustible (peaches) infinite (mushrooms) feta feta feta forever, surely it was hers—it wasn't until her companion suddenly pinched his nostrils together and cried, "He's close by! I have got a whiff!", that Pan made the identification. Why, it was ex-King Whatsizname, that brash upstart from the north, the mad fellow who had gone off—was it fifty, sixty homer years ago?—to spike a petition on death's door. From the looks of him, death had considered his complaint. Well, well . . .

Alobar was then one hundred and two, yet looked half his age, and the vigorous half at that. White hairs continued to populate his noble head, as if they were the familiars, the pale shadows of the chestnut filaments, which continued to dwell there, as well; but the phantoms, impotent, infertile in their ghost sheets, had failed to multiply and seemed content to just hang on, haunting the original inhabitants, who though they once might have quaked, had ceased to be afraid. Alobar had put on a few pounds and no longer carried himself like a warrior—Samye meditations had massaged the tension from his spine, Bandaloop transmissions had turned his spear-arm into a gaily waving thing—but pity the foolish young bully who noticed not the muscles turning and polishing themselves inside the lapidary of his tunic. His beard was trimmed after the Byzantine fashion, his various flashes of scar tissue had taken on a plum's brilliance, his sleet blue eyes looked out upon the world with a cub's curiosity and a papa bear's cunning. He blew playful puffs of slipper smoke through his nose.

Speaking of noses, his consort sported a grandiose banana that was almost musical in the way it curved. Upon a more angular woman it might have been ridiculous, but this dark creature was such a walking barrage of burpy bulges and bending lines that her nose blended perfectly into her contours. From the thick parabolas of her eyelids to the pronounced balls of her now bare feet, she was nonstop curve, three nymphs' worth of curve, a foreign contradiction to Greek geometry. The drool that rained from Pan's lips as he spied on her would have frozen in mid-drip had a reliable source informed him that she was as old as the grandmothers who milked the goats in nearby valleys, toothless skeletons (this one had a mouthful of pearly brights) whose only curves were in backs bent double over walking sticks. Kudra was sixty-six, Pan, and as you were to learn, as much a match for you as any homer girl you had ever piped into a pasture. Of course, you, yourself, Mr. Horny, were long past your prime. . . .

Yes, Mr. Goat Foot, despite the angry split between Rome and Constantinople, the tide of Christianity had not receded, but rather continued its slow, soupy flow into every nook and cranny of the land, until there was scarcely a pagan left whose heart and brain had not been lapped by it, lapped so long in many cases that old beliefs had been eroded, if not washed away, and you, Mr. Charmer, Mr. Irrational, Mr. Instinct, Mr. Gypsy Hoof, Mr. Clown; you, Mr. Body Odor, Mr. Animal Mystery, Mr. Nightmare, Mr. Lie in Wait, Mr. Panic, Mr. Bark at the Moon; yes, you, Mr. Rape, Mr. Masturbate, Mr. Ewe-bangi, Mr. Internal Wilderness, Mr. Startle Reaction, Mr. Wayward Force, Mr. Insolence, Mr. Nature Knows Best, you had been steadily losing your hold on the peasants and were now even weaker in flesh and spirit than when Alobar had seen you last. You were fading, and it was not a pretty sight, for you were a god, after all, with a god's strength; born, laughing and prancing, in the high golden circle where great and terrifying decisions are made. It hurt you to experience your popularity waning, it might have driven you to the wineskin were not the wineskin already, Mr. Sensual License, your lifelong friend; and it added to your misery to observe the effects of estrangement upon your former followers. In losing you, they were losing their body wisdom, their moon wisdom, their mountain wisdom, they were trading the live wood of the maypole for the dead carpentry of the cross. They weren't as much fun, anymore, the poor homers; they were straining so desperately for admission to paradise that they had forgotten that paradise had always been their address. That's why you were attracted to this unlikely couple that came skipping into your meadow, the woman in clear communion with the booming bells of her meat, the man unafraid of appearing frivolous in the eyes of

Christ as he caressed a poppy while puffing on a shoe. You would have admired them even had they not been sniffing you out, which, of course, they were.

Pan suspected, and rightly so, that the couple's gaiety, their cockiness and élan, was somehow the result of Alobar's successful petition against death, and, more than anyone else, the beleaguered god probably could have imagined the anguished expression minted into the other side of the immortalist coin.

To witness Kudra then, giggling and barefoot among the poppies, it would have been hard for anyone to picture her on her knees in a Constantinople pantry, weeping and wailing, shaking like the shuttle in an overachiever's loom, begging Shakti, Shiva, Kali, and Krishna to forgive her for rebelling against divine authority. (And it is divine authority, is it not, that insists that we must die? That grants us consciousness for a few decades, then, no matter how gloriously we have used it, snatches it away? Surely, the human race committed some heinous atavistic crime for the gods to inflict it with mortality, as they have; and isn't it a worsening of our crime, a compounding of our guilt, to try to escape our just punishment?) Even after absorbing the Bandaloop legacy (or part of it, at least), Kudra could never quite overcome the feeling that, in defying death, she was doing something wrong and would be made to pay for it in some prolonged and unspeakably excruciating way. When in Alobar's company, when meditating or bathing, she could exult in a body that remained firm and juicy while thousands about her withered away, but alone in the frottage of twilight, awaiting Alobar's return from the spice docks, fear would ooze out of the brown pit of her chin dimple, and, whimpering, she would turn from one deity to another, even bizarre Ganesh, with his elephant head, pleading for mercy for not having submitted to a widow's death in the rope yard.

Now Alobar had grown up in a more intimate relationship with his gods. His snored in magic tree trunks and twinkled in the constellations, frequently emerging, mossy-haired or moon-burned, to fraternize with humanity, sharing human foibles and appetites. As a king in the forests of what would one day be called Bohemia, Alobar, himself, had been deemed half divine. Still, he, too, felt odd and uncomfortable at times, felt a gulf widening between himself and his fellows who went uncomplaining to the grave. "Am I clinging to my individual being only to have it grow inhuman and strange?" he would agonize. "Am I inviting a revenge worse than simple annihilation?"

On a day such as that one, however, a day popping its seams with sunshine, lust, and adventure, it was difficult for him—or Kudra—to conceive of anything worse than annihilation. So, they advanced in the lavender mountain haze like chatty autograph-seekers closing in on a celebrity's hideaway, but in their secret hearts they wanted something other than your scrawl, Mr. Shaggy; they wanted you to reach into their secret hearts and remove the hard, knobby doggy bone of doubt that their apparent victory over time had buried there.

"We have been living in Constantinople among the Christians," explained Alobar.

"The Christians doth be everywhere," said Pan.

"Not in my homeland," said Kudra.

"They will be," said Pan. A wave of faintness and nausea broke over him. He ignored it to concentrate on Kudra's mounds.

"Prior to that," said Alobar, "we lived in a cave far away in the East. Have you ever heard of the Bandaloop doctors?"

"No," said Pan. "Don't be stupid."

Alobar reddened. "You've been around a while. I thought someone might have mentioned Bandaloop to you."

"I am Pan," said Pan. "People do not *mention* things to me."

"Your point is well taken," said Kudra. Pan grinned at her lasciviously. Alobar glowered.

"I will play for thee," said Pan, producing his reeds.

"We wished to talk to you about immortality," protested Alobar.

"Thou art too late," said Pan. He blew a few weak notes on his pipes.

"Too late for talk or too late for immortality?" asked Kudra.

Pan's instrument made a sound, high and thin.

"Too late for us or too late for you?" asked Alobar. He had noted the god's physical decline.

"Thou art interested in the immortal, *this* be immortal," said Pan, and he commenced to pipe in earnest.

"But—" objected Alobar.

"Your point is well taken," said Kudra.

Alobar glowered.

Before she met him, before they flushed him from his thickets, Kudra had imagined Pan to be a giant, a winged monster with fire-blackened hooves and more arms than necessary for the discharge of polite duties; imagined him smoldering, hissing, uprooting trees and spitting hailstones, instructing humanity in a thunderous tone. She was frankly disappointed when he proved to be slighter in stature than her Alobar, and she could barely keep from sniggering at his foul tangles of wool and his silly tail. Even his stench failed to measure up to Alobar's description of it, striking her as more locally naughty than universally nasty. It wasn't until he began to pipe that Kudra got some sense of Who (or What) He Really Was.

At first, his playing, too, seemed slight; it was so simple, careless, and primitive that one had to sympathize with Timolus, who, judging the music contest between Pan and Apollo, had unhesitatingly awarded the prize to the Apollonian lyre, thereby establishing the tradition that critics must laud polish and restraint, attack what is quirky and disobedient, a tradition that endures to this day. Had Timolus not hooked Pan off the stage so quickly, had he possessed the—the what? the honesty? the humility? (Timolus, after all, couldn't play shit) the nerve? to actually listen to Pan, to respond with something more genuine than his preconceptions, he might have been affected, as Kudra began to be affected, once she stopped smirking at his obvious lack of formal training and quit comparing him unfavorably with the flutist, Lord Krishna. Pan's song, because it served no purpose, because, indeed, it transcended the human yoke of purposes, was, above all, liberating. It was music beyond the control of the player's will or the listener's will; the will, in fact, dissolved in it (which may explain why it was politically necessary for Apollo, with the compliance of Timolus, to drown it out). To Kudra it was the aural equivalent of the rope trick: a giddy ascent up a shaky coil, to arrive in a place of mystery, where the sense of all-encompassing oneness with the natural world and the sense of the absolute aloneness of the individual coexist and commingle. There was a sort of hippity-hoppity bunny rabbit quality to Pan's erratic melody, but also a roaming goatish quality, stubborn, rough, and lean. If at one instance it sounded tender and idyllic, at another, threatening and brutal, perhaps that was because Pan's song was the inner animal's songs, all of them, summed into one seemingly random epiphany. Kudra felt that at Pan's concert she was on less than solid ground, yet, as unsteady as that ground might be, she was driven to dance upon it. (Maybe there is no proper way to react to the inner animal's tunes but dance to them.)

Kudra found herself swaying rhythmically and wiggling her grass-stained toes. She turned to Alobar to find him executing a little shuffle, snapping the fingers of his left hand while with the right he defined a tempo by shaking the charred remains of her half-smoked shoe. Kudra was amused by Alobar's tentative polka until her eyes fell upon the tumescent protrusion dancing with him. *Disgusting*, she thought. *An erection is just inappropriate*. Then she realized with a shock that she was so wet that children could have sailed toy boats in her underpants.

The next thing she knew, she and Alobar were dancing up the hillside, following the Charmer's pipes through thistle bushes and over jagged rocks; and while panic fear erupted with a roar from her deepest places and while she overheard Alobar plaintively asking, "Doesn't it matter to you that she is my wife?" she was incapable of turning back.

The refined erotic engineering taught by the *Kama Sutra* had not prepared Kudra for that night of priapism, but the following morning, after she had sponged her chafed parts in the grotto pool and smeared them repeatedly with the aromatics that she lugged about in the teapot (even so, the goat smell was to cling to her for weeks), she found that she and Alobar could face one another without shame, and she nodded in total agreement when Alobar ventured, "I feel somehow that his lechery was secondary, although to what I cannot say."

For breakfast, Pan served them olives, tomatoes, and cheese, which they ate in the nude without a trace of self-consciousness. Throughout the meal, the sleepy-eyed god kept testing the air, more like a hare than a goat, until at last Alobar inquired what he might be sniffing.

"Flowers, methinks, but unlike any flowers that bloom in these parts. Most strange. Dost thou smell them, too?"

"You are smelling my perfumes," said Kudra, and when Pan looked puzzled, she thrust her shoulder under his nose. His bewilderment increased. "Thou didst not smell like that last night," he said.

Alobar made a move to produce the perfume jars, but Kudra caught his wrist and bade him wait. "We puny homers, as you call us, have some magic of our own," she said. "Tell me, do you find the aroma unpleasant?"

"It be quite pleasing—from a blossom. A woman shouldst smell as thou didst last night."

"Bah! You Western males are all alike, whether you call yourselves gods or men. You've had your noses in too many battles and too many hunts. Alobar used to hate perfumes, but when he came home from the warehouse every evening accidentally smelling of nutmeg and cinnamon and tumeric, he grew accustomed to the idea that flesh is more appealing when not left to marinate in its own rank juices. Here. Close your eyes for a minute. Just for a minute. Go ahead. Trust me."

Reluctantly, Pan lowered his big monkey lids, whereupon Kudra doused him with enough patchouli to stampede a herd of elephants. His eyes flew open like the hatch covers on an exploding ship, and he commenced to sniff at his extremities, as if he were wildly in love with himself. A kind of disorientation seemed to seize him, causing him to walk in circles, repeatedly crossing his own path. The nymphs, who had entertained Alobar during the night while Kudra was being entertained by Pan, laughed nervously from their mossy lounge across the pool. One of the nymphs sidled up to the god and pulled his tail with a petal-picking gesture, only to be flung violently to the ground. At last, Pan sat down between Kudra and Alobar, still inhaling drafts of himself with expressions of disbelief, and began to speak in the most subdued tones Alobar had yet heard him employ.

" 'Tis true, thou homers *do* have magic of thine own, the gods have always known that, known it even better than thee. We gods know how to use our powers, but most men and women do not know how, that be the difference between us and thee. Sniff sniff."

"Forgive me," said Alobar, "but the important difference between men and gods is that gods are immortal and men are not. Is this a result of we men not knowing how to correctly use our powers?"

Pan ran his rather squashed nose along his patchouli-contaminated arm. "Once, a long time ago, when the earth had a flat dark face and a belly of fire, back before the hills had grown so tall that they pushed the moon away, mankind was given a choice between life and death and through trickery or misinformation or something else, made the wrong choice. That is all there is to it."

"But what if," asked Kudra, shooting Alobar a meaningful glance, "but what if we decided now to choose life?"

"Then choose it," said Pan.

Again, Kudra and Alobar exchanged glances. "But would not that anger the gods?" Kudra asked.

"Ha ha ha!" The laughter burst out of Pan like the barking of some obscene dog. "Anger the gods? The gods, those that art still around, wouldst congratulate thee for finally catching on."

"You mean . . . ?"

"I mean that the gods do not limit men. Men limit men."

"We are," asked Kudra, "as deserving of immortality as the gods?"

"Thou hast not deserved immortality because thou hast been too puny in thy mind and heart and soul. Sniff."

"But we can change that?" Kudra's voice was hopeful. "We can expand our minds, and enlarge our souls, and choose life over death?"

"Sniff sniff. Thou hast that potential."

Alobar was nodding his head excitedly, and Kudra wore a

smile that you could mail a letter in. An eleventh-century letter, written on parchment, rolled into a cylinder and tied with thongs. The Charmer was still cruising the patchouli patches.

"Great Pan," said Alobar, with a degree of reverence, "I used to be king over a state, but now I am king over myself."

"Dearest Pan," said Kudra, with more than a degree of intimacy (in the preceding night, after all, she and the god had left no sexual stone unturned), "I used to weave rope, but now I weave my world."

"Methinks thou doth speak from freedom not from vanity," said Pan, "and I lift my wineskin to thee, for thou art rare among humans. Sniff." He squirted a stream of wine into his ugly, yet sensual, mouth. Red rivulets ran into his beard to disappear there, sopped up, perhaps, by whorls of thirsty wool. "Ah, but Alobar, doth thou not recall my telling thee that gods art immortal for only so long as the world believes in them? Thou hast only to look at me to see how a god dwindles when belief in him dwindles. Immortality has its conditions. Immortality has its limits. And immortality has its dangers. Whatever thou hast learned about death from thy wise men in the East, thou wouldst do well to remember . . ."

"Yes? Go on," urged Alobar.

"What, Pan? Remember what?" asked Kudra.

It was no use. Pan had finished speaking and would say no more. Nor would he sniff at himself again, for, incredibly, his native odor had peeled away the perfume that masked it; had slowly burned through the potent excess of patchouli like a sunray blazing its way through a purple fog, and now, after less than an hour of suppression, the goat gas—that chloride compound of barnyard and bedroom—was boiling again, filling the grotto with a sleazy vapor, a steam to press a rooster's pants.

With the return of Pan's stink, there came renewed mischief in his eyes. When he scampered to the cave to fetch his pipes, Kudra and Alobar began hastily to dress. "We have a long journey ahead of us," they explained, and with a curious mixture of relief and regret, they bade their divine host a fast farewell.

Neither of them spoke until they reached the pasture, where they stopped to catch their breath after the rigorous descent. There, sitting against the base of the cliff, sequins of sweat sewn to their brows, they regarded one another as pilgrims—or survivors—do. Kudra folded her hands over her uterus, where some very strange little swimmers had recently drowned. Alobar issued a sigh that was shaped like a funnel: a full quart of beet juice could have been poured through it.

"We shan't forget him for a time," said Alobar.

"We shan't forget him, ever."

"Then you weren't disappointed?"

"You mean disappointed that he wasn't more like Krishna? Not in the end, I wasn't." If Kudra was aware of her pun, she failed to betray it. "The only disappointment I feel is in his reticence to advise us."

"He is Pan. He doth not give advice." At that, Kudra jumped, and so did Alobar, for it was a third party that had said it. The voice, which came from the bushes just above them, was soft and nonthreatening, and in a moment the branches parted, revealing a woman, as bare-assed as butter. Alobar recognized her as the elder—perhaps the leader—of the nymphs; the one who had addressed him on serious matters the last time he was in that neck of the woods.

"Pardon me, my lady, my gentleman, for following thee."

"Pardon granted," said Alobar, "although you did give us a start. Kudra, may I present . . ."

"Lalo," she said, "sister of Echo whose voice, alas, thou hearest repeating thee in all hollow places. Lalo. I only wanted to thank thee for thy visit to Pan. It brought him cheer at a time when his cheer is in short supply."

"Really?" asked Kudra. "From the way he greeted us at the beginning and dismissed us at parting, he did not strike me as overjoyed by our presence."

"He is Pan," said Lalo rather sharply. "Didst thou expect him to bow and kiss thy hand?"

Kudra blushed. Alobar extended his arm to assist Lalo

down onto flat ground. The nymph was not quite as nimble as she once had been. "How grave is Pan's condition?" asked Alobar. "Surely he shan't succumb. Pan is in this land, in its crags, in its cataracts, its winds, its meadows, its hidden places, he can never go from the land, he will be here always, as long as the land is."

"Two things I wouldst say to thee on that account," responded Lalo. "First, the conclusion that a wise homer— forgive the expression, sir—wouldst draw from Pan's admission that he lives only so long as men believe in him, is that men control the destiny of their gods. Thou mightst even say that men create their gods, as much as gods create men, for as I, untutored oread that I be, understand it, it is a mutual thing. Gods and men create one another, destroy one another, though by different means."

A whistle escaped Kudra's lips. "Could such a thing be? Yes, if lack of man's belief is what is ailing Pan, it must be true."

"A warning!" snapped Lalo, who at that moment sounded more like a Fury than a nymph. "Thou must never wax smug or arrogant about thy influence upon the divine. If thou didst create gods, it was because thou *needest* them. The need must have been very great indeed, to inspire such a complex, difficult, and magnificent undertaking. Now, many art the men who think they no longer needeth Pan. They have created new gods, this Jesus Christ and his alleged papa, and they think that their new creations will suffice, but let me assurest thee that Christ and his father, as important as they may be, are no substitutes for Pan. The need for Pan is still great in humanity, and thou ignoreth it at thy peril.

"That bringeth me to the second thing," Lalo continued. Her deep-set eyes were burning, her wine-red nipples were as erect as toy soldiers. "Thou art correct, Pan doth be in the land, he and the wildwoods art a part of one another, but thou art mistaken when thou implieth that the land doth last eternal. There be a time coming when the land itself be threatened with destruction; the groves, the streams, the very sky, not merely here in Arkadia but wildwoods the world over . . ."

"Inconceivable," muttered Alobar.

"If Pan be alloweth to die, if belief in him totally decomposes, then the land, too, wilt die. It wilt be murdered by disrespect, just as Pan is murdered."

Alobar looked around him. In every direction as far as he could see, fierce outcroppings of gray stone, green curves of pasture, uncompromising slopes, spiny shrubs and delicate poppies (unlikely partners in a fling ordered by a reckless breeze), mountains teeming with invisible springs, clouds lying like oatcakes upon the blue tablecloth of sky, all of this seemed so inviolable that he could not entertain the notion of its vulnerability, and he said as much to Lalo.

"Just the same," the nymph answered, "shouldst thee continue to be successful in thy pursuit of long life, thou wilt see it transpire before thine eyes. Thus, I urge thee to protect Pan's dominions and reputations wherever thou mightst go. It be especially thy duty, not merely as a subject of Pan, but because thou, Alobar, art a prime practitioner of individualism, and it wilt be this new idea of individuality that leadeth many future men astray, causing them to feel superior to Pan, and thus to the land, which they wilt set upon to rape and spoil."

A ripple of annoyance like the shock wave from a splat of buzzard guano, zigzagged along Alobar's forehead. "Nymph," he said, puffing himself up like a pigeon, "I do not know if I enjoy you telling me what my duty is."

"Alobar . . ." Kudra's tone was meant to be conciliatory.

"Nor would I describe myself as a *subject* of Pan's. As for your attack on individualism . . ."

"Good sir, I do not attack thy philosophy. I only warn that it be a dangerous instrument in the unfeeling hands of the foolish and corrupt."

"Please inform me, then," said Alobar sarcastically, holding his stuffy pose, "by what authority a cunt-of-the-woods issues warnings concerning the future. Among your more obvious talents—"

"Alobar!" This time, Kudra's voice was prickly with disapproval.

"—do you harbor the gift of prophecy?"

"Alas, I cannot make that claim for myself, sir, but ere I romped in Arkadia, I lived for years at Delphi, where I was intimate with the priests and priestesses who served the Oracle, and where I wast privy to much oracular prognosis. Now I can sense that the boldness of my speech hast ruffled thy feathers, nevertheless thou must hear yet another prophetic plea. Certainly thou dost recollect Pan's words to the effect that mankind hast been too puny in his mind and heart and soul to deserve immortality. Yea? And certainly, also, to have conquered age to the extent that thou hast, thou must have done good strengthening work in thine own mind and heart and soul. Someday, however, a thousand years from today, there wilt be men who seek to defeat death by intelligence alone. They wilt combat age and death with potions and the like, medical weapons that their minds have invented, and age and death will shrink back from them and their medicines. Alas, because they fight with reason only, making no advance in the area of soul and heart, true immortality wiltst be denied them. However, they must not be allowed to attain even the false immortality that their mental facility doth gain for them, for huge evil will be conducted if they shouldst. Thus, thou must vow upon this day that shouldst thou be living still when these events transpire, that thou willst battle them and refuseth prosperity to any immortalist thrust that doth not rise from man's soul and heart as well as his mind. Do promise me now."

"I am sorry," said Alobar, "but I cannot do that. Your intentions are good, so therefore I shall consider your request, but I do not make promises to just anyone about just anything."

The nymph whirled, intent upon returning to the thickets, but Kudra detained her. "Lalo," she called. "My husband claims, with some justification, to be king over himself, yet this morning he has momentarily lost sovereignty over his masculine pride. While he struggles to regain government over that portion of his kingdom, I wish to offer you my own promise, for what it is worth. It is presumptuous to imagine myself alive a thousand years hence, but should that miracle occur, I will do what I can to satisfy your plea. I promise."

"Thank thee, my lady, I thank thee well. If Pan were aware of these matters, I am sure he wouldst express his gratitude at great length." She winked at Kudra. Kudra winked back. For a second, the two women, the one statuesque and umber, the other petite and rosy, smiled at one another knowingly. Then, as quick as a rabbit (a rabbit with a touch of arthritis), Lalo shot into the bushes and was gone.

Alobar made to speak, but Kudra hushed him. "Look up there," she whispered. High above them, barely visible upon the very pinnacle of the mountain, illuminated in the most resplendent manner by noonday sun, heel and horn almost silver, almost holy; stance jaunty yet solemn, regal yet a bit ridiculous; bearded head held at an angle suggestive both of an affection for the variety of life 'round about it and a suffering as primeval and sharp as the peak itself, stood Pan, reeds to lips, and though they scarcely could hear his tune, they felt it in the greasy stirring of the poppies and the mute breath of the snake that sunned itself on a nearby ledge. They watched him in silence for a while, inexplicable tears in their eyes; then Alobar, assisted, it seems, by sister Echo, yelled up the slope, "Lalo! Lalo! I promise, also! I promise! You have my word word ord ord."

Kudra gave him a sloppy kiss. She took his hand. She clasped the teapot. Off they went, over the pastures, breathing in the circular Bandaloop way, locked in a silence finally broken by Kudra's laughter when Alobar lit up her other shoe.

If wild animals could talk, would they talk like cartoons? Would the dismal swamp resound with shrill, befuddled, childlike voices; a cute choir of cuddly Kermits delivering gentle froggy inanities?

Or would beasts converse in the style of Hemingway, in sentences short, brave, and clear; each word a smooth pebble damp with blood; aboriginal speech, he-man speech, an economy of language borrowed by Gary Cooper from frontiersmen who borrowed it from Apache and Ute?

We ask, "Did you see two people pass this way, a man and a woman, walking north?"

The stag shakes its antlers. "Nope," he says.

"The woman was dark with a ripe body, the man had white in his hair. Sure you didn't spot them?"

"Yep."

"Well, how about you?" we ask a fox. "Have you seen a couple in Byzantine garb heading in the direction of Bohemia?"

The fox is slow to speak. "Tonight I dined on loon at the pond," he says. "It was a good meal. Food has an excellent place in my values. Quiet has an excellent place in my values. The forest has been quiet tonight. It is a good thing being a fox when the forest is quiet."

"We apologize for disturbing your peace, but we're searching for a husband and wife, racially mixed, who may be in sort of a daze because they recently had an audience with Pan—you know what that means—and are either wandering aimlessly through the woodlands trying to figure out what to do next, or else are making their way by the stars to Bohemia, where the man at one time—longer ago than you might imagine—had an important job and a large family. They may have passed this way." We pause hopefully.

"The hunt was good," says the fox. "The moon was right. There was a fresh breeze. A man and a woman would have spooked the loon. What a good thing the forest is when it is left to the fox and the loon."

Is that the way animals would talk?

As it turned out, Alobar and Kudra did pass through that forest, before or after the fox's dinner; did hike, guided by constellations, northward across Serbia, Croatia, and the Kingdom of Hungary, arriving in the summer of 1032 (or thereabouts) in that area where the feudal state of Bohemia bordered the Slavic territories. There was no trace of Alobar's former citadel. It had burned, like much of the ancient world, in the medieval furnace, its ashes swept under the rolling carpet of civilization. Compared to Western Europe, Bohemia and the

Slavic territories were still wild and thinly populated, offering many a fox a place to linger over a bit of loon, like some remote animal ancestor of Ernest Hemingway, but even there in the Eastern backwash, the gold-dust twins, Christianity and Commerce, had set up their crooked wheel of fortune.

Kudra had the odd feeling that she had been there before. Alobar stared into the lacquered grapes of her eyes and asked if the name "Wren" meant anything to her. "Nothing," she insisted. They didn't speak of it again, but the *déjà* kept right on *vu*ing. Once, Alobar saw a huge hound at a distance. "Mik!" he cried, running after it. The dog turned on him and might have chewed off some of his best parts had not its owner intervened. Ghosts are good for short-term thrills, in the long run they're boring. Alobar and Kudra departed for Aelfric, but not before purchasing a sack of beets.

Aelfric was four or five times its previous size. It had a wall around it. "Why do you wish to enter here?" asked a soldier at the gate where orchards used to stand. Alobar peeked in at the narrow, crooked streets, deep in garbage, flowing with sewage; dark shadows enlivened by the chirping of rats. *If this is what people must resort to in order to operate their shops and worship their Jesus, perhaps they should return to the hunt and the morning star,* thought Alobar. "State your business," demanded the guard. By then, Alobar had lost considerable interest in searching for his progeny. "Bandaloop business," he said brightly. The guard scowled, but his feet executed an abrupt and completely involuntary dance step, leaving the soldier staring at his own boots, as if he might arrest them for lewd conduct, or, at least, insubordination. Alobar and Kudra hurried away only to pause a short while later near the place where the shaman had lived.

"Why are we stopping in this field?" asked Kudra.

"I have to replace a door," replied Alobar, but what he did was build a fire and roast beets.

"I take it we are not to explore Aelfric," said Kudra.

"Wasn't a glimpse enough? If your grandchildren were citizens of Aelfric, would you be anxious to meet them?"

"Maybe. Out of curiosity."

"My curiosity does not extend to dung beetles, even if they

crawled out of my family tree. Besides, if I am truly immortal, I am my own grandchild, my own descendant, my own dynasty. I am not obliged to live on through what I pass down to others."

"Then pass me a beet," said Kudra. And he did.

The Middle Ages hangs over history's belt like a beer belly. It is too late now for aerobic dancing or cottage cheese lunches to reduce the Middle Ages. History will have to wear size 48 shorts forever.

In the pit of that vast stomach—sloshing with dark and vinegary juices, kindled by a thousand-year heartburn—major figures stimulated acute contractions, only to be eventually digested, adding to the bloat. Clovis, Charlemagne, Otto I, William the Conqueror, Rurik the Viking, Pope Leo, Thomas Aquinas, Johann Gutenberg, and a platter of other renowned generals, kings, philosophers, and popes fermented and dissolved in that mammoth maw. Our little couple, however, our Alobar and Kudra, remained intact and indigestible, like the hard octopus beaks that sicken the stomachs of whales, causing them to vomit the ambergris that bonds the bouquet in great perfumes. Like octopus beaks, our couple. Or maraschino cherries.

More than a decade after his death, Nikolai Lenin's body was removed from its sepulcher in the Kremlin and a belated autopsy performed. Four maraschino cherries were found in Lenin's colon. Perfectly preserved, as whole and candy red as the day (or days) that he swallowed them, the cherries were in better shape than Lenin himself. It is rumored that maraschino cherries are prepared with a chemical resembling formaldehyde, thus can neither be assimilated nor eliminated but must ride in the baggage rack of the bowels for a lifetime, like the seabags of the *Flying Dutchman*. If that is the case, and one is prepared to believe the worst of maraschino cherries, looking, as they do, as if they were picked in the orchards of Pluto; as if they were carved out of spoiled neon; as if they were vegetable visitors from the twenty-third century, beamed here to make us appreciate our old-fashioned beets; if it is true, then we could say that Alobar and Kudra were maraschino cherries lodged in the tubes of history's paunch.

On the other hand, octopus beaks, pointing to the birth of future fragrances, might be a more accurate and lyrical analogy.

At any rate, Alobar and Kudra survived wars, robbers, fires, pillages, plagues (including the Black Death of 1347–1350) and the intolerances of the Church; survived freezing winters, famines, Gothic art, and uncomfortable furniture; survived, most importantly, the "natural" process of aging, which, according to Dr. Wiggs Dannyboy, is so unnaturally cruel that only man could have ordained it—neither nature nor God would stoop so low.

Should one be shallow enough to view existence as a system of rewards and punishments, one soon learns that we pay as dearly for our triumphs as we do for our defeats, and the couple's victory over aging created as many problems for them as did witchhunts and feudal strife. Nowhere could they remain for more than a decade or two. In those rough times, people aged even faster than we do today, making it all the more noticeable when Kudra's and Alobar's gums remained a-bristle with teeth. They did their best to maintain a low profile, but, let's face it, they weren't the most inconspicuous pair to mosey down the medieval pike. For one thing, they were obviously frying with love and lust for one another in an age when romance simply did not exist within the bounds of matrimony. Virtually all marriages in the Middle Ages were arranged between strangers, and the Church disallowed divorce. Therefore, romantic love was almost exclusively a function of adultery. It was for adulterers that troubadours sang their courtly ballads, it was for the attention of another fellow's wife that the jouster risked the lance. When Alobar and Kudra refused to participate in the continental pastime (in their centuries together, Alobar was cuckolded only by Pan, and that was not precisely cuckoldry, that was . . . something else), it escalated the suspicions already aroused by her exotic coloration and his regal manner, by their funny way of breathing and their tendency to wash. So they were obliged to keep moving. A few years in Heidelberg, a few near Rome; green seasons in Flanders, dry seasons on Crete. Fortunately, they subscribed to no magazines. The post office would have gone nuts.

Early in the 1300s, attending the fair at Beaucaire in the south of France, they encountered a group of people whose proclivity for travel made Kudra and Alobar seem as though they were chained to a stump. These nomads rumbled from town to town, fair to fair, in brightly colored wagons. Variously called Logipciens, Bohemians, or Gypsies, they were ostensibly itinerant metalworkers, but music and magic were their true vocations. Although the Gypsies were new to Europe, Kudra had known them in India and could converse in their dialect. Moreover, her pigmentation was the same shade as theirs. Their chief invited her to join them. Reluctantly, he agreed to include Alobar.

For the next half-century (time flies when you're having fun), they lived as Gypsies, bumping over the quasi-roads of the continent in a red and orange donkey cart, sleeping in a tent of woven fabrics kept precariously in place by stones, warming themselves with *tezek*, that charming fuel made of cow dung and straw. They indulged in some serious horse-shoeing and harness making, but more frequently their band earned its living amusing, and sometimes fleecing, visitors to holy sites, festivals, and fairs. The Gypsies danced, they sang and strummed, they navigated a pea beneath a walnut shell so slickly you'd wager your last sou that it was beneath the one next door. When they shook their tambourines and sistrums, in voluptuous poses, feudal barons found them irresistible, but that made them all the more hateful in the eyes of the pious and grave, a reaction that was for Alobar a source of endless delight. Kudra chided him for it mildly, but he was rarely happier than when savoring the fear and disgust that welled up in proper Christians at the sight of their rattling, tinkling troupe.

The opinion that "all good things must come to an end" is a confession of fatalism that the immortalist hand of Alobar would never sign. Nonetheless, he realized his days as a Gypsy were numbered when he surprised several of the chief's sons ransacking his and Kudra's belongings, searching for their presumed "elixir of youth." As a matter of fact, their tent and wagon had been broken into thrice before, but Alobar had written it off to routine Gypsy thievery and to the Gypsies' insistence on treating them as second-class citizens. Claiming to be the direct descendants of the biblical Cain, the Gypsies considered themselves a race elite. It was obvious that their ethnocentricity would never allow complete acceptance of outsiders, no matter how compatible. They not only stole from Kudra and Alobar, but they also served them last at communal meals and required them to perform occasional menial chores. For example, on Saturdays Kudra was expected to clean the chief's wagon and launder his many brilliant scarves.

It was while she was sweeping out the executive cart one day that she noticed that the chief's wife's famous crystal ball had been left uncovered. For a while Kudra managed to ignore the naked sphere, but at last curiosity got the best of her and she peered into it, shyly at first, then so piercingly that the chief's laundry could have been hung out to dry on her gaze. She saw nothing in the ball. There was nothing to see. It was, after all, a mere lump of polished glass. As a point of departure for the psyche, however, a crystal ball has merit, although a mandala, a seashell, or a cigarette pack can be as effectively employed. There are apparently few limitations either of time or space on where the psyche might journey, and only the customs inspector employed by our own inhibitions restricts what it might bring back when it reenters the home country of everyday consciousness. When Kudra shut her eyes to rest them after their intense probing of the crystal innards, a vivid scene unfolded in her mind. She saw Alobar and herself, bound with rope, in the process of being tortured by the Gypsies, who were demanding a map to the fountain of youth.

When she returned to their tent, Kudra told Alobar of her vision. "That settles it," he said. That night, when the moon had set, they stole away. As they disappeared into the woods, they glanced back to see shadowy figures advancing on their tent.

In the excitement of their escape, Kudra had neglected to inform Alobar that she had consulted the crystal ball a second time ere she left the chief's wagon that Saturday. A finely detailed scene had again flashed before her mind's eye as she rested after examining the crystal. This second vision seemed far less urgent, which is why she put it aside, but it was stranger, more difficult to interpret. In it, a tall black man, blacker by several shades than she, was beckoning to her, laughing all the while. The black man wore the oddest clothes she had ever seen, and the oddest item in his wardrobe was his cap. It turned out to be not a cap at all, but a swarm of bees.

Although finished with Gypsies, per se, Alobar and Kudra retained their vagabond life-style, working the European fair circuit on their own. Alongside booths overflowing with cotton, furs, metals, wine, tea, Venetian glass, meat, produce, and livestock, they sold or traded aromatics to a populace that was beginning to appreciate pretty fragrances, despite—or because of—the fact that it had yet to accept the concept of the bath. When business was poor, Kudra slipped into her Gypsy skirt and danced the *dodole*, Alobar accompanying her on tambourine. Less than approving of the leers his wife's dancing elicited from fairgoers of masculine gender, it nonetheless amused Alobar to meditate upon her real birthdate as she undulated those secretly ancient hips and loins; and, of course, it invariably elevated his mood when the priests came by to consign them to hell for their detestable display.

Actually, the priests proved to be good customers after Kudra decided to start manufacturing combustible cones from the raw aromatics in which she customarily dealt. Influenced by the Byzantines, the Western Church had become increasingly fond of the ritualistic burning of incense, ostensibly as an evocation of the sweet oxygens of heaven, but more likely a way of combating the concentrated funk of sweaty congregations. It appeared as if incense might become a rage in the cathedrals of Paris, so Alobar was not overly surprised when Kudra announced one morning that she wished to settle in the French capital and open a permanent shop.

"A shop might be a smart idea," agreed Alobar, "but when you say 'permanent,' you mean, of course, permanent compared to our usual knocking about." They had been on the road for several centuries.

"No," said Kudra. "I mean permanent."

"I needn't remind you of the troubles in store should we hang around long enough to flaunt our perpetual freshness before the envious eyes of our steadily decaying fellow citizens. Ahem. We can realistically expect fifteen, maybe twenty years as Parisian incense merchants. But that will be a welcome change, a nice recess, and when the time comes, we shall move on."

"I am not moving on. I am finished with moving on. I want a shop, I want a home, and I want to stay there."

"Stay," repeated Alobar. "How long, exactly, do you intend to stay?"

"As long as . . . I don't know. As long as it damn well pleases me."

"Well, it better not please you beyond fifteen years or so, because when it dawns on the neighbors that we aren't aging—"

"But maybe I *will* age."

"*What?*"

Kudra gave him a look that you could spread on a bun. Her words, however, pricked him like the knife that does the spreading. "We are capable of aging, if we want to. We stopped the aging process and we can start it again. Haven't we fallen into a rut, being the same age for over five—or is it six—hundred years? I don't know about you, but I am a little fed up with it. I really wouldn't mind aging again."

Alobar couldn't believe how calmly, serenely even, she had spoken the unspeakable. Icy fingers tickled the harpsichord keys of his vertebrae. "You—you don't know what you're saying. Here, let me pour you some tea. You aren't awake yet, that's your problem."

"I am awake, darling. I have been awake most of the night. And the night before. I have thought about this through more sleepless nights than you could shake a tambourine at. And I am ready, willing, and actually eager to settle down in one place like normal people, and grow older like normal people. I am."

Alobar held back, refusing to speak until his vocal cords could be trusted not to quiver. Alas, he waited too long, overshot the mark, and heard his voice go well beyond evenness into petrification. The finest stone carver in France would have been proud to chisel his mark on any word in the following sentence: "Aging seems a high price to pay for normalcy."

"I do not care. I am willing to pay it. Besides, if I do not like getting older, I can always stop."

"Can you?" Simple little question chipped from solid basalt. "How do you know for sure?" Six words weighing in at a ton, not including punctuation. "We believe that we can start it and stop it at will, but the fact is, we have never tried. What if you cannot stop it, what if you just keep on growing older until, until . . ." The voice had become so rigid that it cracked. That's how molecules behave today, and that's how they behaved back then, though in those days nobody blamed molecules for brittleness any more than they credited them for plasticity.

"Until what? Until I die? First of all, Alobar, neither you nor I is convinced that aging has to automatically lead to death. We have talked about that many times. Where is the courage of your convictions? It is not aging that leads to death, it is the *belief* that aging leads to death that leads to death. Do I speak rightly or wrongly?"

"You are probably right," squeaked Alobar, in his newly broken voice. "We do not know for certain."

"There is only one way to find out."

"But what if—"

"What if I die? Then, by Shiva, I die! Dying does not strike me as such a horrible fate anymore."

"I cannot believe you are saying this. You are reverting. You are regressing. You are—"

"I am facing the truth," Kudra interrupted, "and the truth is, there is nothing so almighty wonderful about this long life of ours." He recoiled as if she'd spit on him. She took his hand, kissing each spear-nicked finger in turn. "Darling," she said, "look at us. We are a couple of Gypsies, running from the dogs of authority. From town to town we go, fair to fair, sleeping in fields, eating those awful *mangel-wurzels*, selling pretty smells to hypocrites, and hard-ons to yeomen. Where is the value in that? What is the purpose of—"

"We are alive!" shouted Alobar. "And there—"

"And there is not another couple like us on this whole round planet. Well, so what? Our uniqueness doesn't make the ground softer or give the beets flavor. It doesn't improve feudal conditions or reduce violence or contribute to the welfare of the people. What important thing have we accomplished in all these past six hundred years?"

"We have beaten death," said Alobar, and his tone was as firm and even as it had ever been. More than that, it was proud. "We have beaten death. What everyone who has ever been born since the beginning of time has longed to do, we have done. What could be greater than that?"

"To what end have we beaten death? We can't teach others how to beat it, or else the Church would come down on us and wipe us out, and those we taught in the bargain. We can't sell this grand knowledge, for the very same reasons. We are forced to hide our supreme accomplishment as if it were a shameful crime. Where is the glory in that? Our lives are selfish and covert and none too easy. Methinks that you had a greater life back when you were mortal. You were a king then, Alobar, a leader of men, and every day, every hour, was charged with significance."

"And threatened by the Reaper. Charged, but threatened, because to the Reaper a king is no less fodder than a slave. In my clan, a king was actually an easier harvest."

"Threatened by death you may have been, but look what a life it was that was threatened! And look at it now, my ragged Gypsy—"

"We are about to move to Paris!"

"Yes. I to ply the incense maker's trade, you, noble warrior, to be my assistant."

She paused. Together, they watched the sun break through the morning fog, coming back to the deserted fairgrounds like a dandy returning to the boulevard, prepared, when the moment was right, to strut some stuff. With a clover stem, Kudra traced the pathway of Alobar's veins, through which such endless tides of blood had run; she kissed the forehead that had been greeted by so many rising suns.

"For you," she said, "longevity for longevity's sake is enough.

That is no longer satisfactory to me. Is there a position in the *Kama Sutra* that we have not mastered, a recipe for *mangelwurzel* that our cook pot hasn't memorized? Oh, darling, I know that life is good, and that it still holds surprises for me, but maybe death is good, too; certainly it offers some surprise. Relax, now, don't get upset. My destination is an incense shop, not a tomb. But if I must age to have a happier life, then I will. And should aging lead to death, then I shall explore the planet of death awhile. Certainly I have been on the terrestrial voyage a nice long while. Long enough, frankly, that despite my love for you I do grow bored."

"I will wager that death be a million times more boring than life."

"If so, I shall come back to life. If we are truly immortal, we ought to be able to travel back and forth between both sides."

"Ha!" scoffed Alobar. "Yes, we *ought* to be able to. We ought to, all right, and if we had remained in the caves long enough, we probably could. We might have been able to dematerialize and rematerialize at will. But we cannot. At least, there is no hard evidence that we can. You talk about facing truth. The truth is, Kudra, we hardly know what we are doing. There is so much more to this immortality business, so much more we might have learned from the Bandaloop, but, no, you had to go and see the world, you could not wait, so here we are half-educated and half-assed, conducting the greatest experiment in human annals and not fully qualified to conduct it correctly, just groping in the dark like mice in a bin. Why, oh why, did I let you talk me into leaving the caves before we had all the answers? Well, I can tell you one thing, you are not going to talk me into aging. If *you* want to risk it, go ahead, but you are stupid."

Kudra released his hand. "I may be stupid," she said, "but I am not a coward."

And the sun pulled a cloud down over its ears. And the wind set to whistling a distracting tune. And crows that had been breakfasting on fairgrounds crumbs glanced at some clock or other and realized that they were late for work. And the cookfire flames retreated into the soundproof cellar of ashes. And the tea in the teapot nearly broke its neck in its haste to evaporate.

There's an old axiom: "A couple's first quarrel is Cupid's laxative."

The next worst thing to a quarrel is a compromise. They made one at once.

Since Alobar had been nearly forty chronological years older than Kudra from the start, it was agreed that Kudra could permit herself to age for four decades, more or less, stopping when she had "caught up" with her mate. If she *could* stop, that is. As for Alobar, he would cross his bridges as he came to them.

They did move to Paris, they did open an incense shop. It was located on the rue Quelle Blague, next door to a brewery and perfumery, across the street from a monastery and cathedral. It did all right. Their marriage (it is fair to call it a marriage, though no formal ceremony ever transpired) did all right, too, which is to say the champagne was far from flat, although there were fewer bubbles per sip than there had been before the arguing started. They argued always about the same thing. It's best that way. If lovers have to argue, they might as well specialize. And the arguments usually concluded with Alobar's complaint that they had left the academy of the Bandaloop before they had completed their course.

(Oddly enough, he refrained from pressuring her to return to the caves for additional study, perhaps because he was of the opinion that after so long a time there were no vibrations left to "study." If Fosco of Samye could be believed, the Bandaloop had left the caves for good. Dance craze? Argen-*what*?)

If they ever reached a point where they seriously considered separation, it would have been in the cruel winter of 1664, a season that no amount of firewood nor any variation on the *Kama Sutra* could quite warm. Yet right in the middle of the shivers and the shouts, something came along to bind them, a slapdash patch job by the mason of common cause.

Darkness arrived so abruptly that day it was as if a Gypsy had swept Paris under a walnut shell, good luck, ye gamblers, on guessing which one. By four o'clock, the street lamps were lit. Despite being called to work early, the lamps flickered dutifully, as though lighting a path for the snow. The snow would be along any minute. The clouds promised it and the lamps believed them. Alobar believed them, too. He also believed that there would be no more customers through the door that day, so he bolted it against thieves (a Gypsy who would steal daylight would surely steal incense) and the gales of January. He joined Kudra in the backroom.

Paying him little heed when he entered, Kudra remained bent over a large candle, heating some newly purchased storax resin in a metal cup. "It's cold in here," Alobar said. "Umm," she answered, without looking up. As it relaxed its grip on itself, the wad of storax caused the room to smell like the center of a chocolate cream. Sometimes when a stressful person relaxes, he or she will, in a similar fashion, perfume the air 'round about them. Alobar sat down and tried it.

The candle glow that held Kudra's head like an object in a showcase allowed Alobar to count five silver hairs in her mane. He hadn't noticed them until then. It was all he could do to keep from crying out. He wondered if she knew.

His thoughts flashed back to the afternoon that he met her, eight years old and sobbing, fleeing the funeral pyre. He thought of her in the Himalayas, dressed as a boy; the glossy black explosion her tresses had made when they tumbled from the turban. Then he thought of that fateful day when the concubines' mirror had shown him his own pale intruder. Such a chain of events that little fellow had set off!

So still for so long was Alobar that when he finally spoke, Kudra flinched. She must have forgotten he was there. The corona of candlelight and the vanilla halo of storax ringed her concentrically, as if she were twice blessed, a double madonna.

"Kudra," he said, "I have a splendid idea."

"And what splendid idea is that?" she asked, her head still bowed to the task.

"Let's sail to the New World."

"The New World?"

"Yes, the New World, the land they stumbled upon when they finally caught on that the Earth is round, as I, ahem, was saying all along."

"Only fortune hunters and Christian fanatics go to the New World. We are neither of those."

"Fortune hunters, Christian fanatics, and misfits. That last category describes us rather accurately."

"You may be a misfit, Alobar. I am not. Not any longer, at any rate."

He leaped to his feet and with two swift yanks reduced her silver quintet to a trio. Dropping the strands into the resin cup in front of her, he said, "In the New World, you wouldn't have to sacrifice your beautiful black hair."

Kudra stared at the hairs in the cup. She may have denied that there were tears in her eyes, but the reflection of candlelight upon tearwater proved otherwise.

"See those," said Alobar. "Those are worms from the rot of the grave."

She squeezed her eyes shut. A single teardrop broke through the barricades and made a run for it, only to lose its footing and topple into the cup with the resin and the hairs. Was that a finer place than it had been?

Alobar lay his hands on her shoulders and massaged them gently. "You don't have to go through this," he said softly. "We can sail to the New World."

Kudra shook her head. "We made our own new world," she said, "but something has gone wrong with it. I guess new worlds grow old. Pan was right. Immortality has its limitations."

"If only we had learned more in the caves!"

"Oh, shit," said Kudra. "Not that again."

"But, darling—"

"Alobar, I'd like to be alone for a while."

"But—"

"Please, Alobar!" She picked the hairs from the storax and flicked them to the floor. The teardrop had vanished, whether absorbed by resin, evaporated by candle heat, or welcomed into some mystery dimension, we cannot determine. No reward was ever offered for its return. "Please. Let me be."

So Alobar exchanged his slippers for boots that reached all the way to the hems of his knee breeches, pulled a woolen knee-length coat over his brocade waistcoat, tightened his lace collar until it pinched his Adam's apple, and went out into the night, where, by lamplight, the frosted cobblestone streets resembled marshmallow plantations at harvest time. Although he hadn't a destination in mind, he walked rapidly, soon finding himself in an obscene quarter of Paris, a squalid area without cobblestone or torch, an unpaved district whose frozen mud puddles reflected the shine of red lanterns. From every doorway, the lewd breath of prostitutes rose like hooks of smoke. Huddled against the cold, groups of them called to him as he passed, and he began to get ideas. A misunderstood husband usually is armed with a blunt instrument, its knob painted red like the face of a judge.

The prostitute he eventually approached was tall and blonde. As they discussed rates, her companion, a dumpy, aged woman whom Alobar had not even considered, moved ever closer until she had wormed her way between him and the blonde. She had a rude, animal odor and so many wrinkles she could screw her hat on. Alobar was about to nudge her aside when the blond slapped her with her muff, saying, "Get along, Lalo. This one's not desperate enough to want you."

"Lalo?"

"Alobar! I thought that it be thee!"

They shared a tearful embrace, then and there, while the blonde jeered and the first flakes of snow began to sift through the scarlet lanternshine. Then, he escorted her to the incense shop, walking slowly now for Lalo was a nymph no longer, but an old tart who had quit the brothels of Athens when the demand for her services waned. It was said that in Paris no whore was too old or too ugly to survive.

Kudra was both saddened and delighted by the sight of her. She brought out their best cheese and served tea from the battered but cherished silver pot. Once Lalo was fed and warmed, they questioned her about Pan. The news was enough to sour the cheese.

Pan was a ghost, now, Lalo said; you could look straight through him. His heartbeat was no stronger than a sparrow's.

His pipes could still cause the flocks to shuffle their feet, could still raise the fuzz on a peasant's neck, but he lacked the vigor or the will to play them very often. Pan continued to visit men, according to Lalo, perhaps he always would, but in the modern world he came to them not in person, in sunlight, direct and immediate, but in dreams—erotic nightmares—or in flashes of terror, the kind that cause crowds to stampede for no reason, that they could neither explain nor understand. Lacking a direct relationship with Pan, modern Europeans were estranged from their flocks and their crops, from the natural world and, indeed, from their own natural impulses. "Grieve not just for Pan," said Lalo, in a voice as scratched as the teapot, "but for thyselves, as well."

"And what of the nymphs?" asked Kudra.

"It has been more than a century since Pan last chased a nymph. Without him in pursuit, the nymphs lost their identity, grew thin and mad. Many took their own lives. Others, like me, became whores to homers, seeking in each sexual coupling to recreate the old seduction, the old magic, the old feeling of unity." She sighed forlornly. "I don't know why I hold on, but I do."

They put Lalo to bed in their flat upstairs. Then they took to their own bed, where, as the snow did its sums on the windowsill, they snuggled and talked, eventually formulating a plan of action: they would get Pan out of Europe.

The New World was vast and virgin. They would make a place for him there, beneath smokeless skies where primitive equalities prevailed. Far from any city, they would establish a new Arkadia, complete with flocks of goats; and the pagan Indians, so hounded now by Christian missionaries, could join with them in a free landscape in which the old gods and goddesses would be given their due. Why, they would teach the Indians what they knew of Bandaloop immortality, and, moreover, Kudra would throw away her pennyroyal, and she and Alobar would at last have children of their own. They would found a race of immortals, with Pan as their principal deity. Yes! Wasn't this the grand destiny that had been eluding them all along?! They grew drunk with the vision of it while the sober snow looked on.

When weather permitted, Alobar would strike out for Greece (Lalo could help Kudra with the business) to fetch Pan to Paris. They would nurse him back to health right there in the flat, while they saved and schemed for their passage across the Atlantic.

"How much money have we on hand?" asked Alobar. "Here, let us get up and count it. I cannot wait to get started."

Kudra pulled him back down into the blankets. "We can count when it is daylight," she said. "We have a new world to populate. I cannot wait to get started."

Prior to his departure for Greece, Alobar filled Kudra to the brim. She was saturated. She launched squadrons of sperm every time she sneezed. They circled Paris like microscopic angels, looking for harp concerts in the snow. Wherever she went, she leaked, leaving snail trails, sticky and translucent, upon work stool, carpet, and carriage seat. Needless to say, there was Standing Room Only in her uterus. Nevertheless, she failed to conceive. That the topography of her tummy offered no challenge to his abilities as a climber was the first thing Alobar noticed when he returned from Greece to her embrace. The second thing he noticed, raising his disappointed gaze from the abdominal plane, was that there had been an exodus of gray from her hair and that the skin around her eyes, which had been cobwebbing with crinkles, was now as smooth as custard. In the eight months that he'd been away, she looked to have youthed a good eight years.

"Kudra, you did it! You reversed it!" So pleased was he that he forgot, for the moment, the vacancy in her womb. "Was it difficult? Did you have to labor at it? Will you promise me that you will never backslide again?"

She ignored his jabber and concentrated on Pan, if "concentrated" is the accurate verb. She could determine Pan's whereabouts in the room only by focusing her nostrils upon the epicenter of the caprine aroma that was causing her entire inventory of incense to cry "uncle" and edge toward the door.

"Greetings, Kudra," said a familiar voice from the epicenter. "I thank thee for thy hospitality, puny and human though it be."

"You are welcome, sir," said Kudra. "I think." She turned to Alobar. "It is rather perplexing talking to someone you cannot see."

"Nonsense," said Alobar. "Thousands of Christians do it every day. At least this god will talk back to you." He shoved a wine flask into the eye of the stink storm. The flask tipped and pink Chablis commenced to gurgle out, though not a drop hit the floor. "I know what you mean, however. Traveling with an invisible who smells up the countryside is an ordeal I would hesitate to undertake again. I did not mind the stares and the insults and the occasional stone, but I have not enjoyed a warm meal or a decent night's rest since we left Arkadia. You would think rural innkeepers would be less particular."

"I fear it shall present a problem in Paris, as well."

"Indeed. He seems to have grown less observable and more pungent the further we journeyed from Greece. By the way, where's Lalo?"

Kudra hesitated. "Uh, Lalo. Yes, well, Lalo left. Ran off with a sailor from Brittany."

"How inconsiderate. She was supposed to assist you in the shop."

"Lalo is a nymph, not a shopkeeper," said Pan. "She only did what she was meant to do."

"Yes," agreed Kudra. "And you are a god of the woods and fields. How will you fare in this environment?"

"Perhaps not well," said Pan. "Art thou aware that I be the lone god who never hast had a temple built in his honor? 'Tis true, not a single one. Men have always worshiped me outdoors."

Alobar retrieved the flask, now half empty. "Our shop shall be your temple for a time. As soon as we are able, we shall transport you to greener pastures and wilder company. Meanwhile, you'll have to make do. There are parks nearby where you may roam. We must, of course, contrive a disguise for your odor. Kudra and I shall attend to that right away. Now

that she has come to her senses and stopped aging, I am
confident she can provide a scent for you and a baby for me
with equal ease. Eh, Kudra?"

Kudra nodded in tentative accord. Alas, the tasks assigned
her proved about as easy as skinning a rhinoceros with a set
of false teeth.

She knew from experience that patchouli wouldn't cut Pan's
mustard. Frankincense and myrrh might have reodorized the
diapers of sweet Baby Jesus, but they disappeared in the goat
god's gulf of funk like rowboats in the Bermuda Triangle; and
sandalwood, clean, gentle sandalwood, lasted as long, to the
minute, as a snowball in hell. A resinoid of storax, fixed with
tincture of labdanum (pressed from the fatty arteries of the
rockrose), proved a sufficient camouflage for a walk around
the block, but it had no more staying power than patchouli.
As for civet, it only compounded Pan's indigenous musk,
making his presence felt all the more strongly.

Within a fortnight, Kudra had exhausted her arsenal of
aromatics. There was nothing to do but dip into their savings
(the New World fund was growing very slowly) and purchase
some perfumes from the monks next door. They would be
unable to sail anyhow if they couldn't conceal from curious
and repulsed noses their phantasmal friend.

What was required was a perfume penetrating enough to
obscure the bouquet of rutting goat, yet not so overpowering
that it called undue attention to itself: there was little to be
gained by moving from one extreme to another on the olfactory scale. Ideally, moreover, the scent should have the
capacity to linger, because a free spirit such as Pan could not
be expected to go around dabbing at his wrists and neckbones
every hour, as if he were a husband-hungry marquise at a
Versailles ball.

There were critics who complained that at 23, rue Quelle
Blague the beer tasted like lilac water and the perfumes
smelled of hops. As to the quality of the beer we cannot
testify—perhaps a taste of it today would leave us sadder
Budweiser—but when it came to perfumery, the monks were

not inexpert. They, in fact, laid the foundation for the French fragrance industry. The fragrance house of LeFever descended directly from their early operations. The Quelle Blaque monks were among the principal suppliers to the court of Louis XIV, where enormous amounts of perfumes were consumed. At the height of Versailles, twenty to thirty perfume fountains were gushing rosewater night and day, and the men wore squirt rings loaded with patchouli—when their mistresses approached, they fumigated themselves and the air about them with a fine spray. Louis himself changed his scent every thousand miles. But all this excess failed to compensate for the fact that the royal sewage was disposed of inadequately and that there was not one bath in the court. A visiting English writer wrote of Louis that "all the odoriferous perfumes his courtiers could get him would not ease his nose and still he smelled a filthy stinke." This was a century and a half before the emergence of the great master blenders, but despite the monks' inability to put the Sun King's unwashed nose at rest, the fragrances they distilled were far from primitive. Could they lay the wreath on Pan?

Hardly. Their famous rosewater was no match for his glandular output, and, one by one, he sent lily, lilac, lavender, and linden whimpering off with their l's between their legs. It was a dark day for heliotrope when it was sprinkled upon the transparent god, and hyacinth was reduced to lowacinth in practically a flash. The monks' most expensive product was a recipe that mixed rose oil with cloves, cinnamon, mace, musk, ambergris, citron, and cedar. With some experimenting, Kudra probably could have duplicated it, but Pan was impatient and Alobar was worried, so they further fractured their finances and bought a vial. Expectantly, Kudra rubbed it into Pan's thigh wool, including in one of her passes the smooth underside of his scrotum, a swipe that gave him some pleasure and her some trepidation, for there is nothing quite like the intrusion of an invisible erection to thoroughly unnerve a woman. The old goat might have seized the moment—indeed, he reached for his pipes—had not Alobar threatened to address his private parts with a gesture appropriate to the preparation of eunuchs. So, Pan, richly anointed, departed for the grounds of the Louvre instead, only to return in a couple of hours, smelling all too familiar, and relating how his kibitzing, imperceptible to any eye, had disrupted a fashionable *fête champêtre*.

The most effective scent purchased from the monks proved to be an essence of jasmine. The raw flowers had come from the South of France, where to this day are grown the finest jasmine blossoms in the world (unless one counts the Bingo Pajama Jamaican variety, about which virtually nothing is known). Ah, yes, leave it to jasmine to soothe the savage beast, for jasmine in its delightful way performs an olfactory pantomime of glad animal movements from times gone by. A few other flowers may be as sweet, but jasmine is sweet without sentiment, sweet without effeteness, sweet without compromise; it is aggressively sweet, outrageously sweet: "I am sweet," says the jasmine, "and if you don't like it, you can kiss my sweet ass." Expansive, yet never cloying; romantic, yet seldom melancholy, jasmine has the poise of a wild creature, some elusive self-sufficient thing that croons like an organic saxophone in the tropical night. Pan's glands heard jasmine's sugary howl and were hypnotized into partially suspending secretion.

"Jasmine may stand us in good stead," said Kudra. "Alone, however, it falls short of perfection. Like a grand orator, it requires a somewhat lesser voice to introduce it. I am positive that a qualified master of ceremonies can be recruited, and failing at that, it would not be ruinous should it be forced to introduce itself. But what is a great orator without a strong platform to stand upon, without an enveloping auditorium to hold his words? Do you follow me? Jasmine is longer-lasting by far than any floral we have tried, but we must find a theater to contain it, an anchor, if you will, to keep it in place, because to be efficient it needs to endure at least thrice as long as it does now."

In other words, they could use a top note and absolutely required a fixative and a base.

Since they couldn't afford to commission such a blend from the monks, Kudra must develop it. She had worked with aromatics much of her long life—we are talking seniority here—but having had no experience with distillation, she was not in the true sense a perfumer. Fortunately, jasmine oil is obtained by extraction rather than distillation, and that she could manage. After a period of trial and error, she found lemony citron an acceptable top note; it gave the featured jasmine a brief but flattering introduction. As for fixative, ambergris was already in wide use, and while its detractors might deride it as "behemoth barf," a finer fixative has yet to be discovered. In this case, however, ambergris failed to deliver total satisfaction. It nailed the bouquet to the perfume, all right, but it didn't nail the perfume to Pan—at least not for very long. Since ambergris couldn't be improved upon, what this meant was that the base note, in addition to its usual function as an accommodating and complementing "platform," must also assist the fixative in prolonging the life of the aroma. A very special base note was called for. Kudra didn't find it right away. Months, in fact, dragged by as she experimented and researched.

In the meantime, a sardonic cuckoo was scrambling Alobar and Kudra's nest eggs, replacing them with obnoxious layings of its own.

At the appointed hour when courtiers of Louis XIV were finally to call at the shop to test its wares, Pan returned prematurely from a stroll in the park, his malodor at high mast due to exercise and the sappy influences of spring. The courtiers, three in number, arrived on his heels. "My goodness," said the first courtier; "Snit," said the second; "Phew," said the third. Whatever credibility incense may have held for them was immediately lost. Lost, too, was the most profitable market to which Kudra had ever aspired.

Pan's lasting impression also cost her several smaller sales, and this at a time when expenses were on the rise. As the hunt for an effective base note went on, money was continually being invested in raw materials that were of no use in incense making. And, now, of course, there was another mouth on the premises, a mouth that, though it could not be seen, watered at mealtime nonetheless. They had a cash flow problem, and unless it was solved, they would never ankle up that gangplank in Marseilles.

In the midst of worrying about finances and Kudra's failure to conceive—none of his deposits seemed to earn interest—Alobar was stopped in the street one day by a neighborhood monk who inquired in the rude manner of children, policemen, and journalists if he and his wife employed heathen practices. The monk was no more specific than that, but Alobar instantly assumed the reference was to longevity. "You mean like that old Bandaloop, Methuselah?" he shot back, and as the Christian brother gargled the froth of his bewilderment, he hurried away in a chilly sweat to warn Kudra, rightly or wrongly, that they'd been found out once again.

For all the reaction he got from Kudra, he might as well have told her that the poodle gods were pooping on the paths of the Louvre. She was up to her elbows in a basket of bark, the leprous but fragrant epidermis of some African tree; unraveling its history, reading its fortune, learning its language, its vocabulary of botanical suffering; coaxing from its ancient sores an iridescent pus that smelled of rains and nests and yellow fruits squashed beneath the feet of heavy animals. "This could be it," she confided, milking. A single bead of resin rolled out of an ulcer and was caught in a vial. Somewhere in Africa a tree stood naked. "This could be the one to support the jasmine."

"Little good it will do if the monks set opinion against us."

When she neglected to respond, he said, "Kudra, what is to be our next move?"

"Express the bouquet from the resin."

"No, no, haven't you been listening? There may be trouble over—"

"Oh, that," she said. "Well, Alobar, I have been thinking. . . ." She held another anguished crust of bark over the candle flame, squeezing and pulling until its black boil popped and out bubbled the feverish exudation, hard pearls of honey glistening as if in a prolonged delirium brought on by the pestilence of time. "I have been thinking that the altogether smartest thing would be to dematerialize—and then rematerialize in the New World."

Alobar looked stunned.

"Don't you see, that would save us money and time. We would not require a sou for passage nor would we be forced to bob about in the oceans with a horde of vomiting missionaries. Why, if Pan could dematerialize along with us—he is all but dematerialized already—we would not even need to complete his perfume. Locating the perfect base note may yet prove impossible." She sniffed unconfidently at the wooden warts in her fingers.

"Kudra, we do not *know how* to de- and rematerialize!"

"Then it is time we learned! Have we lived seven hundred years for naught? Except for our longevity, we are no closer to the divine than ordinary folk. Our practices have kept us alive, but they have not revealed to us one divine secret nor one speck of the magic of the gods." She laid down the ugly chips and faced him. He commenced to wring his hands.

"Kudra . . ." he whined.

"But for his age, Alobar the great individualist is just like any common man."

"Kudra! We don't know—"

"What happened to the bold adventurer who seduced me in more ways than one up on the roof of the world?"

"Kudra! You are talking death, I sense that you are."

"There is no death. There are only different levels of life. You must know that by now."

"You who ran away from the funeral pyre! How can you speak with such authority?"

Dealing the bark basket a blow, much as she'd once kicked a wicker of rope, Kudra sent it spinning, setting into motion a brief blizzard of scabious crumbs.

"Damn you, Alobar! By the blue piss of Kali, how you frustrate me! How could any man venture as far as you have and then be unwilling to go further? Is it a failure of imagination that has snipped off your curiosity, or a failure of nerve that leaves you so eager to settle for the one concession you have won from the fates?"

"One concession, eh? You make it sound so trivial. Let me tell you something, Kudra. Each and every morning when I awake, my eyes brim with tears at the realization that I am still here breathing when all who shared my natal day have

for half a millennium been dust; each and every morning
when first I see the dawn ray take your sleeping face tenderly
in its tongs, I tremble in a kind of ecstasy that you and I
continue to lie in love together, century after juicy century,
while every other pair of lovers who have lived has had to
helplessly watch their passion suffocate in the sags of their
sickly flesh. Now that may strike you as some small, unworthy thing . . ."

Kudra took his cheeks in her hands (he was clean shaven
then, in the seventeenth-century style) and kissed him. She
shook her head from side to side, blinking back a few tears of
her own. "No, my darling, it strikes me as magnificent beyond
description." Again she kissed him. "But it happens not to be
the end-and-all. If a person have a glass, does that mean he
should refuse a bottle; if he have a bottle does it mean he
should not want wine? Come now, darling, do not pull away,
but hear me out. We have crossed the threshold of the house
of divine knowledge, yet we linger in the anteroom admiring
its wallpaper and shun the main chambers of the house. Why
is it we resist exploring the mansion to which it has been our
unique privilege to gain admission?"

"Because," answered Alobar, "Death is the master of that
house. My ambition has been to free myself from Death, not
to visit him in his parlor and share tea."

"Death is not a resident of the house. 'Death' is merely the
name we give to certain rooms of the house, rooms that we,
the so-called 'living,' fear for the simple reason that we have
not passed through them."

Alobar righted the overturned basket and began to pick up
pieces of bark. "Again, my little refugee from suttee, I must
question your authority in such matters."

Kudra wished then to tell him the truth about Lalo, that
the nymph had not run off with a mariner while Alobar was in
Greece but had died, peacefully, happily, in the bed where
Pan now slept; that she had attended Lalo's demise and,
indeed, had followed her out of her body, traveling with her
for a ways into the white light of the Other Side, until a
sudden thought of Alobar caused her to turn back. Her
concept of death was altered thereafter, and she wished to

tell Alobar about that, as well, but she had promised the nymph to keep secret her passing. "The world must not think of nymphs as aged or dying," said Lalo, "for that runs counter to the girlish sexual things that we represent." Perhaps Lalo was vain to the end, but it must be noted that she cared about the world, even the modern world (whose replacement of cosmic order with a riotous contest between would-be equals had helped to kill her).

"Listen," said Kudra. "When we were in the caves, we learned by experimenting, by trial and error, guided by some intelligence, perhaps divine, that radiated from the minerals there. What harm would there be in experimenting with dematerialization here in our shop? It is a temple of Pan now, after all. I feel strongly that we will be guided once again. The divine energy doesn't limit itself to some caverns in India. It is everywhere if we are only open to it. Trust my intuition, Alobar. What harm to try?"

"Well, all right, I shall consider it," grumbled Alobar. "Just so long as it does not involve aging."

She thumped him with a look of iron. "Should the monks or any other folk start to trouble us before we have either discovered dematerialization or a base note for Pan's perfume, then I shall age fast and furiously, without hesitation, and you would be wise to follow suit."

At that, their quarreling commenced all over again.

Their quarreling chewed through the curtains, pierced the casements, and rattled over the cobblestones outside. How strange it must have sounded, this quarreling about dematerialization, voluntary aging, goat gods, and immortality, to a city that was primed for the Age of Reason, a populace that was beginning to put Descartes before des horse.

Although the contention that matter can transcend, at will, its material character would have had Descartes spinning in one or the other of his graves, a person who can believe in physical immortality is merely a step away from believing in dematerialization. Kudra believed in it and was prepared to

experiment. Alobar probably believed in it but was reluctant—
frightened, honestly—to pursue it. Wiggs Dannyboy of the
Last Laugh Foundation, trained in the tradition of Cartersian
doubt (deliberate suspension of all interpretations of experience that are not absolutely certain), had, unlike Kudra,
never witnessed the Indian rope trick, nor had he, unlike
Alobar, ever been flabbergasted by Bandaloop, yet to him the
notion of material transcendence was credible. Perhaps that
was because he was Irish.

"Subatomic particles apparently de- and rematerialize fairly
routinely," Dr. Dannyboy has written. "Some of them actually can be in two places at once. Their freedom from the
normal confines of the space-time continuum is thought to be
the result of a weird electricity, an intelligent, creative, playful, and unpredictable interaction among oppositely charged
entities in motion." On at least one occasion, Dr. Dannyboy
has described those energized particles as "fairies," and, unfortunately, there is doubt that he was speaking metaphori-
cally. But, again, he is Irish and, moreover, has swallowed in
his day a lot of drugs.

At any rate, Dr. Dannyboy continued: "We ourselves are
built of subatomic particles (and the spaces in between them),
and our organisms are electrically as well as chemically pow-
ered. Our cells, or something that occupies our cells, transmit an electrical pulse. When we breathe, bathe, eat, make
love, and think the way that Kudra and Alobar did, we alter
the cellular amperage until we find ourselves vibrating at the
frequency of the eternal: *immortality*.

"When interrogated about how they can walk through flames
without being burned, 'primitives' have conveyed to anthro-
pologists that they raise the vibratory level of their flesh to
equal that of the fire. In like manner, then, an adept might
raise—or lower—his or her vibratory rate to match that of
another dimension, thereby disappearing from our customary
universe and popping up in the other: *dematerialization*."

From his vantage point in the twentieth century, Dannyboy
was privileged to marshal a fair amount of scientific evidence
that supposedly explains Alobar's and Kudra's accomplishments. No doubt, such data have their benefits, if for no

other reason than that the couple's immortalist methodology often sounds too simplistic to be feasible: the result was far more dramatic than the process, even though, for all practical purposes, the result *was* the process.

Whether guided by a divine intelligence, as Kudra suggested, or inspired in some supranatural fashion by the absent Bandaloop doctors (maybe the Bandaloop were agents of a divine intelligence), or simply informed by their own intuition, she and Alobar devised, during their residency in the caves, a program based upon the four elements: air, water, earth, and fire. If encouraged, Wiggs Dannyboy will expound upon each element in turn, detailing how it legitimately manifested itself in Kudra and Alobar's program. Dr. Dannyboy is simply mad for the subject of immortality and will yak about it until the cows come home, although the precise time and date of bovine arrival has yet to be reckoned to his satisfaction.

At some later point, it might be rewarding to examine Dannyboy's arguments. For the moment, let it suffice to say that he has connected air to breath, water to bath, earth to food, and fire to sex, supplying a mixture of empirical fact and medical theory to support his case for the life-extending properties of this quartet, when ritualistically and resolutely embraced.

In addition, Dr. Dannyboy has suggested a fifth element: positive thought. Pointing out that their breathing, bathing, dining, and screwing brought Alobar and Kudra much physical pleasure, and that an organism steeped in pleasure is an organism disposed to continue, he has said that the will to live cannot be overestimated as a stimulant to longevity. Indeed, Dr. Dannyboy goes so far as to claim that ninety percent of all deaths are suicides. Persons, says Wiggs, who lack curiosity about life, who find minimal joy in existence, are all too willing, subconsciously, to cooperate with—and attract—disease, accident, and violence.

Enough for now. In urbanized, technologized society—that institutional home for the orphans of Pan—there may be few who can even relate anymore to the Four Elements. At least not in any primal sense. V'lu Jackson, for example, once inquired of Madame Devalier if the Four Elements weren't some Motown jive group, while Ricki the bartender has defined the Four Elements as cocaine, champagne, pussy, and chocolate.

Paris. April. Twilight. A few flat clouds folded themselves like crepes over fillings of apricot sky. Pompadours of supper-time smoke billowed from chimneys, separating into girlish pigtails as the breeze combed them out, above the slate rooftops. Chestnut blossoms, weary from having been admired all day, wore faint smiles of anticipation with the approach of the private night. Or else the blossoms were being tickled by the sleepy insects that were entering them as if they were hotels. Stiff-legged corks squeaked loose from bottlenecks where they'd stood guard since noon. Stiff-legged nags, tiny harness bells jingling, dragged market carts toward the suburbs. At intervals along the boulevards, lamplighters set their gay fires. A wounded tongue licked the shine off cathedral domes. A bat broke loose from a belfry, a loaf broke loose from an oven, six chimes broke loose from a clock. Everywhere a huge, enveloping softness; soft as face powder, soft as petticoats, soft as the snuff in a courtesan's box.

Now, the clock chimed seven times. Nightfall was almost complete. The softness was suddenly interrupted by harsh hoofbeats, not four hooves, oddly enough, but two, striking a stone bridge—clink! clink!—upon which no beast could be seen to trod; and the peachy, powdery softness was further violated by a release of fumes so fetid it seemed almost evil. Clink! clink! Sparks were struck from cobblestones. Clink! clink! To the innocent nostrils of spring there was caterwauled a filthy serenade.

Pan had waited until dark to return home so that he might more stealthily transport the wig stolen from Descartes's redundant funeral. He'd not eaten since early morning, and to the scrape of his hooves (not meant for city streets) and the blast of his stench (meant for no place save the rutting grounds) were added stomach growls, terrible and rude. From grass, he had woven a short rope, which he tied to the wig so that he might pull it along behind him. In the dim light, those pedestrians who saw it scurrying up the street believed it to be blown along by the breeze. Several gave pursuit, only to have it yanked away each time they thought they had it in their grasp. One by one, they gave up. "It stinks, anyway," said the last to quit the chase. And Pan arrived at the incense shop with wig in tow, having painted the gentle April gloaming with shades of Halloween.

Ceremoniously, Pan presented the wig, frescoed now with grit and offal, to Alobar. Were Alobar bewigged, Pan reasoned, he could hold the white hairs of age at bay for as long as he wished, and no outsider would be the wiser. With that pressure removed, maybe Alobar and Kudra would curtail their quarreling, maybe the household would be merry again.

As it turned out, Pan found his hosts in a quite congenial mood already. When, that afternoon, the latest candidate for a base note had fallen short of expectations, they had sat down over a flagon of wine and negotiated an agreement to dematerialize.

For a week, they fasted. They meditated for hours each day and bathed repeatedly. They made love between baths but resisted climax, holding the orgasmic cyclone inside themselves, channeling it up their spinal columns to their brains. Then, one afternoon, the green blush of April still upon the city, they closed the shop an hour earlier than usual and climbed the stairs, one of them for the last time.

The experiment was to be conducted in their small sitting room. After a brief discussion about whether or not they should disrobe, they concurred that nudity might distract Pan, who was to monitor the attempt, and they remained, but for their shoes, fully clothed. Upon the threadbare carpet, a far cry from the rugs that had purred to their buttocks in Constantinople, they sat cross-legged, facing one another. They closed their eyes and . . .

Just then there was a commotion in the street. Excited voices were being raised outside their shop. Alobar asked Pan to investigate. "I be a god not an errand boy," grumbled the old faun, but he hobbled downstairs nevertheless.

The ruckus was caused by the monks. For more than a year, ever since Pan moved into the neighborhood, things had not been right at the monastery. The good brothers had become increasingly plagued by erotic dreams. Dreams of a lascivious nature are fairly common among those of whom the church requires celibacy, but the frequency and intensity of the dreams on rue Quelle Blague had the confession booth smoking. Some monks had begun to resist sleep and walked about heavy-lidded and nervous. Others lived for bedtime and during the day appeared drained, weak, disinterested. Rome dispatched an exorcist to uproot their torment, but the sticky demons mocked his incantations: he, himself, was visited by a succubus of such seductive talent that upon awakening he packed his exorcisory tools and returned to the Vatican.

The abbot, too, was stricken. At least twice a week he was stiffened by creamy visions; the other nights, he told his confessor, he dreamed "of rabbits caught in snares, of snakes that swallow birds' eggs whole, of trailing vines that threaten to trip me up, of rockslides, ewes in foal, yammering hornets, belching vultures, yellow eyes that peer out from hollow trees, and all manner of disagreeable things such as Satan has strewn about God's perfect world, things such as I have not seen since my boyhood in rural Provence."

The monks under his authority were subject to these "rural" nightmares as well. If they weren't being tortured by the rub of feminine thighs, they were being nauseated by the drool of he-bears eating their cubs. Late in the evening, a person afoot on rue Quelle Blague might, by the moans and shrieks and saccadic protests, have imagined themselves passing not a monastery but a hospital or a brothel or a combination of the two.

More and more, the monks came to suspect that the incense shop was the source of their collective possession.

Despite the aromatic stuffs that were its stock in trade, there was often a gamey odor about the place, "a smell," as the abbot put it, "of such wild meats as country rogues doth eat." Never had the shop's owners been seen at Mass, there was a quality of physical well-being about them that was nearly supernatural, and the woman—the woman was perversely proportioned and jiggled shamelessly when she walked. Several monks claimed that she, specifically, haunted their cots of a night.

Still, the two shopkeepers were good customers of the perfumery and were known to cooperate in the acquisition of raw materials. Moreover, the dream epidemic had attacked the monastery but a year before, while the shop had been operating for well over a decade. The superiors urged restraint in placing blame, but accusations were whispered almost daily, and when, with the soft airs and fertile moistures of spring, the dreaming in the cubicles reached a hysterical pitch, small knots of agitated monks began to patrol the block, eager, it seemed, for something demonic to reveal itself.

It was just such a group that on that fateful afternoon descended on a young man who was timidly rattling the latch at the shop's locked door.

"What is your business here, boy?" asked one of the monks.

"I am making delivery, Father."

"Delivery from whom?"

"From the glassblower. I am his apprentice." This last, the boy said proudly.

"And what is in the package?"

"Why, glass, Father. A glass bottle."

"A bottle of what?"

"A bottle of nothing."

"Eh?"

"The bottle is empty. The woman of this shop commissioned it from my master. Someday *I* shall blow fine bottles and—"

"Hush! We shall have a look at this bottle."

"But, your holiness—"

The monk cuffed the lad on the ear. It felt so good he cuffed him again. "We shall see the bottle!"

Confused, the boy drew away, clutching the package to his silica-caked apron. His ear was turning as red as a whore's lantern. The circle of monks closed around him. "The bottle! The bottle!" they demanded. They forced the package from the frightened boy's grasp and tore it open. A shaft of afternoon sunlight illuminated a bluish container, shaped like a perfume vessel, though three or four times larger. As if focusing, the sun ray narrowed its beam upon a finely wrought figure embossed on the glass. It was the monks' turn to pale.

For a moment or two, they were speechless, and there was much trembling of skullcap and rosary. " 'Tis *him*," one managed to whisper. "Him," repeated another, somewhat louder. "The incense shop and him," said a third. " 'Tis what we thought all along. They are allied with Lucifer!"

The monk who was holding the dreadful object raised it, cocking his arm as if to dash it against the cobblestones, but, lo and behold, the bottle squirmed free from his fingers and floated away, flying under its own power—or so it seemed to the terrified monks—about five feet above the street. Slowly it bobbed down the block, rounded a corner, and disappeared. Only then, crossing themselves so furiously that it was a wonder no wrists were sprained, only then did the monks become fully aware of the vulgar aroma—naturally, they assumed it was sulfur or brimstone—that the bottle left in its wake.

Entering the shop from the rear (a familiar route for a Greek), Pan fetched the bottle up to the sitting room, where Kudra admired it at length. Normally, Alobar would have been too concerned about the monks to pay much attention to an oversize perfume bottle, but preparations for the dematerialization attempt had so tranquillized him that he brushed aside all thought of events in the street, concentrating, instead, on the pale fruit of the glassblower's rod.

"How exactly the fellow copied your design!"

"Yes," said Kudra, "isn't it splendid? Pan, it is you on the side. What think you?"

Pan rarely replied to direct questions, but in this instance he did stampede a flock of little sighs, hairy and wistful: full udders and quick feet running over a cliff.

"The rendering flatters you, I daresay," joked Alobar to Pan. Then, to Kudra he said, "It is a marvelous container for a potentially marvelous liquid, but, alas, it is all academic now. We still haven't the what-you-call-it, base note, and, besides, if the three of us can rematerialize ourselves in the New World, Pan shall not require a cover for his stink."

"Oh, I would not be so sure of that. He might find a cover handy even in a wild and distant land. And should he need it not, well, still I want that base note, I want that perfume, I want this bottle filled with its intended contents. I want it for you and me, now, as much as for Pan."

"But, why?"

Slowly, Kudra turned the bottle in her hands. Then, she sat it on the floor between them. It was about six inches tall, square-bottomed but rounded at the shoulders, with a short, flared neck tightly fitted with a glass stopper. There was a ridge down each side of the body, seams left by the wooden mold in which it was formed. The neck, lip, and stopper were seamless, having been formed by hand and added after the blowing. On the bottom of the bottle was a scar not unlike an umbilicus, where an iron pontil rod had held the hot, freshly blown bottle while its neck was being shaped. The cute little pontil scar measured one cubic centimeter, the same, on the average, as the human navel that it resembled. (A Harley-Davidson motorcycle with a 1000cc engine has room in its chamber for a thousand belly buttons, a piece of information that may or may not interest the Hell's Angels.) The bottle glass was clear but had a bluish tinge because of impurities, and it contained the odd bubble, ripple, and tiny bit of stone. One side of the body was embossed with an oval "frame," within whose boundaries there was an image of none other than Mr. Goat Foot himself, in a jaunty stance, his horns freely displayed, his reeds pressed to his leer, a garland of weeds encircling his bushy brow.

The bottle was between them, and Kudra spoke over the top of it. "Suppose, just suppose, that we should become separated in our—our journeys into the Other Side. If we were marked by a unique scent, a fragrance all our own, we could always identify each other, even if the light was not clear, even if our vision was clouded or our shapes physically altered; we could find each other no matter if we were lost in the rooms of Death."

That kind of talk was a bit spooky for Alobar's taste. He suggested that they get on with the experiment while he was still in the mood. So they shut their eyes again and reset their breaths upon a circular track. Kudra's plan was that they should slow themselves down until their "humors" buzzed at a rate below that of the visible world, then merge with the vibrations and broadcast themselves through a crack. Which crack? Why, the crack at the top of the Indian rope trick. Okay. Alobar would give it a whirl. After all, his goal always had been to be complete, and were he restricted to occupancy of this one world, as round and fully packed as it might be, he supposed he could not claim completion. He was as nervous as a praying mantis at an atheists' picnic, but he bore down gently, intensifying his concentration, letting go of his attachment to gravity, applying the brakes to his bodily functions. Just before he abandoned himself to the process, however, he heard Kudra whisper, "The bottle must be filled."

From corner to corner, silence webbed the room. Gradually, there commenced a ringing in Alobar's ears. The sound was produced, no doubt, by his central nervous system, though he imagined it the ringing of the spheres. Stars, in fact, had begun to colonize the darkness behind his lids. At first they were as faint and icy as the pimples on an albino's backside, but they grew in brilliance and size until a sewing basket of flaming buttons spilled on his head, and the Great Bear raked him with her sidereal paws.

Motionless, he sat inside himself as if in a planetarium. Neither a twitch nor a flicker, a pulse nor a discernible breath marred his smooth facade. His heart slowed until it seemed to have frozen in its burrow. His lungs were as immobile as sponges. The wheel rolled to a stop, and bubbles of oxygen slid off of it to skitter upon the surface of his stagnant blood like waterbugs attending to some dizzy business. He tingled, he sparked, and he rang. He felt light and loose and large. The more static his functions became, the more he seemed to expand, as if he had entered a state where there was progress without duration, advance without movement.

He was becoming unstuck, he was sure of that—his bones were no longer wrapped in flesh but in clouds of dust, in hummingbirds, dragonflies, and luminous moths—but so perfect was his equilibrium that he felt no fear. He was vast, he was many, he was dynamic, he was eternal.

Then, suddenly, he was falling, not downward but outward, beyond the horizon—as if the earth had an edge after all. And with that thought, his life started to unreel before him. He saw himself as a babe, gnawing at the nipple of his great golden mother; as a child, rolling in pine needles; as a youth, swimming rivers. He witnessed himself in battle after battle, smoke winding 'round his helmet, his right sleeve stiff with gore. He occupied the throne, skinned a fox, drained a mead goblet, spread the yellow short-hairs of Alma, Ruba, and Frol. There, over the watchtower, was the winter moon in its ermine snood; here, in the harem mirror, was his good old beard, unsullied by silver; yonder was Noog sawing a chicken in half; here stood Wren, advice forming in her mouth like spittle; and—oh joy!—up bounded the huge hound, Mik, jowls a-drool and tail a-wag. Alobar embraced the dog and buried his face in its coat, only to be knocked back by an overpowering odor.

Upon first contact, the smell was acrid and offensive, but by the second or third whiff it was acceptable enough, and by the fourth or fifth, downright agreeable. A shock of olfactory recognition reverberated in Alobar, and he said to himself—his light, loose, large, and falling self—"Ah, 'tis late in summer and the dogs have been in the crops."

The pageantry of his life continued to flash by, but he clung to the brief encounter with Mik, galvanized, somehow, by the familiar smell. And then it hit him. "That is it!" he cried. "That is it!" So deep was he in "his" time, so removed from exterior time, that he made no sound in the room, but he cried "Methinks I have found it!" with force enough that

the breath wheel was jarred into motion again, a wild thump
rattled his heart, and all at once his trajectory reversed itself
and he came flying back, shedding stars like dandruff, gaining
weight, contracting, shrinking, until he tumbled back over
the edge into the shallow bowl of our reality, his plasma
sluggish in the pump, his eyes pasted shut with some atomic
glue, but voice finally audible in the little sitting room: "Kudra!
I have got it."

   A beet, by and large, has little odor; its leaves, stalk, and
famous red root are, to the nose, equally, relatively bland.
Around August, however, when the plants go to seed, a
pungent and singular aroma rises from them, like a gaseous
wrench that gives the surrounding atmosphere a sharp turn
to the left, twisting it into strange new configurations. When
dogs run through August beet fields, the pollen dusts their
coats, and they return to their masters so strongly scented
that no scour brush, however vigorously wielded, will leave
them fit to sleep in the house. As Alobar recalled, only
time—days of it—would relieve the dogs of their odd olfactory burden, "odd" because once the nose was past the initial
shock of it, it was not unpleasant; yet, unless substantially
diluted, its pleasure was difficult to endure.
   If the waft that streams from a freshly opened hive is
intimate to the point of embarrassment (ask any sensitive
beekeeper), so it is with beet pollen. There is something
personal about it, and something primeval. If there is a
comparable odor, it is, indeed, the moldly inner sanctum of
some fermenting, bursting hive; but beet pollen is honey
squared, royal jelly cubed, nectar raised to the nth power;
the intensified secretions of the Earth's apiarian gland, reeking of ancient bridal chambers and intimacies half as old as
time.
   However, on Nature's cluttered dressing table, there is no
scent to truly match it, not hashish, not ambergris, not decaying honey itself. Beet pollen, in its fascinating ambivalence, is
the aroma of paradox, of yang and yin commingled, of life and

death combined in vegetable absolute. And Alobar intuited that it was the missing link in the evolution of the perfect perfume. "Beet is our base note," he said. "Why did I not think of it before?"

Maybe he was right. Beet pollen had the muscle, the stamina, the tenacity to both establish the jasmine and to stand up to its detractors. Like that rarity, the wise husband, it was strong enough to possess its mate, secure enough to allow her her freedom. If Pan's musk was the dark and convulsive essence of animal behavior, then beet's musk was its floral counterbalance, the olfactory interface where the fuck of beast and the pollenization of plant became roughly equivalent. "Kudra, methinks I have found it!

"Kudra.

"Kudra?"

With effort, Alobar forced his lids apart. The light was piercing, but the pain passed quickly. He squinted, striving to focus. Slowly, the walls came into relief and, in turn, the fireplace, curtains, furniture, and empty bottle at his stockinged feet. Kudra, alas, was not to be seen. He blinked furiously and rubbed his eyes with his fists. His vision was back to normal. That wasn't the problem. The sun was setting, but the room was still adequately lit. That wasn't the problem. Kudra was gone.

Life is too small a container for certain individuals. Some of them, such as Alobar, huff and puff and try to expand the container. Others, such as Kudra, seek to pry the lid off and hop out.

"Both of thee wert going," said Pan from his post in the corner. "Thou stopped and came back. She went."

Naturally, Alobar was tempted to restart the experiment, to try to join her—wherever she might be. Upon reflection, however, he submitted to his truer nature and elected to wait for her return.

As darkness fell, he lit candle after candle in the sitting room, indifferent to what the monks might think of the con-

centrated brilliance. Should any tiny part of her wink on, he
didn't want to miss it. When, by midnight, not so much as a
chin dimple had shown up, he experienced alternate states of
panic and relief; panic that her disappearance might be permanent, relief that *he* had not disappeared.

At dawn, he blew out the candles, which had come to
resemble the fingers of careless mill workers, and continued
the vigil by sunlight. Above Pan's cataractous snoring, he
could hear carts creaking to market, birds blowing the bugs
out of their pipes, and monks marching to and fro in front of
the shop, but he couldn't hear a peep from the Other Side.
There was simply nothing left of Kudra but a pair of empty
shoes. In some kind of desperate attempt to get her attention, he set fire to the left shoe and smoked it.

He had just blown a ring about the size of her left breast
when—how embarrassing!—the gendarmes arrived. They ar-
rested Alobar, charging him with heresy, blasphemy, satan-
ism, and witchcraft, and confiscated the new perfume bottle
as evidence.

Breaking into the Bastille was as easy as falling off a ewe for
the invisible Pan. Less than twenty-four hours after the arrest, before the whips and lashes had gotten limber, Pan had
liberated Alobar, and the bottle as well, leaving nothing in
their place but an awful smell.

Immediately, they made their way to the incense shop. It
was boarded up, and a heavy wooden cross was propped
against the front door. Prying boards loose from a rear window, they hurried upstairs. The sitting room was just as they
had left it. Kudra's right shoe lay upturned on the thin
carpet, like a boat washed up on a desolate shore.

It was barely four in the morning, but already candles were
exercising their little flames, *left, right, flicker, sputter, left,
right,* in the monastery halls across the street. Alobar knew
he must get out of there, but first he bundled up as much
fragrance equipment as he could carry, and left a note in
Kudra's shoe telling her to look for him in the beet fields of
Bohemia.

To Alobar's mind, there were several possible reasons why Kudra hadn't rematerialized. To wit:

(1) Once she had fallen over the edge (Alobar was assuming that her experience paralleled his own), she had just kept falling, growing lighter, looser, and larger until she became nothing—or everything—and was, therefore, in a rather grandiose way, "dead," or, at least, irretrievable.

(2) In the world of the nonliving, she had been reunited with her parents, with Navin the Ropemaker, and with her abandoned children, about whom she felt, Alobar knew, continued remorse. (Alobar secretly blamed himself—no seventeenth-century male would publicly admit to such a shortcoming—for Kudra's failure to conceive in their recent efforts, but, of course, the fault lay with the pennyroyal that she had ingested for over seven hundred years and which had left a contraceptive residue that would bash sperm in the head for a long time to come.) In that case, she would choose not to rematerialize for a while, if ever.

(3) She had landed safely on the Other Side and was searching there for him. Since she had no way of knowing that his dematerialization had been aborted, perhaps she feared that he was lost.

(4) She had landed on the Other Side and become lost there, herself. Maybe she longed to come back but couldn't find her way.

(5) Since their practical objective in learning to dematerialize was to transport themselves across the Atlantic, it could be that Kudra had crossed directly and was waiting for Pan and him to join her in the New World.

In the event that it was reason number one that detained her, there was nothing Alobar could do but grieve. If it was number two, he could only carry a torch, as they say, and hope that his love would eventually draw her back to him. To deal with possibility three or four might or might not require him to dematerialize, but, in either case, he instinctively felt that their long-sought perfume would be the key to their finding one another again. For that matter, if it was number five that was correct, if she had taken advantage of a free and easy passage to the New World and was counting on Pan and him following her, the perfume would also be necessary, both as a mask for goat gas and as a signal in case their seeing one another directly was prevented by natural or supernatural obstructions.

Well, at least he could provide the perfume now. Or could he? That question—and a sack of beakers, tubes, crucibles, industrial-strength candles, citron, jasmine oil, and a five-ounce bottle with Pan on its side—weighed him down on the long trek to Bohemia.

The beet harvest was right on schedule. Toward the tail of July, peasants were in the fields from morning until night, ripping whiskered fetuses from the planetary mud. A steady parade of oxcarts wound toward the villages, bearing baskets of smokeless coals and sacks of idol eyes. Concealed in a hillside thicket, Alobar kept one eye on the harvest, one on the road to the west, down which he expected at any moment to see an hashish-colored woman jiggling and swaying: jumping beans in aspic, a satin ship rolling in a tide of licorice sauce.

The harvest petered out, the woman never appeared, but the Bohemian farmers, as they had done since Alobar could remember, left a few acres of beets undug so that they might complete their cycle and provide the seed for next year's crop. There was a patch of seed-beets here, a patch there, often miles apart. Alobar mapped the countryside, X-ing the fields where the treasure lay. He needn't have bothered. By mid-August, his nose could have led him blindfolded to the places where the pollen was congregating.

In the dark of night, Alobar and Pan collected the viscous powder from the plant tops, filling beakers that they stashed in a particularly dense thicket. Twigs and branches jabbed at their eyes, briers tore Pan's flesh and Alobar's clothing, but each dawn they kicked and shoved their way into the coppice, where they added another couple of beakers to the stash and lay down to sleep in a chaos of sweating vines, mucous leaves, and maggoty logs. Mistletoe dripped an unsavory liquid on them, a living confetti of spiders and earwigs dotted them from head to heel, curds of mushroom and scrumbles of lichen soiled them to the bone, but Pan slept as if he were to that foul manor born, and Alobar was too desperate to care. His fitful dreams were all of Kudra, and when he lay awake in the rot and tangle, he sniffed at the contrasting clouds of musk that billowed from the god and the beakers of beet pollen, noting with immense satisfaction that they nearly cancelled one another out.

After a dozen containers had been filled, they hiked into the high hills, where smoke would not be noticed, and, while Pan lay on the humus, noodling his pipes (Alobar had fetched them in his sack, and they put the local fauna into a tizzy), Alobar constructed a crude laboratory. He boiled down the beet pollen into an extract, gray, gooey, and possessed of a *basso profondo* that could have brought the rafters down in the grand opera of smell.

When all the extract had been made, Alobar shook the wood lice out of his britches, washed his face in a creek, and set out for a large town on the Russian border, where he knew a vodka master to reside. Pan was left behind to guard their equipment. Without the feeble god to slow him, Alobar reached the town in a week. There, he approached the vodka maker, who, in return for the last of Alobar's French gold pieces, agreed to distill the beet pollen extract, an operation that, to Alobar's displeasure, consumed the better part of a month.

The job at last complete, Alobar tied a gallon jug of distillate to each end of a stout pole, rested the pole across both shoulders, and left the town at a trot. Were it not for the preciousness and weight of his cargo, he might have left at a gallop. He was anxious about Kudra, who could have returned in his absence, anxious about Pan, who could have

strayed. In as much as his health would permit, Pan had
cooperated in the venture to disguise his malodor and transport him to the New World, but he hardly could be rated
enthusiastic. He was, in fact, so nonverbal, so distant, distracted, solitary, and, even in his invisibility, especially in his
invisibility, charged with psychic shock, that nothing he might
have done would really have surprised Alobar, who had little
choice but to withhold trust. Stopping neither to eat nor
sleep, his brain hot with imagined disasters, the man who
once was a king in this land flapped through the countryside
in his filthy rags, his boots falling away from his feet, his
latest beard flying in the wind like a nauseated Chinaman
losing his bird's nest soup.

Their camp proved blessedly intact, Pan present and ac-
counted for, molesting a confused doe that he had attracted
by his piping. As the poor deer sprang into the bushes,
Alobar lifted the pole from his raw shoulders. " 'Tis done," he
said, and lay down in the lean-to, falling immediately into a
wife-infested slumber.

Twelve hours later, he awoke and set at once to mixing the
beet pollen distillate with jasmine oil and citron essence, in
varying proportions. After five days of experimenting, he hit
upon what seemed the ideal mixture: one part beet to twenty
parts jasmine to two parts citron, a ratio that inspired him to
name the scent K23. The K was for Kudra.

Like a lobster with a pearl in its claw, the beet held the
jasmine firmly without crushing or obscuring it. Beet lifted
jasmine, the way a bullnecked partner lifts a ballerina, and
the pair came on stage on citron's fluty cue. As if jasmine
were a collection of beautiful paintings, beet hung it in the
galleries of the nose, insured it against fire or theft, threw a
party to celebrate it. Citron mailed the invitations.

If Alobar could trust his nose, K23 stopped Pan in his
tracks. It seemed to throw a mantle—gossamer in places,
heavily embroidered in others—over his funk, and however
long and hard the goat musk might squirm beneath that

cloak, it could not wriggle free. "I wonder if I am only imagining that it is so effective?" worried Alobar. "Perhaps it is wishful smelling." There was nothing to do but submit it to objective testing.

Into a sack, Alobar packed a gallon jug of K23, what remained of the beet pollen distillate (the jasmine and citron were used up), the empty bottle that Kudra had designed, some roasted beets to munch on on the road, and his companion's innocent-looking reeds. Then, at Pan's pace—out there in the back country the peasants still secretly honored him, a fact that put a tad of pep in his step—they set off in the direction of France. In every village through which they passed, Pan—freshly sprinkled with K23—walked ahead, Alobar following at a distance of nine or ten yards. Directed by Alobar, Pan endeavored to brush as closely as possible to people in the street. From Bohemia to Paris, the results were invariably the same.

As the invisible Pan walked by, people's eyebrows would raise, their noses would tilt, and they would begin to turn toward the source of the scent, looks of expectation or ill-concealed delight forming on their faces. Halfway into the turn, however, that expression would be abruptly dislodged by a twitch of embarrassment, and, reddening slightly, the person would turn away, as if to look directly at the origin of such a fragrance might violate an intimacy sacred even to an unrefined yokel. Bemused smiles involuntarily parting their lips, they would continue on their way for a few yards, when, at a safe distance and no longer able to resist, they would stop and slowly look back, smiling all the while, only to find that the emanator of the aroma had—so they believed—turned a corner or disappeared through a doorway. Off they would go then, not really disappointed, some fantasy or other obviously drawing a grass blade lightly along the genitals of their minds.

Now Alobar was hardly expert, but he realized that he had concocted a unique and genuinely amazing perfume, a fragrance whose possibilities extended far beyond its worth—praise the morning star for that worth!—as a cover-up for the Horned One's fetid ooze. Kudra had predicted it, had she not? She had said, at least, that she wished the perfume for Alobar and her as much as for Pan.

On the outskirts of Paris, where they rested beneath a stone bridge, waiting for darkness before daring to enter the city, Alobar filled the bluish bottle to the brim with *K23*. He put its stopper in. He pressed it to his tear-wet cheeks.

It was late September, there were tambourines of frost in the air. Alobar and Pan crossed the great city, their breath always one step ahead of them. Man's breath and god's breath looked identical, congealed in the urban night. Their footsteps, on the other hand, were distinctly different—the bum flap of Alobar's boots, the blacksmith chisel of Pan's hooves—but they led to the same destination over the rigid effervescence of cobblestones.

The incense shop was just as they had left it, boarded up and blocked by a crude wooden cross. Apparently the monks were giving it a wide berth. Had Alobar stopped off at the neighboring brewery/perfumery, he would have caught the abbot discussing the sale of the business to an enterprising fragrance broker named Guy LeFever. At that very moment, LeFever was inquiring about the possibility of locating the owner of the incense shop and purchasing it as well, for he had heard that its inventory was quite valuable and in disuse, but the abbot, who was sleeping better those nights and taking no chances, wrung his lily hands and cried, "No, no, do not pursue it."

As deftly as possible, Alobar pried open a rear window. He and Pan crawled in. Alobar's heart was beating more loudly than Pan's hoofbeats as they climbed the stairs. The door to the sitting room was opened with a creak. Alobar did not recall that it had ever creaked before.

It seems there should have been a harvest moon that night, but not a cuff link of moonlight was in evidence. Perhaps the moon was spending the evening at Versailles. In any case, Alobar didn't really require a moon to see that nothing in the room had changed. The pale reach of a streetlamp was sufficient to illuminate the sad tableau: his note, the single shoe, the balls of dust.

He avoided going inside, but, rather, leaned across the threshold just far enough to set down the bottle of *K23*, having first removed its stopper. He shut the door briskly, as if the breeze from the door might speed a waft of perfume toward the Other Side.

Upon the bed where he, a latecomer to kissing, had kissed so much of her, he lay the night, weeping, dozing, waking to weep once more. Throughout the morning he lay there, a pillow, which he imagined to bear some scent of her ebony hair, pasted to his face. It was past noon when he finally released himself from the twist of marriage-stained sheets. Lint in his beard, burrs of salt in the corners of his eyes, he padded barefoot to the sitting room to fetch the bottle. Pan was up and would be needing a fix.

As bait, *K23* had failed—for the time being, at any rate. Alobar had heard no sound from the sitting room during the night, and now, creaking open the door, he saw that his note still lay there, beneath the forlorn shoe. But wait! Hadn't he tucked the note *inside* the shoe?! And hadn't the shoe been placed in the very center of the carpet, whereas it now lay somewhat off to the right, closer to the fireplace!?!

Shaking like a wedding announcement in a misogamist's fist, Alobar examined the shoe, unfolded and reread the note. He turned them over and over. He even sniffed them. There were no marks, no odors, nothing unusual in any way. Yet they had been moved, he was positive of that! The question was, had they been moved during the night —in which case, the perfume was a lure, after all—or sometime during the preceding five months? The light had been so dim, his emotions so swollen on the previous evening that he easily could have overlooked such a slight, though significant, displacement.

Unable to learn anything from the slipper or paper, he scrutinized the room itself, patrolling the carpet, inch by dusty inch. Nothing. The walls, too, were a tabula rasa. When his gaze settled on the fireplace, however, his spine was straightened by a fulminous jolt. On the mantelpiece, next to Kudra's beloved silver teapot, a word had been written in the dust!

Yes, someone, using a fingertip as implement, had plowed

a grafitto on the surface of the marble, where the dust lay thick as fur. The script, while instantly familiar, was not Kudra's style, however, nor was the word in her single written language. When Kudra had finally become literate, it was French that she learned to read and write. The word on the mantelpiece was from the Slavo-Nordic tongue that his clan had used to speak of battles, bear hunts, beet harvests, and broken mirrors, and the handwriting was that of the only woman in his kingdom with the ability to write that language: Wren.

For a long time, Alobar just stood there, grasping the mantel ledge for support. So shocked was he by the implications of language and penmanship that he didn't even consider content. When at last he turned his attention to it, his bafflement only increased. The word was a transitive verb, an exclamation, a command, of which an exact English translation is impossible. The closest equivalent probably would be the phrase:

Lighten up!

Lighten up, indeed. Against his better judgment and to Pan's chagrin, Alobar remained in the flat for a week, subsisting on crusts of stale bread and flakes of moldy cheese. Each night he placed the open bottle of K23 in the sitting room, each morning he rushed in and searched for messages in the dust. There were none. That is, there was but one, the one and only: *Erleichda*. "Lighten up!"

Alobar watched the last grain of green cheese work its way down Pan's invisible gullet while some morbid hymn about the gore of Christ drifted over from across the street. He chewed a mouthful of dried blossoms from the shop's supply. They tasted like Grendel's underpants. He spat them out, wiped his beard with his sleeve, and asked, "What shall we cook for dinner? The drapes?" Had Guy LeFever, who was next door closing his deal with the abbot, overheard him, the businessman might have snapped, "Not drapes, you idiot, draperies. Drape is a verb." LeFever did *not* overhear him, but Alobar knew that it was merely a matter of time before one of the monks did hear him, or spot him through a window (the upper ones were not boarded), a prospect that caused his empty stomach to rattle its chains.

He was sitting there in the universal slouch of hopelessness, the old droop of despair, when he felt the pressure of Pan's hand on his arm. The god had never touched him before, and Alobar had to confess that his first reaction was that he must defend himself against intended buggery. Pan simply squeezed him, however, and remarked, "Death hath more than one way to defeat a man, it seems. Death bests thee even while thou liveth." Then he walked away, his hooves beating a slow rat-a-tat on the floorboards, pausing to call over his presumed shoulder, "Puny homer."

That must have done it. Alobar slumped there for another quarter-hour, then rose, bathed, shaved off his tear-encrusted beard, donned his finest clothes, polished his spare boots, pulled on and powdered the frazzled wig that Pan had dragged home from Descartes's funeral, and beckoning to the god, who may or may not have been smiling, slipped recklessly out of the shop while the sun's seal was still affixed to the scroll of the horizon.

Packing the perfume, beet distillate, and little else, the pair made its way to Marseilles, where the last ship of the season was preparing to sail for New France.

For more than a decade, the French had dominated the Great Lakes region of what would eventually be called North America, but unlike the English and Spanish, the French tended to view the New World in terms of its spoils—furs, fish, Christian converts, and a possible westward route to the Indies—rather than as a place to build homes, towns, and a new life. Disease, attacks from hostile Iroquois, and a major earthquake in Quebec in 1663 had brought its fur-trading company to the brink of ruin and set weary settlers to crying "Back to France!" before Louis XIV stopped waltzing long enough to rectify matters. Rumors of a mighty and mysterious river flowing southward from the Great Lakes, perhaps as far as the Pacific, had reached King Louis, and, murmuring "Mississippi, Mississippi" into his scented hankie, he raised New France to the status of a royal province, secured it with a regiment of highly trained soldiers, and appointed a capable

executive to oversee its internal affairs. Henceforth, Louis
decreed, qualified settlers (those with skills) would take precedence over missionaries and trappers on the ships to
Montreal.

When Alobar approached the captain of the *Mississippi
Poodle*, he found that it had space for several more single
male passengers—most families were waiting for spring before emigrating, not wishing to begin colonial life at the onset
of a harsh northern winter—and were he deemed fit, he
could not only travel free of charge, he would be paid a small
bonus for his commitment. Alobar contended that he was an
aristocrat who'd recently lost his fortune, and since he had a
gentlemanly manner, and since there was another fellow
aboard in an identical situation ("Sieur de La Salle by name,
is he a friend of yours?") the captain believed him.

There was some worry about Alobar's age, however. "Just
how old *are* you, sir?" inquired the chief immigration officer.
Alobar didn't know what to say. He had no idea anymore
what age he looked to be, and God knows he couldn't tell the
truth. He stammered a bit, finally blurting out, "Forty-six," a
figure arrived at by doubling *K23*. "A hale and hardy forty-
six, accustomed to leading men."

Up the gangplank he went, aromatic liquids gurgling in his
sack, suppressed laughter gurgling in his throat. Pan followed.

The *Mississippi Poodle* slid across the Mediterranean as
slickly as an asparagus spear gliding through a serving of
hollandaise sauce, but once past Gibraltar and into the open
Atlantic, she ran headlong into a mass of cold air and choppy
water. With each dark day, the waves grew more pugilistic.
Passengers could imagine her hull turning blue from the
chilling and the pounding.

It was routine sailing for that time of year, of course, and
the seamen not only took it in stride, they seemed as content
a crew as the captain had ever commanded. There was a
curious sweet aroma aboard that, while it could neither be
identified nor pinpointed, lifted everyone's spirits in a shy,

private way, fostering the secret hope that some wonderful encounter waited just below deck (if one was above) or on deck (if one was below). Like habitual snuff users, the men sniffed as they went about their work. "This tub smells like a Bombay whore," grumbled one old salt, but the younger men, who'd never seen Bombay, only grinned and, being sailors, lost little sleep over the pornographic nightmares that with increasing frequency invaded their hammocks. Homosexual impulses, which normally didn't surface until the men had been parted from their wives for several months, began to flicker a few days past Gibraltar, more to the amusement than disturbance of those so visited.

Alobar spent much of the voyage seated alone behind the bowsprit, enjoying the energy of the waves, refreshed by the salty sprays that needled him. For him, the blustery days provided calm introspection, a time for putting his long, strange life into some sort of perspective.

"Pan is right," he thought. "Death can ruin a man's life even though he go on breathing." The sea hissed at him, but he didn't flinch. "If Kudra is dead, dead as all the others who have died, then I must refrain from driving myself mad by wishing her alive. I do not know why the dead do not come back to life. Perhaps death is so wonderful, in ways we cannot comprehend, that they prefer it over and above their friends and loved ones, although I am inclined to doubt that be the case. If Kudra is dead like all the others, then it does me well to curtail my grief, lest my life become a deathly imitation through depression and sorrow." He wiped a piece of foam from his eye and, without malice, flicked it back into the waves.

"Ah, but suppose she is dead in the manner of the Bandaloop, able to pass back and forth freely between This Side and the Other Side. Although six months have gone, that still is a reasonable speculation due to her unusual abilities and to the very significant fact that she did not leave behind a body to molder in the sod: she took it with her. Hopeful I am, yet to ride that hope each day from dawn to sleep the way this vessel rides the bucking ocean is also a kind of death. Certainly I sail to New France, with my lure of

K23, intent upon meeting her there, but I should be prepared to thrive even if she fails to appear."

On every side of him, the cold viridian waters stretched as far as he could see, and for every wave that reared and whinnied upon those waters, there was a question to rear and whinny in his mind. Did the Bandaloop *really* come and go as they pleased, with no regard to normal distinctions between "life" and "death"? Where was the proof? Who *were* the Bandaloop? Where were they now? Was Kudra with them? A swell of jealousy pitched him, as if *he* were a ship upon an autumn sea.

He had placed a lot of emphasis on the perfume, but what if its scent could never reach Kudra? Or, if it could, what if she was powerless to react, or, worse, what if perfume no longer mattered to her?

And, yes, what was the connection, if any, linking Kudra and Wren? Now there was a mystery. If Wren had written in the dust of the sitting room, wouldn't that mean that she, too, was alive behind that curtain that separates us from the Other Side? And since Wren knew nothing about dematerialization, since she regarded the notion of immortality as unnatural and vain, wouldn't her message on the mantelpiece mean that a person need not harbor immortalist ambitions in order to survive after death? Did the so-called Bandaloop practices merely provide a different brand of life—longer, healthier, more flexible—and have little or nothing to do with death per se? Suppose Kudra, not Wren, had written that word (*"Erleichda!"*) employing Wren's language and handwriting, which she had somehow appropriated in the afterworld? Did a man's wives all blend into a single entity after their deaths? Would *he* blend with Navin the Ropemaker if and when he died? Was it wife soup and husband soup on the Other Side? Or was it simply soup?

At that moment, La Salle, the penniless young nobleman, approached the bow, intending to engage Alobar in genteel conversation, but Alobar's gaze was sweeping the Atlantic, and so absorbed was he in trying to imagine a soup as vast as that ocean that he heard not a word of the fellow's greeting. Miffed, La Salle walked away, his stride, despite the heaving of the deck, revealing the stubborn pride that a few years later would prevent him from admitting that he was lost in Texas when he was supposed to be exploring Louisiana (his frustrated men finally assassinated him, depriving him of the opportunity to found New Orleans, America's perfumed metropolis).

Alobar continued to survey the sea. Was that wave over there Kudra and this one Wren? Or was there a drop of Kudra, a drop of Wren in each and every wave that rose and fell? Wren. He had loved Kudra so long and so well that he'd almost forgotten how he'd once loved Wren. It had been Wren who comforted him when that first white hair slithered like a viper into his happy garden, Wren who had aided and abetted his subsequent subterfuge even though she'd been shocked by his crazy notions of personal identity and survival, Wren who had plucked him from the burial mound—and that very night spread her legs for his successor. Ah, women: the mystery of them sometimes seemed greater than the mystery of death.

One thing was certain, had it not been for Wren he wouldn't be here, seven hundred—yes, seven hundred!—years later, embarked upon the strangest adventure of his strange life. And now, after all that time, Wren had contacted him. To tell him what? *Lighten up!*

Very well. He'd lighten up. As a matter of fact, he felt as light as the bubbly froth that flew from the lips of the waves. Whatever else his long, unprecedented life might have been, it had been fun. Fun! If others should find that appraisal shallow, frivolous, so be it. To him, it seemed now to largely have been some form of play. And he vowed that in the future he would strive to keep that sense of play more in mind, for he'd grown convinced that play—more than piety, more than charity or vigilance—was what allowed human beings to transcend evil.

Quite damp now from the spray, Alobar took no step to go below. He had made one promise in the teeth of the sea, and he would stay to make another. He thought that he would persist in his devotion to his individual consciousness. Perhaps it was selfish. Perhaps someday, despite his efforts, he would end up in the one big soup, anyhow. Yet, looking at his life and the life of the world from the vantage of seven continuous and well-traveled centuries, he would say this to anyone with ears brave enough to hear it: the spirit of one individual can supersede and dismiss the entire clockworks of history.

"Our individuality is all, *all*, that we have. There are those who barter it for security, those who repress it for what they believe is the betterment of the whole society, but blessed in the twinkle of the morning star is the one who nurtures it and rides it, in grace and love and wit, from peculiar station to peculiar station along life's bittersweet route."

If there was any crack in his conviction, a seam opened, perhaps, by remembered teachings of the Buddhists at Samye, it closed when he turned his face from the stiff salt air and caught a whiff of *K23*.

Alobar was benefiting from the voyage, but for Pan it was a sea horse of a different color. It was, in fact, the most terrible experience of his life.

The old god had endured severe setbacks in the past: the disdain of Apollo and his snooty followers, the rise of cities, the hostility of the philosophers—from Aristotle to Descartes—with their smug contentions that man was reasonable and nature defective, and, most damaging of all, the concentrated efforts of the Christian church to discredit his authority by identifying him as Satan. The arrogant attacks, the dirty tricks, the indifference had rendered him weak and invisible, and might have destroyed him altogether had not an unreasonable affection for him persisted in isolated places: hidden valleys and distant mountain huts; and in the hearts of heretics, lusty women, madmen, and poets.

Recently, he'd been yanked from his indigenous crags and set down in an urban environment, a move that some might have thought would apply the coup de grace. Indeed, it was hard on him, but one cannot truly escape nature by paving streets and erecting buildings, and Pan found in Paris enough grass and trees in its parks and vacant lots, enough animal compulsions in the souls of its citizens, to sustain him. A ship, however, was a different matter.

Never had he felt so confined. The crowded hold, the unrelieved ocean. He was totally out of his realm, totally in weird Poseidon's. It was foreign and insubstantial. Were he free to play his pipes, he might set fish to jumping, might roust a mermaid from the deep (if mermaids had not died out like the nymphs). But he dare not pipe. He dare not move about or cause mischief. Even if he were free to do so, he was in no condition. He was seasick.

If that were only the worst of it. . . . The idea of an invisible leaning over a rail, broadcasting green bile from a stomach nobody could see, is almost comic. Alas, something more insidious than the rocking ship was sickening Pan. He was becoming emotionally ill, as well. And the cause was the perfume.

Pan had hit upon the perfect disguise, all right. He no longer knew who he was. The perfume separated him from him, dismantled his persona. Invisibility itself was alienating. When he drank from a spring, only waterbugs looked back at him, and whose body was that that itched, whose hand that did the scratching? In his invisibility he had become increasingly attached to his odor, occupying it as though it were a shell, a second body, familiar and orienting, home foul home. From the start, the various perfumes had had a confusing effect on him, but his native aroma made short work of them, generally, and it was seldom very long before he was cheerfully, securely stinking again like an old furnace stoked with gonads. K23 was a different matter. It obscured his house of smell the way a mist would sometimes erase his favorite crag; a cloud without pockets, drifting in the direction of the Void.

Ironically, he rather liked the new perfume. The jasmine blew like a soft wind from Egypt across the scruffy pastures of his mind, the beet thumped a dance drum with scrotum-tightening rhythms. Together, they dulled the ache that had pierced his breast since birth. But could it be that that ancient sadness was as necessary to his identity as his odor?

On dry land, he had managed to keep some bearings. The rocks and leaves had seen to that. At sea, however, he was lost. He retched and did not recognize who was retching. Twice a day, Alobar came to anoint him, sniffing him out at whatever rail he clung to or in whatever rope bin he lay groaning. Pan realized that each application of the scent only made him foggier, but, like a drug addict, he was already too foggy to resist further fogginess.

As the *Mississippi Poodle* approached New France, smelling sweeter by far than any ship ever had after a transatlantic crossing, its crew whistling as it worked, its mates hiding behind some barrels in tender embrace, Alobar on the bow facing the future with a silly grin, Pan was curled in pukey delirium close to dying.

What caused him to suddenly leap to his wobbly hooves? What burst of madness fired his motor? Two things, probably. A gull, the first they'd seen in weeks, swooped low over the mastpole, shrieking loudly. At that very instant, one of the few women aboard walked by the corner where Pan lay. She happened to be menstruating. Perhaps the smell of blood, dark and chthonian, at the precise moment that the bird screamed, awakened something deep and intrinsic in what remained of Pan's consciousness. Perhaps it would have spoken to something inside us, as well, were our barriers down, and perhaps we had just as soon not probe that primal pie. In any event, the god sprang up, possessed. Stumbling and reeling, he rushed through the bulkhead toward Alobar's hammock.

Pan snatched up Alobar's sack, threw it over his shoulder, and, not caring how the sight of a levitating bag might frighten the passengers, climbed the ladder to topside. Heading directly to the rail, over which he'd spewed every morsel Alobar had fed him since Gibraltar, he opened the sack and hurled the jug, the one and only jug, of *K23* into the ocean.

Then, as Alobar looked on in horror, Pan pulled out the bottle. He held it aloft for a second or two, as if admiring (or puzzling over) the image of himself piping clownishly, mockingly, sensually, powerfully, in some forgotten time. A sunbeam struck the bluish glass and caromed off the weedy brow of the figure embossed there, the creature that seemed to be laughing, even as it piped a poignant tune; laughing at the puny endeavors of man. A second sunbeam bounced off its stopper. Then it fell.

Whereas the heavy jug had plummeted without hesitation

to the bottom, Kudra's bottle, barely half full of perfume, bobbed to the surface. And stayed there. Clinging like lint to the blue serge shoulder of the sea.

Away it bobbed, swiftly out of range of net or hook, floating southward on the current, sparkling, scenting, bumping the occasional whisker or fin, destined to eventually loop the Floridian peninsula, where it would languish in waters well suited to its contents—until the night when hurricane tides would beach it. And bury it. In the Mississippi mud.

SEATTLE

"ORDER IN! Hi, Ricki. I'd like . . ."

"Nine Fantasy Islands, six steel-belted radials, one Aztec ceremony with obsidian swizzle stick, twelve makes-you-invincibles, and an emergency landing with a cherry."

"Whoa! *You're* in a good mood tonight."

Ricki leaned across the mahogany, resting her arms on the chrome rails that separated the waitress station from the rest of the bar. It was a fine, old bar, long and curved like a tusk and so solid that the entire membership of the Fraternal Order of Belligerent Drunks of America could not make it budge. Ricki's bare arms, damp and rather hairy, seemed frail against the monolithic bar, but her smile more than held its own.

"Good mood? Honey, my antlers are in the treetops. And yours are gonna be there, too, when you hear the news."

Priscilla set down her tray. "What news?" she asked.

"Two pieces of news, actually. The first is that the Daughters of the Daily Special are meeting Monday. And I have it on good authority they're gonna approve your grant."

The brickload of fatigue that Priscilla was carrying suddenly turned into brick soufflé. "You're kidding."

"Nope."

Hummingbird soufflé. Cobweb soufflé. "How much? Do you know?"

"Twenty-five hundred is the figure I've heard."

Nitrous oxide soufflé. "No lie?!" Priscilla didn't require a pocket calculator to determine that twenty-five hundred dollars would purchase three ounces of prime jasmine oil and leave enough to support her for a couple of months while she devoted all her time to identifying, and perhaps acquiring, that enigmatic base note. It would also mean that she wouldn't have to rely on her stepmother for assistance. "God Almighty, that's wonderful!"

"I thought you'd be pleased. Gimme your order and I'll tell you the rest of the news."

"Three Carta Blancas and a 'rita is all."

Ricki began to mix the margarita. "That's a 'rita and three Carta Blancas, Pris," said Ricki sternly, reminding her of the hierarchy of ordering.

"Sorry," Priscilla sighed. "I'm just excited," she explained, knowing full well that this was destined to be a shift like any other, complete with dropped menus, spilled cocktails, botched orders, undercharges, overcharges, pinches from the lecherous and insults from the chaste. Ah, but there was relief in sight. A twenty-five-hundred-dollar rainbow with perfume at one end and, who knows, maybe the perfect taco at the other.

"Now," said Ricki, uncapping the beers and placing them on Priscilla's tray, "the crowning mojo is, the clinic says my infection is totally cleared up. So you and I can stay together tomorrow night."

Priscilla labored to fake a smile. "Gee, that's great, Rick. But you do remember that I have something going tomorrow night. It's that dinner party at the Last Laugh Foundation."

"You mean you're actually gonna go to that?"

"Well, yeah. It's got my curiosity up."

"Okay, if you wanna waste your time, go ahead. Bunch of druggy weirdos putting on the ritz for some big scientist who's probably also a druggy weirdo, if the truth be known. It's not my cup of cake."

"Well, I've decided to go."

"All right. I'll meet you afterward."

"It might be late."

"So what? I'll wait up for you."

Priscilla shrugged with resignation. *It looks like it's just my destiny to turn queer,* she thought. *Why fight it?* To Ricki she said, "Your place or mine?" not caring that two other waitresses were lined up behind her, impatient to place their orders but savoring every word.

"Yours is closer."

"It's a mess."

"It's always a mess."

"I guess it is. How come your place is always so neat? How do you do it? With mirrors?"

Ricki shook her head. "My lunar sign is in Virgo," she said. "Every month when the moon is full, I'm driven to balance my checkbook and straighten up my apartment. I can't help myself. Instead of a werewolf, I turn into an accountant."

"Who can only be killed with a silver dildo," called Priscilla, walking away with her drinks while her fellow employees, now four deep in front of the waitress station, looked on in disgust and bewilderment.

She completed the Saturday shift with no more than the usual mishaps. There was a birthday party at one of her tables, which meant that she had to deliver a complimentary cake with lighted candle and sing "Happy Birthday" to the recipient, a chore that she always despised. She felt better, however, when she overheard another customer, a famous young fashion photographer from Madrid, who was being treated to El Papa Muerta's Uncle Ben paella by some Seattle department store executives, proclaim, "How embarrassing, how gauche! In Europe such vulgarity would never happen. A birthday is a private affair. Only in America would it be a cheap public display." The last thing she did before she went off duty was to order a birthday cake sent to the photographer at his table.

On the way out, she gave Ricki her spare key so that the bartender could let herself in to wait for her on Sunday night. "See you after the party," Pris said. "Thanks for the good news."

"I'm sure you'll find a way to repay me," said Ricki. She winked.

Priscilla bicycled home, where, relieved by the absence of beet at her door and bolstered by the prospect of financial aid, she allowed herself the rare luxury of going straight to bed. In her dreams, however, she mixed fragrances continuously, awakening the next morning, still in uniform, feeling almost as tired as if she had worked through the night.

Having slept with her tips in her pocket, she found red welts the size of quarters on her thigh when she showered. "Marked by the Beast!" she exclaimed. "Well, there's one thing to be said for money. It can make you rich."

After a breakfast of half-fresh doughnuts and canned Carnation milk, she attacked the apartment with sponge and cleanser, with mop and broom, with organizational tactics for which she'd previously exhibited little aptitude. She would not settle for less than spick-and-span. "Won't Ricki be surprised," she said.

In the afternoon, she napped. She dreamed of her father. They were in his palace in Mexico. He was rubbing salve into the welts on her thigh. V'lu Jackson was down on all fours, scrubbing the palace floor. There was a strong odor of ammonia. The odor was still there when Priscilla awoke. For a whole minute, she did not recognize her own apartment.

The least wrinkled garment—and even it had as many folds as the waddles of a Republican president—in her closet was a green knit dress given to her by her ex-husband, the Argentine accordion ace, Effecto Partido. She hung it in the bathroom with the shower on hot and full, until the steam performed the equivalent of one of those partially successful face-lifts administered to aging actresses. The dress looked good on her. It called attention to the violet in her eyes. She applied eye shadow and lipstick and as a finishing touch, forced earring wires through the virtually grown-over holes in her lobes. The earrings were also a gift from Effecto. They were tiny accordions.

With a tingle of excitement, she decided to call for a taxi. The Last Laugh Foundation was only a dozen blocks away, but it was raining, as usual, and she just couldn't ride her bike in her best dress. She turned the latch, checking twice to ascertain that the door was tightly locked, then went downstairs to wait for the cab. "If a beet comes tonight, that carnivore Ricki can deal with it," she said. She was chuckling softly when she climbed into the Farwest taxi.

The cab streaked through the wet streets with a noise like an asp. Alas, before Priscilla could fully enjoy the blur of neon, the crisp vinyl upholstery, the mystery crackle of the two-way radio, she was at her destination. She showed her invitation to one of a half-dozen security guards—triple the usual number—and was immediately let through the iron gate, while from the excluded crowd that spilled out front, even in the chilly drizzle that was falling, there arose loud grumbles and cries of "Who the hell is she?" Her lungs filled momentarily with a sort of golden gas, that righteous helium that inflates the diaphragm of any honest person who finds himself or herself suddenly one of an elite. Slightly giddy with privilege, she stumbled along a gravel path that wound through a rhododendron garden and led to the front steps of the mansion. She was beginning to have visions of Wally Lester's Mexican palace. They ceased when she noticed a squashed slug on the steps.

The brass door-knocker was in the shape of a fairy. Little wings and wand and everything. "Hmm," said Priscilla. She thought that she would feel silly, putting it to its intended purpose, but it was okay. She was still regarding the knocker when a girl about eight years old opened the door and admitted her. "My daddy believes in fairies," the child said. "Hmm," replied Priscilla.

Although the ivy-covered exterior of the Last Laugh Foundation led one to expect brown leather furniture, worn but expensive Oriental carpets, carved wood ceilings, and Flemish tapestries depicting medieval stag hunts or mythological rowdies, the interior proved to be bright and modern: chrome, smoked glass, canvas couches in bold primary hues. The floors were polished hardwood. The walls were pure white. "White as alkaloid crystals," Wiggs Dannyboy was to say. "White as yeti dung, white as the Sabbath, white as God's own belly. Floral patterns, they're for your doomed. Your immortalist wall is a white one." Here and there were prints

by M.C. Escher, a multiplication of stiff, metamorphic images that assured the viewer that the world is a puzzle and
life a loop and that is that. (Escher is sneered at by critics,
but he may be one of the few artists who didn't lie to us.)
Above the fireplace, in which Pres-to-logs were smoldering,
was a display of headhunting equipment, probably relics of
the days when Dr. Dannyboy was a working anthropologist.
"Would you care for a cocktail?" the little girl asked. You bet.

Standing about the large room were approximately twenty
people, none of whom seemed any more at home there than
Priscilla. She thought she recognized one of the guests. He
was, oddly enough, a fragrance wholesaler, the only one in
the Pacific Northwest. She had made modest purchases from
him. It was he who would order French jasmine oil for her, if
the educated waitresses did, indeed, grant her the funds with
which to buy it. She was about to approach him, gulping
bourbon and ginger ale all the while, when Dr. Dannyboy
fairly burst into the room, introduced himself loudly, and
called the gathering to table.

The dining room was formal in character, despite the fact
that its long table was made of red plastic, the chairs of
chrome tubes and purple canvas. The walls here were white,
as well, adorned by another Escher or two, commenting
again on the poetic transformations that occur systematically,
if mysteriously, in the seemingly endless loop of life. Candles
blazed in a plastic candelabrum. The last chrysanthemums of
autumn hung their heads apprehensively over the rim of a
vase, like voyagers whose crowded boat was steaming into a
strange and possibly dangerous port. The chrysanthemums
were part of a centerpiece that included some beets.

Priscilla failed to notice the beets right away. Her gaze was
concentrated upon Dr. Dannyboy. That a one-eyed man of
fifty could be so handsome! Dannyboy was slender, svelte,
and nimble, a tanned, athletic man with an Airstream nest of
silver curls, teeth like the spots on dominoes, and more
twinkle in his single eye than most men have in a pair. A
high-voltage blue, the eye color was in aesthetic contrast to
the patch that he wore on the right side, the patch being
white vinyl with a painted green shamrock in its center.

Priscilla had seen photographs of him, of course, taken both before and after he lost his eye, but they had barely hinted at the charm that spilled out of him like foam out of an ale mug.

Of his background, she knew a little. Brilliant young anthropologist who left his native Dublin to teach at Harvard, where he experimented with mind-altering chemicals beyond the call of academic duty. Lost his professorship, journeyed to the Amazon to munch vision vine with the Indians, returning to the United States as a self-styled psychedelic prophet, or "electronic shaman," as he called himself, appearing on TV talk shows, lecturing on campuses everywhere, promoting with considerable flair the notion that certain drugs can raise consciousness and that persons with elevated consciousness are less apt to be violent, greedy, fearful, or repressed. Since it was hardly in the best national interest to relieve citizens of their violence, greed, fear, or repression, the government acted to silence Dr. Dannyboy by arresting him on a phony marijuana charge and checking him into the steel hotel. Escaped, only to be nabbed two years later on a Costa Rican orchid farm, and imprisoned again. Paroled after nearly a decade, during which time he lost an eye to a sadistic prison guard and impregnated his wife by smuggling out his semen in a dinner roll. Turned up in Seattle a couple of years back to quietly (for him) found an institution devoted to "immortality and longevity research."

All this Priscilla knew, but it seemed to have nothing to do with the attractive man who sat at the head of the table in Irish tweeds, sipping red wine, tapping from time to time his garish eye patch with his salad fork, and holding forth on a variety of topics. "England!" she heard him bellow with distaste. "How can a country that cannot produce ice cubes in abundance be hopin' to palm itself off as a major civilization?" Moments later, he had turned his attention to grammar: "There are no such things as synonyms!" he practically shouted. "Deluge is not the same as flood!" After each of these pronouncements, he erupted with laughter, almost as if making fun of what he'd just so passionately proclaimed.

At the other end of the table, acting as hostess, was Dannyboy's young daughter, Huxley Anne. Priscilla sat to

Huxley Anne's left. The place directly across from Priscilla
was vacant. "There was a colored woman supposed to eat
there," volunteered Huxley Anne, "but she didn't come.
Maybe she's late. She lives long away." The place to the right
of Dannyboy was likewise unoccupied. "That's Dr. Morgenstern's dish," explained the little girl. "He'll be downstairs
soon as he finishes jumping."

"Jumping?" asked Priscilla.

"Uh-huh," said Huxley Anne, giggling. Before she could
say more, Professor Morgenstern entered the room and made
to take his place. A tall, thickset German, gray-suited, be-
spectacled, bald as a bomb, the noted chemist might have
appeared the epitome of the cold, clear-eyed, methodical,
reasoning man were he not panting like a Saint Bernard on
avalanche patrol. His face was as red as a Christmas sock, and
his heart was pounding so hard that his bow tie was bouncing.

Despite the fact that the guest of honor was obviously and
oddly out of breath, the others at table were relieved to see
him. They were, for the most part, members of Seattle's
scientific fraternity—department heads from the University
of Washington, Boeing Aircraft physicists, research chemists
at Swedish Hospital, mayoral advisers on medicine and
technology—and they had been ill at ease in the company of
Wiggs Dannyboy, what with his careless pronouncements
and boisterous laughter. Wary of Dannyboy's reputation, the
good academics probably believed their host loaded on some
arcane substance, though Priscilla had been around both
French Quarter trippers and Irish Channel blarneymongers
long enough to recognize that this particular brand of bullshit
was not artificially induced.

At any rate, the guests were visibly relieved when Dr.
Morgenstern joined them, and they applauded when Wiggs
lifted his much-consulted wineglass and said, "Ladies and
gentlemen, let us be welcomin' to Seattle, to the Last Laugh
Foundation, to our pleasant company here on this rainy November eve, the world's only double Nobel laureate, your
Dr. Wolfgang Morgenstern."

As the applause died out and the chemist sat down to
analyze the minestrone soup, little Huxley Anne leaned over

to Pris and whispered, "Wolfgang, show us some tricks on
your Nobel lariat. That's what my daddy says. Hee hee."
Priscilla laughed at that. Wiggs must have heard her laugh,
because he grinned approvingly in her direction and waved at
her with his soup spoon.

The salmon linguine was tasty, and Huxley Anne, who was
edging toward roly-poliness, got seriously involved with it.
The seat across from Priscilla remained vacant. The other
guests attempted to converse with the rather taciturn Dr.
Morgenstern. Most of their questions were fielded by Wiggs
Dannyboy, who, after a rational sentence or two, would issue
some immortalist epigram, such as, "If you can't take it with
you, don't go," or "Death is a grave mistake," followed by a
jolly roar from deep within his tweeds—and pained smiles
from the polite diners. Eating in silence, Priscilla was mildly
amused by it all—until she spotted the trio of raw beets in
the centerpiece.

Could Dannyboy be behind the produce deposits at her
doorsill? And if so, to what possible end? She sank into a
swamp of spooky speculation, from which she emerged with a
start when a maid inquired if she wanted chocolate mousse or
apple slices for dessert. "Uh, er, beg your pardon?" mumbled
Priscilla.

"How do you feel about calories?" asked the maid, display-
ing the dessert tray.

"Well, there are more of them than there are of us," said
Pris. She selected the mousse.

Huxley Anne squealed at this, and for the second time
during the meal, Wiggs wagged a utensil at Priscilla and
regarded her warmly.

After coffee, the guests thinned out rapidly. They had
obviously come solely to meet Wolfgang Morgenstern, and
having accomplished that, to greater or lesser degrees of
disappointment, they made for the exit. (Exit, not egress.
There are no such things as synonyms.) "Interesting," thought
Priscilla, "these people wanting out so badly and all those
others on the street wanting in." She elected to join the
small, brave group that gathered in the front room for brandy
and tobacco. She thought perhaps there might be a tour of

the laboratories later. Mostly she wished to inquire about those beets on the table.

"I have to go to bed now, Miz . . . ?"

"Partido. Miz Partido. But you can call me Priscilla."

"I have to go to bed now, Priscilla. It's after ten and the cigar smoke makes me dizzy."

"Goodnight, Huxley Anne. It's been totally awesome." She shook the child's chubby hand. "Say, do you think your daddy will let us have a peek at his laboratories?"

The little girl looked puzzled. "*What* labbertories?" she asked.

"Hmm," said Priscilla. "No labs? Well, I guess I shouldn't be surprised. Can you show me where you hung my raincoat? Cigar smoke makes me dizzy, too."

She downed her cognac in a single gulp, causing evidence of alcohol trauma to roll down her cheeks as she donned her yellow vinyl slicker. She waved goodbye to the blurry figure of Huxley Anne that was ascending the stairs, and somewhat timidly, despite being three-quarters drunk, approached her host. He was stationed in front of the fireplace, pointing out some feathered skinning knives to an academic-looking couple that was trying its best to get away in order to speak to Dr. Morgenstern. "Your cannibal gourmet is partial to the palm o' the hand," Wiggs was saying, "but his piece de résistance is the testicles. Tried them myself once. Bloody delicious!" The woman gasped.

"Excuse me, please. Dr. Dannyboy . . ."

Wiggs turned to face Priscilla, his good eye, so bright with intelligence and rebellion, swinging like a beacon. The shamrock patch followed in its wake. "You're not leavin'?"

"Yep. I don't know what I'm doing here in the first place. But thanks for dinner. Bloody delicious."

The couple fled. Dannyboy grinned. "Sure and go on with you. The likes of you is a wee bit o' delicious, as well." O' delicious is what he said and o' delicious is probably what he meant, o' palatable, o' savory, and o' delectable being unacceptable synonyms. "Do you have to be runnin'?"

The glint in his eye! The lilt in his voice! Her estrogen level accelerated from zero to sixty in one-point-nine seconds. The gravity force was so great it snapped her pelvis back and stiffened her nipples. It was with difficulty that she replied, "I do. I have a date."

"A date, eh? You're actin' none too happy about it. As a matter of fact, darlin', if I may say as much, you strike me as an unhappy woman overall. And I say as much even though you were the only guest here this evening with a sense o' humor. Which is to say, you were the only guest with any wisdom about you."

Priscilla was rather taken aback. She didn't know whether to feel insulted or flattered. "I'm fine," she said. "I've been kinda tired. You're jumping to conclusions. Besides, unhappiness is natural. I'm not one of those bubbleheads that spend all their time trying to avoid the normal misery of life."

She moved toward the front door, but none too swiftly. He followed.

"Sure and life is a lot o' misery, all right, and death is more misery, yet. Dread, fear, anxiety, guilt, even a bit o' neurosis, are perfectly natural responses to a life that promises such an unacceptable end. The trick is not to take such responses too seriously, not to trivialize your all too short stay in your carton o' flesh by cooperatin' with misery."

"Seems to me," said Priscilla, snapping and unsnapping the collar of her slicker, "that the so-called happy people are the ones who are trivial. Avoiding reality and never thinking about anything important."

"Reality is subjective, and there's an unenlightened tendency in this culture to regard something as 'important' only if 'tis sober and severe. Sure and still you're right about your Cheerful Dumb, only they're not so much happy as lobotomized. But your Gloomy Smart are just as ridiculous. When you're unhappy, you get to pay a lot of attention to yourself. And you get to take yourself oh so very seriously. Your truly happy people, which is to say, your people who truly *like* themselves, they don't think about themselves very much. Your unhappy person resents it when you try to cheer him up, because that means he has to stop dwellin' on himself and start payin' attention to the universe. Unhappiness is the ultimate form o' self-indulgence."

Did he think she was an *audience* or something? Couldn't he tell that she was an off-duty waitress full of mousse and booze, and stuck on a collision course with the lips of a pretty Italian bartender? "Jesus," she said. "You talk like a book."

"That's not surprisin'."

"You mean you read too much?"

"There's no such thing. Unless it's prissy academic novels that you're readin'. No, I mean that when I was a wee lad, I used to climb into my parents' bed of a morning early, crawl in between my mum and dad, and each o' them would immediately roll over and turn a back to me, just like they were a pair o' bookends. It's only natural I grew up thinkin' I was a bloody volume."

"Parental rejection, uh? There's a subject I know inside out. It doesn't appear to have slowed you down."

"Would you be likin' to discuss it?"

"No," she said. She saw her opening and went for it. "I'd be liking to discuss beets."

A laugh went off in his throat like a rat-bomb, sending the last of the guests scurrying for their bumbershoots. His eye closed and then slowly opened, a process that took so long that by the time his iris was up to full glint, the house had been cleared of Seattle scientists and Wolfgang Morgenstern was halfway up the stairs. "Beets, you say?"

"Right! I want to know why I was invited here tonight and why the center of your dining room table bears a striking resemblance to my doorjamb."

Her tone was so firm that he could have set his brandy on it.

"Ah. Indeed. Yes. Well, to be perfectly frank, Miss Partido, darlin', there was a ration o' beets on my table tonight *because* there has been beets at your very own door—but, alas, I'm not sure o' the connection myself. Except that it has something to do with the thousand-year-old janitor and his perfume."

She looked him over pore by pore. He was slightly sloshed and terribly flaky (and cute in that daddy way that always made her heart roll over), but he wasn't surfing the psychedelic billows, she was reassured of that. Moreover, he seemed sincere. "What are you talking about?" she asked.

"Sure and what am I talkin' about, indeed. I was hopin' we could get into that tonight, but only one o' you showed up. Actually, I've known all week that Marcel LeFever wouldn't be here until *next* Sunday, but I really was expectin' the other—"

"Wait a minute. Marcel LeFever? The perfumer?"

"The one and the same."

Priscilla had heard Bunny LeFever speak at a perfumers' convention. It had been quite a speech. It had, in some crazy way, changed her life. She unsnapped her slicker. "I think we need to sit down and talk," she said.

"All right, then," he said, helping her out of the coat. "I'll be gettin' us a splash o' something. And, say, Miss Partido, though I know it's an affront to the Virgin Mary to be mixin' business with pleasure, pleasure *is* my business—the extension o' pleasure, indefinitely, eternally—and my immortal soul is warmed by the loveliness o' you, you're a sight for sore eyes, so to speak"—he tapped his shamrock patch with his empty snifter—"and I deserve to be chained by night in a church basement without company o' cassette player if I am not man enough to ask you for the teeniest, slightest brush of oral-muscular affection."

Jesus, she thought. *I bet the son of a bitch does believe in fairies*. But she couldn't help herself. She kissed him.

Meanwhile, a dozen blocks away, Ricki, carrying a pound of gift-wrapped chocolate, had let herself into Priscilla's apartment. There had been no trick to that. The door wasn't locked. It had been slightly ajar, in fact. Ricki shook her head. "Where is that girl's mind *at*?" she wondered.

In addition, the apartment was in the worst state Ricki had ever seen it. True, no gnarled old beets were in evidence, and it smelled as if it had been recently scoured—the odor of ammonia cut right through the floral fragrances in the makeshift laboratory—but drawers were out of the dresser, the kitchenette cupboard looked as if it had been rifled by a starving ape, and possessions were scattered everywhere. There were sanitary napkins all over the bathroom, that's how bad it was.

Ricki rolled up her sweatshirt sleeves and set to putting the place in order. It took her the best of two hours—lucky it was only a studio apartment—but her Virgo exactitude finally prevailed. "Won't Pris be surprised," she said. "It's after midnight. I hope she gets home soon."

NEW ORLEANS

THE MINUTE YOU LAND IN NEW ORLEANS, something wet and dark leaps on you and starts humping you like a swamp dog in heat, and the only way to get that aspect of New Orleans off you is to eat it off. That means beignets and crayfish bisque and jambalaya, it means shrimp remoulade, pecan pie, and red beans with rice, it means elegant pompano au papillote, funky filé z'herbes, and raw oysters by the dozen, it means grillades for breakfast, a po' boy with chowchow at bedtime, and tubs of gumbo in between. It is not unusual for a visitor to the city to gain fifteen pounds in a week—yet the alternative is a whole lot worse. If you don't eat day and night, if you don't constantly funnel the indigenous flavors into your bloodstream, then the mystery beast will go right on humping you, and you will feel its sordid presence rubbing against you long after you have left town. In fact, like any sex offender, it can leave permanent psychological scars.

You would think that the natives would be immune, and to a certain extent they are, but even a lifelong resident of New Orleans must do his or her share of Creole consumption or suffer consequences. The cuisine is glorious, of course, and the fact that the people of New Orleans are compelled to dine out so often should not be considered a hardship in any sense other than financial. Ah, but there are underlying motives about which southern gentry will not speak. Even riffraff are hesitant to acknowledge the disgusting specter that haunts their city. They feed the loa and make the best of it.

When citizens have been out of town for a while, they know by instinct that no matter how well they may have dined on their journey, they must fend off the beast immediately upon their return. Thus, V'lu Jackson stepped off the jetliner from Seattle to find herself craving a fancy platter of Arnaud's daube panée, accompanied by a glass of Bichot Chass-Montrachet (with maybe a squirt of hurricane drops for the zoom that was in it). However, to Lily Devalier, who met her at the airport, she said, "Mmm, ah sure would lak to stop by Buster Holmes, git me a mess a ribs 'fore we goes home."

And Madame Devalier said, "Gracious, cher, I dropped everything and spent a small fortune to dash all the way out to Moisant Field"—she still called New Orleans International by its original name—"to meet you, and now you want me to sit around that hole-in-the-wall while you slop and slather over ribs. Didn't they give you a meal on the plane?" She complained, but she ordered their taxi to Buster's because she secretly understood.

What Madame did *not* understand was why V'lu requested that she come to the airport. Indeed, she didn't fully understand the circumstances that had led to V'lu traveling to Seattle in the first place. She had ignored the card inviting the staff of Parfumerie Devalier to a dinner party at some Seattle place that sounded like a comedy nightclub. She suspected it was a publicity stunt for a dump where Priscilla was working. "Dr. Wolfgang Morgenstern" was probably one of those loud Jewish boys who got paid for telling dirty jokes in public. Then an envelope arrived containing a round-trip plane ticket, and a guest list that included scientists, perfumers, and, yes, Priscilla Partido. Very curious. Still, Lily refused to consider attending, but V'lu began pestering her to allow *her* to go, and while the idea of V'lu sitting down to dinner with gentlemen of science seemed ludicrous to her, curiosity, concern for Priscilla, indigestion or something else got the better of her, and she let that poor simple bayou girl go jetting off to make a fool of herself—and the shop—in a distant city that as far as Madame could tell was barely civilized.

She had worried the entire time her assistant was gone. When the telegram came asking her to meet V'lu's flight, she grew as edgy as a thirty-dollar diamond. But there V'lu was, waltzing through the terminal looking as pretty and composed as Miss Tanzania on a TV beauty pageant, and smiling like the catastrophe that swallowed the Canary Islands. And every time Madame attempted to question her about the trip, she just smiled in that smug but guilty fashion and said, "Ah powerful hungry, ma'am. We talks 'bout it after Ah eats."

Of course, V'lu wasn't threatened by starvation, it was just that she didn't fancy anything hot and nasty rubbing up against her—unless it belonged to Marcel LeFever. Or maybe Bingo Pajama. By the time the first ounce of rib sauce had slid down her gullet, the beast was slinking away, and she felt safe enough to elucidate. "Dee troof is, ma'am, to answer yo question, *no*, Ah didn't see her."

Madame was incredulous. "You didn't see Priscilla?! Wasn't she at the party?!"

"Yes, ma'am, she wuz."

"Well . . ."

"But Ah wuzn't."

Lily Devalier would have been beside herself except that there wasn't enough room at the table. (Madame D. was carrying more tonnage than any woman to dock in Buster's since Velma Middleton, or maybe Bessie Smith.) "What in God's name are you talking about, child?! You didn't go to the party?!"

"No, ma'am."

"*Sacrebleu!*" Lily pulled a handkerchief out of her old-fashioned black purse and mopped her brow. The hankie was scented with something—Bingo Pajama jasmine? Jazz powders? Or worse?—that caused several dark heads to look up knowingly from their beans and rice. "Well, what happened? What went wrong?" She was entertaining visions of V'lu getting lost in Seattle, failing to find this "Last Laughing" place, or being barred at its door.

"Nuffin. Nuffin went wrong." She let her lips stretch into that infuriatingly mysterious and self-satisfied smile. "Sompin' went right."

"*Merde*," snapped Madame Devalier, who would never permit herself to swear in English. "You better get out with it, right now—out with it!—what is going on?!"

V'lu let the words slide slowly through barbecue-colored saliva and perfect teeth: "Ah gots dee bottle."

There was scarcely any response from Madame Devalier. She merely blinked once or twice and looked dumb, or stunned, like a baby whale washed ashore on a fashionable beach.

"Ah gots dee bottle," said V'lu again.

Clearly confused, Madame blinked a few more times. She seemed almost senile. "But that is Pris's bottle," she protested weakly.

"Not any mo, it ain't!"

"You stole it from her?"

"Ah *libberated* it," said V'lu. "Dat bottle belong to our shop, it nebber wuz Miz Priscilla's, you know dat as good as me."

Madame was uncertain if she knew that or not. Having paid scant attention to the bottle, the circumstances surrounding its arrival and departure were vague to her. She squeezed her eyes shut and sniffed at her hankie, trying to remember.

Yes, it was after Pris's marriage to that old tango-wango fell apart, after her daddy died. Pris had announced, with a certain pathetic bravado, that she was going to become a perfumer after all. Nothing could have pleased Lily more. But the girl didn't want to apprentice in her stepmother's floundering shop, oh, no, she intended to enter college to study chemistry. She had a settlement from Effecto Partido and was going to use it to learn modern fragrance manufacturing. None of that old-fashioned, small-potatoes, storefront Devalier perfumery for her. Lily was a little hurt, but she was aware that times had changed and that to a younger generation her ways were quaint, if not obsolete. In the end, she sent Pris off to Vanderbilt University with her blessings.

Although she earned straight A's, Priscilla had remained restless and melancholy, and upon completion of her freshman year had returned to New Orleans, claiming that she was through with college and wanted to take over Parfumerie

Devalier. In the meantime, however, Madame had accepted as her assistant a young black woman from Belle Bayou, the plantation owned by a branch of the Devalier family. V'lu Jackson was eager and bright, though almost laughably countrified, and Madame had grown fond of her. She wasn't going to kick V'lu out the door in favor of Pris when Pris was liable to change her mind at any moment and go chasing after a fortune, an older man, or both. Moreover, V'lu functioned as Madame's maid as well as her shop assistant, a duty for which Priscilla would have neither instinct nor inclination. And when it came to loyalty and respect, V'lu was more like a daughter to her than Priscilla had ever been.

Madame informed Pris that she could stay for the summer, providing she earned her keep, but that come September she would have to make other arrangements. Pris was none too happy with that, but Effecto's settlement was fast dwindling and she hadn't much choice. She worked diligently, if clumsily, and minded her manners, although she often walked around with her lower lip sticking out so far she could have eaten tomatoes through a tennis racket.

It was during that summer, yes, that was when it was all right, that there arrived the bottle over which there has been such a silly commotion. Some beachcombers brought it in, Madame recalled, a retired couple. They had dug it out of the mud near the mouth of the Mississippi, and since it was obviously quite old, they thought it might be of interest to someone in the perfume trade. Having recently moved into a mobile home, they had little room for bric-a-brac, and besides, the fellow on the side of the bottle was some sort of devil whose image didn't belong in a Christian household. They were donating their find to the Parfumerie Devalier, they said, because they had purchased a small vial of scent there forty-five years earlier on their honeymoon.

Yes, yes, it was as clear to Lily now as dew on a shoelace; Pris and V'lu had been standing behind the retail counter, and Pris was saying, "College is fun and you can learn a lot of interesting stuff, but if you really want to get rich, you've got to get out in the world and start something up on your own." Sniffing her handkerchief, Madame could hear those words as plain as if they were on Buster's menu. And it was right then, she remembered, that the beachcombers had come in with the bottle and made their little presentation.

She'd been busy at her desk, working on the books, figuring if there was any way to put the shop back on its feet, put it back to showing a profit from perfume so she wouldn't have to dabble in that . . . that other work. From the rear of the shop, she thanked the couple for their nostalgic gesture, but she didn't get up. She could tell at a distance that the bottle was too large to have held a truly fine perfume; that, in any case, there were only a few drops left in it, and time and tide had no doubt rendered those drops impotent long ago. It had a pleasing shape, all right, and its bluish tint lent it a mystic aura. What with that weird horned figure embossed on the side, it would make an excellent container for mojo lotion or moon medicine were she forced by cruel circumstances to add to the hoodoo pharmacopoeia. She would examine it at her leisure, evaluating then its possible use to her. Meanwhile, speaking of hoodoo, she had some red ink to turn black.

Her face was deep in the ledger, as it was now deep in her scented hankie, when Pris and V'lu pulled the stopper out of the bottle and began oohing and aahing over the aroma it released. What did they know, a rustic plantation pickaninny and a dropped-out college girl? She would put her professional snout to the vessel when she had a moment, but really, what olfactory excitement could there be in a virtually empty curiosity exhumed from the mud?

Having wrestled with the balance sheet until dinner, Madame had begun to nod almost upon swallowing her last spoonful of gumbo. She went to bed without ever having tested the depleted contents of the antique. And during the night, Priscilla had eloped with the bottle much as she had with Effecto Partido (only this time nobody had had to play an accordion outside her window). Well, summer was ending, anyway, so good-bye, Pris, honey, and God bless. Her exodus was probably for the best. As for the bottle, it was unimportant, although in the ensuing three years, V'lu had found endless occasions to squawk about it.

When Lily removed the hankie from her face and snapped out of her trance, she found V'lu gnawing delicately at the corner of a rib. Diners who had been staring returned to their meals. One, with a mouthful of cornbread, whispered to his companion, "That ol' Madame D. got plant powers." He didn't specify which plant.

"V'lu, I don't especially approve of what you've done. It was dishonest and unnecessary. That bottle obviously meant something to Priscilla, it was part of her fantasy. Little value it is to us."

"Ah doesn't wants you to say anubber word until you smells it, ma'am. You ain't nebber smelled it!"

"Well . . ."

"It gots a jasmine theme, a *mighty* jasmine theme, near bouts as good as our Bingo Pajama flowers. It gots a citrus top note, lak our boof gots. And it gots something else, ma'am, it gots a bottom note. It gots a base whut does dee job!"

"Just the same, Priscilla was—"

"Smell it."

"But—"

"Smell it!"

"All right. But not in here."

They walked out onto Burgandy Street as the sun was setting. It was late November, and there was a chill in the air, but there were people on balconies and people on stoops. They were in one of the few sections of the French Quarter where blacks still lived, most of them having been driven across the North Rampart Street boundary by escalating rents. It seemed the sleazier the Quarter got, the more it cost to live there.

Of the buildings on Burgandy, most were four-room Creole cottages that lacked the shady courtyards where, out of sight of tourists and photographers, the true social life of the Quarter transpired. Here, residents sat on their stoops instead, yet even thus exposed, they managed to protect their privacy. A stranger could watch their languid movements, hear their laughter and music, smell the spicy foods they ate, but could never expect to be a part of those things. And when they went inside and shut their doors, their habits became as unknowable as those of ancient Congolese. The historian Kolb has called New Orleans "a city that has never truly been in the mainstream of American life." Although an indoors city to a large extent, New Orleans watches less television than any town its size in the nation. What does it do, then, behind those closed shutters? What, indeed?

If New Orleans is not fully in the mainstream of culture, neither is it fully in the mainstream of time. Lacking a well-defined present, it lives somewhere between its past and its future, as if uncertain whether to advance or to retreat. Perhaps it is its perpetual ambivalence that is its secret charm. Somewhere between Preservation Hall and the Superdome, between voodoo and cybernetics, New Orleans listens eagerly to the seductive promises of the future but keeps at least one foot firmly planted in its history, and in the end, conforms, like an artist, not to the world but to its own inner being—ever mindful of its personal style.

Turning down St. Ann Street, toward Jackson Square and the river, the two women—the older, white, painted, and bejeweled one simultaneously lumbering and waddling, as if the bear and the duck on the animated Hamms beer commercial had coupled and issued an illicit offspring; the younger black one wiggling pertly on sleek hams—were together an expression of the city's style. And it was completely in character when they stopped beside a tall wrought-iron gate, spiky with fleurs-de-lis, so that the younger could remove a bottle from her weekend bag and pass it furtively to the other.

"Let go of it, I have it," said Madame Devalier. "*Mon Dieu*, you'd think it was going to run away." She scrutinized the bottle for a while in the waning light, scowling at the devilish figure that seemed at once so mischievous and so forlorn. "Harumph," she snorted. His image sat no easier with her Catholic sentiments than it had with the superstitions of the Southern Baptist beachcombers. "Harumph."

"We gots to be careful. Miz Priscilla coulda call dee po-lice or somethin'. Dat's why Ah ax you to meets me at dee airpote. You thinks it okay to take it to dee shop?"

Madame didn't hear a word. She had removed the tight stopper, and her nostrils were hovering, quivering; the open bays of a mother ship beaming up cargo. Indeed, her nose, her whole head, seemed to be growing heavier, larger as she inhaled; and her pulled-back hair, dyed as black as Satchmo's coronet case, was actually rippling in the Tabasco dusk.

Like a baby grand in a town without piano movers, Madame had settled firmly into place, her bulk as transfixed as a wild hog in truck lights. A jazz funeral could have marched through the gates of her corset, and she wouldn't have squirmed. To a passerby, to V'lu, perhaps, she was a dumpy old lady with her feet in black lace-ups and her nose to a bottle top, but inside her swelling head, up among the rafters of the spheno-ethmoidal recess, a music was rising, a happiness was rising; her dumpy old heart was rising, made buoyant and girlish again, a lost beach ball blown miles along a levee, illuminated by heat lightning.

V'lu waited patiently. She knew that it was a good sign that Madame was taking so long. She could almost feel the energy radiating from the unfashionable pleats of Madame's midnight blue chemise, she could sense it etching lines in Madame's thick rouge and collecting in the colored hollows of the gems she wore. V'lu tapped her Tootsie Roll toes and waited.

The sun had set, and St. Ann Street was in darkness by the time Lily restoppered the bottle and handed it back to V'lu. Her face was radiant, although whether from memory or expectation nobody could tell. "I wish Papa could have smelled it." Her voice was both shaky and blissful, and for quite a while that was all she said.

They walked in silence, the old woman swinging her purse. As they reached Royal Street and turned left toward the shop, she said, "I'm proud of you, V'lu, and Pris, too. You recognized its magnificence right away. It's for the two of you that I am going to interpret that base note. Right now I am mystified as to what it might be. There's not enough liquid left in the bottle to have it analyzed by a chemistry lab. But I shall find it, you can count on that! Lily Devalier may not be a celebrated nose like Bunny LeFever, she may have indulged in practices for which any respectable perfumer would hang their head in shame, but she knows her perfume, believe her, she knows the bricks of perfume and the mortar of perfume, and she knows each and every one of the circuits and emotions of perfume." She paused. "I think this stuff must be Egyptian. I've been told some of their perfumes have retained their boof after three thousand years. And then the bottle!" She crossed herself, still swinging her purse. "Some sex demon out of pagan Egypt. They'd love his kind at Mardi Gras. His boof is heavenly, though. That poor little Pris. Such an amateur. She had about as much chance as a snowball in Gulfport of tracking down that base note. Right?"

"You right."

"But I will track it down. I will recreate this great perfume—with our jasmine it will be even greater—and I will dedicate it to you and Pris."

She lumber-waddled on down the block, her handbag whirling in an even wider arc. There were neighborhoods in the world, perhaps even in New Orleans, where she would have attracted attention, but the French Quarter was not one of them. There were in the French Quarter, after all, gay men who wore dog collars and were led around on leashes by their lovers, there were heavily tattooed women who draped themselves with snakes, Dixie mystics who sewed their eyelids shut and would tell your fortune for a beignet, and people who wore their Mardi Gras costumes three hundred and sixty-five days of the year. No, the French Quarter was hardly the neighborhood to take particular notice of an overly made-up stout woman swinging a purse. For that matter, the Quarter took no particular notice of the lanky black man wearing a strangely whirring, pulsating, undulating skullcap who stepped from the shadows and approached the stout woman, extending to her a huge bouquet of jasmine branches, wrapped in soggy newspaper.

That is, the Quarter took no particular notice until two men in suits emerged from shadows on the opposite side of the street and shot the black man dead.

PARIS

". . . NINETY MILLION YEARS AGO, give or take twenty million, there occurred . . ."

What was that? Was that Bunny's voice?

". . . two events that should be of interest to all perfumers. It was then, toward the end . . ."

It *was* Bunny's voice.

". . . of the Cretaceous Period, that . . ."

Who but Bunny had a large, deep, soft, hot, suffocated voice, a voice like coal being formed in the swamps of the Cretaceous Period?

". . . the flowers wiped out the dinosaurs."

Perhaps Bunny talked that way because, unlike the majority of Frenchmen, he refused to talk through his nose. Bunny believed the nose designed for grander things. But how could Bunny be in Luc's office? Bunny was supposed to have caught the morning flight to America.

Upon hearing his cousin's voice, Claude LeFever's hand had gone as stiff as Medusa's optometrist. Now he commanded motor function back into its fingers and slowly turned the knob. There at the presidential desk, his scow of a head thankfully relieved of its whale mask cargo, sat his father, listening to a cassette player. Luc LeFever nodded to his son and pushed the Pause button. The cassette silenced, Claude could hear the blood singing in the old man's clogged arteries like the choir aboard the Titanic.

"Sit down, son, and listen to this. I trust your liver is strong this morning."

"If this is the speech Bunny made at the convention, I've heard it once, and that was once too often."

"I know," said Luc, "but I'm looking for clues. I suspect that it was this fool speech that got Marcel invited to the Last Laugh Foundation. I'm trying to determine what it might have been they heard in it." He pushed Rewind.

Claude didn't give a big quiche about the Last Laugh Foundation, about Bunny's visit to it, or Luc's morbid interest in it. Claude had come to his father's office to discuss the so-called agent file. He was disturbed that one V'lu Jackson was listed as a spy for their company. He wondered if Luc was aware that Bunny was mad about V'lu. Had the old man instigated their affair? Had Bunny played a role in recruiting V'lu? That seemed unlikely, yet Claude had an annoying feeling that business had been conducted behind his back. He was intent upon answers, but it appeared that he would have to wait until they'd listened, once again, to the address that had so embarrassed them when Bunny had delivered it to the Eighth International Congress of Aromatics (the biannual perfumers' convention) in New Orleans during early June.

"Do I have to sit through this? I need to talk to you about—"

"Shush." Luc aimed his cigar as if it were a laser. Having zapped Claude's vocal cords, he pushed Pause, then Play.

The tape had rewound farther than necessary, and the first sounds to escape the transmitter were those of the chief executive of a large New York fragrance corporation concluding a talk on the future of the industry. "In selecting fine fragrances, the perfumer has the most knowledge as to what new compounds and materials are available, but I don't believe he is close enough to the marketplace or the consumer to apply this knowledge correctly. Finished goods manufacturers have begun almost exclusively to put full responsibility for fragrance selection for their products in the hands of marketing people rather than technical people or fragrance compounders. This trend has made for more commercial, and somehow more successful, fragranced products having been launched in recent years."

Claude smiled to imagine how Bunny must have been fuming over those assertions.

". . . fragrance must be styled just as fashions are, or automobiles, or table settings, or anything else. Fragrance styles, like fashion styles, are cyclical, but new developments in chemicals, like new developments in fabrics, mean a return-with-a-difference. Thank you."

During the applause that followed, Claude pictured Bunny clinching pale, manicured fists. In Claude's picture, his cousin was the only member of the audience not clapping. In real life, however, that was not the case. Wiggs Dannyboy had not applauded because he had heard nothing that astonished him (he had, in fact, been bored and disappointed with his introduction to perfuming). V'lu Jackson and Priscilla Partido had not applauded because they, in separate parts of the auditorium, were so close to sleep that their breathing was locked into snore-launch modes. They nodded through the introduction of "master perfumer Marcel LeFever," twitching into wakefulness only when their respective subconscious minds were pricked, for some odd reason, by the words, "It was then, toward the end of the Cretaceous Period, that the flowers wiped out the dinosaurs."

Oblivious to the fact that he'd shaken two attractive amateurs from the mosquito nets of drowsiness and reversed an outside observer's decision to go to the men's room for a toke of marijuana, Bunny continued: "Science knows that the disappearance of dinosaurs and the appearance of flowers occurred simultaneously, yet, strangely, it has never drawn much of a connection between the two events. It is up to perfumers to correct the oversight.

"Vegetarian dinosaurs dined on ferns, floating water plants, and the palmlike cycad. They were not very intelligent, and certainly not very French, having developed a limited, strictly specialized diet. When the great mountain building took place during the Cretaceous Period, seaways drained and swamps dried up. First the aquatic plants, then the ferns and cycads succumbed. Insufficient surface water. Some new plants had been gradually moving in, however. These plants were inconspicuous at first, and neither the dinosaurs nor the swamp plants paid them much attention. Ah, but they had plans for the future. They began to grow their roots longer and longer, sink them deeper and deeper, until they could reach the moisture trapped beneath the surface, and when their stringy little exploratory organs hit the water table—POW!" (Bunny smacked the podium; if V'lu and Priscilla hadn't been awake before, they were now.)

"POW! They exploded in a scandalous display of sexual invitation.

"The old claw-and-fang world of drab, predatory, reptilian repression had never seen anything like this. Lasciviously colored, scandalously scented blossom after blossom flaunted its genitalia openly, enticing with visual and heretofore unknown *olfactory* charms any who might be inclined to sample its pleasures.

"With their appalling genius for adaptability, insects responded enthusiastically to the outbreak of sensuality. So did the smaller birds. Dinosaurs, however, were repulsed. Although their reproductive equipment must have been monumental—the penis of a Brontosaurus would have been only a couple of yards shorter than the thirty-foot organ of the great blue whale—it was kept out of sight and infrequently used. The dim-witted, thin-blooded dinosaur was not a hot lover, another way in which it differed from the French." There was a soft ripple of laughter. Very soft. "It mated once a year, barring headaches. So put off was the prudish dinosaur by the sexy smell of flowering plants that it starved to death and went extinct rather than eat them."

Claude was particularly bothered by this part of the speech. Claude did not enjoy being reminded of whale penises and dinosaur peepees. The very thought of big dumb clumsy dinosaurs engaged in sexual intercourse was enough to flash-freeze his gonads, making him temporarily unreceptive to his wife. For that matter, Claude resented the fact that dogs and cats and chickens were allowed by nature to indulge in sexual practices not so terribly different from his own. In a perfect world, according to Claude, coitus would be the exclusive prerogative of humans. Even most humans weren't fit to participate in an activity so sacred, so personal, so sublime.

Often, Claude simply could not imagine the couples he met at parties or passed on the street ever being locked in carnal embrace. It was not merely disgusting, it seemed impossible. Had they not had children, he would have been convinced that they cohabited platonically. This was especially true if the people were fat or stupid. Claude believed that only smart, attractive people had the right to fuck, and it sincerely hurt him when he discovered evidence to the contrary.

Claude was shaded by a revulsion as dark as his socks, but the tape rolled merrily along.

"I shall not ask you to believe that an evolutionary intelligence developed flowers for the specific purpose of ridding the world of dinosaurs (and incidentally, the carnivorous dinosaurs quickly joined their vegetarian relatives in oblivion, since, with the plant-eaters gone, *they* had nothing to dine upon), or that that intelligence was trying to teach our planet a lesson, to wit: it is better to be small, colorful, sexy, careless, and peaceful, like the flowers, than large, conservative, repressed, fearful, and aggressive, like the thunder lizards; a lesson, by the way, that the Earth has yet to learn. That is not really my point. Nor is it the point that the largest, most terrifying animals that ever lived were eradicated by fragrance.

"No, the point is that the aroma of flowers, from which we have borrowed our perfumes, while extremely powerful, has been from the beginning entirely seductive in its intentions. A rose is a rose is a rogue.

"Perfume, fundamentally, is the sexual attractant of flowers, or, in the case of civet and musk, of animals. Squeezed from the reproductive glands of plants and creatures, perfume is the smell of creation, a sign dramatically delivered to our senses of the Earth's regenerative powers—a message of hope and a message of pleasure.

"Small wonder that the Church came to equate perfume with sin, stench with holiness. It is said that certain saints so completely neglected the normal requirements of personal hygiene that Satan himself fled in terror when approaching them from downwind—thus, their reputation for sanctity. The Church periodically favored incense and oils. LeFever purchased its original perfumery from an order of Catholic monks in 1666. Fragrance has long been an important element in ceremony and ritual. Overall, however, the Church has had to oppose perfume because it could not escape the conclusion that perfume is an implicit invitation to forbidden sexual license. As perfumers, we must face up to that reality, as well.

"There is little difference between the Zulu warrior who smeared his body with lion's fat and the modern woman who dabs hers with expensive perfume. The one was trying to acquire the courage of the king of beasts, the other is attempting to acquire the irresistible sexuality of flowers. The underlying principle is the same."

Claude shuddered. Lion's fat. Ugh. Where did Bunny come up with these things?

"What we are really talking about, then, is *magic*, is it not so? In the anthropological understanding of homeopathic magic, perfume is the medium by which the lady magically usurps the sexual powers of the blossom. As with the warrior's lion fat, there is also more than a little fantasizing going on, for however undetailed, a potential result of the use of the magical medium is being projected onto the wearer's screen of consciousness.

"Since the perfumer is dealing in sexual magic and romantic fantasy, he or she is operating in a realm that is both deeply primitive and highly exalted. This realm has its rhymes and reasons, and they are not quite the same, I regret to inform you, as the rhymes and reasons of the marketplace."

The last remark was ad libbed, apparently. In spite of himself, Claude felt a tingle of pride in his cousin. He turned to Luc, shaking his head and chuckling. "That Bunny is a quick one," he said. "And afraid of nothing." Luc did not reply. Luc had other things on his mind. Luc had been awake most of the night. Luc had money to invest, and now that Morgenstern had hooked up with the Last Laugh Foundation . . . well, it was worth investigating. Surely, the foundation needed funds. Who knew, maybe it *could* do something for him. Luc chewed his cigar and listened intently. Luc felt rotten. The circles under his eyes were the purple of bad meat.

"Now," Marcel the Bunny was saying, "I wish to call your

attention to yet another prehistorical event. About two hundred thousand years ago, the human brain tripled in size. Science has been unable to explain this relatively sudden enlargement, since beyond a certain size, a size that the brains of our ancestors had already reached two hundred thousand years ago, intelligence does not increase with brain volume. What evolutionary purpose was served, then, by tripling our cerebral real estate?"

Bunny paused for effect, then went on. "I submit that the brain was enlarged in order to store more memories. We have learned in recent experiments that memory is stored not in specific neural centers but, holographically, *throughout* the brain. As the human mammal came to live longer, and to widen the scope of its intellectual activities, it had more to remember. It needed more closet space, so to speak. But the interesting thing is, the increase in memory capacity was far beyond what was needed at the time. It was, in fact, far beyond what is needed today, although we now live on the average more than three times as long as our prehistoric ancestors, and the range of our activities has increased geometrically. Could it be that evolution was preparing us for a time in the future when we will live considerably longer than we do at present? Could the mushrooming of memory space have been long-range longevity planning? An immortalist ploy?"

Luc grunted. "This must be the part," he said. "I passed over it the first time." He sat up in his chair. The movement made him dizzy. (Five months earlier, Wiggs Dannyboy had been pulled forward in his seat by the same remark. Wiggs had crashed the convention on a hunch, and it looked as if the hunch was paying off.)

Bunny: "We may only speculate about such matters. We do know, however, that of our five senses, the one most directly connected to memory is the sense of smell. Although man has become increasingly visual in his orientations, although his olfactory receptor has shrunk until it is no larger than an American dime, sight simply cannot compete with smell when it comes to the ability to awaken memory. Memories associated with scent are invariably more immediate and more vivid than those associated solely with visual imagery or sound. Psychiatrists have begun, in fact, to use perfume to aid the patient in recreating the suppressed memories of early childhood."

The old man cocked his head. Bunny was speaking in English, and what with the Blood Pressure Chorale caroling in Luc's temples, he had difficulty comprehending every word. English was a language fit only for narrating animated cartoons and inciting crowds at sporting events, according to Luc.

Bunny: "Scent is the last sense to leave a dying person. After sight, hearing, and even touch are gone, the dying hold on to their sense of smell. Does that sharpen your appreciation of the arena in which we perfumers perform?

"Fragrance is a conduit for our earliest memories, on the one hand; on the other, it may accompany us as we enter the next life. In between, it creates mood, stimulates fantasy, shapes thought, and modifies behavior. It is our strongest link to the past, our closest fellow traveler to the future. Prehistory, history, and the afterworld, all are its domain. Fragrance may well be the signature of eternity."

"That's laying it on a bit thick," commented Claude. Luc made an effort to nod in agreement, but his head was so full of hot, noisy, polluted blood that it felt like a bistro on a weekend midnight, and he could not move it.

The tape was enjoying perfect health, however. It stuck steadfastly to its pace. "There is a long-standing argument about whether perfuming is a science or an art. The argument is irrelevant, for at the higher levels, science and art are the same. There is a point where high science transcends the technologic and enters the poetic, there is a point where high art transcends technique and enters the poetic.

"A perfumer, of course, is neither a quantum physicist nor a painter, but at his best, when his purposes are high purposes, when his imagination is liberated, his choices inspired, he, too, enters the poetic. And it is revealed to him, then, what the ancients meant when they said with conviction that the soul receives its sustenance via the sense of smell.

"I have spoken to you this afternoon of poetry and of sexual magic. Not too many years ago, the names of our perfumes bore testimony to such things. There was a popular scent called *Tabu*, there was *Sorcery*, *My Sin*, *Vampire*, *Voodoo*, *Evening in Paris*, *Jungle Gardenia*, *Bandit*, *Shocking*, *Intimate*, *Love Potion*, and *L'Heure Bleue*—The Blue Hour. Nowadays what do we find? *Vanderbilt*, *Miss Dior*, *Lauren*, and *Armani*, perfumes named after glorified tailors"—there were murmurs and gasps in the audience—"names that evoke not the poetic, the erotic, the magic, but economic status, social snobbery, and the egomania of designers. Perfumes that confuse the essence of creation with the essence of money. How much sustenance can the soul receive from a scent entitled *Bill Blass*?

"*Vanderbilt* and *Bill Blass* are what the 'marketing people' have given us."

Marcel paused, as if trying to contain a coiling rage. Claude slapped the creased thigh of his expensive gray trousers. "Give them hell, Bunny," he said, with a mixture of affection and mockery. Luc, meanwhile, had laid down his cigar so that he might employ both his hands to massage his exploding temples.

"*Vanderbilt* and *Bill Blass*, alas. But you know, you perfumers, in the deep unfolding rose of your hearts, you know that fragrance is no automobile or table setting, no insurance policy, no Preparation H. Attempts to reduce perfume to a predictable product with which cost accountants can safely deal; attempts to own it, control it, and make it happen when the mysterious spirit is not there are fated to end in crude failure and coarse farce.

"Perfuming is most unlike manufacture. And perfumers should be proud to assume our historic roles as enchanters, soul feeders, sacred pimps, and alchemists. 'Marketing people' are fine enough when it comes to peddling wares, but let us remember always that it is the perfumer, the flowermaster, the guardian of the Blue Hour, who can charm the birds and bees in the human spirit—and destroy its dinosaurs."

Scattered applause. Shocked murmurs. Nervous laughter. Then, the white-on-white whirr of blank tape.

"That's that," said Claude, relieved that it hadn't been worse than the first time that he heard it. "The wonderful Wizard of Oz. My guess is that Wiggs Dannyboy identified with Bunny. Someone told him about the speech, and he thought, 'Here's a man who's as big a bedbug as I am.' That must have been why Bunny was invited to that clinic."

Luc said nothing. Like a paper snake with a white spark on its tongue, the tape hissed on.

Claude stretched and turned to look at his father. "Oh, no!" The executive was slumped over his desk, his face in the alabaster ashtray. The cigar was smoldering against Luc's cheek, burrowing like a red-hot worm into the head that was now the color and texture of one of Bunny's beets.

If Claude was slow to react, it was because the smell transported him, helplessly, to a distant summer evening when he and his young bride were strolling between the braziers of kabob hawkers grilling mutton on an Algerian beach, consumed by romance but unable to see either stars or sea because of the fatty smoke.

PART
IV

DOWNWIND
FROM
THE
PERFECT
TACO

THE CITADEL WAS DARK and the heroes were sleeping. When they breathed, it sounded as if they were testing the air for dragon smoke.

Except that the "citadel" was Concord State Prison and the sleeping "heroes," who had been damaged by sorry environments and shoddy genes long before they had had a chance to wax heroic, were testing the air for tear gas. These were men who didn't *care* if the world was round or flat. Their dreams were haunted by jack handles and cash registers, and those who had been incarcerated for five years or more dreamed only in black and white.

Alobar did not dream at all. He was as awake as the guards on the cell block. More awake, actually, for the guards dozed over their detective magazines, dreamily musing about the long Thanksgiving weekend that was approaching, while Alobar was kept fully conscious by the smell of his body aging.

Yes, he could smell it. During the first year of his sentence, he hadn't aged a notch. His body was still running on the impetus of a millennium of immortalist practices. With the exception of breathing techniques, he was unable to continue those practices in prison, however, and one day it dawned on his cellular bankers that the immunity accounts were overdrawn and there hadn't been a deposit in fifteen months. The DNA demanded an audit. It was learned that

Alobar's figures were juggled. He had successfully embezzled more than nine hundred years.

Outraged, the DNA must have petitioned for compensation, because within a week, Alobar's salt-and-pepper hair had turned into a pillar of sodium. Wrinkle troops hit the beaches under his eyes, dug trenches, and immediately radioed for reinforcements. Someone was mixing cement in his joints.

Now, in his third year behind bars, he could smell, taste, and hear the accelerated aging going on inside him. It smelled like mothballs. It tasted like stale chip dip. It sounded like Lawrence Welk.

That very morning, Doc Palmer (five-to-ten for Medicare fraud) had said to him, "Al, you looked your age when you got to Concord." (In prison records, "Albert Barr" was listed as forty-six years old.) "Now, I swear you're looking twice that much. You want a slip for the infirmary, let us have a look?"

"No, I'm okay."

"But your skin . . ."

"Must have been something I ate."

Doc Palmer shook his head. "If you say so, Albert."

Alobar smiled. He enjoyed being called "Albert." It reminded him of all the nights he spent cleaning up after Einstein.

Looking back, it was amazing how few male friends he had had in his lifetime. Some men make more friends in a day than Alobar had made in a thousand years. There was Pan, of course, if one could describe their odd association as friendship. There had been the shaman, but they'd met only once. Fosco, the Tibetan artist, might be included, although Fosco had been often withdrawn and enigmatic, and as for Wiggs Dannyboy, well, he just wasn't sure about Dannyboy. Albert Einstein, on the other hand, was a pal.

Sort of a pal. They never went bowling together or guzzled beer in a bar, but Einstein had lent him money, as a true friend will do, and they'd had some wonderful talks. If you and another guy know things about each other that nobody else knows, and you keep those things confidential, then you and the guy must be pals.

Only a month or two before, while leafing through a magazine in the day room, Alobar had chanced upon an article that began, "When Albert Einstein died in Princeton Hospital at 1:15 on the morning of April 18, 1955, having mumbled his last words in German to a night nurse who knew no German . . ." He couldn't help but laugh. The magazine implied that Einstein's last words were tragically lost to history. Alobar conceded that such might be the case. But *he* knew what Einstein's last words were.

Did they imagine that the dying Einstein suddenly pulled himself up in bed and uttered, "E equals MC *cubed*"?

Did they think that he had mumbled, "Der perfekt Tako"?

On numerous occasions during the past three centuries, Alobar had come to the brink of suicide, driven there not by despair, or even boredom, but by the longing for reunion with Kudra and the wish to prove incorrect her accusation that longevity for longevity's sake was for him a limiting obsession. To some degree, Kudra's charge must have been accurate, because he never lowered the shade. He would decide that he was finally ready to die, or, at least, to dematerialize, for he had no intention of leaving his dear body behind to be poked at by policemen and lied over by priests, but always something would come up at the last minute to change his mind.

Alobar was fairly certain that he could manage a dematerialization. He was uncertain that he could rematerialize. Since Kudra had failed to reappear, he supposed that it must be impossible. His ego prevented him, except in rare moments of self-doubt, from believing that Kudra had remained on the Other Side by choice.

In any case, Alobar would decide to board the spook express at last, and he'd dust off his antique lab equipment in order to whip up some *K23*. He had to be reeking of the perfume when he reached the Other Side, he reasoned, to insure that Kudra would recognize him. So, he'd proceed to assemble the ingredients, which was not quite as easy as making cherry pie, since citron was scarce, quality jasmine oil scarcer, and beet pollen scarcer yet (it was available only a few weeks out of the year, and then in widely scattered locations). Invariably, before he had his aromatics together, he'd find a reason to postpone the journey.

That was exactly what had happened the last time, back in 1953. It was the Eisenhower Years and things were slow. The Eisenhower Years were so slow that if they fell off a cliff they'd only be going ten miles an hour. The Eisenhower Years were a slow boat to Abilene, and it looked as if it would be many a crewcut moon before America turned lively again.

For nearly half a century, Alobar had owned and operated a spa outside Livingston, Montana. This enterprise afforded him daily access to mineral springs. Hot baths, remember, are part of the immortalist process. In rural Montana, he also was convenient to the disintegrated spirit of Pan, which roamed the Wild West in the company of the disintegrated spirit of Coyote. Occasionally, Pan and Coyote would blow by (for they were like the winds), stirring things up (for Coyote was an agent of mischief) and causing spa guests to clamp towels against their faces (for Pan still stank to the stars).

It had been quite a while since Pan had come to call, however. If the Eisenhower Years bored Alobar, imagine what they did to Pan. If anything could finish Pan off, it was the vibration of all those self-righteous Eisenhower puritans shuffling canasta decks and defense contracts. This was no time for the strong of heart. If Alobar was ever going to take the step, if he was ever going to kick the longevity habit and rejoin his beloved Kudra (or Wren, or Kudra *and* Wren: who knew how heavenly the Other Side might really be?), 1953 was opportune.

Moreover, while he had arrived in Montana with his hair

dyed ebony, gradually allowing it, over the decades, to return to its natural salt-and-pepper (he had learned a *few* tricks in his millennium), fifty whole years had passed, and curiosity was rising among neighboring ranchers. The same old problem alas, that back around 1031 had ejected him from Constantinople just ahead of a mob. It was time to move along.

So, Alobar sent away to New York for citron and jasmine, and, from inquiries, pinpointed where Minnesota beet fields would be ripening in a matter of weeks. He had never actually concocted a single drop of *K23* since the original batch, but he was confident that he could reproduce it.

Ah, but then, a fortnight before he was to set off for Minnesota to procure the beet pollen, an outhouse copy of *Reader's Digest* called his attention to the news that geneticists at Princeton University seemed to be on the verge of discoveries that could more than double human life span. Toward the end of the article one of the scientists was quoted as saying that if the experiments panned out, he imagined that the White House would assume direct control, assuring America's leaders primary access. Federal grants, after all, were funding much of the research.

Small wonder that Alobar was alarmed. Consider the prospect of Ike, John Foster Dulles, and Dick Nixon indefinitely preserved. Consider the prospect of the Eisenhower Years going on forever.

Such frightening thoughts might have been by themselves enough to motivate him. However, it was the promise that he had made to Lalo the nymph nine hundred years earlier that caused Alobar to cancel his trip to the beet fields, sell his spa, desert his current mistress, and head for Princeton to become Einstein's janitor.

"Someday," Lalo had said, "there wilt be men who seek to defeat death by intelligence alone." She warned that huge evil would result if those men should attain immortality, or rather, "false immortality," since true immortality requires advancement of heart and soul as well as mind.

Were the Princeton geneticists the false immortalists of whom Lalo had prophesied? To find out, Alobar wrangled a job as assistant custodian at the Institute for Advanced Study, where the geneticists had their offices and lab. Assigned originally to boiler room duties, Alobar had to bribe the chief custodian to be allowed to clean the wing in which the geneticists worked. Upon finding documents that proved White House and Pentagon interest in the experiments, Alobar began to throw monkey wrenches at the delicate machinery. He flicked drops of dirty mop water into culture dishes, waxed the guinea pig's protein pellets, unplugged incubators, and altered figures on charts. Once he fed a prize long-lived white rat one of Einstein's cigar butts. The rat was kaput by morning.

Professor Einstein's office was down the hall from the genetics area. It was a mess. And not just a common two-plus-two-equals-four mess. Einstein's office was a genius equation mess. (A disarray in which Priscilla might have felt at home.)

Books, reports, binders, sheaves, scrolls, periodicals, letters, and uncashed checks were piled, layers deep, all over the floor and furniture, making it virtually impossible to sweep or dust. It was especially frustrating because the place sorely needed a sweeping. In amongst the piles of paper were strewn orange peels, banana skins, Dixie cups, chalk sticks, pencil nubs, sweater lint, violin strings, and drifts of cigar ash (the snows of El Producto). To make matters worse, Einstein himself was usually in the office until well past midnight, and should so much as a sheet of paper be disturbed, he became agitated.

Alobar began postponing the cleaning of Einstein's office to the very end of his shift, but still the professor was there, 2:00 A.M., slumped in his chair, looking like a musical teddy bear with its springs and stuffing flying out. By and by, Einstein confessed that he waited for Alobar so that the two of them might talk. His wife mothered him, he complained, and denied him his cigars. Mrs. Einstein thought that a pipe was more dignified. Her favorite topic of conversation was bowel productivity.

They had some fine discussions, Alobar and Einstein. The special theory of relativity, the general theory of relativity, the unified field theory, they were what Einstein was famous for, but they were not his best work, he said. Einstein told Alobar that he had thought of many more wonderful things than relativity, but he wasn't going to let "der kats out of der bag" because he didn't trust politicians to put his ideas to moral uses.

Upon hearing some of the unpublished theories, Alobar agreed that they were wonderful, if difficult, and had best be saved for a more enlightened age. Made bold by Einstein's revelations, the janitor told the professor some secrets of his own.

Whether Einstein actually believed the janitor's stories is questionable, but he relished them. He was fascinated by Alobar's views on life and death. His depression was relieved by Alobar's cheerful nature and strongly regal bearing. When Alobar disclosed, cheerfully, that his financial nose was in the mud, Einstein dropped to his knees, rummaged in his papers until he found a royalty check from *The Physical Review*, and promptly endorsed it to his late-night friend.

The reason Alobar was short of cash was because he was being blackmailed. The chief custodian, suspicious of the new janitor from the onset, eventually had caught him tampering with experiments in the genetics lab. Soon he had extorted from him every penny of the proceeds from the spa sale and was demanding the bulk of his salary. It was expensive business, keeping a promise to a nymph.

That the longevity experiments at Princeton's Institute for Advanced Study were terminated in 1956 probably was due as much to faulty procedures on the part of the geneticists as to Alobar's sabotage. In trying to increase human life span by building virus-resistant cells in rodents and dogs, the scientists were barking up the wrong chromosome. In any event, by the time the custodian turned in Alobar to the police, nobody cared very much about the experiments. Alobar was questioned and released. He lost his job, of course. It was just as well. His buddy was dead.

Einstein's office was now a museum. It was very clean and very tidy. There was a rack of pipes on his desk.

Alobar hadn't been allowed to visit Albert in the hospital. He was hanging around the waiting room, however, when word came that the professor had refused surgery for the rupturing aorta that was wiping his personal equation off the blackboard of life. "It is tasteless to prolong life artificially," Einstein had told his physicians.

Alobar's reaction was summed up ten years later by a British fashion designer named Mary Quant, who, in a different context, announced, "Good taste is death. Vulgarity is life."

Saddened by Albert's decision, disappointed that his own philosophy had had no stronger influence upon his friend, Alobar returned to the institute to mop and mope. The following week, after the funeral (which Alobar, on principle, refused to attend), he heard a local radio interview in which the nurse who had ministered to Einstein on his deathbed attempted to recreate the German that the patient had mumbled with his last breath.

Alobar seized his broom and danced it around the boiler room. His laughter echoed through the heat ducts of the Institute for Advanced Study. No wonder they didn't understand Einstein's last words! Einstein's last words weren't in German at all. Einstein's last words were in the language of an obscure and long-lost Bohemian tribe, and had been taught to him by Alobar.

Einstein's last words were, *"Erleichda, erleichda."*

Memories of Einstein, and of his own first (but, alas, not last) exploits as a science saboteur, distracted the prisoner "Albert Barr," permitting him to escape momentarily from the two cells in which he was locked; the chamber of steel, cold and indestructible; the chamber of flesh, feverish and deteriorating.

The instant the reminiscence faded, the symptoms of deterioration took over, grabbing the limelight like an insecure celebrity, drowning out, with Welkian schmaltz, the shy snores of embezzlers, the out-of-sync rasps of homicidal maniacs, the nocturnal whimpers of lifelong bullyboys. The noise of aging came from deep inside him, and although it was relatively soft, it had an urgency that the distant country/western of the guards' radio did not.

More disturbing was the odor. What chemical evil could be working in his tissues to cause them to smell like the bottom drawer in a maiden aunt's dresser?

At that moment, Alobar became aware of a new symptom. His ears had started to burn. Of itself, it wasn't a ruinous sensation, and he recalled the folk wisdom that attributed ear heat to gossip. If your ears burned, it meant that someone was talking about you. That would be okay, Alobar thought, especially if it were the parole board. But at this saw-log hour of the morning, who on Earth could possibly be talking about *him*?

Who, indeed?

"A thousand years old," said Priscilla. "No-oo! He was feeding you a whopper."

"Your man here is a scientist," said Wiggs. "I am trained in skepticism. I'm not the chap to be swallowin' whoppers."

"Ha! I've heard from informed sources that you believe in fairies."

Wiggs reddened slightly. " 'Tis an entirely different matter," he said.

"Maybe not."

"Myths explain the world." He cleared his throat in a pedagogic manner. "Both the psychic and physical world. The world past, present, and future. When your ancient Celts spoke o' fairies, they were describin' the photon. Not the unintelligent pulse o' light that is the basis, the creator, o' all matter, but the pulse o' light charged with consciousness, the new photon that is evolvin' *out* o' matter. Faith, don't be gettin' me started on quantum physics and the wisdom o' the Irish. Alobar, for all his age, was no bloody fairy."

"You know, your brogue is getting worse by the minute."

" 'Tis the drinkin'. And I shouldn't be drinkin'. Alcohol runs counter to me immortalist aspirations."

Priscilla looked at her own glass of spirits. She thought of Ricki, waiting—perhaps worrying—at her apartment. "I shouldn't have anymore, either. Here, I'm gonna go in the kitchen and get us some ice water."

"Arraugh!" Wiggs grabbed his collar as if he were strangling. "Water?" He rolled off the couch, still clutching his throat. "Water! Of all the liquids on Earth, the only one chosen for scrubbin' and flushin'. The liquid they rinse the baby's nappies in, the fluid that floods the gutters o' this cloud-squeezer town; a single drop o' water discolors a glass of Irish, and you, false friend, are wantin' me to pour this abrasive substance into me defenseless body!"

Priscilla giggled, which delighted him. His heart thought it was an electric toaster, set for "tan." In *her* heart, the yeast was rising.

"Okay, okay, no water. What *can* I get you to replace the booze?"

Dr. Dannyboy straightened his tie and his eye patch, and reoccupied his seat on the sofa. The only illumination in the room was from the fireplace. It lent a cheerful glint to the cannibal cutlery above the mantel. "Another nice wet kiss would be fillin' the bill," he said quietly.

Pushing aside anxiety about Ricki and curiosity about beets, she slid into his arms.

Across the continent, near Boston, in a cell inside Concord State Prison, Alobar's ears abruptly ceased burning.

"Ahh, I do love zippers. Zippers remind me o' crocodiles, lobsters, and Aztec serpents. I wish me tweeds had more than the single fly. . . . Zippers are primal and modern at the very same time. On the one hand, your zipper is primitive and reptilian, on the other, mechanical and slick. A zipper is where the Industrial Revolution meets the Cobra Cult, don't you think? Ahh. Little alligators of ecstasy, that's what zippers are. Sexy, too. Now your button, a button is prim and persnickety. There's somethin' Victorian about a row o' buttons. But a zipper, why a zipper is the very snake at the gate of Eden, waitin' to escort a true believer into the Garden. Faith, I should be sewin' more zippers into me garments, for I have many erogenous zones that require speedy access. Mmm, old zipper creeper, hanging head down like the carcass of a lizard; the phantom viper that we shun in daytime and communicate with at night."

"Here, let me help you with that."

Throughout Dr. Dannyboy's monologue, he had been trying to unzip Pris's dress, to part the teeth of the Talon that ran down the length of her green knit back; trying to maneuver it cooly, unobtrusively, as if Pris, suddenly noticing her dress falling away, would regard it as a spontaneous act of nature, organic and ordained, but he couldn't budge the damn thing, though he tugged until sweat burst out on his brow, and finally, she said . . .

"Here, let me help you with that."

And with one smooth stroke, she separated the interlocking tracks, the 'gator yawned, and, lo, there she sat in her underwear.

Her bra was rust-stained and more than a size too big.

Is that a brassiere or a flotation device? Wiggs wondered.

At least it was a cinch to remove. He simply pulled it over her head without unhooking it, catching her breasts as they tumbled out, like croquet balls from a canvas bag. They were as smooth as peeled onions and perfectly pinked. He squeezed one, nuzzled the other. The pink did not lick off.

There was a run in the seat of her nylon panties. Neither of them seemed to notice. His hand passed over the run like a streetsweeper passing over a skid mark, maintaining momentum, registering nothing. The longest finger on his left hand

curled like a celery stalk and dipped into the bowl of her
buttocks, a bowl in which metaphors were easily mixed.

"Sweet Jesus, 'tis wonderful you feel!"

"Wiggs . . . you're still dressed for dinner."

In a minute he was wearing nothing but his eye patch.

"You feel wonderful, baby," he said, fingering her again.
He had dropped his brogue with his shorts.

Priscilla had forgotten how it was with older men. The last
man with whom she had lain was a twenty-year-old dish-
washer from El Papa Muerta. During a single evening, he
had made love to her four times—for three minutes each
time. Perhaps it is noteworthy, she thought, that the performance of a young man in bed is roughly the same length as a
rock song on AM radio.

"I . . . had . . . ummm . . . forgotten . . . how . . . it is
. . . with . . . older . . . men."

That must have been the wrong thing to say. Wiggs paused
in midstroke. "Age," he grumbled. "There are only two ages.
Alive and dead. If your man is dead, he should go lie down
somewhere and get out o' the way. But if 'tis alive he is . . ."

He completed the stroke, then paused again. *Oh, no,*
thought Priscilla. *Surely he isn't going to get pedantic at a
time like this?*

Her worry was soon abated, for although Wiggs cleared his
throat and tapped his patch with his finger, a clear signal that
he was on the verge of expounding, he became distracted by
the wiggly thrust of her pelvis, and gradually, after mumbling
something about senility being wasted on the old, and something else about never having met an adult who really liked
him, he fell silent, except for the occasional sweet grunt, and
gave full attention to the further stoking of the hot box in
which he found himself.

"Yes, God, yes," moaned Pris. This was the way Effecto
had loved her: muscular and tender, relaxed and confident,
carefully modulating rhythm and tempo, prying her apart
with sweet determination, kissing her adoringly all the while;
a far cry from those young guys who were either trying to

score touchdowns in bed or else practicing to join the tank corps. "Daddy!" squealed Pris.

"Daddy?" asked Wiggs.

"Uh, no, *Danny*," said Pris. "Dannyboy."

"Your man," said Wiggs.

Effecto had played Priscilla like an accordion. Wiggs worked her as if she were an archaeological dig: spading, sifting, dusting, cataloging. Now, lying in a puddle on the sofa, she felt like she was ready to be shipped to the British Museum. Accompanied by a crate of late twentieth-century come shards.

Wiggs covered her with a Sepik war blanket and lay down beside her. A fresh Pres-to-log sputtered in the fireplace, and rain tapped messages in Morse code against the window-panes. "You can't stay indoors forever," and "There's plenty more where this came from" was what the rain was sending.

"Did you invite me here to seduce me?" asked Pris. She didn't care, at that point, she was merely curious. She caressed his flaccid shillelagh, wondering if Ricki would ever forgive her; wondering, too, if she would have felt half this good after sex with Ricki.

"I wish I could say yes, but the truth is, darlin', I wasn't that smart. This was an unexpected bonus."

"Then why *did* you invite me?"

"Smell," said Wiggs.

"I beg your pardon."

"Now don't be takin' offense. Personally, you smell dainty as a lamb." Dr. Dannyboy ducked his head beneath the blanket and took a vigorous whiff. "They can have their loaf o' warm bread, their new-mown hay. Nothin' beats the smell of a lassie freshly laid."

"Hey . . ."

"Again, no offense." He surfaced, and kissed her with earnest affection. "See here, Priscilla, I have an interest in smell. That is, I have an interest in the evolution o' consciousness. Smell is the only sense to communicate directly with the neocortex. It bypasses the thalamus and the other middlemen and goes direct. Smell is the language the brain

speaks. Hunger, thirst, aggression, fear, lust: your brain in-
terprets these urges with a vocabulary o' smell. The neocortex
speaks this language, and if we can learn to speak it, why we
may be able to manipulate the cortex through the nose."

"For what?"

"For expeditin' the evolution o' consciousness."

"For what?"

"So's we can be happy and live a long, long time and not
be bloody blowin' each other to bits."

"You're going to disappoint a lot of generals."

"Worse. It could mean the end o' Monday Night Football."

"Well, fuck the Dallas Cowboys if they can't take a joke.
But, Wiggs, wait a minute. What does any of this have to do
with me?"

"You make perfume, don't you, darlin'?"

Priscilla raised herself on one elbow. "Uh, yeah, sort of.
How did you know that?"

"I've learned a lot about perfumers since I met Alobar."

"Alobar. The guy in prison."

"Him."

"The janitor."

"And former king."

"Who's a thousand years old."

"Yes."

She sat completely upright. "This is the nuttiest thing I've
ever heard. I'm getting more confused by the minute. . . ."
She sounded genuinely distressed. Wiggs gripped her sticky
thigh.

"'Tis a long story."

"I don't care. And cut the brogue, please. You talked like
an American when we were making love."

"Sure and 'twas because your wild little wooky sobered me
up. Now the grape has got hold o' me tongue again."

"All right, fine, I don't care if you talk like Donald Duck.
Just tell the story."

"Should I start at the beginning?"

"If that's not too traditional."

"But what about your date?"

"You've already eaten her share."

"*Her?*"

"Never mind. Talk to me. Now."

"I'll start with the sixties."

"Fine. You were probably more interesting then. I understand *every*body was."

"I'll start with the seventies."

"I like you, Wiggs."

"Sure and I like you, too."

He cleared his throat and, tapping his patch with a wooky-scented knuckle, commenced to pin a tail on the beet.

By then, it was that part of the day that is officially morning but which any dunce can see is purest night. The streets of Seattle were as wet and greeny black as freshly printed currency. Despite the hour and the weather, people were lined up outside the Last Laugh Foundation as if the Last Laugh Foundation were a radio station giving away rock stars to pubescent girls. Some of the people looked at Ricki's tea strainer of a car as it ever so slowly rattled by. Others persisted in gazing expectantly at the darkened mansion.

Squint as she might, Ricki could detect not a glimmer in the house. She bit her lip to keep from crying. "It's two-thirty," she said sorrowfully, as if "two-thirty" were the name of a fatal disease. "It's two-thirty in the son-of-a-bitching morning."

Were Ricki concerned with precise expression, and she was not, she might have added, "here," for while it was indeed, two-thirty in Seattle, in Massachusetts it was half past five, a time of night that could lay some legitimate claim to morning, and a cold crack of oyster light was beginning to separate the sky from the Atlantic. Still awake, Alobar lay upon his prison cot, practicing Bandaloop breath.

That's what he called it, what he and Kudra had called it all those years: Bandaloop breath. Of course, there was an absolute lack of evidence that the Bandaloop ever breathed in that manner. For that matter, there was precious little evidence that the Bandaloop ever existed. Absence of proof failed to faze Alobar, however, since, thanks to the Bandaloop, he had witnessed three hundred and eighty-five thousand, eight hundred and six sunrises in his life, and judging from the milky molluscan glow seeping through the barred window, was about to witness yet another.

Moreover, if he concentrated on his breathing, and the parole board soon ruled in his favor, he might go on witnessing sunrises indefinitely, despite the aging that worked in him now like naphthous bees in a leathery hive. That was his hope, although, considering his prospects, why he should want to go on—and on and on and on—was a question he could not easily answer. One thing was certain, he didn't intend to risk the Other Side without a splash of *K23*, and he was starting to wonder if he shouldn't have gone ahead and given Wiggs Dannyboy the formula for it. Dr. Dannyboy could have had some made and smuggled it in to him. His intense secrecy about *K23*, his long-standing refusal to tap its commercial potential, was a bit irrational, he must admit. But, then, were he a rational man, he would have been dead a thousand years. Ho.

Joints creaking like the lines of a storm-tossed ship, Alobar arose and hobbled to the window. He looked for his old benefactor, the morning star, but the window was tiny, and the only celestial light in the slice of sky available to his scrutiny was a blinking satellite circling the Earth. "The world is round-o, round-o," he started to sing, but embarrassment shut him up. "If the parole board doesn't act soon, I'll send Dannyboy the formula," he promised.

Alobar wasn't the only person thinking about a secret formula that morning (or night). Distracted by first one thing and then the other, Wiggs and Priscilla hadn't gotten around to it yet, but in New Orleans—time: four-thirty—Madame Devalier lay in her canopied bed, bejeweled hands crossed upon the vault of her belly, pondering a possible bottom note, mixing dozens, scores of ingredients in her mind's nose, not ever imagining how simple it could be; and not imagining, either, that in a cheap motel near the Seattle-Tacoma airport, where it was, yes, two-thirty, thank you, Ricki, V'lu Jackson slept with the answer—a drop or two of the answer—in an ancient bottle beneath her vinyl-wrapped, foam rubber pillow; and, of course, neither of them, Madame, awake, formulating, nor V'lu, dreaming, fist pressed against lonesome labia, could imagine that before they lay abed again, Bingo Pajama would be shot at their feet and that his little swarm of bees, masterless, would be frightening New Orleans half to . . .

. . . death. Arrgh! How Wiggs Dannyboy hated that word.

His reaction to "death" was neither terror nor resignation, avoidance nor morbid longing, shock nor denial, but, rather, fury. Controlled fury. Challenge, if you please. Combat. Wiggs was at war with death and had vowed never to surrender.

The declaration of war had been drawn up while he was in Concord State Prison. He had been transferred to Concord from a federal penitentiary in the Midwest at his own request after the incident in which a guard had poked out his right eye with a matchstick.

In the investigation that followed the blinding, it was revealed that Dr. Dannyboy had been subjected to almost continuous physical and mental harassment during his months in federal custody. The media, which, while it may have condemned Dannyboy's life-style and philosophy, had always found him good copy, fanned the story into a scandal. In addition, there was the threat of a multi-million-dollar lawsuit. The government was hardly in a position to deny the request for transfer.

At Concord, Wiggs was near friends, mavericks who had managed to remain on the Harvard faculty or who had entered one or another of the "New Age" businesses that flourished in Cambridge and Boston. His pals kept him supplied with books from the university library and with the latest journals and papers in his fields of interest: anthropology, ethnobotany, mythology, and neuropharmacology. They paid him gossipy visits, monitored his health, and delivered his occasional contributions to *The Psychedelic Review*. They smuggled out the half-frozen dinner roll into which he had freshly ejaculated, rushing it to the parking lot where his ovulating wife (who was eventually to jilt him for a more available partner) received it and immediately did with it what she had to do: the origins of Huxley Anne.

It was, despite the many difficulties of prison life, a reasonably productive and stimulating period. There was plenty of time for contemplation, however, and Dr. Dannyboy used it to review what had been accomplished in the sixties, by himself and like-minded others. Then, he placed those accomplishments within the context of history, not merely the official history, with its emphasis on politics and economics, or the more pertinent history of the various ways that we have lived our daily lives since we first crawled out of the ooze or swung down from the foliage, but also the higher, more complex history of how our thought patterns, our nervous systems, our spiritual selfhoods have developed and changed.

This much Wiggs concluded: illumination, like it or not, is an elitist condition; in every era and in almost every area, there have resided tiny minorities of enlightened individuals, living their lives upon the threshold, at the gateway of the next evolutionary phase, a phase whose actualization is probably still hundreds of years down the line. In certain key periods of history, one or another of these elitist minorities has become sufficiently large and resonant to affect the culture as a whole, thereby laying a significant patch of brick in the evolutionary road. He thought of the age of Akhenaton in ancient Egypt, the reign of Zoroaster in Persia, the golden ages of Greece and Islam, the several great periods of Chinese culture, and the European Renaissance. ("The Celts would have produced a major culture, too," he told Priscilla, "if the Church hadn't got hold o' them first.") Something similar was brewing in America in the years 1964 to 1971.

Maybe it was sentimental, if not actually stupid, to romanticize the sixties as an embryonic golden age, Wiggs admitted. Certainly, this fetal age of enlightenment aborted. Nevertheless, the sixties were special; not only did they *differ* from the twenties, the fifties, the seventies, etc., they were *superior* to them. Like the Arthurian years at Camelot, the sixties constituted a breakthrough, a fleeting moment of glory, a time when a significant little chunk of humanity briefly realized its moral potential and flirted with its neurological destiny, a collective spiritual awakening that flared brilliantly until the barbaric and mediocre impulses of the species drew tight once more the curtains of darkness.

Moreover, Wiggs believed that the American womb eventually would bear fruit. The United States was the logical location of the next enlightened civilization. And since the sixties phenomena had at least prepared the soil—many of the individuals who had successfully mutated during the sixties were carrying on, out of view of the public eye—the next flowering was probably no more than a decade or two away.

Even though, in social terms, the sixties had failed, in evolutionary terms they were a landmark, a milestone, and Wiggs was proud that he had been able to lend a helping hand in ushering in that dizzy period of transcendence and awareness (transcendence of obsolete value systems, awareness of the enormity and richness of inner reality). Still, he was dissatisfied. Anxious. Unhappy. It wasn't prison or the blinding that was bothering him, they were small sacrifices to make for what had been accomplished. It was something else, something that had haunted him since boyhood, undermining his every triumph, dulling his ecstasies, amplifying his agonies, mocking his optimism, spitting in his ice cream.

It was, he came gradually to realize, the specter of death.

If a person leads an "active" life, as Wiggs had, if a person has goals, ideals, a cause to fight for, then that person is distracted, temporarily, from paying a whole lot of attention to the heavy scimitar that hangs by a mouse hair just above his or her head. We, each of us, have a ticket to ride, and if the trip be interesting (if it's dull, we have only ourselves to blame), then we relish the landscape (how quickly it whizzes by!), interact with our fellow travelers, pay frequent visits to the washrooms and concession stands, and hardly ever hold up the ticket to the light where we can read its plainly stated destination: The Abyss.

Yet, ignore it though we might in our daily toss and tussle, the fact of our impending death is always there, just behind the draperies, or, more accurately, inside our sock, like a burr that we can never quite extract. If one has a religious life, one can rationalize one's slide into the abyss; if one has a sense of humor (and a sense of humor, properly developed, is superior to any religion so far devised), one can minimize it through irony and wit. Ah, but the specter is there, night and day, day in and day out, coloring with its chalk of gray almost everything we do. And a lot of what we do is done, subconsciously, indirectly, to avoid the thought of death, or to make ourselves so unexpendable through our accomplishments that death will hesitate to take us, or, when the scimitar finally falls, to insure that we "live on" in the memory of the lucky ones still kicking.

Wiggs wasn't buying that "live on in memories" number. He had typed himself a small footnote in academic and social history. More important, he had, in his opinion, contributed to the evolution of consciousness in his time. But that sort of immortality was a hollow prize. If what he had accomplished in his "electronic shaman" days in the sixties was destined to have an impact on the future, he wanted to be around to enjoy it.

Not that he hadn't enjoyed himself already. He'd had more fun than an electric eel in a public bath, and, prison or no prison, eye patch or no eye patch, doom or no doom, he was confident the joy wasn't over yet. (As Wiggs related this sentiment to Priscilla, he patted her bare bottom for emphasis.) What's more, he didn't classify himself as a greedy fellow. It was simply that aging was so rapid and death so final that ultimately they robbed life of any meaning.

PHYSICAL PLEASURE
SCIENTIFIC DISCOVERY
ARTISTIC MASTERPIECES
SOCIAL IMPROVEMENT
TECHNOLOGICAL INNOVATIONS
even
LOVING RELATIONSHIPS
or even
SPIRITUAL ECSTASY

Could any or all of these balance the dark weight? The certainty that the most gifted, the most beautiful, the most wise, the most virtuous of us must grow old and die?

"It was then and there, wallowin' on me cot in Concord Prison, that I decided to do somethin' about it," Wiggs said.

"Because every bloody thing else is secondary to the creepin' chill o' personal extinction.

"Death is the fly in everybody's ointment.

"Death has never been acceptable to humanity, and 'tis less so today.

"To the religious chap, I say, if God loves ye, he wouldn't sicken ye and then murder ye. To the rational fellow, and to the hedonist, as well, I say, death makes a mockery of your logic and your pleasure, alike.

"Folks can never be truly happy, or truly free, or even truly sane as long as they got to be expectin' the vigor to decline and the swatter to fall.

"So, darlin', I pushed aside everything else, cleared me jail cell o' professional journals and scholarly books and, yes, girlie magazines, too, although Alobar was to teach me that was a mistake, and I vowed to dedicate me every erg o' energy to this modest pursuit: the eradication o' death."

Priscilla looked at him with respectful disbelief. "Well, frankly," she said, "I've got to classify that under the label of beating the old head against the old brick wall."

"Indeed?"

"Why, yes, Wiggs. Of course. Everything that's alive was born, and everything that was born has got to die. There's no getting around it. It's the law of the universe."

Nude though he was, Dr. Dannyboy drew himself up like a bank president. He tapped his patch portentiously, like a master of ceremonies testing a microphone. Then, in a surprisingly soft and even tone, he said:

"The universe does not have laws.

"It has habits.

"And habits can be broken."

Above Seattle, the many-buttocked sky continued to grind. It taxed the wipers, ragged and lame, that limped, complaining every step of the way, back and forth across Ricki's windshield; first plangent, then lambent, then plangent again, it addressed the tarpaper roof of V'lu's motel, adding an extra dimension to her dreams; it stacked its liquid telegrams against the windowpanes of the Last Laugh Foundation.

Ricki pulled the VW into the driveway of her duplex, killed the engine (a mercy killing), and dashed for her door. She ran not to minimize rain-soak but in order to catch the ring of the telephone should Pris be on the line.

A horned man with the haunches of a goat forced his way into V'lu's dream. The dreamscape was lit by a yellow flame, and there was a *suck suck* sound as the creature, advancing on her, pulled his hooves in and out of soupy mud. V'lu was awakened by the pounding of her own heart. She was surprised and disturbed to find her pussy quite wet. Realizing that the man in the dream and the man on the bottle were the same, she wisely removed the bottle from under her pillow and buried it beneath the neatly folded clothes in her suitcase. In the darkness, tinted slightly by a seepage of NO VACANCY neon, she walked to the window. Although it was permanently sealed, through it she could smell the rain. Seattle rain smelled different from New Orleans rain, thought V'lu. She was right. New Orleans rain smelled of sulfur and hibiscus, trumpet metal, thunder, and sweat. Seattle rain, the widespread rain of the Great Northwest, smelled of green ice and sumi ink, of geology and silence and minnow breath.

Except to the extent that it enhanced the coziness of their fireside chat, Priscilla and Wiggs were oblivious to the rain. It was simply there in the background, like the feeble fire in the grate. In the foreground were hormones, questions, and wild ideas.

Priscilla was willing to accept Dr. Dannyboy's notion that mortality was the principal source of misery for the human race. She might, moreover, sympathize with his painful conclusion that his previous philosophy had been a sham because it had been friendly to death, accommodating it, making excuses for it, even celebrating our vulnerability to it. But his apparently sincere conviction that he could snatch the mouse hair and remove the scimitar struck her as the kind of high-pitched delusion that can shatter a man's mind like a cut-glass punching bag.

"Wiggs," she said, "all those strange drugs you took, jungle berries and Amazon sap and stuff, not to mention regular old LSD, do you think they might have, you know, physically, uh, barbecued your brain?"

"Oh, no, darlin', none o' that. Sure and they destroyed some cells, no doubt about it, but 'twas for the good. If you want your tree to produce plenty o' fruit, you've got to cut it back from time to time. Same thing with your neural cells. Some people might call it brain damage. I call it prunin'."

At that, even the rain backed away.

Things were quiet for a while, what with the slack in the weather and a conversational pause. After a bit, Wiggs took her nipple in his lips, applying a rubbery, rolling pressure, like Captain Queeg worrying those steel peas in his fingers during the *Caine Mutiny Court Martial*. Boing! The little pink pea stiffened with pleasure, much as an aged veteran will sometimes stiffen with patriotism. Pris was beginning to experience a resurgence of powerful urges in her loins when all at once there was a thumping noise from the floor above them.

"What's that?" she asked.

Wiggs spat out the nipple. "Morgenstern. I hope he doesn't wake Huxley Anne."

"What's he doing up there?"

"Oh, 'tis a dance that he does, a dance against dying."

"Wiggs, what is going on in this nuthouse? I mean, you don't have a laboratory on the whole blessed premises, but you've got a Nobel chemist dancing with himself at three in the morning—or is he dancing with a full-grown kangaroo? It sounds like it—and do you actually believe you're going to live forever? Tell me you don't believe it. Please."

"I don't believe it."

"You don't?" She sounded relieved.

"No, I don't believe that Wiggs Dannyboy will be livin'

forever, but future generations will, Huxley Anne quite likely
will, and even so, I expect to outlast me detractors. I could
see me hundred-and-twentieth birthday, I could easily."

"But how? And why? Is this some sort of grandiose and
rococo midlife crisis? Are you that afraid of getting old? Aging
is the most natural thing in the world."

He snorted. "Sure and there's where you're bloody mistaken, me darlin'. There's where you're as wrong as garters
on a nun." He snorted again, and his knuckle began rapping
at his eye patch like a mongoloid woodpecker drilling for
worms in a poker chip. "Agin' is a disease. Maybe disease *is*
natural, but health is natural, too, and a hell of a heap more
desirable. Rust is natural, wouldn't you say? But rust can be
prevented. And if you don't be preventin' it, it will ruin your
machinery. 'Tis the same with agin'. Your man ages because
he lets his body rust."

"Rust? I don't—"

"I'm talkin' about the degeneration o' cells. I'm talkin'
about the gumming up o' cells with superoxide free radicals
and toxins, I'm talkin' about the gradual breakdown o' healthy
cell reproduction due to progressive deterioration o' nucleic
acids. 'Tis all a form o' rustin'."

"And it can be prevented?"

"It can."

"Why don't doctors know about it then?"

"You might as well ask why didn't mariners in the Middle
Ages know the world was round?"

"A few did."

"Sure and a few doctors today know the truth of agin'." He
paused, gazing into the fire. Eventually, he smiled and said,
"Your man, Alobar, he knew the world was round way back
then. And in his own fashion, he knows the truth about age."

"Ah, yes, Alobar: the janitor who never rusts."

"Well, until recently he didn't. I should be gettin' back to
me story."

"That's for sure."

"A kiss first."

"Mmm."

At Concord, Dr. Dannyboy had cleared his cubicle of journals and papers relating to his erstwhile (and some said, alleged) profession, only to gradually replace them with material relating to gerontology, genetics, and life extension. From prison, he became privy to the latest longevity research at universities in North America, Europe, and Japan, and at private institutions such as the Bjorksten Research Foundation, Montesano Laboratories, the Menninger Clinic, and the Institute of Experimental Morphology in Soviet Georgia. Allowed one telephone call per week, he found himself, guiltily, dialing a biologist at Cornell or a gerontologist at the University of Nebraska Medical School, rather than his wife and infant daughter in nearby Boston.

It was far from easy, keeping pace with the leading edge of some of the most esoteric science, but Dr. Dannyboy was resourceful and, despite his unfashionable address, charming. What he learned encouraged and delighted him. To be sure, it also frustrated him in the saddest way that there wasn't more effort and money behind rejuvenation research. With an immense national effort, such as the project that brought us the atomic bomb, we could add fifty years to the average life span in no time at all, he was convinced of that. Wiggs also was depressed by the fact that he was unable to benefit personally from the information that he was accumulating. Nutrition was one area, for example, where he might have done some immediately salubrious work, but, alas, there were few diets on Earth so perfect for rusting out the machinery as the starch-and-sugar blizzard, the fatty acid monsoon of prison fare.

Wiggs began to fall prey to wide swings in mood. One day, brightened by the latest report from the UCLA Medical Center or some such place, he would be as optimistic as a newborn fly in a Mexican restaurant (an insect that might have its own vision "the perfect taco"), but the next day, crushed by the realities of the slowness of underfunded research and the deadliness of prison life, he'd be aboard that nickel submarine that is anchored at the bottom of the Black Lagoon.

Then, late one evening, as Wiggs whispered coarse curses at the Capital of Adjectives—the moon—there was an explo-

sion across Middlesex County at MIT, at one of the very
laboratories that Wiggs was monitoring; and about three months
later, as if in slow motion or delayed reaction, that blast blew
into Concord Prison a new inmate named Al Barr, who would
soon have incandescent beet leaves curling out of the eye of
Dannyboy's periscope.

When he first learned about the bombing of the MIT lab,
Wiggs was irate. A lot of progress was being made there at
MIT. Those guys had molecules jumping through hoops like
poodles in a circus. While other experts in the field spoke of
"the challenges presented by the mysterious and implacable
process called aging," scientists in the MIT experiment talked
about slowing down aging as if that feat were already possible, and they stated publicly that in the future, "society
might be able to abolish death from natural causes entirely."
Dannyboy admired people who could rescue themselves from
modest objectives.

He had expected the "middle-aged" janitor convicted of
destroying the lab to be a fundamentalist Christian fanatic, a
sexually repressed lout driven loony as an outhouse rat by
charlatan evangelists and the ambiguous poetry of the Bible;
a knife-nosed, tight-lipped, lost-eyed ignoramus on a self-
appointed mission to punish scientists for playing God, like
those peasants who burn down the mad doctor's castle at the
conclusion of countless monster movies.

When Wiggs thought of lodging with this yahoo under a
common roof, the green Spanish worm of revenge began to
turn in his heart.

Therefore he was not only surprised but a bit abashed
when Al Barr proved to be the most dignified prisoner in
Concord. Straight of spine and sapphirine of eye, Barr appeared poised, intelligent, and master of a certain smile.
Whereas Wiggs, on his good days, had a smile that snipped
the tense prison air like musical scissors, Barr's smile was on
the order of those stone-cut enigmas that, wired to a heroic
nerve, grace the faces of classical statues. He wore an air of
mystery and some very interesting scars.

Having decided that this chap was no ordinary janitor (although it was known that he had swabbed the tiles of Boston's Turkish Bath House for years), and having become increasingly curious about the motives for the vandalism at MIT, and, further, having had little luck in generating conversation with Barr in the exercise yard (where the new inmate was occupied with a strange kind of yoga), Wiggs pulled some strings (had Wiggs been Geppetto, Pinocchio never would have left home) and arranged for Barr to become his cellmate.

The arrangement was acceptable to Alobar, who intuited that the one-eyed Irish drug maniac would be better company than the blue-collar sister-raper with whom he had previously been bunking. Although Alobar never trusted Wiggs completely (Wiggs was open and eccentric in ways the more closed and conservative Alobar found unsettling), the pair slowly, gradually became such friends that Alobar told him his life story. All thousand years of it. Everything.

Well, not quite everything. He told Wiggs more than he had told Albert Einstein. He told him of exploits in Asia, adventures in French Canada (when Pan, half-mad from the lingering effects of *K23*, was still close by), which even the reader of these pages has not been told. He told him, more than once, of the perfume that was so strangely significant in his life. But he never told him how to make the perfume.

He told him *almost* how to make the perfume. He told him of the jasmine theme, the citric top note, and how he had finally discovered the great elusive and startling base note of beet. Ah, but Alobar, the fox, left something out. He said "beet" to his bunky, but he did not say "beet pollen." If he had, things would have gone differently for several people that we know.

What's more, Alobar forced Wiggs to swear upon his mother's grave, his wife's knickers, the *Book of Kells*, the fairy hills of County Dublin, his one good eye, and everything else that he held holy, including whiskey, vision root, the true universe, Huxley Anne's future happiness, and the Salmon That Fed on the Nine Hazel Nuts of Poetic Art, that he would never ever mention to anyone that beet was the secret ingredient in an allegedly unique and wonderful perfume.

Therefore, Wiggs kept the word *beet* to himself, fine and private, despite his sensitivity to Priscilla's burning curiosity about the comet-tailed vegetable that had extended its crimson orbit into her atmosphere. He did, however, tell her the rest of Alobar's life story. Rather, he told her the *highlights* of Alobar's life story, for to tell the whole of it would have taken months. As it was, it took a full two hours, what with Pris getting up twice to pee, and Wiggs tiptoeing upstairs three times to check on Huxley Anne.

By the end of the story, Dr. Morgenstern had long since ceased his immortalist jitterbug, the fire was out, the windowpanes nearly dry—and Priscilla was practically faint from the knowledge that she was in possession of the ancient bottle that had held the Kudra-baiting, Pan-deodorizing *K23*.

Finding herself stunned and upended by that knowledge, like a myopic houseguest who has walked into a patio door, Pris groped for sturdy furniture with which to right herself. "But—" she said, "but if they really truly did live all that time, all those centuries . . . I mean, how? It's medically impossible, isn't it? How could they have done it?" She was stalling. She wasn't prepared to talk about the bottle just yet.

"Medically impossible 'tis not. Humanly impossible 'tis not. Can it be done? ye ask. Does koala-bear poop smell like cough drops?"

Wiggs then went on, applying an occasional rat-a-tat to the shamrock, to explain Alobar and Kudra's program and how it was based upon the Four Elements. He took each element in turn and did a little number with it.

AIR

"We relate to air through the breath. Most of us don't breathe properly, which is to say, we take in too little or too much and fail to consume it efficiently. Alobar and Kudra developed a method o' breathin' whereby the inhale and exhale were connected in an uninterrupted rhythm, a continuous, circular, flywheel pattern like a serpent swallowin' its own tail. Their breathin' was deep and smooth and regular. When they brought air into their bodies, they visualized suckin' in as much energy and vitality as possible; when they expelled air, they visualized blowin' out all the staleness and flatness inside o' them.

"Simple, 'tis true, but hardly simplistic when we understand that much o' the cellular damage that leads to tissue breakdown—agin', in other words—is caused by the accumulation in our bodies o' the toxic by-products o' metabolizin' oxygen. Superoxide free radicals, which is what these garbage molecules are called, combine with fatty acids to produce lipofuscin, which is an unstable, repulsive gunk that clogs up a cell like grease clogs a drain. The more goop ye have gummin' up your cells, the greater the strain on your metabolism, and the more taxed the metabolism the easier 'tis for still more poisons to accumulate.

"Biological studies have proven that the animals with the longest life spans are those with the lowest rates per body weight of oxygen consumption, apparently because they dump fewer superoxide free radicals in their cells. Since we're stuck with havin' to breathe oxygen until somethin' better comes along—laughin' gas is me own nomination, but so far Nature's not seen fit to make the improvement—we need to learn to consume less of it and to burn it more efficiently. Sure and that is precisely what your couple, oblivious though they were to the putrid perils o' lipofuscin, succeeded in doin'.

"Proper breathin', in addition, reduces stress, and stress is a major contributor to agin', disease, and death. Alobar had been introduced to the virtues o' slow, relaxed breathin' at Samye lamasery. 'The lungs are not plow yaks,' the lamas said, 'so do not drive them. Neither are they potting sheds, so keep them free of cobwebs.' What the Bandaloop 'told'

him, on the other hand, is impossible to translate, but 'tis
obvious, 'tisn't it, darlin', that if a serpent of air is to swallow
its tail—thereby perpetuatin' the circle o' life—it must be
flexible, not tense."

WATER

"Water, too, is helpful in alleviatin' stress. How many
bloomin' times have ye heard, 'Why don't ye get into a nice
hot bath and relax?' Sure, but relaxation may not o' been the
primary result of Alobar and Kudra's bathin' rituals, nor was
the psychological benefit o' ceremonial purification the main
thing, although neither should be underestimated for their
effect in promotin' salubrious longevity. O' greater benefit
may have been the ability o' the bathin' ceremony to lower
blood temperature.

"Research at Purdue University, the UCLA Medical Center, and other lovely places has demonstrated that agin' can
be forced into the slow lane, if not off the road altogether, by
decreasin' the body's temperature. Hypothermia not only
slows down the metabolic pump, allowin' it to coast a bit and
refresh itself, it puts a lid on the autoimmune reactions that
contribute to an organism's deterioration. You see, darlin',
our immune systems tend to be trigger-happy, especially at
high or 'normal' temperatures, frequently attacking the very
cells they hired on to defend—not unlike your police department or your FBI. When body temperature is depressed, the
immunological cops remain in the station house playin' check-
ers, respondin' with their pistols, tear gas, and billy clubs
only to genuinely threatenin' situations. The wear and tear
this saves on the body is the difference between a cherry and
a beater.

"Now, being European, Alobar was less than an enthusiastic participant when Kudra discovered a thermal spring in
one o' the caves, but gradually he came to appreciate the
contribution o' the bath to their program. Their procedure
was to soak for a half-hour or so, then withdraw to shade for a
quarter-hour, repeatin' the process four or five times. The
hot water caused their blood to rise to the skin surface,

where, once they left the tub, it was in a position to be rapidly cooled. Ye understand? Over a period of centuries, this regular cooling down o' the blood may well have reset their internal thermostats—their hypothalamuses—so that they registered permanently two or three degrees below borin' —and debilitatin'—old ninety-eight point six. In Concord, alas, I never got a chance to take your man's temperature.

" 'Tis not the whole of it, though. Our bodies, splendid though they be, are as gullible as your widow in love or your farm boy on Broadway. The body will fall for the same line from the same slick-talking placebo over and over again. Fortunately, it is usually as much to our advantage to be conned by a placebo as to be blarnied by an Irishman, and that was the case when the hot tub fooled the DNA of Alobar and Kudra into reactin' as if its hosts were back in the womb again. The temperature o' womb fluid is a fairly constant one hundred degrees. That happened to be the temperature o' the cavern spring where your couple bathed in India, and they duplicated it as precisely as possible whenever they heated baths in Constantinople or Europe. Floatin' suspended in one-hundred-degree water as often as they did may have conned their DNA into believin' they were neoembyronic, thus supplyin' them with the strongest and freshest hormones and enzymes, because 'tis the nature of DNA to lavish life-enhancin' goodies upon the fetal and the young, while deprivin' us that is over twenty.

"In the centuries when they traveled the fair circuit, they carted a barrel about with 'em, going to the trouble to fill it nightly with bathwater heated in Kudra's silver teapot. Their patience and persistence paid off. Every time the teapot whistled, your Pale Figure would lay down his scythe and mop his bony brow with a black bandanna: quittin' time on the corpse plantation, the most productive farm on Earth. Sure and Alobar stuck to his bathin' throughout his years in America."

EARTH

"Trees and houses and diamond mines may attach themselves like lice to this element, but ye know that soil itself is fastened to the belly. Dirt is the mother o' lunch.

"There's probably no subject with quite so many conflictin' opinions about it as there are about food, and 'tis better to swap bubble gum with a rabid bulldog than challenge a single one o' the varyin' beliefs your average human holds about nutrition, but 'tis obvious that diet must've played an important role in Alobar and Kudra's long-run performance.

"By now, even congenital idiots shut up in cellars in Saskatchewan grain towns are aware that excess body fat promotes infirmity and shortens life expectancy, but are ye familiar with the experiments at Cornell, Montesano Laboratories, the University of California, and the Nebraska Medical School? Severely reduced calorie intake and restricted ingestion o' certain amino acids by laboratory animals *drastically* altered the process of agin'. There was an unfortunate side effect: your animals who were deprived of amino acids suffered from weakened immune systems. However, ye might recall that Alobar and his woman were, in perfect bloomin' counterbalance, strengthenin' their immunological effectiveness by coolin' their blood.

"Your man and his wife ate simply, but apparently they ate with gusto. They consumed small amounts o' food at a time, and let me impress somethin' upon ye, darlin', 'tis the best kept secret o' nutrition that 'tis healthier to eat small amounts o' 'bad' food than large amounts o' 'good.'

"Alobar told me that they fasted for five days each month. Now there's nothin' like periodic fastin' for cleanin' out your pipes, and remember 'tis the accumulated death o' cells—their failure to reproduce—that ages and kills a body, and 'tis the accumulation o' toxins that kills a cell. How does your sweet little cell get polluted with toxins? From improper breathin' and improper diet.

"One other thing about your couple's menu. Ye'll be rememberin', o' course, that they were eaters o' beets. They were your original beetniks, ha ha. Well, 'twas only a few years past that Dr. Benjamin S. Frank discovered that beets build

up the blood, stimulate the liver (which is our main organ o'
purification), and supply a body with nucleic acid, nucleic
acid being absolutely essential to the efficient reproduction o'
youthful cell structure. Ta-*da*!"

(Dr. Dannyboy felt a wee bit guilty about bringing up
beets in the context of nutrition while saying nothing about
their application in perfumery, a subject that, for the present,
at least, was a hell of a lot more interesting to Priscilla. In the
near darkness, he watched something flicker in her tired
violet eyes at his mention of beets. Surely the poor girl didn't
think that a good samaritan was sending her beets in order to
improve her diet?)

FIRE

"With the element o' fire, sex enters the picture."

A little too obviously, he squeezed the cheeks of her ass.
Not to be outdone, she squeezed the cheeks of *his* ass. She
closed her eyes and tried to imagine sex entering the picture.
Would sex enter the picture in a silk robe, or would it be as
nude as a platter of cold cuts? Would sex enter the picture
from the left or the right? Would it ring first, or would it just
slide in slyly, too quick and slippery to be denied; or, would
sex barge in forcibly, red-faced and green-bereted, pushing
all other things aside? She was very tired . . .

"Now we know that sex can ease stress, and we know that
stress wears out the rubber on the wheel o' life. But sexual
fire, like the breath of air and the bath o' water, makes other
contributions to the immortalist program.

"The human organism is designed by DNA to maintain an
optimum of strength and health to sexual maturity—and just
a few years beyond. Once it has presumedly done its procre-
ative duty, (and the perpetuation o' the species may be the
only thing DNA really cares about) 'tis kissed off, abandoned
to steadily deteriorate. What Alobar and Kudra did was to
keep their sexual fires so hotly stoked that DNA was fooled
into believin' that they were just entering into sexual maturity. The fact that, despite their adolescently high hormone
levels, they never actually produced a pregnancy, only con-

tributed to the ruse. What with their womb soaks and sex spurts, their DNA couldn't get a clear fix on their age. 'Twas only aware that they had somethin' going, and to be safe, it had better support them.

"You're yawnin'."

Priscilla stretched. "You know what *time* it is?"

"I hope I've not been borin' ye—"

"Oh, no . . ."

"—with me gab. But ye wanted to know if 'twas medically possible for your man to live a thousand years, and I had to make me case. Next you'll be wantin' to know how 'tis medically possible for a tongue to wag incessantly without comin' unhinged. Me ex-wife said, 'Wiggs, you talk so much that when you die they'll have to beat your tongue to death with a stick.' I resent that remark. She should've said, '*if*' you die."

Pris made two small fists and rubbed her eyes. "Oh, Wiggs," she said.

"Hey, 'tis true! Your man programs himself to die. Almost with our first breath, we're taught to expect our last. The power o' suggestion will pack you up if nothin' else does. Check the statistics sometime on how many people die at the same age that their parents died, the parent whom they most identified with. Your man Elvis Presley not only packed it up at the same age as his mum, but the very same day o' the year. The body is the servant o' the mind, and if we keep tellin' our bodies that they're probably goin' to croak, age seventy-two, then come seventy-two, croak they will. Maybe the main reason your Alobar lived on was because he *believed* he could. It doesn't matter how ye take care o' yourself, beets and baths and breaths and whatever, if ye think that your death is inevitable, it will be. Attitude, attitude. 'Tis the death wish that nails 'em, every bleedin' time."

Wiggs actually paused for a moment, but before Pris could take advantage of the situation, he coughed up a couple of chuckles. "Funny thing," he said, "but that's where Alobar went wrong."

"Where? Did he go wrong?" Her voice was limp and

webby, as if it were being filtered through mummy wrapping. "I was under the impression that he did everything right."

"Sure and 'twasn't right puttin' the torch to that laboratory. Landed him in Concord, where he's in a bloody fix. And 'twas completely unnecessary."

"He gave his promise."

"No matter. 'Twas in vain. Ye see, even if MIT, or any other institution, should come up with a purple elixir, some formula for indefinitely extendin' life, it wouldn't help those old boys in the White House and the Pentagon. Not a whit. The death wish is so ingrained in 'em, in every polluted cell o' their shriveled old brains, that nothin' could make a difference. They can change their diets, change their chemistry, but they can't change their fundamental attitudes. If ye could peek at their personal TV listings, ye'd find they've got a fiery finish scheduled on every channel. What's more, they're lookin' forward to it."

"But why?" she asked weakly.

" 'Tis their religion. To a man, your leaders believe that life on this ball o' clay is merely a test. An entrance exam for eternity. 'Tis the *next* life they're interested in, a life spent swappin' tales o' power with God, sittin' around the lobby o' the Paradise Hotel. That's why they're so dangerous, those righteous old farts. If they pushed the button and furnaced the Earth, they'd say the Earth had it comin'. Sin and immorality and all. Most o' them are secretly wishin' for it. Fry those of us who are at ease with Nature and enjoyin' ourselves, then harpsichord off to their reward. No wonder people are scared silly. Most o' them won't let it show, but they're scared. Look at the line outside this house. It grows longer week by week."

"What do they want?"

"Those people in line? They want somebody to tell 'em they have a chance at the i-n-g of life and not just the e-d."

"Are you going to tell them, Wiggs?"

He sat upright and ran his fingers through his copse of chromium curls. "Me? I don't know. I had a fling with messiahhood once. The Caesars tried to crucify me, but they only got one eye. Ha! Still, I wonder if 'twas worth it. If you look this good to me out o' one eye, darlin', imagine how ye'd look out o' two." As if releasing a pigeon from a cage, he freed a sigh. The pigeon was so heavy it could barely fly. Priscilla stroked his jaw. Sensing some pity in the gesture, he brushed her hand away.

"At any rate, 'tis too early to help the poor bastards. If I let 'em in here now, they'd only feel ripped off. Just like you, they'd be lookin' around for the laboratories. How could I make 'em understand that *I* am the laboratory? And not a very good one. I drink too much. And I let me daughter get chubby.

"When I established the Last Laugh Foundation, it was to research the psychological barriers to immortality. Because what I learned from Alobar was that we have to evolve beyond our death consciousness if we expect to claim our divine right to life everlastin'. If we expect to be i-n-g instead of e-d. When I met Professor Morgenstern six months ago and found that he'd become a bloomin' nonstop immortalist, I invited him, at great expense, to take up residency here, not merely because o' the credibility he'd lend to the joint but because I thought he'd be settin' up a lab, and we *could* run some test-tube experiments out o' here as well. Oh my, and the fairies tricked me on that one! But it all fits together. Do ye know what 'tis called, that jig Morgenstern is always doin'?"

There was no response from Priscilla. Unless "Zznnphh" may be considered a response. She was snoring.

It was a pretty little snore. A rustling of scarabs in the mummy wrappings. Wiggs listened attentively. Most snoring is composed by Beethoven or Wagner, although a few times Wiggs had heard heavy metal rock performed on the somnambulate bassoon. But Priscilla's snore, it had a Stevie Wonder sound. A lyrical scrap left over from "My Cherie Amour." Wiggs tried to hum along.

For a while, he listened and watched, marveling at the manner in which the dawn light seemed to cling to her lashes, at the tiny shadow cast by her Frito nose.

Then he slid gently off of the couch and gathered his tweeds. Huxley Anne would be waking soon, and he must be there. There were nine bedrooms in the Last Laugh Foundation, but he shared a room with his child. Never did he want her to go looking in the morning for a parent who was really a bookend.

Before he climbed the stairs, however, he tiptoed into the dining room and surveyed the centerpiece. Selecting the largest of the beets, a specimen that weighed as much as the skull of a lemur, he fetched it back to the den and laid it upon the cushion next to Priscilla's snore.

Pris slept for about two hours. The length of a Stevie Wonder concert and a few minutes more. When she was awakened by a thud-a-thump on the ceiling, she knew, even before opening her eyes, exactly where she was.

She caught a whiff of *Irish Spring* cologne. She sensed the presence of a face beside her own. Smiling, she turned toward the face and kissed it.

Blech!

What she kissed was rough and cold and flavored of topsoil.

Her lids popped open. Any morning light that might have been stuck to her lashes fell away like spilled sugar.

For a long time, she sat there regarding the beet, looking at it with optimism, misgiving, wonderment, bewilderment, and slight disgust, like a beginning medical student confronting her first anatomical drawing of a prostate gland.

At that moment, in Concord, Massachusetts, Alobar was likewise engrossed in anatomical scholarship. He had very nearly reported to sick call that morning, but changed his mind when his ears suddenly cooled. Instead, he decided to consult his library of *Penthouse* magazines.

As he had pointed out to Dr. Dannyboy, frequent sexual stimulation was essential to a youthful physiometry. And for a heterosexual behind bars, what stimulation was there besides memories and magazines?

On page 83, a young actress was bent over like a map of Florida, affording an unobstructed view of the inland waterway around Cocoa Beach. Sailing in those backwaters would be sunny and brisk. But at the end of the voyage, he'd be searching the horizon for Kudra again.

He was thinking of Kudra, her courage, her character, her crazy wisdom, when a guard rattled his cage. "Barr! From the warden!" The guard shoved an official-looking envelope into the cell. "They're gonna hang ya first thing tomorrow. Tough luck. Ha ha."

"I regret that I have but one life to give for my country," said Alobar, mouthing what to him, from the vantage point of having seen hundreds of countries come and go, come and go, was one of the most shortsighted utterances for which a man was ever remembered.

The letter informed him that his hearing before the parole board was being postponed until "after the holidays."

Which holidays? Did they mean Thanksgiving, which was only three days away, or *all* the holidays, Christmas and New Year's as well as Thanksgiving? He sat down on his bunk with his head in his hands. If they kept postponing parole, they might as well hang him. A lump formed in his throat. It was as large as a beet. It was imperative that he dissolve it.

He ripped up the letter. "I am immortal," he said, ignoring the granny's wedding dress smell that streamed from each of his pores.

He returned to *Penthouse*, opening it to the centerfold. In this photograph, the actress reminded him of Alaska, the centerfold of states: big, beautiful, unrefined, empty—and absolutely irresistible to the type of man who shoots a lot of pool in taverns while dreaming constantly of striking it rich.

"Now, Kudra . . ."

The beet reminded Priscilla, rather rudely, that Wiggs had managed to talk until sunup without ever explaining her connection to his obsessions. She rose, dressed (feeling pleas-

antly sordid as she wriggled into the green party dress), and
went searching for her host.

Had she thought clearly about it, she might have realized
that it was Monday morning and Wiggs had doubtlessly taken
Huxley Anne to school. There remained, however, a yard or
two of mummy bandage festooning her brain, so she went
about the ground floor of the house calling, none too loudly,
"Wiggs."

Unsuccessful, she ascended the stairs and repeated the
procedure. No response there, either. She did, however,
hear a thumping and bumping noise emanating from the
master suite and assumed that it was Wolfgang Morgenstern.

The door to the suite, thrice her age, was graced by an
old-fashioned keyhole. In secretive New Orleans, keyholes
were always plugged, but this one was as open and inviting as
a prostitute's kimono. She laid a bloodshot peeper to it.

Dr. Morgenstern, fully dressed, was skipping and bounding about the suite in a kind of exaggerated, athletic polka.
Every once in awhile, he would stop, execute a little backward and forward jitterbug step; then, necktie flapping, an
exultant yelp springing from his heaving breast, he would
jump straight in the air, up and down, five times.

Well, she'd witnessed some crazy dances during Mardi
Gras and all, but this one took the cake, and the coffee, too.
Actually, it looked like fun, although on a morning such as
this it would surely put her in the morgue. Nervously, she
spied a bit longer, then pulled away. There was an imprint
upon her upper cheek that resembled an archway in a sul-
tan's palace.

Downstairs, slipping into her raincoat, she noticed that the
beet still lay on the sofa, but now, unless her nostrils were
playing games with her, there hung a vulgar odor about it,
the familiar beet-delivery stink, which she was positive had
not been present earlier.

The genius waitress walked home through sunlit traffic.
Puddles shrank before her eyes and she could practically hear
the pavement drying. "The mountains were out," as they said
in Seattle, meaning that the overcast had lifted and snowcapped
peaks were flashing flossed fangs from every quadrant, as if
Seattle were the object of some cosmic plea for dental health.

It was one of those glorious days that, had they occurred less rarely, would have led to Seattle being more populous than Tokyo or India. Gulls circled downtown skyscrapers, derelicts with faces like soup bones luxuriated on jewel-bright park benches, and out in the glittering bay, flotillas of sailboats showed off for watercolorists. Despite her bedraggled condition, or because of her bedraggled condition, men smiled at Priscilla as they passed, and she could not help smiling back.

To be sure, she was exhausted; obviously, she was confused; but she was excited, as well. She felt that she was caught up in some chaotic but grand adventure that was lifting her out of context and placing her beyond the normal constraints of society and biology.

The idea of a thousand-year-old convict with a dematerialized wife and Pan for a pal was difficult to swallow, and the goings-on at the Last Laugh Foundation were enough to strain the elastic on the cerebral panty hose. Ah, but then there was the bottle! In the past, the bottle had meaning to her only as a means of getting rich—of getting even—but now . . . now, she sensed that the drop or two of exquisite fragrance in that weird old vessel had greater worth than she had imagined. The bottle seemed charged with omen and portent, it had a mojo working, as Madame Devalier and her black friends used to say. That bottle was a link to something. It could melt the ice on the dog dish of destiny, and it was hers!

She was glad that she hadn't told Wiggs about the bottle. It would give her an excuse to see him again soon. It would undoubtedly elevate her in his view, and, speaking of links, it would serve to hook them up like sausages in this Alobar adventure.

For the first time since she learned the truth about her daddy, Priscilla felt lucky, blessed. Furthermore, unless she was misreading the symptoms, she was *in love*.

A rat-bite of guilt accompanied the admission of her amorous state, and she decided that she had better call Ricki right away. To that end, she nipped into Market Time Drugs on Broadway and made for the pay phone, which, as reality would have it, was just across the aisle from the perfume counter.

Ricki's phone rang three or four times, and then Pris heard that click and moment of artificial silence that meant she was about to be the recipient of a recorded message.

"Hello, this is Adolf Hitler. I'm out of the country right now, but I'll be happy to return your call as soon as I'm back in power. If Aryan, leave your name and number at the beep."

After hanging up, Priscilla entertained the notion of taking a bus over to the Ballard district for a meeting face to face. She was reasonably certain Ricki was at home. Then, the last strip of mummy wrap fell away from her brain: Hey! It was Monday, there was a meeting of the Daughters of the Daily Special at the 13 Coins at 11:00 A.M. Ricki would be there. Moreover, the waitresses were going to vote that very day on candidates for a twenty-eight-hundred-dollar grant.

She looked at the drugstore clock. Jesus, Mary, and Pepto-Bismol! It was ten already.

Priscilla had been looking forward to fishing out the bottle and, well, studying it, adoring it, consulting it or something, but she barely had time to soap away (a bit reluctantly) the dried and aromatic frosting of coital secretions, to comb her tangles, apply cosmetics, and change into sweater and jeans. As it was, she arrived at the 13 Coins twelve minutes late.

"They're hiring at that new seafood restaurant on Lake Union," Trixie Melodian was saying. "What's it called? Fear of Tuna."

"Forget it," said Sheila Gomez. "I've seen the menu. They're serving Bermuda triangles with shark dip."

"So what?" countered Ellen Cherry Charles. "I caught the special yesterday at that pit where *you* work: 'spaghetti western.' "

"It actually wasn't bad," said Sheila.

"Yeah? Well, hang 'em high, honey."

Priscilla surveyed the room. Ricki wasn't there yet.

"We've got live music now, three nights a week," said Doris Newton.

"Improve your tips?"

"Are you kidding? Stark Naked and the Car Thieves?! Bunch of kids look like they're dressed to invade Iwo Jima. Sound like a cat with its asshole on fire."

"I know that band," said Trixie. "They're fun to dance to."

"Is that dancing or walking in a mine field?"

"People can't dance and eat at the same time."

"Worse, people can't dance and tip at the same time."

"Car Thieves' fans don't tip. They garrote and strafe."

There were no windows in the banquet room, so Priscilla put her ear to the walnut paneling. She thought that she could hear Ricki's clunker maneuvering for a parking space.

There was a new member present. She was skinny, bepimpled, getting rapidly drunk, and didn't look as if she'd been to college. Of course, looks can be deceiving. The girl gulped a swallow of wine large enough to drown a parakeet, then announced, "Dear Abby is a man."

"Pardon," said Ellen Cherry.

"Did you know that? Dear Abby is really a man."

"Yeah," said Ellen Cherry. "Say, anybody get any tempting and entertaining propositions this week?"

"In real life, I mean," said the new girl.

"Right," said Ellen Cherry, turning her back and trying again to change the subject. "Come on, ladies. Didn't anybody get invited to spend Christmas on Christmas Island?"

"I got invited to the Fountain of Youth," said Priscilla. She couldn't help it, it popped right out. "A gentleman asked me to join him in achieving something more than mere animal succession, in perpetuating indefinitely the distinctive personality, the individual self. What do you all think of the idea of human beings living to be a thousand years old? What do you think about death?"

A silence as thick as an Eskimo throw rug fell over the gathering.

Fingering her crucifix, Sheila Gomez looked as if she wanted to comment, but the air in the banquet room was so taut she couldn't spit a word out. Finally, Ellen Cherry turned to the new girl. "Are you sure?" she asked.

"Huh?"

"Are you sure Dear Abby is a man."

The girl brightened. "Oh, yeah," she chirped. "Bald old guy in a wheelchair. Lives in Australia or someplace."

"How about her sister?" asked Doris.

"Huh?"

"The other one. Ann Landers. The sister."

"Oh, Ann Landers," said the new girl. She smiled triumphantly. "Ann Landers is a man, too."

Conversation skittered along for a few minutes, Doris wondering, aloud, what university might have given the girl credit for reading *The National Enquirer*, and Priscilla wondering, to herself, when Ricki was going to arrive. Then President Joan Meep, the driftwood poet, called the meeting to order, and they turned to the business of awarding the grant.

"We have three contenders," said Joan. "There's Amaryllis Tidroe, who wants to complete her portfolio of photographs of wrestlers' wives; there's Trixie Melodian, who, by the way, was a winner year before last, and she's choreographing a ballet based upon the social habits of lemmings—"

"Ought to have a *spectacular* ending," put in Doris.

"—and there's Elizabeth Reifstaffel, who wants to research her master's thesis on the effects of the menstrual cycle on dream content. Okay . . ."

"Wait a minute!" shouted Priscilla. "What about my project? What about me?"

There was a bloated pause, after which Joan said, "I'm very sorry, Pris, but Ricki Sinatra, who was your sponsor, called this morning and withdrew your nomination."

Priscilla wept all the way home. Pushing her bike up Olive Way, her tears threatened to refill the puddles that the unseasonal November sunshine had been evaporating. At one point, she passed a dilapidated building in front of which Tito, the famous Spanish photographer, was posing some local fashion models. "No! No!" Tito screamed at an intimidated young beauty. "Do not smile! Do not smile! Look

sophisticated." Priscilla wanted to yell "Happy Birthday, Tito"
—she wanted to yell, "Are any of you girls married to
wrestlers?"—but her throat was too choked with sobs.

At the top of the hill, she stopped at a telephone booth and
dialed Ricki. A few rings, then that mechanical click and the
canned silence: "Hello, this is Ricki Sinatra. I've been stricken
with eight varieties of virus, including the Mekong Delta
chills, the Mongolian railroad flu, and the Hong Kong rubber
pork chop. I'm under doctor's orders not to be disturbed.
The AMA joins me in requesting that you honor . . ."

"Screw her!" said Priscilla, slamming down the receiver.
"Screw all of 'em!" Through the disappointment, the humiliation, the fatigue, and the guilt, there surged a voltage of
defiance. "I have the bottle," she said. "I don't need Ricki, I
don't need her goddamned educated waitresses, I don't need
Stepmother Devalier and her pickaninny. I don't need any of
'em. I have the bottle!"

But, of course, she did not have the bottle.

She made that devastating discovery immediately upon
returning to her studio apartment, where the refrigerator
made noises at night like sea cows ruminating, where the
toilet sounded like the audio portion of a white-water rafting
expedition, where fallout from fifty failed base-note experiments perfumed the peeling wallpaper, and where the Kotex
box on the bathroom shelf was empty now, except for a
couple of frayed and yellowing pads.

Priscilla did not have the bottle, not anymore, and if she
hadn't the bottle, she hadn't hope or dream, and lacking hope
or dream, why would she wish to live to be a thousand? Or
twenty-five? for that matter. The bottle, once a flagon of
fulfillable fantasy, once the repository of ambition and pur-

pose, was falling into the category of galloping mind-fuck—and a woman really didn't need more than one "perfect taco" in her life.

CALENDAR OF EVENTS

Monday afternoon, November 26: Priscilla Lester Partido traveled to Seattle's Ballard district, where despite pounding, kicking, and screaming that aggravated the murmuring hearts of every old Norwegian in the neighborhood, she was denied admission to the duplex of Ricki Sinatra.

Monday evening, November 26: Priscilla contacted police, who informed her that they could not interfere without a warrant. The judge on duty refused to issue a warrant directing authorities to search for an old perfume bottle for which there was no proof of ownership, which, by the complainant's admission, contained only a few drops of perfume, and which had been concealed, prior to alleged disappearance, in a Kotex box.

Monday night, November 26: Priscilla resisted the impulse to call Wiggs Dannyboy, for fear that he might doubt her story.

Tuesday morning, November 27: Priscilla met with an attorney. The lawyer telephoned Ricki, who assured him that she had no perfume bottle, never wore the stuff, was unaware of the existence of the antique bottle in question (having, in numerous visits to the client's apartment, neither seen nor heard mention of such a bottle), and invited the attorney to personally search her duplex, her car, and her locker at the Ballard Athletic Club. The attorney was convinced.

Tuesday evening, November 27: Ricki the bartender and Priscilla the waitress got into a shouting match in the cocktail lounge at El Papa Muerta, the waitress calling the bartender "a thieving, vindictive dyke" and the bartender characterizing the waitress as "a liar, a two-timer, and a clumsy slut." They were separated by fellow employees and reprimanded by management.

Midnight, Tuesday/Wednesday, November 27/28: Priscilla found a note under her door inviting her to Thanksgiving

dinner at the Last Laugh Foundation, where the celebrated
French perfumer Marcel LeFever was to be feted along with
Dr. Wolfgang Morgenstern. The note was typed and quite
formal, but was signed, in an eccentric scrawl resembling the
markings made by the muddy tail of a water buffalo, "Love
and Kisses, Wiggs."

Wednesday evening, November 28: A second heated exchange at El Papa Muerta, during which the waitress Priscilla
repeatedly demanded that the bartender Ricki relinquish a
purloined perfume bottle, resulted in the waitress Priscilla
being fired. She was escorted from the premises and informed that she was to return her sailor dress within twenty-
four hours or face prosecution. The waitress Priscilla offered
to doff the uniform on the spot, but the manager, despite a
twitch of prurient interest, insisted that it be laundered first,
as it was badly dappled with *salsa suprema.* "That's ketchup
and you know it," said Priscilla.

Wednesday night, November 28: Priscilla stopped off at
Ernie Steele's Bar & Grill, where she proceeded to get
intoxicated enough to forget where she had parked her bicycle (which she then abandoned), but not so intoxicated as to
give in to the burning desire to call Dr. Dannyboy.

Midnight, Wednesday/Thursday, November 28/29: Priscilla,
on foot—and wobbling—returned home to find another note,
this one imparting the information that Marcel LeFever,
upon arrival in New York, had learned of the death of his
uncle, Luc, head of LeFever Odeurs, and rushed back to
Paris. Thanksgiving dinner was canceled. Wiggs added that
he, nevertheless, hoped to see Pris soon. Accompanying the
note was a beet. Accompanying the beet was a raunchy
aroma. Priscilla hurled the beet the length of the hall. It
rattled some innocent tenant's door, probably interrupting a
Johnny Carson monologue.

Thursday morning, November 29: Priscilla flopped on the
sofa, flopping, further, into a drift of sooty snow; sinking into
the placid nightlife of a city of wool, a subterranean Venice
flooded by ink, where a language of bubbles was spoken, and
misfortunes, like furniture in storage, were draped with heavy
blue coverlets.

Thursday afternoon, November 29: The dying gobble of a

hundred million Thanksgiving sacrifices could not awaken her.

Friday morning, November 30: Still sleeping.

Friday afternoon, November 30: Ditto.

Friday night, November 30: Priscilla was pulled to the surface by a banging at the door. She stood, stretched, and admitted Wiggs Dannyboy. She greeted him with a kiss. The inside of her mouth was as white as a swamp snake's. He didn't seem to mind, but, rather, prodded her coated, sluggish tongue with his fresh, lively one. He slipped off her panties and fucked her on the floor in her sailor dress. Refreshed now by forty hours of slumber and a spine-shuddering orgasm, she could scarcely believe how well she felt. She lay in his arms, purring like a Rolls-Royce that has learned it isn't going to be sold to an Arab, after all. "Tell me a story," she said. "Sure and one time in the jungles o' Costa Rica, me voice was stolen by a parrot. For six months, durin' which time I could utter not a syllable, I beat the bushes for that bird . . ." "No," said Priscilla, sweetly. "Tell me a story about beets." "Very well then," said he.

Upon his release from Concord State Prison, Dr. Dannyboy had moved to Seattle, where eventually he leased the proper mansion and established his longevity clinic. Some eighteen months later, he traveled to New Orleans, where a perfumer's convention was about to commence. His motives were vague. "I had vowed to devote me life to immortality work," he said, "and me conversations with Alobar had led me to believe, for some peculiar reason, that perfumery was somehow connected to the mystery o' mysteries. I mean, I knew that the sense o' smell played a role in the evolution o' consciousness, and thought perhaps . . . I'm not sure what I thought. 'Twas just a hunch. I was searchin' for clues. 'Twas intuition led me there. Intuition being the most reliable instrument in science."

Discouraged initially by the focus on merchandising, Wiggs was about to give up on the convention when he heard a speech delivered by Marcel LeFever.

"Yes, that was some speech," interrupted Priscilla. "Up until that point, I'd always hated perfumery. I'd gotten involved with it again because I had a little understanding of it, and for reasons I won't go into now, I believed I had a chance to make a lot of money from it. But I was contemptuous of it, due to childhood experiences and all. It was simply a means to an end. But LeFever's speech . . . boy, he gave me a whole new attitude about perfumery. He made it sound so magical, so special, so important . . ."

"Your man did that, all right," said Wiggs.

After the speech, Wiggs had caught up with Marcel in the corridor adjacent to the auditorium. He had bombarded him with praise and expressions of his own interests. Marcel responded enthusiastically, especially when Wiggs pointed out that the dolphin has no sense of smell. Dolphins have larger brains than humans, and their rudimentary fingers suggest that at one point in prehistory, they might have been the equal of men in more physical ways. Yet, while humanity has gone on to ever more complex achievements in philosophy, athletics, art, and technology, the nonproductive dolphin has apparently swum into an evolutionary cul-de-sac. Could it be, asked Dannyboy of LeFever, that the dolphin failed (in an evolutionary sense) because it neglected to develop an olfactory capability?

" 'Twas obvious I was on your man's wavelength, and he was invitin' me to dine with him at Galatoire's, when *you* approached. Yes, darlin', that was me standin' there, but you didn't notice me. And after you showed up, LeFever didn't notice me, either. Your man has an eye for fine flesh, or, rather he has a nose for it, because all the time you and him were speakin', I could see him sniffin' you up and down, smellin' you out, as it were. Well, bless you, you mustn't o' been his type. He listened politely, wrinklin' his nose all the while, as you told him that you lived in Seattle and were developin' a great jasmine-theme perfume with a citrus top note, but was lookin' for somethin' a wee unusual in the way of a base, and did he have a suggestion o' bases to explore, bases that might o' been used long ago and forgotten. Yes, and he was tellin' you that 'twas a complicated matter, and some base notes had as many as eighty-five separate ingredients in 'em; not bein' very helpful, I'd have to say, when this lovely young black woman walks up.

"Well, 'twas apparent you and your black woman were on familiar terms, familiar but not especially friendly." (Priscilla nodded, vigorously.) "But your man ignores your frosty exchange, and he begins to sniff *her* up and down, only this time the deeply scalloped wings o' his snout are beatin' like a fat swan trapped in a wind tunnel, flappin' like an archangel on Methedrine, *she* is gettin' through to him on the olfactory level. The comic thing is that she is givin' him almost the same exact story as you. She's speakin' French, and me French is a wee rusty, but I hear her say she lives there in New Orleans and has got a wonderful jasmine-theme perfume brewin', only she's havin' difficulty with locatin' somethin' special and unusual to bottom it out, and the sly devil tells *her* that he's gettin' interested in jasmines again himself, and maybe he can lend a hand. Lend a prick is more like it. Next thing I know, your man is invitin' your woman to dine with him at Galatoire's, only there's no mention o' me, in French or English."

Thereupon, Dr. Dannyboy was on the verge of asking Priscilla to dinner at Galatoire's: "complicate the scene a bit, if you can't get any enlightenment out of a situation, you might as well get some fun." At that moment, however, the handle on a nearby emergency-exit door began to jiggle, as if someone in the alley outside wanted to be let in, so Wiggs opened the door. There was nobody there. But, with the opening of the door, a rank odor rushed in, an odor embarrassing in its suggestion of unwashed genitals and bestial glands. Wiggs recognized the smell.

"One morning in Concord, I woke before me accustomed hour. I came into consciousness holding me nose. There was a bloody rotten smell in our cell, as if the warden had put a herd o' goats in with us. I asked Alobar what was goin' on, and your man said, 'It was Pan. Pan came to visit me during the night.'

" 'No joke? What did he say?' I asked. 'Why, he didn't say anything,' said Alobar. 'Pan can no longer speak. He just dropped by. I suppose to show me that he wasn't finished yet.' Can ye imagine? The smell hung around for nearly an hour. And 'twas the very same smell that blew through the door in New Orleans that day. I turned to remark on it, but you had gone. And a minute later, LeFever was escortin' the black girl toward the main entrance and the street.

"I went out in the alley and looked around, but there wasn't a sign o' anythin'. So I got me hands on a list o' convention attenders—it listed Marcel's address and yours and V'lu Jackson's, too—and took a night flight back to Seattle. There was a lot o' funny business goin' on in this blarney-stone head o' mine."

I know the feeling, thought Priscilla. Her relaxed state was giving way to a video arcade of blinking wonderments and beeping forebodings. A chill, like current from a nuclear icicle, vibrated her sex-softened spine.

"Wiggs," she asked, after a while—she was clearly afraid to phrase the question—"Wiggs"—her brain stem was quivering as if it were being prodded by a jewel—"Wiggs, is it . . . Pan . . . who's leaving the beets?"

"No," he answered, without hesitation.

Somewhat relieved, Priscilla raised herself on one elbow. In the process, she accidentally struck her worktable, causing lab ware to tinkle and slosh. It was a miracle, she thought, that they hadn't dumped the whole enterprise in the throes of their passion.

"But the smell . . ."

"The smell is Pan's, all right."

"It is?"

"Indeed. Though it isn't old Pan who's deliverin' the beets. As a matter o' fact, Pan is tryin' to *prevent* the delivery o' the beets. Pan is tryin' to interfere with the delivery o' the beets. Only your god is weak and limited, nowadays, and there's little he can do but leave a reminder o' himself—and the powers that he represents—to discourage the recipient and him that *is* leavin' beets."

"And that is . . . ?" She sounded calm enough, but she was quaking inside.

"Me."

"You?"

" 'Tis me left all the homely little vegetables at your door. 'Tis me leavin' 'em with V'lu Jackson. I've spent a small fortune flyin' to New Orleans and back. Fortunately, I have me royalties. And 'tis a friend o' mine from the acid days been droppin' 'em off for Marcel LeFever. He's a professor in Paris and his son works in the mailroom at the LeFever Building. Were ye aware that Marcel and V'lu have been gettin' beets, as well?"

"Well, no. Hell no, I wasn't aware—"

"I'm sorry, but ye didn't have an exclusive contract, ye know."

"Why, Wiggs? Why the goddamn beets?"

"I can't tell ye, darlin'. I'd dearly love to tell ye, but I can't. I gave Alobar me word. The fairies would cause me terrible sufferin' if I broke me vow."

"But—"

"Listen. Don't fret. Ye can figure out for yourself. If you think about it real hard and be puttin' two and two together, it will come to ye. Clear as the tap water that spoils your man's whiskey. Just give it some thought."

Priscilla agreed and set into thinking, but Wiggs suggested they chew up some geoduck first. Since she hadn't eaten in a couple of days, she agreed to that, also.

After tidying themselves a bit, they set out by taxi for Never Cry Tuna, the new restaurant on Lake Union. Sure enough, Trixie Melodian was working there.

"Amaryllis Tidroe got the grant," Trixie said.

Priscilla wasn't surprised. "Oh, goody! I can't wait to see eight-by-ten glossies of Mrs. Masked Marvel."

"You're taking it awfully well," said Trixie.

"Not to mention Mrs. Garp—"

"I thought he wrote books."

"—and the various loving helpmates of the midget tag team."

"I could eat the midget tag team," said Wiggs.

"One order of shrimp with mussels," said Priscilla.

"Jesus," moaned Trixie. "If I'd gotten that grant, I wouldn't be here listening to this."

Priscilla wanted Wiggs to spend the night at her place, but he claimed that Huxley Anne would be needing him bright and early. "But tomorrow's Saturday," said Pris.

"We watch cartoons together," said Wiggs.

Since no invitation to join them appeared forthcoming, she kissed him good night in the lobby and climbed the lonely stairs, stumbling often enough in her ascent to insure exclusion from all future Everest expeditions.

As she lay on the sofa digesting the goeduck, she figured out that beets *must* be the secret ingredient, the elusive base note, in *K23*. Why else would Wiggs be bombarding perfumers with them? Yet, how could that be? A beet had no memorable aroma, and it would turn a perfume the color of Dracula's mouthwash.

It was puzzling. And it might be academic, as well, if she couldn't recover the bottle. The loss of the bottle was one of those "harsh realities" with which she was not unfamiliar. If she was relatively equanimious about it, it was because Wiggs was teaching her that "harsh realities" were not the only realities: that there were many different realities, and to a certain extent, with the proper focus of energy, one could choose which reality one wished to live. One might even outwit the harshest reality of all.

For the third night in a row, Pris fell asleep in El Papa Muerta's sailor dress, its wine-dark ketchup stains now counterbalanced by scrumbles of chalky semen. As she drifted into sleep, she had the feeling that she was waking up.

In the week that followed, Priscilla fiddled with her lab equipment, meditated upon the beet, spent the funds that she'd been saving to purchase jasmine oil on a private detective ("I'm positive Ricki Sinatra has my bottle"), and worried, progressively as each day passed, that she'd not hear from Wiggs again. On Saturday, however, her presence was requested at the Last Laugh Foundation to participate in "the Alobar-Kudra bath ritual."

Out of the frying pan and into the hot tub, she thought.

The line outside the Foundation walls seemed slightly longer and considerably more agitated than usual. People hollered rude things at her when she was let through the gate.

" 'Tis the news background," explained Wiggs. "The Middle East is smokin' cigars in the fireworks stand again, and that shallow jackass in the White House is waggin' his nuclear-headed peepee at the Russians. People are nervous."

"I don't get it, Wiggs. I mean, if there's such a universal longing for immortality, if the human race is going bananas because it can't accept any more that it has to die, why do we still have wars? All this military violence seems to contradict your theory."

"Not in the least," he replied, loosening, like an iguana butcher, the spinal column of one of his beloved zippers. "Your common man is willin' to go to war only because he hates death so much."

Having successfully filleted his own trousers, he seized the triangular viper-head of Priscilla's fly and rib by rib, pulled it apart. "Don't you see? The enemy represents Death to 'em. The government propaganda mills paint the enemy as an unfeelin', devourin' monster. So, when we go to war we go on a noble mission, a life-affirming mission, whose object is the destruction o' death. And 'tis precisely because we hate death so much that we're too crazed and irrational to see the irony in it. We hate death so bloody much that we will kill—and die—in order to try to halt its march."

In unison, they stepped out of their pants. Their gap-toothed zippers, split like the vertebrae of a temple sacrifice, made a tiny clink when they hit the tiles of the tub-room floor.

"As a grandiose self-deception, war is o' the same magni-

316 TOM ROBBINS

tude as religion. We embrace war or religion—usually both at the same time—as a means o' defeatin' death, but neither o' them do a blinkin' thing but sanction dyin'. Throughout history, Death's best friend has been a priest with a knife."

At their feet, the zippers shuddered.

They lowered themselves into the steaming water, tensing at first from the shock of the heat, then relaxing until they were as buoyant as sausages.

"Ahhh. How many can you get in this tub?"

"Ahhh. Six, as a rule. You can fit eight, but 'tis rather crowded."

"If it wasn't for death, the world would be eight in a tub."

"Uh?"

"Overpopulation. If nobody died, pretty soon it would be standing room only."

"That's one o' the standard arguments in favor o' death, but it doesn't hold water. Or whiskey, either. We don't have an overpopulation problem, we have a land-use problem. We're sprawlin' out all over the place, like hogs in a rose garden, takin' up a thousand times more space than we need. If we were to stress vertical growth instead o' horizontal, if we were to build tall apartment complexes instead of acres o' one-story ticky-tackies, there'd be more than enough room. If we built tall enough, and we have the technological capability, we could double the world's population and still fit every single one of us into the state o' Texas. *Comfortably*, I might add. The rest o' the planet could be given over to agriculture and recreation. And wilderness. We could have elephant herds again. Buffalo on Main Street."

"That would be nice," she said. "Speaking of vertical development, I thought hot water was supposed to take the starch out of this." She slipped her fingers around his half-hard penis. It immediately grew taller. Were it an apartment building, they could have moved another hundred families in.

"Love, little darlin', defies the laws o' physics. Or, rather, it breaks the habits."

As she stroked him, he tapped his moisture-studded eye patch and, with some difficulty, continued to hold forth on his favorite theme.

"Besides, not everybody is goin' to give up death. The death wish is very strong, and a lot o' people prefer to die. You'd be surprised at the number who say their lives are so miserable they couldn't bear the thought o' lengthenin' 'em."

"Speaking of lengthening . . ."

"Alobar says you aren't supposed to do this until *after* the soak."

"Sorry. You know, my daddy used to say, 'Life is rough, and then you die.' "

"Bad attitude," said Wiggs.

"Then he'd wink and say, 'But, meanwhile, there's Mardi Gras.' "

"Your father was willin' to enjoy some crumbs, but not the whole cake."

"But his life *was* short and rough. Maybe most lives are. I read once that it takes a chicken-plucking machine barely forty seconds to complete the job."

"Indeed. But remember, at that point the chicken is only naked, not dead."

"Speaking of which . . ."

"Okay, darlin'. Okay."

Wiggs placed his palms beneath her reddening buttocks and, assisted by the water, lifted her up, centered her, then lowered her slowly onto the length of his shaft. When she struck bottom, she emitted a primitive cry, coming almost immediately. He lifted her off again. The entire procedure occurred in the span of time it would have taken a chicken-plucking machine to defeather a drumstick.

When she could speak, she said, "If we did die—you and me, I mean—you could come back as a lily pad, and I'd be a very happy frog."

"A pleasant arrangement, but let's not be countin' on it."

"I'm surprised you don't believe in reincarnation."

"Why? 'Tis probably just another rationalization. Reincarnation—or the transmigration o' souls—was an idea spawned in one o' the most rigid social systems humanity has ever devised. Your ancient Hindu was stuck like a gnat in amber. Durin' his lifetime, he was obliged to live in a prescribed place with a prescribed family and practice a prescribed occupation. The possibility o' mobility did not exist. The hand you were dealt at birth was the hand you played. Everythin' was predestined, and you couldn't change a bleedin' dot o' it. Since they had no chance o' change in life, 'tis only natural they fantasized about change in the afterlife. Reincarnation was simply a fantasy your Hindu perpetuated to keep his rigid reality model from drivin' him mad.

"That's why Kudra, by the way, was such a remarkable figure. Can you imagine the odds against a tenth-century Hindu, especially a woman, breakin' out o' those fetters? When it comes to liberatin' the Indians, Kudra's example is worth a barrel o' Gandhis."

"I can appreciate that. But how can you be positive we don't reincarnate?"

"Oh, I can't. You can't be positive about *anything* regardin' an afterlife. There's not a dot o' proof anywhere."

"Well, now, what about those people who die temporarily on the operating table? They seem to have very similar experiences. Leaving their bodies behind with relief, feelings of great tranquillity and love, reuniting with deceased friends and relatives. And most of them describe an encounter with some kind of light . . ."

"Who knows? Maybe it signifies that the best *is* yet to come, which suits me, I guarantee. On the other hand, we know that the brain remains electrically alive for up to thirty minutes after the heart and other vital organs have ceased to function. So these 'heavenly' experiences o' the temporarily dead may be merely an archetypal drama unfolding upon the stage o' departin' consciousness, a farewell performance of a powerful mythological allegory. And when the brain turns the juice off a half-hour later, boom, the curtain falls once and for all; the show is over, and there's no waitin' up for the reviews. Ultimate solitude. As for the light, well, all o' matter is condensed light. We came from light, each of us, so where's the wonder that we return to it in death?"

"So, you're saying any way we slice it we're doomed."

"Not at all, Pris. I'm sayin' that we don't know what the afterlife is like, we absolutely do not know. Therefore, until we do know, we ought to do our best to go on livin'."

"But how will we ever know?"

"Should your man Alobar make contact with Kudra, we'd learn a lot, we would. 'Tis a long shot, but I believe it might still be done. Part o' the secret lies in the perfume."

They climbed from the tub to allow their blood to cool. The tiles pressed like frozen petals against their flesh. Their bodies gave off a painterly glow. An Old Master glow. *Still Life With Boiled Beets*.

"Amazing, Wiggs."

"What's that?"

"Amazing. After all that talking, your pole is still up."

"I'm not Gerry Ford, ye know. I can do more than one thing at a time."

Grinning, she hovered over him. Then, like a fist closing around a doorknob, her grin closed around him. With her lips, she turned the knob first one way and then the other: left, right, open, shut; left, right, open, shut. The knob did not squeak. In fact, Wiggs was unusually quiet.

Now, falling into rhythm, she sucked the knob from its axle, sucked the axle from its door, the door from its hinges. Out onto the lawn, tempo increasing, she sucked up the flagstone walk, the rosebushes, the petunia bed, the sprinkler, the driveway, and the small Japanese car parked in the driveway: Oh, what a feeling! Toyota! Wiggs moaned as the neighborhood disappeared.

The towers of the city began to sway, and soon, the planet itself fell victim to the force, swelling at its equator, throbbing at its poles. It wobbled violently on its axis, once, twice, then exploded. The Big Bang theory, proven at last. Continuing to impersonate a black hole, she pulled in every drop and particle—she'd never had a man in such entirety—and it wasn't until the final spasm had subsided and the cosmos was at peace that she loosened her grip and, lips glistening like the Milky Way, looked up to see—the legs of a third party standing there.

"Ach! I am fery sorry."

Wolfgang Morgenstern, nude except for a towel about his hips, turned stiffly and strode, with steps of Prussian exactitude, from the tub room. Dr. Morgenstern was red-faced, sweaty, and breathless. Presumably, his condition was due to his jumping—his immortalist dance, his solo jitterbug—and not to the effects of the cosmic spectacle that he had stumbled upon.

"God! I'm mortified. I'm so embarrassed I could die." Priscilla covered her face with her hands, surreptitiously wiping the corners of her mouth.

"Did you hear what you just said? 'Mortified. I could die.' Pris, ye must never use such expressions. They are unconscious manifestations o' the death wish. You're signalin' the universe that death is not only acceptable but deserved."

"Oh, Wiggs!"

"And as for your Nobel laureate, 'tis high time he had a taste o' quality entertainment. He *does* seem to be gettin' younger, to tell the truth, but I don't know what good 'tis doin' him, cooped up in his room."

Wiggs pulled her hands away from her face and kissed her. "Darlin', ye were magnificent."

"I was?"

"Truly. Ye must promise me now, no more expressions such as, 'I'm so embarrassed I could die' or 'The suspense is killin' me.' "

"I'll try. But how will I ever face him?"

"With pride," said Wiggs. "With pride."

They slid back into the Jacuzzi.

Minus the extra heat of desire, the water seemed cooler now. They submerged to their chins in the tropical broth, the pot of doldrums, the horse latitudes that modern landlubbers had domesticated and miniaturized, wrapping themselves willingly in its enervating ripples.

"You know, Wiggs," she said, her voice softened to near inaudibility by the sultry climate, "it seems like with you everything leads back to the subject of death."

"Sure and show me the person's road that does not lead to death. We try to divert our attention, to pretend 'tisn't so, but the very air we breathe is vulture's breath. Please don't be insinuatin' your man is morbid. I dwell on death in order to defeat it."

"But suppose death is necessary to evolution. What if we have to give up our bodies so that we can evolve off the earth plane, move on to a higher plane? It might be foolish and regressive to cling to our physical bodies."

"Might be. Although life on the astral plane has always held a minimum o' charm for me. No whiskey, no books, no Frederick's o' Hollywood. And if it should turn out that there *is* no astral evolution, where does that leave your poor dead self? 'Tis a gamble I'm not willin' to take."

"After the gambles you've taken with vision root, all those psychological deaths and rebirths, how could you still be afraid of regular old dying."

"Sure and I'm *not* afraid o' dying. Never have been. Death can't do anything to us because death is dead. What's dead can't hurt ye. Fear is not the issue. Like your man Alobar, I'm less scared than resentful. We've got ourselves stuck in a cyclic system that makes true freedom, true growth impossible. In the arts, a period o' classicism is followed by a period o' romanticism. Then 'tis back to the classical again. 'Tis as simpleminded as a bloody pendulum, and for me, at least, it robs art of any real meaning. Same thing in society. A conservative cycle, a liberal cycle, then a conservative cycle again. Action and reaction, back and forth, like the tides. As long as we're trapped in these cycles, we can't expect much in the way o' liberation, we can't even expect fundamental change except the awful slow variety where each step takes a million years or more. For most of our history, we were trapped by the seasonal cycles, the weather cycles. Now, however, we can at least move south for the winter, north for the summer. The seasons still operate cyclically, but we don't have to submit to 'em. All I'm askin' is for that kind o' mobility in life as a whole. I'm askin' for the opportunity to break out o' the birth-death cycle. Ye see what I mean? 'Tis far too rigid and predictable to suit me. Cycles take the meaning out o' life, just as they do in art. Me hope is this: certain individuals have always managed to break out o' the artistic and social cycles—that's why I love and respect your individual more than I love and respect humanity at large. Maybe, maybe, the time is ripe for certain individuals to escape the birth-death cycle, as well. And I don't mean by vaporizin' into the void o' Buddhist Nirvana, either. Maybe Alobar has done just that. Maybe I can do it, as well. And maybe—as long as I'm into the maybes—some cycle-buster will come along to rescue mankind from the hollow tides o' mortality."

"We deserve a break today?"

"We do."

"Dying is a bad habit?"

"Yes, and must be broken."

"Good luck, Wiggs."

"Thanks. You know, there is one condition under which I might willingly die. Might even take me own life."

"You're joking?"

He shook his head as somberly as an elephant. "If anything ever happened to Huxley Anne, I think I would choose to die, too, just on the chance that we could be together."

"Oh."

Wiggs was quiet for a while. A tear bubbled up, like a syllable from a flounder, in his single eye. It hung upside down from his lower lid, like a transparent sloth from a ledge, until gravity finally pried it loose, sending it plunging, silently, headlong, salt and all, into the anonymity of the steaming tub.

"One last thing about death," said Wiggs.

"What's that?" Pris asked rather morosely. She was still staring at the spot where his teardrop had hit the water.

"After you die, your hair and your nails continue to grow."

"I've heard that."

"Yes. But your phone calls taper off."

Once more, they climbed out onto the tiles to cool. Then, another hot soak and a final cooling. They toweled and slipped into their underpants, his as crisp and green as a shamrock, hers a faded, indeterminable color ringed with sagging elastic. They donned their pants, his of tweed, hers of denim, and, with the hands of miracle workers, restored to wholeness the golden salamanders that held the pant fronts together.

He'd made it clear she was not to stay the night. Seemed he and Huxley Anne had plans for early morning. So she embraced him at the door, feeling a trifle, well, vulnerable, insecure, and was steeling herself for the walk home when he asked, "Well, how's it comin' with the perfume?"

She hadn't wanted to speak of perfume for fear she might blurt out something about the bottle. She dare not tell him of the bottle, but, rather, must show it to him, must hold it up to that gleaming orb of his and watch the silver hairs stand on his head like the bristles of a robot's toothbrush. How she looked forward to that moment!

"I've come to the conclusion," she said, "that beet is the bottom note in K23. Am I right?"

Hesitant to respond, he eventually nodded in the affirmative, trusting that the fairies, that the Salmon That Fed on the Nine Hazel Nuts of Poetic Art, that his ex-wife's knickers would not regard a nod a breach of promise.

"I thought so. But how in the world is it used? I really can't figure out . . ."

"You're the perfumer."

It was Priscilla's turn to nod in agreement, but to herself she said, "Ha! I'm an unemployed waitress without an ounce of first-rate jasmine to my name. And if I don't get lucky, and fast, this time next week I'll be hustling nachos at someplace like Gourmet de Tijuana."

The way she backed through the door, waving good-bye,

sort of burdened and flustered, you'd have thought that she had suddenly and inadvertently cornered the world market in refried beans.

In truth, Priscilla felt a twinge of resentment that she had to return to her little studio apartment. Certainly there was plenty of room for her at the Last Laugh Foundation. Why, Christ and all twelve disciples could have dwelt in the Last Laugh Foundation, although Judas would have had to sleep on the sun porch.

. She walked down the path feeling like three-fourths of two pieces of slug bait. As she passed the letter box at the guard gate, she had an urge to stick a stamp on her forehead and mail herself to the Abominable Snowman.

On the street, it was worse. The crowd of aspiring immortalists was restless and surly. They glared at her as if she were a piece of modern art at a county fair. A hostile sneer here, a puzzled laugh there, and not a blue ribbon in sight.

Apparently, there recently had been a provision run, because many in line were munching on fast-food hamburgers. They were old enough to know better. Some of them were old enough to remember when old McDonald had a *farm*.

People used to die from germs. Now they died from bad habits. That was what Dr. Dannyboy said. Heart disease was caused by bad personal habits, cancer was caused by bad industrial habits, war was caused by bad political habits. Dannyboy believed that even old age was a habit. And habits could be broken. Priscilla felt like lecturing the crowd on its habits and sending it home, but, of course, she did not.

Toward the end of the line, she thought she heard a white-haired guy on crutches remark that it was December 7, "the thirty-fifth anniversary of the Japanese attack on Pearl Bailey." He was wrong. It was then December 8.

Five days later, on December 13, Pris gave Wiggs Dannyboy a call. She was in a funk about their "relationship," a snit compounded by the detective's lack of progress, and was desperate enough to try to force a talk.

"Pris, me darlin', 'tis happy I am that ye called!"

"Really?"

"Sure and I couldn't be happier was I to learn that God and the Devil had settled out o' court, endin' once and for all the ridiculous notion of a struggle between good and evil that has provided the religious o' the world with a pious excuse to kill and plunder and has spoiled the plot o' many a novel. I couldn't be happier was I to grow another eye, one that shines in the night like a wolf's eye and can twist on its stalk to look up a lassie's skirt. I couldn't be happier was Alobar to be released from the nick, which, indeed, he may be next month, if it's not too late. As fortunate as I am to be born an Irishman and thus possess a license to broadcast this brand o' pseudolyrical bullshit, that's how fortunate I am that you—I mean, ye—called. I would have called ye but ye haven't a phone."

"Don't mock the afflicted."

"Or I would've dropped by, except I've been to New Orleans to deliver a certain vegetable. Ye know what I mean?"

"All too well."

"I do have good news. Marcel 'Bunny' LeFever has successfully buried his Uncle Luc and has aimed his wondrous nose again in our direction. Dr. Morgenstern and I—he sends his regards, by the way—are planning another dinner party, if we can coax the university scientists away from their research for the CIA. A week from tonight, I think, and ye must come. Only this time ye must sit next to me; to me left, would be proper, so's I can rest me left hand on your tender thigh while I am liftin' a sociable glass with me right."

"Wiggs?"

"Yes, love?"

"You've had me to dinner, and now Marcel LeFever is coming. I'm curious why you haven't had my stepmother or V'lu."

"Oh, I invited them. As a matter of fact, I just learned on this trip to New Orleans that V'lu actually flew to Seattle to attend the last dinner. I have no idea why she didn't show up."

"Wait a minute. V'lu was in town the night of that party?"

"Yes. Stayed overnight and returned home the next day."

Adrenaline welled in Priscilla with such pressure it was practically shooting out of her major orifices.

"Wiggs," she said, "I have to make a trip to New Orleans myself."

"When?"

"Right away."

"Will ye be back in time for the party?"

"I hope so. If I am, I'll have a surprise for you."

"Goody. I love surprises."

"Good-bye then."

"Bye-bye, Pris. Have a lovely trip and watch out for the bees."

After she hung up, she thought, *Watch out for the bees? Whatever did he mean?*

She would find out soon enough.

The Chinese discovered gunpowder by accident while trying to invent a potion that would alchemically lengthen life.

It is unclear what the Chinese were trying to invent when they discovered spaghetti. Perhaps the spaghetti noodle, too, was a byproduct of longevity research, of an effort to live a won, won ton; a futile attempt to avoid facing the question, "Who's going to chop your suey when I'm gone?"

No matter. It may be prudent, however, for would-be immortals to bear in mind the Chinese experience. Seeking prolonged existence, they ended up with gunpowder, the elixir of death, not life; the propellant of history's innumerable tragic bullets, including the ones that felled Gandhi, John Lennon, and Bambi's mother—and the one that left Bingo Pajama facedown on Royal Street.

Figuratively and literally, New Orleans was buzzing. It was an angry black buzz in counterpoint with a terrified white buzz: historically typical of that city where slaves liberated themselves long before Lincoln, where a black aristocracy flowered to rival the only true white aristocracy in America, where a black voodoo queen once ruled as completely (if covertly) as any Catherine of Russia; where African mystery, large, organic, and powerful, has provided a soundtrack of primeval rhythm against which all metropolitan life—stodgy white commerce as well as fierce black pleasure—has had to unfold.

Even in slavery, the blacks called the tune. Proud and virtually fearless, they danced in Congo Square in such a graceful abandon, in such harmony with unseen forces, that their owners acted to outlaw African dancing lest it escalate into rebellion. And all the while, even as the owners drafted proclamation after proclamation of wiggle prohibition, their white toes tapped in their shoes. White folks have controlled New Orleans with money and guns, black folks have controlled it with magic and music, and although there has been a steady undercurrent of mutual admiration, an intermingling of cultures unheard of in any other American city, South or North; although there has prevailed a most joyous and fascinating interface, black anger and white fear has persisted, providing the ongoing, ostensibly integrated *fête champêtre* with volatile and sometimes violent idiosyncrasies.

Due to their poverty, anger, and moral imperatives, some New Orleans blacks were disposed to create a jazz of robbery. Due to their insecurity, fear, and religious philosophy, some New Orleans whites were disposed to compose hymns of brutality. The thieves tooted out of the federal housing projects—they were young, spirited, and pessimistic. The cops lumbered out of the bayous—they were paunchy, insensitive, and easily manipulated by authoritarian dogmas. On the one side, playground slam-dunkers, jive-talkers and second-line parade dancers with an easy propensity for redistributing wealth; on the other, good ol' boys who, up until getting their badges and patrol cars, went slender-pole fishing by day and slammed each other around by night. Clashes were inevitable, but the white boys had the law on their side.

Umm, but the air here is getting thick with sociology. We are discussing New Orleans, after all, the city Louis Armstrong said "has got that thing." (As for the identity of "that thing," Louis said, in the most Zen statement ever made by a westerner, "If you have to ask, you'll never know.") Perhaps it is time for a riff.

"New Orleans"

> She went to the school of Miss Crocodile
> Where she learned to walk backwards
> And skin black cats with her teeth.
> Soon she could wear the loot of dead pirates
> Cook zee perfect gumbo
> And telephone the moon collect.
> But it took sixty-six doctors to fix her
> After she kissed that snake.

New Orleans was buzzing. A Jamaican flower peddler and street singer named Bingo Pajama had been shot and killed by two off-duty policemen who claimed they were trying to make an arrest. Pajama, a suspect in the bizarre death of a fellow officer, made a threatening move, according to the cops. They pulled down on him with their .38 Specials.

The black community was not swallowing that trash. Too often, in Louisiana, blacks suspected of having killed policemen were themselves slain by their arresting officers. It smacked of revenge by execution, and it had become routine. Also routine were the hearings in which the cops were cleared of any wrongdoing. It was the sort of situation that turned a second-liner's bile a dangerous hue, the sort that could build into a "race riot."

Although Bingo Pajama was from out of town, a foreigner with a funny accent, a bum who kept bees but had no hive; a mysterious, clownish figure known well by none, the blacks of the city adopted him posthumously. They went so far as to send him off with a jazz funeral.

Mourners poured out of the projects, out of the shotgun

houses below Canal Street, out of barrooms and gumbo parlors, out of the Baptist church at Liberty and First and the Hoodoo church on Rampart, and with a mighty brass band leading the way (horns wailing in the modes of both Satchmo and Bird, drums recreating the phantom energies of the Congo), with umbrellas twirling (although the day was dry), feathers flashing, joints smoldering, bottles gurgling, and fingers snapping, they strutted and stomped, rambled and hooted, all the way to the French Quarter, through the Quarter, and back to the Central City again. A horse-drawn hearse bore the coffin, but there was no corpse in it. The police had the corpse and wouldn't release it. Inside the coffin was a bouquet of jasmine branches, crushed and faded but so potently sweet it perfumed the length of the parade.

Although the funeral was typically merry, a wild, winding party ("In yo' face, Mr. Death") enjoyed by all, it was fueled by an ill-concealed cache of anger. Dark curses were shouted at police cars, and placards of somber protest appeared along the way. That night, an ancient work began behind locked shutters. Black candles were burned, bitter powders were sprinkled, crude objects were fashioned of wood or wax, pythons were addressed, and chickens were put to uses that would have shocked the pants off Colonel Sanders, not to mention Julia Child.

There were formal protests, as well. A steady stream of black community leaders visited the police department and city hall, demanding justice. So great was the outcry that the mayor wasted little time in scheduling a hearing. At the insistence of blacks, and of white liberals, a special commission was appointed to conduct the investigation. To the dismay of "law-and-order" factions, only one policeman was named to the panel.

According to reports, several people had witnessed the shooting of the Jamaican. Two had viewed it at close range. Two women, the story went, one white, one black. And the white woman was said to be tight with blacks. Why, it was ol' Madame Devalier, the French Quarter perfumer, a one-time supplier of Special Delivery Oil, she who was rumored to possess the secret of hurricane drops!

So New Orleans buzzed. Black folks buzzed. White folks buzzed. Bingo Pajama's bees buzzed. And the bee buzz was the most disturbing of all.

It was a tiny swarm: fifty bees at the outside, maybe only forty. Their number was to their advantage. A swarm of many thousands, as is customary in a honey colony, would have been easily tracked and cornered, but a fist of forty, flying in excess of a dozen miles per hour and climbing to altitudes loftier than New Orleans' tallest building, could be elusive, evading entomological patrols and escaping DDT barrage or apiarian capture.

With his life, the bees left Bingo Pajama. Nobody saw them go. They flew away in the night with his soul. Only the pollen grains that the coroner found in the slain man's hair indicated that they had ever existed.

Ah, but the next morning! When the streetlamps went out, the bees lighted up. Wearing the dawn like silver on their wings, they returned in a glassy phalanx to the scene of the crime. Like a glass spearhead come suddenly to life, like an animated dagger with an angry voice, like an electrified pineapple spike; like a darting fish made of noisy sparks, half full of fire and half full of cold, the swarm circled the death scene, diving and looping, again and again, a crazed cactus loose in the air, humming defiance, forty little spines dripping poison and pain.

For most of the day, reporters, photographers, police investigators, sympathizers, and curiosity-seekers were held at bay. Those who challenged the swarm's territorial claim retreated quickly with burning welts about the neck and face. From time to time, the swarm would settle on the map of dried blood where their master had lain. It was as if they were feeding there. A newsman or a cop would grow brave, but at his approach—*banzai!*—the missile would launch itself, screaming toward target.

In late afternoon, beekeepers were brought in. Like brides behind their protective veils, they wooed the golden phallus, but it would not surrender to them. It scorned their traps of honey, its forty tongues preferring to lick crusty blood.

Curses and consternation abounded. From a nearby telephone booth, calls were made to universities and the Department of Agriculture. "This is not your common North American honeybee," said an entomologist gazing through binoculars. He was probably correct. According to an official handbook, "Stinging requires a bee to use twenty-two different muscles." These bees used twenty-three.

At nightfall, the swarm departed, but it returned the next day. So did the media and the crowds. Barricades were set up. Traffic was snarled. The proud pragmatism of civilized intelligence was being insulted again by goofy nature. It was time for might to make things right.

Spray teams were dispatched. Foggers from the swamplands. Experts at gassing mosquitos. Their Jeeps pulled trailers with compressors and hoses and metal tanks full of gaseous insecticides. They wiped out every cricket in the neighborhood and mutated countless future generations of mockingbirds. But the swarm took to the sky, disappearing through a trapdoor in a low-flying, and ominously dark, cumulus cloud.

Thirty minutes later, it flew through an open window at city hall, where the chief of police was explaining to the district attorney that that very swarm had been used as a murder weapon by Bingo Pajama and would be useful as an exhibit during the hearing for the courageous officers who, in self-defense, had eliminated the mad Jamaican. "Here's your exhibit, Chief," yelled a mayoral aide, diving for cover. Exhibit B.

Faces swollen and painted pink with calamine lotion, the city fathers looked like buffoons that evening on the six-o'clock news.

The bees were not seen again until the next afternoon, when they followed Bingo Pajama's funeral parade along its entire route. None of the marchers was stung, and it was reported by a trombonist and a couple of second-liners that the swarm kept time with the band.

After that, the bees played hide-and-seek. They were observed all over the city. They appeared in the Garden District, in the Irish Channel, uptown, downtown, in Audubon

Park, along the lakefront, the riverfront, on Metairie Ridge, and in the forgotten voodoo groves of Bayou St. John. Nobody could guess where they would strike next. They harassed cops on the beat, dive-bombed adulterous judges on the patios of Lake Pontchartrain love nests, interrupted work on the Mafia wharfs, and sent tourists running from Jackson Square, portraits half-painted, Sno-Kones half-eaten and spilled on the bricks. The press began to speak of the swarm as if it were a terrorist band.

Like a necklace of gouged-out crocodile eyes—yellow-green and menacing, shiny and ancient—the renegade bees encircled New Orleans, a mosaic albatross that wouldn't lie still.

Such was the situation in New Orleans when Priscilla arrived: a buzz of black anger, a buzz of white fear; a buzz of multicolored rumor, panic, and superstition; a buzz of bees.

Initially, she scarcely noticed. After two days and three nights on a Greyhound bus (the detective had refused to refund her retainer, and she was functioning far below the summit of her economic potential), her homecoming was rather numb.

She headed directly to the Quarter, to Royal Street, to the Parfumerie Devalier, only to find the shop dark. It was shuttered and locked. After a night's rest on a lumpy mattress at a YWCA, she returned to the shop, truly expecting it to be open for business. Still it was closed. Moreover, with Christmas hardly a week away, the quaint little perfume-bottle nativity scene that had graced Madame Devalier's show window every December for as long as Priscilla could remember was nowhere in sight.

Lingering over a café au lait at Morning Call, she speculated that the shop's closure was connected to the bottle of K23. It was not. It was connected to the buzz.

I'll bet they're in Paris or New York, making some kind of deal, thought Priscilla.

In fact, Lily Devalier and V'lu Jackson were nowhere near Paris. They were in Baton Rouge.

A few hours after Bingo's shooting, threatening phone calls began to jangle into the shop. Rough voices warned Madame and her assistant not to testify against the policemen who had blown the Jamaican down. "Whatever are we to do, cher?" asked Madame. "It could be the cops threatening us, or it could be the Klan."

"Whut's de difference?" asked V'lu.

As the public furor increased, so did the threats. Madame grew woozy and could no longer answer the phone. She would have her nose parked on the rim of Kudra's bottle, saying something such as, "You know, cher, I believe this to be a deceptively simple boof. A fine jasmine middle, a citrus top, and a single bottom. Oui, single. Three ingredients only. But, ooh-la-la, what could that bottom . . ." And the phone would ring, and she'd turn woozy. V'lu would lift the receiver, and clear across the room Madame would hear the man. He had a voice like a biceps.

"Who dat say dat?" V'lu would inquire.

"The man who's gonna love lynching your black ass." *Click.*

When Wiggs Dannyboy's most recent beet hit the floor upstairs, V'lu nearly fainted alongside Madame. Both were so convinced it was a firebomb that they actually smelled gasoline.

Madame was conditioned not to complain to the police. Eventually, however, she complained to the press. The press told everybody in Louisiana. And when it was through telling them, it told them again.

Meanwhile, the governor suggested to the mayor that it might be wise to move the hearing out of New Orleans, move it, say, to Baton Rouge. The mayor suspected the governor of wanting to bale a bit of political hay, but he didn't care. The mayor was scared of that hearing. He admitted to the governor that he was scared of demonstrations, scared of protests and violence. The governor could tell that the mayor was also scared of the bees.

Although the hearing was not scheduled to commence until after the holidays, the governor had Madame Devalier and V'lu Jackson moved to a motel near the capital. They had separate rooms and were guarded by state patrolmen around the clock. V'lu spent the days reading Edgar Allan Poe in French. Madame sniffed at the bottle and addressed Christmas cards. She addressed no less than three to Priscilla in Seattle, for as the holiday approached, she felt increasingly guilty about the bottle. "It is Pris's boof, too," she said. Quote V'lu, "Nevermore."

Priscilla, living close to the bone at the New Orleans Y, had her own guilt going. She wrote a long letter to Ricki, apologizing for having accused her falsely. She didn't post it, however. She decided she'd better first make sure Madame and V'lu had the bottle.

Once she took notice of the buzz about her, the contentious whirr, the apprehensive whisper, the unpredictable golden hum, the vibrating mantras of panic and revenge, once her ear focused on the buzz, and her brain examined its origins, variations, and ramifications, Priscilla quickly learned that Madame and V'lu were in Baton Rouge. The address of their motel was a secret, however. Incoming calls were forbidden, and inquiries were curtly discouraged. Resigned to a wait of several weeks, she settled in at the Y and began to look for part-time work as a waitress.

Naturally, she missed the dinner party at the Last Laugh Foundation. The party went on without her. A fresh group of scientists were introduced to Wolfgang Morgenstern, in the hope that this meeting would elevate the prestige of the foundation.

Dr. Morgenstern showed up at table so breathless from jumping that he could barely chew his lettuce.

Huxley Anne told everyone who'd listen about how she'd cleaned out the old greenhouse behind the mansion and was planning to cultivate flowers there: "My daddy's going to smuggle in rare jasmine plants from Jamaica, and I'm gonna be in charge of making them grow." The biologists on either side of her raised their eyebrows. "Jasmine, all right," whispered one to his wife. They'd heard the stories about Jamaican marijuana.

Dr. Dannyboy presided, consuming impressive quantities of wine and issuing periodic pronouncements, usually preceded by a knock on his eye patch with whatever inanimate object lay handy. "The most glarin' failure o' the intelligentsia in modern times has been its inability to take comedy seriously." Things such as that.

At one point, Dannyboy announced, "Paris is yet another contribution o' the Irish. Look it up in your history books, gentlemen. A Celtic tribe called the Parisii founded the place some centuries before the birth of our Lord and Savior. 'Twas a gift from the Micks to the froggies to give them something to justify their arrogance." Several guests were offended by this, but Marcel LeFever was amused, and fully intended to get a lot of mileage out of it when he returned to France.

In fact, Marcel and Wiggs hit it off famously. When a lonely (and horny) Priscilla telephoned Wiggs on Christmas Eve, Marcel was still there. "Your man is goin' to remain until after New Year's," Wiggs informed her. "He's infected with perfume, he's its master and its slave. Perfume is beauty to Marcel, 'tis his glory, his opiate, his *samadhi*, his breakfast sausage as well as his midnight champagne. Oh, to feel about something as passionately yet coherently as your man feels about perfume! That, darlin', is the key to the piggybank o' life. How I wish I could speak to him directly about beets."

Priscilla felt a pinch of jealousy. "But what about me?" she very nearly whined. Then she recalled the bottle, the ace she might yet play.

"Merry Xmas, Pris. If only I was there to put a little somethin' in your sock."

"A *big* something," corrected Priscilla, feeling sweaty and weak. "And 'tis in me pants you'd be puttin' it." Her vulnerability to Wiggs was opening her up (as voluntary vulnerability often can) in unexpected ways.

"Ha ha. Indeed. And, say, have ye had a glimpse o' the bees?"

"Well, no, not personally . . ."

But just then the swarm rounded the corner, flying in

wedge formation, silhouetted against the sunset, screaming
like a cutting tool, and a few paces ahead of it, running for his
life, his beard and cap flapping wildly, his belly spilling
feathers and his tin cup spilling coins, dashed Santa Claus.

The old pagan festival came and went. Neither Seattle nor
New Orleans would consent to strike a seasonal pose. Seattle
was mild and rainy and as green as Bing Crosby's royalties.
New Orleans was mild and sunny and quite accustomed to
stringing lights in banana trees.

Snows and ices decorated Concord, Massachusetts, you
may be certain, but Alobar could spy no acre of greeting card
tableau from his cell. He could see the famous Star of the
East, however, and its gelid twinkle reminded him of his first
Christmas, that commoner's winter in Aelfric when he learned,
with some astonishment, that the face of an executed Eastern
rabble-rouser had been carved in the pagan pumpkin.

Marcel and Wiggs sat before a yule log, in a room in which
there was scant necessity for blaze, and night after night, in
conversation after conversation, rebuilt "reality" from the
ruins they'd left it in the night before. They slept late.
Afternoons, they assisted Huxley Anne in the greenhouse,
where the child was tending, with precocious expertise, an
enlarging accumulation of exotic plants. Dr. Morgenstern
jumped for something approximating joy.

Priscilla made the rounds of Mexican restaurants, but while
there was no shortage in New Orleans of imperfect tacos, she
failed to land a job. On New Year's Eve she got drunk and
got laid. Upon that, it would be indiscreet to dwell, except to
pass along the advice that before going home with a person-
age one has met in a French Quarter bar, one should make
absolutely certain of their gender. Later, she was to refer to
the episode, without bitterness, as "Ricki's revenge."

Alobar boycotted the cell block Christmas party, preferring
to sit alone in his cubicle and breathe, even though, thanks to
his escalated aging, the sterile steel cubicle had begun to
stink like a mouse nest or a potato bin.

The "season" crab-walked by in its emotional shoes, then it

was over, it was January 2, the Western world blew its nose, took two aspirins, packed pagan ornaments and plaster mangers to the attic, and set about finding ways to finance the recent indulgences. Bing! The clock, after its celestial wobble, was back on mechanical time, and precise, or, at any rate, measurable, or at least, normal things could happen. Alobar was paroled from prison, the hearings got underway in Baton Rouge, Wiggs (with some help from Bunny LeFever) figured out Where We Are Going and why it smells the way it does, and Huxley Anne became the youngest member ever of the Puget Sound Orchid Society.

Upon learning of Alobar's release, Wiggs and Marcel jetted to Boston to greet him. Over bowls of borscht that resembled the steaming blood of Beowulf's monster, Alobar consented to accompany them back to the Last Laugh Foundation.

"He almost looks a thousand," Wiggs said to Priscilla over the wire that night. "He's as wrinkled now as a lemon-suckin' prune, his hair has gone white, his torso has shrunk, and he walks stooped over like a dentist. Ah, but he's got the spirit still, and he claims he can recover his youth if he cares to. I've asked him in private if he won't pass the beet to Marcel, let him in on the *K23* and all. He's thinkin' it over."

Again, Priscilla felt an inflation of the green balloon. Striving to conceal her resentment and insecurity, she said, "Wiggs, remember that I said I was going to have a surprise for you? Well, the surprise is for Alobar, too. It's a great big surprise, and it will mean even more to Alobar than to you. It's not quite ready yet, but I think he should see it before he makes any major decisions."

"Sure and that sounds swell to me, little darlin'. Maybe I'll be bringin' him to New Orleans in a week or two. Marcel is headin' there himself. To see V'lu. They've stayed in touch, and it would seem your man is bloody moo-eyed over her."

"Ha ha," said Pris, thinking all the while, *I wish you were bloody moo-eyed over me*.

The hearings in Baton Rouge lasted ten days. Hardly a session passed in which the two suspended policemen did not protest that the jasmine bouquet that the late Mr. Pajama pointed in their direction could have concealed a gun.

"Yes, it *could*," the panel chairman finally agreed. "And the blind man's cane *could* hide a sword, and the wife's chicken and dumplings *could* be laced with razor blades, and the lunch boxes of school children *could* be ticking with bombs."

It was the panel's recommendation that the cops stand trial, although as a compromise, they would be charged not with murder but manslaughter. When news of the compromise reached New Orleans, it did not exactly turn the Mississippi River into diet soda.

Roosters were heard to squawk at midnight in Central City storefronts.

A cross was burned in front of Parfumerie Devalier, blackening its show window and charring its door.

The bees, which except for a daily fly-by of the *Times-Picayune* offices had been little seen of late, attacked in a single afternoon six policemen, five politicians, four whiplash lawyers, three used-car salesmen, and two fast-talking disc jockeys—and put the fear of Beelzebub the Bug God into an agnostic from Dallas.

It was decided by the court that the trial should be conducted in Baton Rouge. The judge scheduled it for the middle of February. Concerned by the cross-burning, he ruled that Madame Devalier and V'lu Jackson be kept in protective custody until after the trial.

With difficulty, Priscilla resigned herself to a wait. Yet she did not stand still. Having exhausted the Mexican restaurants of New Orleans as a potential source of gainful employment, she suddenly spun on her dais of habit and set off in a relatively new direction. Abandoning her long-standing obsession to the same fate as the cottage cheese she'd left in her refrigerator in Seattle, she accepted a job in a coffeehouse near Tulane University, where the clientele played chess, wrote poetry, and debated matters of cosmic import (subjects forbidden to "mature" intellectuals unless they first sign an oath to be dry and dispassionate). Inclined to insert her own opinions, especially when a discussion broached issues of life and death, Priscilla rapidly revived her reputation as a genius waitress. For example, she dazzled a party of students one evening by declaring, "To be or not to be isn't the question. The question is how to prolong being."

And she almost believed it.

Next thing you know, I'll be drumming on my eyelid with an espresso spoon, she thought.

Since the spirit of Wiggs Dannyboy was upon her, and since Wiggs contended that longing for the future was as antilife as dwelling in the past ("nostalgia and hope stand equally in the way of authentic experience"), Priscilla decided that she must de-emphasize the role in her life of the perfume bottle and its promise of future financial bliss. She refused, however, to relegate her ambition for wealth to the back of the fridge where she'd shoved the allegedly perfect taco. After all, it was Wiggs who once said, "I love the rich."

Actually, his statement in its entirety was, "The rich are the most discriminated-against minority in the world. Openly or covertly, everybody hates the rich because, openly or covertly, everybody envies the rich. Me, I love the rich. *Somebody* has to love them. Sure, a lot o' rich people are assholes, but believe me, a lot o' poor people are assholes, too, and an asshole with money can at least pay for his own drinks."

Priscilla was forced to admit that she missed such pronouncements. *The radium-tongued rascal has contaminated me*, she thought.

The radium-tongued rascal who had contaminated her, the windy cyclops who had brought both tornado and calm, fog and clear sky into her life, the defrocked anthropologist whom everybody, including Priscilla, suspected of having a bit too much fun, was on a collision course with death and tragedy.

Disaster struck while he was high above the world and its

cares, relaxing aboard a Boeing 747 in the company of Marcel
LeFever and King Alobar. Sometime during that flight, as
the fields and peaks soaked up sweet darkness beneath them,
the crowd outside the Last Laugh Foundation in Seattle went
mad.

Somebody had supplied beer, cases of it, and many in the
crowd had lost their reason in it. About seven o'clock, as
much of Seattle was finishing its dinner, a dense, hot, rustic
odor swept through the street, and as if it had one mind, one
nose, the crowd spontaneously panicked. Something snapped
in it, and it rushed the gate, tearing it from its hinges and
throwing the guards aside.

Disturbed and anxious, pursued by the smell, the people
ripped loose the fairy door knocker and streamed into the
mansion, where they raced from room to room, looking for
the divine magic that had been denied them. And when they
found nothing—no gurgling test tubes or sparking coils, no
vials of purple elixirs or leatherbound books bursting with
esoteric information, no files, even, that they might plunder;
when they found merely a posh modern residence lacking so
much as a hint of scientific activity and occupied only by a
red-faced man who'd been skipping and leaping about in a
bizarre dance, and a young girl playing with potted plants,
then they truly panicked.

They ravaged the furnishings, smashing chairs, coffeetables
and lamps, defiling the white immortalist walls, hurling Escher
prints through stained-glass windows. As mirrors shattered
and food flew, several in the midst passed into further frenzy,
went beyond the hot madness of disappointment and longing
into the cold madness of fear and loathing, and seizing Papuan
war clubs from above the fireplace, they bashed the skulls of
Wolfgang Morgenstern and Huxley Anne Dannyboy.

Like a fertilized condor egg, filled with blood and promise,
the bald head of Dr. Morgenstern split open. He died instantly.

Huxley Anne was not so heavily damaged, although when
police arrived she was exhibiting no vital signs and was believed as dead as the professor. Nevertheless, oxygen and

CPR were administered. After twenty discouraging minutes, a tiny birthday-candle flame of pulse began to flicker.

She was taken to Swedish Hospital, a few blocks away, and by the time her father got there, physicians were venturing that she had a twenty-five-percent chance of living, although only a ten-percent chance of having escaped permanent brain damage. Should she survive, which was improbable, she would likely be, in terms most disparaging to the consciousness of beets, "no more than a vegetable."

Naturally, the news traveled swiftly. It involved a famous scientist and the child of an infamous heretic, it involved the "occult" (for that is the context in which the press placed immortalistic research), it involved murder, a guarded mansion, and, probably, drugs. The media snatched it up and streaked with it, galloping toward tons of pay dirt, and Priscilla knew about it almost as soon as Wiggs did.

She heard about it at work. When it had sunk in, and that took a minute or two, she set down her tray, tables away from its destination, untied her apron, and walked out of the coffeehouse. "Where are you going?" yelled the fellow who operated the espresso machine. "Seattle," she replied.

Of course, she had practically no money. Within minutes, she was back at the coffeehouse, pleading with the manager for an advance on salary. He refused, but when he saw the tears breaking loose, when he recognized that they were massed in huge numbers and might be expected to march, two abreast, for hours, he allowed her to call Seattle on the office phone.

After hacking through several thousand feet of red tape, she managed to reach Wiggs at Swedish Hospital.

"I'll be there as quick as I can get there," said Priscilla.

"It isn't necessary," said Wiggs. He spoke with hardly any accent at all. "I appreciate it, but it isn't necessary."

"I don't care. You'll need help."

"Marcel and Alobar are with me. Marcel's left an open bottle of her favorite scent by her bed. To call her back.

Alobar has some ideas, too. Bandaloop stuff. I'm confident, Pris."

"You sound pretty good. But I'm sure I can help you."

"No. Huxley Anne's mum will be here by morning. She'd probably be uncomfortable if you were around."

"Screw her comfort! Don't you care about me?" The instant she said it, she regretted it.

"I do care. But right now my energy is totally with my daughter."

"I'm sorry. I understand. You can call me if you need me. Here, or else they'll take a message at the Y."

She hung up and after a heroic belt of the manager's bourbon, returned to duty. If Huxley Anne died, however, she'd proceed to Seattle with all possible haste, even if she had to steal the funds, because she and she alone knew that if Huxley Anne went, Wiggs would go, as well.

At birth, we emerge from dream soup.

At death, we sink back into dream soup.

In between soups, there is a crossing of dry land.

Life is a portage.

That was the way Marcel LeFever had always looked at it. After his encounters with Dr. Dannyboy and Alobar, after the experience with little Huxley Anne, Marcel began to suspect that it might be more complex than that. He went so far as to consider that there might be more than one type of afterlife experience, that there might be several, that there could be, in fact, as many different death-styles as there were life-styles, and "dream soup" was merely one of dozens from which the dead person might actually choose.

It was pure conjecture, of course. Moreover, he much preferred to think about fragrance. Yet, wasn't fragrance somehow involved? In the case of Huxley Anne, at least it seemed to have played a part. Alobar and Dr. Dannyboy agreed that it had, although the physicians were equally convinced that it had not.

The physicians had no explanation of their own, however,

so Marcel was prepared to attribute the miraculous recovery to fragrance, or, rather, an interaction between the powers of fragrance and the powers of human spirit. Why not?

It *was* a miraculous recovery, no one would deny that. The child lay comatose for nearly a month, neither advancing nor receding, just sort of standing hip-deep in the dream soup, connected to shore by, as they say, "artificial means," and then, toward midnight on Saint Agnes's Eve, her eyes popped open, she asked, in a completely normal voice, for SpaghettiOs and chocolate-chip cookies, and demanded to know why there was no television in her room. "Mmm, smells good in here," she said. Within days she was walking the corridors. Were there damaged parts in her brain, they were well concealed.

When he felt that she was strong enough, Wiggs inquired if she had felt at any time, especially during the minutes immediately following the attack, that her soul had left her body. "Oh, Daddy!" she said, "Don't you know that when you die, your soul *stops* leaving your body?"

"Uh, no. What do you mean?"

"Our souls are leaving our bodies all the time, silly. That's what all the energy is about."

"You mean the energy field around our bodies is the soul being broadcast out of the body?"

"Kinda like that."

"And at death this transmission stops?"

"Yes. Can I have some ice cream?"

"In a minute, darling. When your soul stopped leaving your body, what did it feel like?"

Huxley Anne screwed up her face. "Well, kinda like a TV set that wasn't quite off and wasn't quite on. You know, the TV had cartoons in it, but it couldn't send them out."

"But your, ah, TV set, it didn't go completely off?"

"No. That would have been something different, being all the way off. I didn't want to go off without you, Daddy. I tried hard to stay on. I knew where you were because I could smell my *White Shoulders*, but it took a little while to get back on all the way and warmed up and everything. Can I have my ice cream now?"

They say that February is the shortest month, but you know they could be wrong.

Compared, calendar page against calendar page, it *looks* to be the shortest, all right. Spread between January and March like lard on bread, it fails to reach the crust on either slice. In its galoshes—and you'll never catch February in stocking feet—it's a full head shorter than December, although in leap years, when it has growth spurts, it comes up to April's nose.

However more abbreviated than its cousins it may look, February *feels* longer than any of them. It is the meanest moon of winter, all the more cruel because it will masquerade as spring, occasionally for hours at a time, only to rip off its mask with a sadistic laugh and spit icicles into every gullible face, behavior that grows quickly old.

February is pitiless, and it is boring. That parade of red numerals on its page adds up to zero: birthdays of politicians, a holiday reserved for rodents, what kind of celebrations are those? The only bubble in the flat champagne of February is Valentine's Day. It was no accident that our ancestors pinned Valentine's Day on February's shirt: he or she lucky enough to have a lover in frigid, antsy February has cause for celebration, indeed.

Except to the extent that it "tints the buds and swells the leaves within," February is as useless as the extra *r* in its name. It behaves like an obstacle, a wedge of slush and mud and ennui, holding both progress and contentment at bay.

James Joyce was born in February, as was Charles Dickens and Victor Hugo, which goes to show that writers are poor at beginnings, although worse at knowing when to stop.

If February is the color of lard on rye, its aroma is that of wet wool trousers. As for sound, it is an abstract melody played on a squeaky violin, the petty whine of a shrew with cabin fever. O February, you may be little but you're small! Were you twice your tiresome length, few of us would survive to greet the merry month of May.

Confined to its usual length, February *still* extracted a toll from Priscilla and New Orleans. On Groundhog Day, a carpetbagger freeze turned banana plants as black as seminary shoes, and night after night, the Mississippi exhaled Yukon breath. The small boys who tap-danced for coins on Bourbon Street were forced to compete with their own chattering teeth. Aside from tap and chatter, the Quarter was so quiet it might as well have been in Salt Lake City. Even the bees took refuge from the chill. Where, was anybody's guess.

As for the frost on Priscilla's personal pumpkin, it was neither thick nor withering, but typically Februarian, it was a long time melting.

Once a week, approximately, she received a letter from Wiggs: one paragraph about Huxley Anne (she appeared to be completely healed, but the doctors, "taking no chances," were keeping her out of school); one paragraph about the restoration of the Last Laugh Foundation (Marcel made financial contributions, while Alobar, who had acquired carpentry skills over the centuries, helped with the actual work); a couple of paragraphs alluding to his new ideas about evolution; and a phrase or two of sexual innuendo. All in all, it wasn't enough to get a young woman in love through a lingering funk such as February. Nevertheless, she wrote him daily and practiced a fairly strict fidelity.

About the time the trial began in Baton Rouge, she learned the exact whereabouts there of Madame and V'lu, but made no attempt to contact them lest she tip her hand. When they returned to New Orleans, she'd retrieve that bottle. If they had it, that is. February is the month for doubt.

Because she was no longer up until dawn trying to make perfume, she was rested and energetic, and since meeting Wiggs, she mainly looked at life, even when it was studded with failures and misfortunes, with a subdued, irrational cheerfulness. So, though she had to battle impatience on several different fronts, and though February lay about her shoulders like a cloak of lead, Priscilla stayed afloat.

Then came March.

On the very first day of March, Wiggs telephoned to announce that Marcel and Alobar were heading to New Orleans for Mardi Gras. Wiggs himself would be joining them in a week or ten days, whenever the doctors gave Huxley Anne the green light. "Take care of them until I get there, please, Pris. Show them the sights. Once V'lu is back in town, you won't have to worry about Marcel, but in the meantime, he and Alobar will need a place to stay and a good spot to watch the parades. You know the city. Alobar's a touch high-strung. Still holding out on the *K23*. If you've got that surprise for him, it might do him good."

"I'll do my best. When you come, will you . . . will you stay with me?"

"Huxley Anne and I."

"Oh. All right. Hurry."

A contrarian, the owner of the coffeehouse made a practice of leaving town during Mardi Gras. He had a three-bedroom flat in the Garden District, and assuming that Marcel would pay, Priscilla sublet it for the first half of March. The master bedroom she claimed for Wiggs and her. And Huxley, damn it, Anne.

She took a bus to the airport and met the flight from Seattle. Marcel deplaned first. She recognized him from the perfumer's convention. His hair was still slicked back and parted in the middle, his suit was expensive, his cologne turned heads, his Vandyke beard shoveled the air in front of him as if he were digging in it, turning it over, searching for diamonds. Or worms. With an elegant gesture, he kissed Priscilla's hand. Then he wrinkled his sturdy nose as if he didn't quite approve of her smell.

Alobar soon followed. Cocooned in the ill-fitting Robert Hall suit that he'd been issued upon parole from Concord Prison, he was obviously an old man—Priscilla would have guessed seventy-five—yet he revealed not a tremor of the fear or fragility that so often causes us to look with pity, or disgust, upon the old. If he was less arrogant than Marcel, he was no less self-confident. He moved through the world as if he was intimate with it, as if he belonged in it, as if there was not the remotest chance that he would fall down in it and break a hip. His manner was vague, but it was the vagueness of a mind distracted by important issues, not enervated by insufficient oxygen supply. In fact, his breathing was deep and smooth, so rhythmic as to be almost hypnotic, and when introduced to Priscilla, he drew in an especially long breath. And winked.

They collected luggage, rented a car, and drove, bumper to bumper, into the hubbub and jubilee of Carnival.

Technically, Carnival had commenced January 6, with the ball of the Twelfth Night Revelers, and had been underway throughout the downcast days of February, but so far Carnival had been a matter of club parties and society balls, closed to the public and made all the more private, all the more small, by the unusually low temperatures. Now, on the Thursday before Mardi Gras, itself—five days before climactic Fat Tuesday—it was sewing on sequins, dusting off cowbells, and ambling into the streets. On Saturday, ninety-six hours of uninterrupted spectacle and debauchery would begin. The parade of the Knights of Momus would, that very Thursday evening, prepare the way.

Priscilla, Marcel, and Alobar were able to watch the Momus parade from the balcony of the sublet flat, where they sipped champagne and munched Cajun popcorn. For the Friday parade, they had to fight for space on the curbs of Canal Street. Saturday evening, they were back on the balcony for a third parade, and later that night, the three of them, *en costume*, attended a minor but nonetheless ornate ball to which Pris had wrangled invitations. There was something just a trifle unreal about dancing with a thousand-year-old man, Priscilla thought, particularly when the man was dressed as an astronaut chipmunk.

No less than four major parades were scheduled for Sunday. As they sat around the kitchen table Sunday morning, deciding which one they would attend, Marcel thanked Pris for her hospitality, admitting to her that the festivities in New Orleans were grander in every way than Carnival in Nice.

That statement prompted from Alobar an expression of disappointment.

"New Orleans Mardi Gras is a sham," he said. "So is Mardi Gras in Nice. It's all a sham these days. No, I am not living in the past, but believe me, some things have changed for the worse."

He unbuttoned his shirt, for he was preparing to soak in a tub of hot water. "In olden times, Carnival had meaning. During the forty days of Lent, the forty days before Easter, almost the entire population would abstain from eating meat and drinking spirits. Many of them gave up sexual intercourse, as well, a most unhealthy expression of self-denial, I can attest, after my recent experience behind bars. Anyway, Carnival was a final fling, it was a last indulgence of rich foods and wine and lust before the severe austerity of Lent. When you're facing a forty-day fast, that last spree can be intense. It has physical significance as well as deep psychological penetration. The old Mardi Gras was charged with real meaning. Today . . ." He sighed. "It's entertaining, but it's empty. It's just another big party. An opportunity for some to spend money and others to make money. It isn't connected to anything larger than itself. I've been a foe of Christianity all my life, but Christianity gave meaning to the fun and the rowdiness, made it more fun and more rowdy. You can't raise hell when you don't believe in hell."

"Pardon, Alobar," said Marcel, "but Carnival predates Christianity, does it not?"

"Ha ha. I'll say. By fifty centuries. It goes back to ancient Hellas—Greece—to the shepherds who worshipped a certain god named Pan. Pan." He sighed again. "We don't have Pan in our lives anymore, either."

"So you say we have kept the form of Mardi Gras but lost the content?"

"Yes. It's a shallow experience nowadays, and inevitably unsatisfying."

Alobar excused himself and went to his bath.

"He seems sad," said Priscilla.

"He is not used to being old."

"Even after a thousand years?"

"During most of that time he was a man in the prime of

life. He is amazing. He is stronger than he was a month ago. Younger, also. But, you see, Mademoiselle Pris, he needs a woman if he is to recover his youth. Perhaps every man does." Marcel closed his eyes. Priscilla could tell that he was thinking of V'lu. "Ah, yes, but Alobar cannot get a woman because he is too old. The double bind, they call it. You are correct, he is sad."

Feeling even more despondent after his soak-and-cool, Alobar elected to forgo the parade, sending Priscilla and Marcel downtown alone. On Monday, he complained that the continuous beating of drums and frequent drunken whoops had kept him awake all night, and he might have remained in the flat again were it not for two unexpected events.

"The Krewe of Pan is parading today," said Priscilla. "I'd forgotten there was a Krewe of Pan."

"With so many krewes, it is only fair," said Marcel.

"It'll be a sham," said Alobar. "A desecration, in fact. But I suppose I ought to go."

While they were studying a map of the parade route, deciding exactly where they should station themselves for the most auspicious view, a United Parcel Service delivery van pulled up outside, and its driver rang their bell. Priscilla signed for the package. It was from Seattle. From Wiggs Dannyboy.

The note inside was handwritten in red ink. It resembled something Noog the necromancer might have scratched into the lungs of a hen. Marcel and Alobar were baffled. "Let me have a peek," said Priscilla, wondering if an addled land crab had not deposited its string of eggs upon the page.

"Here are your . . . Mardi Gras . . . costumes," she read.

They unfolded the three piles of green satin, crimson velvet, and chicken wire and held them at arm's length, looking from one to the other in a manner both a- and be- mused.

Beet suits.

The three beets made their way through the French Quarter, seeking to root themselves at the intersection of Royal and Canal, where the Quarter met the business district. It was slow going. For blocks, they would be swept along by the throng, only to have the tide reverse itself so that they were forced to fight the current and barely moved at all.

Through eyeholes in their stems, the beets were bombarded by garish colors and flashes of light popping from sunlit sequins, rhinestones, and glass. They passed among the swaying and bobbing fronds of a forest of feathers, overshadowed at times by towering headdresses that must, each one, have left a hundred birds shivering in their birthday suits, and at other times were caressed or tickled by wayward ostrich plumes. The muffled echo of an ocean of mythology welled up around them; a surf of Orientalism broke over them, spraying them with sultans and caliphs, prophets and potentates, gladiators and porters, harem girls and dragons, licentious Babylonians and passive Buddhas. This strange Asia shimmered in the sun, and the river of gods and monsters overflowed its banks, knocking the pinnings from under tourists and photographers.

Countless pictures were snapped of the three beets, countless hands waved at them, countless lips smiled. Who among the thousands might have guessed that inside the ambulatory vegetables were a genius waitress, the world's finest perfumer, and a man older than the first mosquito to preen its proboscis in the fever marsh that was once New Orleans? But, then, who could guess the identity of any of the costumed or the masked? And wasn't that—and not the lust and the gluttony—the true beauty of Mardi Gras? A mask has but one expression, frozen and eternal, yet it is always and ever the *essential* expression, and to hide one's telltale flesh behind the external skeleton of the mask is to display the universal identity of the inner being in place of the outer identity that is transitory and corrupt. The freedom of the masked is not the vulgar political freedom of the successful revolutionary, but the magical freedom of the Divine, beyond politics and beyond success. A mask, any mask, whether horned like a beast or feathered like an angel, is the face of immortality. Meet me in Cognito, baby. In Cognito, we'll have nothing to hide.

There was a definite distance, a gulf, between those in costume and those in daily dress. In the caste system of

Carnival, the unmasked were instantly relegated to a position of inferiority. They were peasants, outsiders, mere spectators no matter how energetically they attempted to participate. For example, gangs of college boys, in beer-wet T-shirts and vomit-encrusted jeans raced through the Quarter shouting "Show yer tits! Show yer tits!" and when some woman upon a balcony would oblige, pulling up her front in a gesture of mammary theater, the boys would go berserk, hooting and slobbering, scratching themselves, slapping their thighs, punching one another and rolling on the cement, like a band of baboons shorn of its baboon dignity, but although these raunchy gangs had become increasingly a dominant force in Mardi Gras, there was a sense in which they were not a part of it at all; for all their lewdness, they were unconnected to the true lewd heart of Carnival, which must beat behind a disguise, grand or grotesque, in order to be heard by the gods, for whom Mardi Gras, ultimately, is defiantly and lovingly staged.

As the beets neared Canal Street, the jostle of the multitudes grew turbulent. According to the news, it was the largest attendance in the history of New Orleans Mardi Gras. City fathers had feared that the bees might keep people away, but widespread stories of the swarm had had just the opposite effect. Thousands came to New Orleans with the expressed desire of seeing the bees. And bee costumes were the most popular, by far, that holiday. Human bees, solitary or in swarms, were everywhere. Legion were the pretty girls who were "stung" by insects six feet in height.

As for the real bees . . . well, who knew? Numerous sightings were reported throughout the city, but officials were unable to confirm a single one. Madame Theo, a fortune-teller on St. Philip Street, claimed that the swarm had returned to Jamaica, a prospect that relieved many people and disappointed still more.

In the all-black Zulu parade, at least one float had borne a sign, REMEMBER BINGO PAJAMA.

The beets managed to reach Royal and Canal without being pulverized or pollinated. They pushed to curbside, where the espresso brewer from the coffeehouse, with his kid brothers, had staked a narrow claim. As prearranged, the beet named Priscilla gave each of the boys ten dollars of Marcel's money, and they whooped off to buy beer and to yell, "Show yer tits!" to anyone who was suspected of legitimately possessing tits. The beets took their place at the curb.

Since the Pan krewe's parade had not yet begun to pass, the trio waited there, gaping through their stems at the intoxicated fantasy surrounding them. All at once, two vegetable cries penetrated the jazzy din. Not thirty feet from them, also on the curb, stood a beautiful black woman, less than *en costume*, yet not wholly straight. Apricot and artichoke were the colors of her gown, which clung to her like a child about to be separated from its parents, and cream was her turban, fastened with a glass jewel the size of half a peach. Aside from gown and turban, and spiky, pink, rather vaginal shoes, she wore no adornment, but she appeared as much a creature of Carnival—mysterious, alluring, fanciful—as any befeathered Sheba or she-bee in the multitudes. Perhaps it was because disguise and deception were second nature to her, or it could have been simply that she was one of those persons destined to be exotic even should they never stray from home. It was V'lu.

At the sight of her, there was an immediate and abrupt schism among the beet population of Mardi Gras. One beet peeled off to the left, heading for V'lu. A second beet whirled, if one could be said to whirl in so dense a congregation, and began to fight its way down Royal Street, in the direction of Parfumerie Devalier. The third beet, abandoned, stood its ground to await the passage of Pan.

Parfumerie Devalier was at the opposite end of Royal Street from the Canal intersection. It took the beet more than forty minutes to wade through the baboon boys, Dixieland high-steppers, and glittering transvestites who blocked its route to the shop. When it at last arrived, it found the shop unlocked. Madame Devalier was in the rear, seated upon the lime love seat, filling the space of two lovers, fingering rosary beads and nodding dreamily from the effects of the first hurricane drops she'd ingested in fifteen years.

The cop trial had ended on Friday with a verdict of guilty. Seizing the opportunity, the judge issued sentence on Saturday: two years, suspended. The judge was well aware that there could be no race riot during Mardi Gras. Potential participants would be too distracted, too dispersed, too happy, too drunk. The sentencing barely made news. Without fanfare, Madame and V'lu had returned on Sunday, in time to dust off their hundreds of perfume vials and attend the Bacchus parade.

Now, both under the influence of drops, V'lu had wandered off to view Pan, while Madame rested in the eye of the hurricane, hallucinating about Jesus, Wally Lester, a Mardi Gras baby, *gris-gris*, zombie butter, and the way things used to be. When the giant beet burst into the shop, she crossed herself and chanted:

> "Eh, Yé Yé Conga!
> Eh! Eh! Bomba Yé Yé!"

With deliberation, the beet bustled to the rear, snatched the ancient perfume bottle from the table where Madame had been contemplating it, off and on, and before the stout woman could revive enough to shriek in protest, rushed out of the shop and into the masquerade melee.

> "Eh! Eh! Bomba Yé!
> Hail Mary, Full of Grace!
> Help, police! Police!"

Cradling the precious bottle, shielding it from the flailing appendages of dancers and drunks, it took the big beet the better part of an hour to navigate the treacherous human river, but when it reached the Canal Street intersection, its fellow beets were there, one on either side of V'lu.

"Alobar! Alobar!" Priscilla cried. She held the bottle up for him to see.

Alobar blinked inside his beet stem, scarcely comprehending what he saw. More from instinct than reason, he reached out for the bottle, trembling with excitement, fear, and desire as visions of jasmine boughs, goat hooves, and lost love swam past his brain.

At that moment, Priscilla tripped, pitching forward on her velvet-and-wire encircled belly. The bottle slipped out of her stubby fingers and went rolling into the path of the parade.

Later, Priscilla swore that she'd been purposefully shoved, and she clung to that story even though Marcel insisted that no one had touched her, even though V'lu testified, "Her *always* had butterfingers and two leff feets."

Alobar was more sympathetic. Just as Pris fell, he imagined that he'd registered a strong goaty odor, and while he automatically attributed it to the nostalgic atmosphere of the float that was passing—a lofty wagon decorated with enormous plaster sheeps' heads and festooned with purple grapes as big as cannonballs, and on whose pinnacle there pranced in pastoral splendor, attended by nymphs in filmy tunics, the living image of old Goat Foot himself—Alobar was to consider, in retrospect, that the smell had been real and had originated at curbside. Was it an invisible arm that shoved her?

The question was probably academic. What mattered was that the bottle rolled beneath the tractor wheel of the heavy float, and as the Great God Pan (to be sure, an insurance adjuster who'd once played linebacker for LSU) looked down upon the prone beet in the gutter with the clownish contempt that the ribald deity has forever held for the puny failures—and accomplishments—of humanity, it was crushed. There was a *pop!*, a gritty crunch, an earthy, mocking laugh from Pan above, and it was over.

Two of the beets tore off their stems and leaves and ran into the street. The third beet quickly followed, pulled by V'lu. The four of them dropped to their knees in the wake of the float, surrounding a tiny pile of ground blue glass as if it were a sacred spoor that they were worshiping.

Kudra's bottle, Pan's bottle, the K23 bottle, the bottle that three hundred years earlier had terrified an order of monks, beckoned to the Other Side, and negotiated the fishy seas, was now no more than a dust of glitter that might have sifted from a Carnival transvestite's cheeks.

But from the sparkling blue powder there wafted a marvelous aroma, an effluvium both sweet and bitter, a fragrance as romantic as the pollen-stained teeth of the floral Earth, the sexual planet; wafted the secret fetish and daring charm that creates a new reality for men and women, transcending and transforming nature, reason, and animal destiny.

In a matter of minutes, policemen forced the quartet back to the curb. Three of them moved reluctantly but with minimal resistance. The bottle had meant much to them, and they were in shock. The fourth, Marcel LeFever, to whom, on the other hand, the bottle had meant nothing, had to be dragged, kicking and screaming.

"That scent, that scent!" he exclaimed, his voice inflamed by passion. "What is that scent? *Le parfum suprême! Le parfum magnifique!*"

Several hours later, in the rear of Parfumerie Devalier, there occurred something akin to a wake. In turn, Alobar, Priscilla, Madame Devalier, and V'lu eulogized the bottle. And right when everyone was feeling its loss most keenly, Alobar, who, alone, still wore a beet costume—it was the most fulfilling garment he had worn since he was forced to abdicate his kingly ermine—lifted everyone's spirits by spilling the beans. Or, rather, the beets.

"Beet pollen. Yes. Simply beet pollen. Beet pollen and nothing else. The pollen of the beet plant, if you please. Exactly, positively, emphatically beet pollen. Beet pollen, don't you see? The answer is beet pollen."

"*Incroyable!*" exclaimed Marcel.

"*Sacre merde!*" gasped Madame.

"Why didn't I think of that?" asked Priscilla.

"Beets, don't fail me now," said V'lu.

"The theme was jasmine, of course. A deluxe jasmine, rare and costly. But the top note was merely citron—"

"Would tangerine work as well?" inquired Madame.

"Oh, tangerine is *charmant*," put in Marcel. "It might be superior to the citron."

"—and the bottom was beet pollen. Good old everyday beet pollen."

"Hardly everyday," said Priscilla. "I've never seen a speck of beet pollen in my life."

"Me neever."

"Imagine, cher! Vegetable spore in a fine boof!"

The little group was so amazed by the revelation, and so fascinated by Alobar's subsequent tale of the intertwined roles of beet and fragrance in his life, that it failed to notice V'lu when she slipped out the door, a conspiratorial and purposeful set to her jaw.

That edge of the Quarter at that hour was fairly free of Carnival congestion and noise, and V'lu was detained only by the lump that rose in her throat when she passed the place where Bingo Pajama, prince of blossom and song, had fallen bleeding at her feet. She paused briefly, bit her lower lip, and then proceeded to the telephone booth. It was occupied, but she was next in line.

While she waited for the camera-laden tourist to complete his call, she focused on the sunset and calculated what the time of day must be in Paris, where it was already Fat Tuesday. She knew that Luc LeFever wouldn't have minded a call at an inopportune hour, but she wasn't sure about his successor, Claude. Still, how could Claude complain, once he'd heard the news? This perfume, this *K23*, could justify, a million times over, every cent they'd ever paid her.

Born at Belle Bayou into a family of ex-slaves who'd elected to remain on the plantation as paid servants, generation after generation, V'lu grew up with the plantation owner's daughters. They were an old Creole clan who refused to speak English. The servants spoke mostly French, as well. When the owner sent his daughters to school in Switzerland, V'lu, age eleven, was sent with them—as companion, schoolmate, and unofficial maid.

Upon graduation, the white girls went on to the Sorbonne, but V'lu, who'd piqued the girls by earning higher academic honors, was returned to Belle Bayou. The owner didn't know quite what to do with her. She was pretty, mannered, had an aptitude for chemistry and French literature, and could speak no English beyond the dialect she'd picked up in the rural ghetto. "Niggertown" English. He and his wife were trying to decide what might be best for her when his second cousin, Lily Devalier, arrived for a weekend visit and confessed she needed an assistant—and heir—in her perfume business. *Voilà!*

For fear she'd appear overqualified, the Belle Bayou owner hid her accomplishments from Lily, palming her off as a simple plantation girl. Moreover, he advised V'lu to speak only English in New Orleans, so that she'd fit in. V'lu followed that advice (she even changed her name to Jackson from Saint-Jacques), except when she might encounter some interesting visitor from France.

Such a visitor was Luc LeFever, who'd come to Parfumerie Devalier one afternoon while Madame was napping, met V'lu, and swiftly recognized her worth. He took her to dinner that evening, seduced her (she'd had a few sexual encounters in Switzerland and found them to her liking), and put her on the payroll. Luc, after all, had had dealings with Lily Devalier and her fragrances and recognized that she had the potential, at least, to produce something of commercial interest.

As an industrial spy, V'lu earned one hundred dollars a month, with the promise of a fat bonus should she deliver a formula LeFever might profitably market. With some misgiving, Claude saw to it that the arrangement continued after his father's death, and it was to fulfill her obligation and collect her bonus that V'lu now stepped toward the public telephone to dial Paris, collect.

As V'lu reached for the door of the booth, a small yellow cloud materialized between her hand and the door. She drew back her arm. The cloud fragmented into forty or fifty "drops," spread like oversize dew upon the glass door. For a second, V'lu thought she might be experiencing a flashback hallucination, because the hurricane drops had worn off only an hour before, but just then someone in the street yelled, "The bees! It's the bees!"

A crowd began instantly to form. "The bees!" "Where?" "There!" "Look, it's the bees!" The way the pedestrians were acting, the bees might have been Michael Jackson and Katharine Hepburn. Any minute, someone in the crowd would ask the bees for their autograph.

V'lu swung her pink plastic handbag in the swarm's direction. "Shoo!" she said. "Shoo, bees! Go on now!"

As one, the swarm lifted off the glass and with wings vibrating furiously, fell into their infamous saber saw formation. The flying blade splintered the air around V'lu's head. She yelped and ran for cover.

Through the plate-glass window of a boutique across the street, she waited and watched. For nearly five minutes, the swarm patroled the space between the telephone booth and the boutique, then it flew off into the spreading bruise of dusk.

V'lu was patient. She waited until it was completely dark. She waited a little longer. It was common knowledge that bees ceased to function at sunset. At last, when night lay on the Quarter like a fallen horse, V'lu cautiously opened the boutique door and slowly crossed the street. The coast was clear.

Safely in the booth with the door shut, she reached out with a slender, magenta-nailed finger to dial the overseas operator. A bee lit on her finger.

It appeared to be alone, a sleepy straggler left behind by the swarm. She snapped her wrist and flicked it off. She went to dial again, but there was a bee in the "O" hole. Uh-oh!

Single file, they were invading the booth through the crack

between the door and the pavement. Quickly, the booth was full of them. They swarmed over V'lu, squirmed up her nose, into her ears, down her cleavage, and under her armpits. A solitary bee, kamikaze all the way, buzzed up her dress and drilled its toxic stinger through her cotton underpants and into her perineum, that exquisite corridor separating a woman's back door from her front door, that smooth, hidden cusp that may be the most holy spot on the human body.

V'lu screamed, dropped both the receiver and the card with Claude's number on it, and bolted from the booth. Swaying dangerously upon her pink, spiked shoes, she ran all the way back to Parfumerie Devalier, where she found the others in such a state of happy excitement that they neglected to notice that she was out of breath and sobbing.

In V'lu's absence, important decisions had been made.

Alobar had decided to dematerialize. Should he fail, then he would simply permit himself to die. "I have nothing else to prove by remaining alive," he said, "but a great deal to prove—and gain—by pursuing Kudra. Finally, I'm ready for that adventure. I've seen the bottle again, and I'm ready. I feel that Pan has, for better or for worse, made his parting gesture, and it would behoove me to do the same."

It was his plan to attempt his dematerialization in Paris, on the rue Quelle Blague. He suspected it might be advantageous to leave this plane near where Kudra had left it.

Meanwhile, he was turning over the *K23* formula to Marcel. "That's overwhelmingly generous of you," said Marcel. "But what if you change your mind about this dematerialization?"

"I won't. Nothing short of Kudra's return could change my mind."

For his part, Marcel decided that LeFever would distribute the perfume internationally, it was ideally suited for that, but he insisted that Parfumerie Devalier actually produce the fragrance. It would be marketed under the Devalier label. At that, Madame Devalier began to blubber.

Under Marcel's plan, LeFever would claim thirty percent

of profits. Lily Devalier would be awarded fifty percent, with Priscilla and V'lu each receiving ten percent, until Madame's death, at which time they'd split her share.

My, did V'lu feel bad. And it wasn't just the throbbing in her perineum.

"How about Wiggs Dannyboy?" asked Priscilla.

"Eh?"

"He's done as much as anybody to get this perfume made—and he's never even smelled it." Pris described the trouble and expense to which Dr. Dannyboy had gone in delivering his clues—his beets—to those in the best position to duplicate *K23.*

"Quite right," said Alobar.

It was agreed that LeFever and Madame would each award Dr. Dannyboy four percent of their share, while Priscilla and V'lu would give him one percent apiece.

"Live by the heart if you would live forever," said Alobar.

They toasted to that with champagne, after which Madame and Priscilla went into a corner to hug and cry and reconcile; Alobar fell asleep on the love seat, dreaming of his lady; and V'lu took Marcel up to her room, where, in the best French tradition, he sucked the venom from her bee sting.

The next day was Mardi Gras, but in the shop nobody really noticed. They held their private celebration, a celebration of the heart and the nose, which honored neither mindless excess nor neurotic asceticism, and from which neither church nor state would benefit—at least, not in any way that their leaders might have imagined.

Madame introduced Marcel to the Bingo Pajama jasmine. His nostrils opening and closing like the flaps of an airplane in distress, he pronounced it more precious than any in the South of France and swore that he would send a team of botanists to Jamaica to track it down. "So this is what Wiggs and his little girl were wishing to grow in their greenhouse. Ooh-la-la-la-la-la-la-la."

At noon they uncorked more champagne. They toasted Bingo Pajama. "And to *mangel-wurzel,*" added Alobar. "Long may it wave," said Pris. Regarding Alobar in his beet suit, now crumpled (and flat in places) from having been slept in, Marcel said, "I wish I had my whale mask." Everyone was too polite to ask what he meant. In truth, Marcel no longer owned a whale mask. He had stuffed it into Uncle Luc's coffin just before it was sealed.

The party agreed that it would call the perfume *Kudra*, a more romantic name than *K23*. Alobar was touched and pleased, although at one point Priscilla, only half facetiously, suggested christening it *The Perfect Taco*.

Madame looked at her long and hard.

They drank more champagne and sang breezy songs, mostly in French, for they spoke the language fluently except for Priscilla, who knew only six words in French, and that was counting *ménage à trois* as three.

They ate jambalaya (protection against the Humping Beast), drank yet more champagne, and waxed sentimental over Alobar, lamenting his proposed departure.

"It's been a huge adventure, an exploration of possibility, the invention of a game and the play of the game—and not merely survival. But I don't mind going now. This is not the best of times, you know."

"You're referring to the political situation?"

"Oh, no, not that. Our political leaders are unenlightened and corrupt, but with rare exception, political leaders have *always* been unenlightened and corrupt. I stopped taking politics seriously a long, long time ago, therefore it's had practically no effect on the way I've lived my life. In the end, politics is always a depressant, and I've preferred to be stimulated.

"No, my friends, what bothers me today is the lack of, well, I guess you'd call it authentic experience. So much is a sham. So much is artificial, synthetic, watered-down, and standardized. You know, less than half a century ago there were sixty-three varieties of lettuce in California alone. Today, there are four. And they are not the four best lettuces, either; not the most tasty or nutritious. They are the hybrid lettuces with built-in shelf life, the ones that have a safe, clean, consistent look in the supermarket. It's that way with so many things. We're even standardizing people, their goals, their ideas. The sham is everywhere.

"But wait, now. Don't let me spoil the party. Things will change, eventually, believe me. You can count on change. Even now, I'm curious about what's going to happen next. And I'll be back, if I can get back. The perfume will guide me back, I feel that it will.

"So make our perfume, my friends. Make it well. Breathe properly. Stay curious. And eat your beets."

"Right," said Pris, under her breath. "And don't smoke in bed."

Thus, their Fat Tuesday passed with some sadness, some gaiety, and much optimism. In the garbage-strewn, hungover hush of Ash Wednesday, a letter arrived from Wiggs Dannyboy. It slid through the slot with an appropriately soft sound, like a headachey matron folding her Mardi Gras fan.

Wiggs and Huxley Anne would fly in on Friday, the letter said. It said that it was raining in Seattle and that the greenhouse had been completely repaired. It concluded with a joke, an obscene suggestion, and a pronouncement or two. The pronouncements concerned Dr. Dannyboy's new theory of the evolution of consciousness. Perhaps because she had received the theory in bits and pieces, Priscilla hadn't paid much attention to it. Now, however, she sensed that Wiggs was attempting to make a major, radical statement, and she wondered if she shouldn't put it into focus.

Gathering all the letters that he'd written to her since she came to New Orleans, she snipped out the relevant sections, placed them in her handbag, and left the sublet flat. She walked through the Garden District, stopping finally at a park bench in front of Charity Hospital. There, almost directly beneath the window of the ward where her daddy died, she pieced together the fragments of Wiggs's hypothesis.

She wasn't positive that she accepted it or understood it. She wasn't positive that anyone else would accept it or understand it, or that anyone would care. She only knew that despite the numb torture of a champagne hangover, it made her want to go on living, a feeling she never quite got from the theories of Thomas Aquinas, Freud, and Marx.

DANNYBOY'S THEORY

(Where We Are Going and Why It Smells the Way It Does)

To put it simply, humankind is about to enter the floral stage of its evolutionary development. On the mythological level, which is to say, on the psychic/symbolic level (no less real than the physical level), this event is signaled by the death of Pan.

Pan, of course, represents animal consciousness. Pan embodies mammalian consciousness, although there are aspects of reptilian consciousness in his personality, as well. Reptilian consciousness did not disappear when our brains entered their mammalian stage. Mammalian consciousness was simply laid over the top of reptilian consciousness, and in many unenlightened—underevolved, underdeveloped—individuals, the mammalian layer was thin and porous, and much reptile energy has continued to seep through.

When our remote ancestors crawled out of the sea, they no doubt had the minds of fish. Smarter, more adventurous and curious than their fellows who remained underwater, but fish-minded, nonetheless. On the long swampy road to a primate configuration, however, we developed a reptile mind. After all, in those tens of millions of years, reptile energy dominated the planet. It culminated in the dinosaurs.

As Marcel LeFever suggested in his address to the perfumers' convention, reptile consciousness is cold, aggressive, self-preserving, angry, greedy, and paranoid.

Paul McLean was the first neurophysicist to point out that we still carry a reptilian brain—functional and intact—around in our skulls today. The reptile brain is not an abstract concept, it is anatomically real. It has been carpeted over by the cerebrum, but it is there, deep within the forebrain, and consists of the limbic lobe, the hypothalamus, and, perhaps, other organs of the diencephalon. When we are in a cold sweat, a blind rage, or simply feeling smugly dispassionate, we may be sure that, for the moment, our reptile brain is in control of our consciousness.

As the Age of Reptiles was drawing to a close, the first flowers and mammals appeared. Marcel LeFever believes that the flowers actually eliminated the great reptiles. Mammals also may have contributed to their egress (not "exit"), because for many early mammals there was nothing quite like a couple of dinosaur eggs for breakfast.

At any rate, our ancestors had by then evolved brains that were both mammalian and floral in their formation. For reasons of its own, evolution allowed mammalian energy to hold sway, and the recently developed human midbrain or mesencephalon, which had folded over the old diencephalon, could be accurately labeled a mammal brain.

Characteristics of mammal consciousness are warmth, generosity, loyalty, love (romantic, platonic, and familial), joy, grief, humor, pride, competition, intellectual curiosity, and appreciation of art and music.

In late mammalian times, we evolved a third brain. This was the telencephalon, whose principal part was the neocortex, a dense rind of nerve fibers about an eighth of an inch thick that was simply molded over top of the existing mammal brain. Brain researchers are puzzled by the neocortex. What is its function? Why did it develop in the first place?

LeFever has postulated that the neocortex is an expanded memory bank, and it certainly possesses that capability. Robert Bly thinks that it is connected somehow to light. If the reptile brain equates with cold and the mammal brain with warmth, then the neocortex equates with light. Bly's hunch makes a lot of sense because the third brain is a floral brain and flowers extract energy from light.

Even prior to the mysterious appearance of the neocortex, our brains had strong floral characteristics. The whole brain is described in science as a *bulb*. The neurons of which it is composed have *dendrites: roots* and *branches*. The cerebellum consists of a large mass of closely packed *folia*, which are bundles of nerve cells described in the literature as *leaflike*.

Not only do the individual neurons closely resemble plants or flowers, the brain itself looks like a botanical specimen. It has a *stem*, and a *crown* that unfolds, in embryonic growth, much in the manner of a *petaled* rose.

In the telencephalon—the new brain—the floral similarity increases. Its nerve fibers divide indefinitely, like the branches of a *tree*. This process is called, appropriately, *arborization*. In the proliferation of those twiggy fibers, tiny deposits of neuromelanin are cast off like *seeds*. The neuromelanin seeds apparently are the major organizing molecules in the brain. They link up with glial cells to regulate the firing of nerve cells. When we think, when we originate creative ideas, a *literal blossoming* is taking place. A brain entertaining insights is physically similar, say, to a jasmine bush blooming. It's smaller, and faster, that's all.

Moreover, neuromelanin absorbs light and has the capacity to convert light into other forms of energy. So Bly was correct. The neocortex is light-sensitive and can, itself, be lit up by higher forms of mental activity, such as meditation or chanting. The ancients were not being metaphoric when they referred to "illumination."

With the emergence of the neocortex, the floral properties of the brain, which had, for millions of years, been biding their time, waiting their turn, began to make their move— the gradual move toward a dominant floral consciousness.

When life was a constant struggle between predators, a minute-by-minute battle for survival, reptile consciousness was necessary. When there were seas to be sailed, wild continents to be explored, harsh territory to be settled, agriculture to be mastered, mine shafts to be sunk, civilization to be founded, mammal consciousness was necessary. In its social and familial aspects, it is still necessary, but no longer must it dominate.

The physical frontiers have been conquered. The Industrial Revolution has shot its steely wad. In our age of high technology, the rough and tough manifestations of mammalian sensibility are no longer a help but a hindrance. (And the vestiges of reptilian sensibility, with its emphasis on territory and defense, are dangerous to an insane degree.) We require a less physically aggressive, less rugged human being now. We need a more relaxed, contemplative, gentle, flexible kind of person, for only he or she can survive (and expedite) this very new system that is upon us. Only he or she can participate in the next evolutionary phase. It has definite spiritual overtones, this floral phase of consciousness.

The most intense spiritual experiences all seem to involve the suspension of time. It is the feeling of being outside of time, of being timeless, that is the source of ecstasy in meditation, chanting, hypnosis, and psychedelic drug experiences. Although it is briefer and less lucid, a timeless, egoless state (the ego exists in time, not space) is achieved in sexual orgasm, which is precisely why orgasm feels so good. Even drunks, in their crude, inadequate way, are searching for the timeless time. Alcoholism is an imperfect spiritual longing.

In a hundred different ways, we have mastered the art of space. We know a great deal about space. Yet we know pitifully little about time. It seems that only in the mystic state do we master it. The "smell brain"—the memory area of the brain activated by the olfactory nerve—and the "light brain"—the neocortex—are the keys to the mystic state. With immediacy and intensity, smell activates memory, allowing our minds to travel freely in time. The most profound mystical states are ones in which normal mental activity seems suspended in light. In mystic illumination, as at the speed of light, time ceases to exist.

Flowers do not see, hear, taste, or touch, but they react to light in a crucial manner, and they direct their lives and their environment through an orchestration of aroma.

With an increased floral consciousness, humans will begin to make full use of their "light brain" and to make more refined and sophisticated use of their "smell brain." The two are portentously linked. In fact, they overlap to such an extent that they may be considered inseparable.

We live now in an information technology. Flowers have *always* lived in an information technology. Flowers gather information all day. At night, they process it. This is called photosynthesis.

As our neocortex comes into full use, we, too, will practice a kind of photosynthesis. As a matter of fact, we already do, but compared to the flowers, our kind is primitive and limited.

For one thing, information gathered from daily newspapers, soap operas, sales conferences, and coffee klatches is inferior to information gathered from sunlight. (Since all matter is condensed light, light is the source, the cause of life. Therefore, light is divine. The flowers have a direct line to God that an evangelist would kill for.)

Either because our data is insufficient or because our processing equipment is not fully on line, our own nocturnal processing is part-time work. The information our conscious minds receive during waking hours is processed by our unconscious during so-called "deep sleep." We are in deep sleep only two or three hours a night. For the rest of our sleeping session, the unconscious mind is off duty. It gets bored. It craves recreation. So it plays with the material at hand. In a sense, it plays with itself. It scrambles memories, juggles images, rearranges data, invents scary or titillating stories. This is what we call "dreaming." Some people believe that we process information during dreams. Quite the contrary. A dream is the mind having fun when there is no processing to keep it busy. In the future, when we become more efficient at gathering quality information and when floral consciousness becomes dominant, we will probably sleep longer hours and dream hardly at all.

Pan, traditionally, presides over dreams, especially the erotic dream and the nightmare. A decline in dreaming will be further evidence of Pan's demise.

Returning to information efficiency, science has learned recently that trees communicate with each other. A tree attacked by insects, for example, will transmit that news to another tree a hundred yards away so that the second tree can commence manufacturing a chemical that will repel that particular variety of bug. Reports from the infested tree allow other trees to protect themselves. The information likely is broadcast in the form of aroma. This would mean that plants collect odors as well as emit them. The rose may be in an olfactory relationship with the lilac. Another possibility is that between the trees a kind of telepathy is involved. There is also the possibility that all of what we call mental telepathy is olfactory. We don't read another's thoughts, we smell them. We know that schizophrenics can smell antagonism, dis-

368 TOM ROBBINS

trust, desire, etc., on the part of their doctors, visitors, or
fellow patients, no matter how well it might be visually or
vocally concealed. The human olfactory nerve may be small
compared to a rabbit's, but it's our largest cranial receptor,
nevertheless. Who can guess what "invisible" odors it might
detect?

As floral consciousness matures, telepathy will no doubt
become a common medium of communication.

With reptile consciousness, we had hostile confrontation.

With mammal consciousness, we had civilized debate.

With floral consciousness, we'll have empathetic telepathy.

A floral consciousness and a data-based, soft technology are
ideally suited for one another. A floral consciousness and a
pacifist internationalism are ideally suited for one another. A
floral consciousness and an easy, colorful sensuality are ideally suited for one another. (Flowers are more openly sexual
than animals. The Tantric concept of converting sensual energy to spiritual energy is a floral ploy.) A floral consciousness
and an extraterrestrial exploration program are ideally suited
for one another. (Earthlings are blown aloft in silver pods to
seed distant planets.) A floral consciousness and an immortalist
society are ideally suited for one another. (Flowers have
superior powers of renewal, and the longevity of trees is
celebrated. The floral brain is the organ of eternity.)

Lest we fancy that we shall endlessly and effortlessly be as
the flowers that bloom in the spring, tra-la, let us bear in
mind that reptilian and mammalian energies are still very
much with us. Externally and internally.

Obviously, there are powerful reptilian forces in the Pentagon and the Kremlin; and in the pulpits of churches, mosques,
and synagogues, where deathist dogmas of judgment, punishment, self-denial, martyrdom, and afterlife supremacy are
preached. But there are also reptilian forces within each
individual.

Myth is neither fiction nor history. Myths are acted out in
our own psyches, and they are repetitive and ongoing.

Beowulf, Siegfried, and the other dragon slayers are aspects of our own unconscious minds. The significance of their
heroics should be apparent. We dispatched them with their

symbolic swords and lances to slay reptile consciousness. The reptile brain is the dragon within us.

When, in evolutionary process, it became time to subdue mammalian consciousness, a less violent tactic was called for. Instead of Beowulf with his sword and bow, we manifested Jesus Christ with his message and example. (Jesus Christ, whose commandment "Love thy enemy" has proven to be too strong a floral medicine for reptilian types to swallow; Jesus Christ, who continues to point out to job-obsessed mammalians that the lilies of the field have never punched time clocks.)

At the birth of Christ, the cry resounded through the ancient world, "Great Pan is dead." The animal mind was about to be subdued. Christ's mission was to prepare the way for floral consciousness.

In the East, Buddha performs an identical function.

It should be emphasized that neither Christ nor Buddha harbored the slightest antipathy toward Pan. They were merely fulfilling their mytho-evolutionary roles.

Christ and Buddha came into our psyches not to deliver us from evil but to deliver us from mammal consciousness. The good versus evil plot has always been bogus. The drama unfolding in the universe—in our psyches—is not good against evil but new against old, or, more precisely, destined against obsolete.

Just as the grand old dragon of our reptilian past had to be pierced by the hero's sword to make way for Pan and his randy minions, so Pan himself has had to be rendered weak and ineffectual, has had to be shoved into the background of our ongoing psychic progression.

Because Pan is closer to our hearts and our genitals, we shall miss him more than we shall miss the dragon. We shall miss his pipes that drew us, trembling, into the dance of lust and confusion. We shall miss his pranksterish overturning of decorum; the way he caused the blood to heat, the cows to bawl, and the wine to flow. Most of all, perhaps, we shall miss the way he mocked us, with his leer and laughter, when we took our blaze of mammal intellect too seriously. But the old playfellow has to go. We've known for two thousand years that Pan must go. There is little place for Pan's great stink amidst the perfumed illumination of the flowers.

Just recently, a chap turned up in New Orleans who may have been the prototype of the floral man. A Jamaican, they say, named Bingo Pajama, he sang songs, dealt in bouquets, laughed a lot, defied convention, and contributed to the production of a wonderful new scent. In some ways, he resembled Pan. Yet, Bingo Pajama smelled good. He smelled sweet. His floral brain was so active that it produced a sort of neocortical honey. It actually attracted bees.

When Western artists wished to demonstrate that a person was holy, they painted a ring of light around the divine one's head. Eastern artists painted a more diffused aura. The message was the same. The aura or the halo signified that the light was on in the subject's brain. The neocortex was fully operative. There is, however, a second interpretation of the halo. It can be read as a symbolized, highly stylized swarm of bees.

On Thursday, Priscilla packed her belongings, including Dr. Dannyboy's theory, and moved into Parfumerie Devalier. The coffeehouse owner was returning and wanted his flat back. Marcel and Alobar checked into the Royal Orleans Hotel for their remaining days in New Orleans.

Thursday night, Madame cooked a gang of gumbo (Down, Big Fellow, down, boy!), and they dined together above the shop. After dinner, Marcel presented Madame with a check for $250,000 so that she might get *Kudra* underway: modern equipment and additional employees would be required. V'lu and Priscilla received $25,000 apiece as advance on royalties.

The money filled Pris with a great Buddhistic calm. It left her no less klutzy, though. On her way to the toilet, she walked into a door, loudly and painfully banging her head. Her eye required an ice pack, her headache required something stronger than aspirin. Madame administered a single hurricane drop in a glass of orange juice. "This is the last, cher," Madame said to V'lu, who was trying to work up a headache of her own. Madame washed the rest of the foamy liquid down the sink. V'lu shed a silent tear, but somewhere near the terminus of the sewer line, a Lake Pontchartrain fish or two would soon be nodding out in school.

Thanks to the dream powers of the drop, Priscilla overslept on Friday. By the time she bathed, dressed, deposited her check in the bank, and snared a taxi, the early flight from Seattle had already landed.

Wiggs and Huxley Anne waited in the sunshine outside the terminal. They were patient. They felt relieved to have escaped the rain. If raindrops were noodles, Seattle could carboload Orson Welles and have enough left over to feed Buffalo on Columbus Day.

It's unclear who saw the swarm first. A porter, perhaps, or a post-Carnival tourist catching the shuttle to the Holiday Inn. Maybe several people saw it simultaneously, for when the cry went up, "The bees! The bees!" it was a chorus of voices. This was a sober group of businessmen, convention delegates, redcaps, and drivers, and nobody seemed particularly thrilled by the sudden appearance of the famous insects. Nobody except Wiggs Dannyboy, that is.

Wiggs stepped out onto the asphalt and lifted a benign, expectant face skyward, like the good-guy earthling in a flying-saucer movie. The bees ignored his gesture. They buzzed the area two or three more times, then flew directly for Huxley Anne.

Many in the group screamed, but a horrified hush fell over them when the bees landed on the little girl's head.

"Don't move!" someone said, in a stage whisper. "Don't move!" Huxley Anne wasn't moving. The bees weren't moving much, either.

Once they had established their position, evenly distributed, rather like a skullcap atop the child's head, the bees stilled their wings, drooped their antennae, bent their knees, rested the thousand facets of their compound eyes, withdrew their tubed tongues and barbed stingers, and sort of settled in.

Huxley Anne looked at Wiggs. He smiled encouragingly

The paralysis of the onlookers was finally broken when a driver started up his van. "I'll get the cops," he yelled out the window.

"You do and I'll rip your esophagus out," said Wiggs. He moved toward the van. "Turn that engine off."

The startled driver did as he was told. Nobody else in the crowd moved a muscle.

Slowly, Wiggs walked over to Huxley Anne. "You're okay, aren't you, darling?" he asked. When she nodded, the onlookers gasped. But the bees didn't stir. At close range, Wiggs could detect a slight pulsation of each bee's abdomen, as if it were absorbing something through osmosis.

"Where can you rent a car around here?" Wiggs asked.

A redcap pointed nervously.

Wiggs took Huxley Anne's hand, and as the others looked after them with bulging eyes, they walked off toward the airport perimeter.

While Dr. Dannyboy filled out the required forms, Huxley Anne stayed out of sight at the rear of the car agency, admiring some hibiscus that grew there.

By the time Priscilla's taxi arrived at the airport, father and daughter—and bees—were pulling out of the lot, burning rubber, and scattering the crushed oyster shell that New Orleans used for gravel.

"This is the big one!" Wiggs sang from the wheel. "This one is bigger than Carlos Castaneda and Levi-Strauss put together! Bigger than the bomb! Bigger than rock 'n' roll!" Then he added, "Of course, the next time she goes to the hairdresser, there may be a bit of a problem."

Priscilla didn't hear him. In fact, she never heard from him again, although rumors were later to reach her that he had moved to an orchid farm in Costa Rica, or else a jasmine plantation in Jamaica.

Priscilla took to her bed and remained there all weekend. She felt like a can of cheap dog food that had been ruptured by a railroad spike. Something mealy and ugly might have oozed out of her, except for the fact that the twenty-five-thousand-dollar deposit receipt made a highly effective Band-Aid.

Material things anchor one in life much more firmly than purists would like to believe.

We seem to face an enemy who, no matter how many times we win, will best us in the end. He has so many allies: time, disease, boredom, stupidity, religious quackery, and bad habits. Maybe, as Dr. Dannyboy has postulated, all these things, including disease and our relationship with time, are merely bad habits. If so, an ultimate victory is possible. For individuals, if not for the mass. And maybe evolution—playful, adventurous, unpredictable, infuriatingly slow (by our standards of time) evolution—will rescue us eventually, according to a master plan.

Meanwhile, we are beleaguered. We hold the pass. The fragile hold the pass precariously, hiding behind boulders of ego and dogma. The heroic hold the pass a bit more tenaciously, gracefully acknowledging their follies and absurdities, but insisting, nevertheless, on heroism. Instead of shrinking, the hero moves ever toward life. Life is largely material, and there is no small heroism in the full and open enjoyment of material things. The accumulation of material things is shallow and vain, but to have a genuine relationship with such things is to have a relationship with life and, by extension, a relationship with the divine.

To physically overcome death—is that not the goal?—we must think unthinkable thoughts and ask unanswerable questions. Yet we must not lose ourselves in abstract vapors of philosophy. Death has his concrete allies, we must enlist ours. Never underestimate how much assistance, how much satisfaction, how much comfort, how much soul and transcendence there might be in a well-made taco and a cold bottle of beer.

The solution to the ultimate problem may prove to be elemental and quite practical. Philosophers have argued for centuries about how many angels can dance on the head of a pin, but materialists have known all along that it depends on whether they are jitterbugging or dancing cheek to cheek.

By Sunday evening, Priscilla was feeling slightly better, feeling less like a dented can of cheap dog food than like a dented can of expensive dog food. Alpo instead of Skippy.

For the diversion that was in it, she switched on the television. On the Sunday Night Movie, a small boy named Jesse Jonah was pedaling his bike into the voracious vacuum of a black hole with a message from the Security Council of the United Nations. "I've been here before," said Priscilla. She changed channels and found a magazine-format documentary program.

After exposing corruption and chicanery in two governing bodies and three major industries, the program focused on a new dance craze that was sweeping Argentina.

"They call it the bandaloop," said the announcer, "and everyone is doing it."

Priscilla sat up in bed.

On the screen, the dancers were skipping and bounding about the floor in a kind of exaggerated polka. Every once in a while, they would stop, execute a little backward and forward jitterbug step, then, yelling "Bandaloop!" they would jump straight in the air, up and down, five times.

Priscilla sat more erect. "Morgenstern," she whispered.

"But the bandaloop is more than just another dance fad," the announcer said. "It's a health fad, as well. Supposedly, it can add years, even decades, to your life."

A familiar face appeared on the screen.

"The man who is singularly responsible for the bandaloop epidemic is a veteran Argentine accordion virtuoso named Effecto Partido."

Priscilla leaned forward.

"A respected amateur ethnomusicologist, Señor Partido last year accompanied a small group of scientists, including the late Nobel prize-winning chemist, Wolfgang Morgenstern, into the most remote area of the Patagonian wilderness.

Partido's interests were musical, but the scientists were there to investigate the habits of a little-known tribal people whose average life span was said to exceed one hundred and forty years. The scientists have yet to comment, but according to Partido, the secret of the tribe's longevity was the dance they performed several times each day: the bandaloop."

The camera panned to dancers in a Buenos Aires night spot, then back to a close-up of Effecto, who, Priscilla perceived, was looking youthful and fit, indeed.

"Theese dance she make zee blood happy, zee bones happy. I don't know how explain eet, but theese dance she celebrate that we are not, you know, died already."

As the announcer chuckled, the camera panned to a warehouse, painted bright pink. "The bandaloop requires so much space that the traditional tango clubs of Argentina can only accommodate three or four dancers at a time. So Effecto Partido acquired an empty warehouse near the Buenos Aires waterfront and converted it into a bandaloop club. The place is jammed every night of the week—and Effecto Partido, who also leads the band and takes frequent accordion solos, is South America's newest millionaire. His nightclub, by the way, is called Priscilla."

"I call it for zee only woman I ever love," said Effecto.

Priscilla bandalooped out of bed.

For fifteen minutes or so, the former genius waitress paced the floor. Then she got the idea to telephone Ricki.

"Hello."

"Bartender, I'd like some Alpo on the rocks with a twist of railroad spike."

"I don't make house calls. Who is this?"

"You don't recognize the one who did you wrong?"

"Pris! Maybe I do make house calls. Where are you?"

"Still in Louisiana. Ricki, it's so good to hear your voice."

"It's good to hear *you*. You asshole."

"I'm sorry, Ricki. I was positive you had my bottle. I'm prepared to eat a lot of crow."

"I'd rather you eat something else."

"You're a dirty-talking woman."

"It's not just talk."

"Can you forgive me, Ricki?"

"Hey, I was a jerk myself. But, look, the Daughters got another grant coming up. This time—"

"No, I don't need it anymore. How're things at El Papa Muerta, by the way? Customers still complaining that there're only nine hundred islands in their thousand-island dressing?"

"Yeah, they don't realize the peso's been devalued."

"Ricki, you want to go to Argentina?"

"Does the Pope want to play Las Vegas? What're you talking about?"

"I'm not kidding. I'm going. You would not *believe* the past four months of my life. The people I've met, the stuff I've learned, the things that have been happening to me. . . ."

"Try me."

"Okay, what would you say if I told you a dying god knocked me down and broke my perfume bottle?"

" 'Don't cry for me, Argentina.' "

"You want to go to Argentina?"

"What's happened to your junkie boyfriend?"

"He's not a junkie, and he's not my boyfriend! I guess he never was my boyfriend. I don't know anymore. He's amazing. Incredibly amazing. But he's sure not in love with me. He came to New Orleans Friday and then turned right around and left, without seeing me. I think it has something to do with his daughter—"

"The gift of the Magi."

"What?"

"In the Bible. The Magi brought frank incest and mirth."

"Ha ha. I didn't know you read the Bible."

"Only the good parts. There's a lot about me you don't know."

"You want to go to Argentina tomorrow?"

"I'm off tomorrow. Why not? Why're we going to Argentina?"

"To join my ex-husband."

"Wait a minute. Are we talking *ménage à trois?*"

Priscilla paused. "I'm not sure what we're talking. I only know that I seem to require a man of a certain age—and that you're the only real friend I have. I don't know what we're gonna do in Argentina, but one thing I can tell you . . ."

"What's that, Pris?"

"Whatever it is, it may be possible to do it for a long, long time."

The night sky over Paris was the color of beet juice, a result of red lights and blue lights reflecting upon the gunmetal gray of the clouds. The sky was sorrowful and disheveled, like the head of an old musician. Heavy with music, it nodded uncontrollably, strands waving, as if keeping time, against its will, to the cabaret piano that was the heartbeat of Paris. Through breaks in the overcast, a dandruff of pale stars could be seen.

Emerging from the dim lobby of the LeFever Building into the dimmer street, Claude LeFever didn't notice the sky, but looked first left, then right, then left again. He knew that he was early, but he hoped that his car and driver might be early, as well. No such luck.

Claude turned up the collar of his cashmere topcoat. It might have been spring in Nice, but winter winds had not moved completely off the rue Quelle Blaque. Chilled and impatient, still Claude was fond enough of the street to stand in it, his back to the edifice that smell had built.

Although the law prohibiting skyscrapers had been amended for thirty years, the LeFever Building remained the sole high-rise in that neighborhood. The rest of the block was oblivious to what, in the modern world, passed for progress. With a mixture of frustration and affection, Claude surveyed the cafés and bicycle shops, and the cathedral, of course, and wondered how a city whose name meant fashion to the world could, decade after decade, get away with conforming to archaic ideas. Paris was like his cousin Bunny, he thought: faithful to tradition, on the one hand, in a constant state of upheaval on the other.

As his eyes swept the street, the door of the darkened bicycle shop next door creaked slowly open, and a somnambulistic figure, as evocative as a silhouette in a period cinema, joined him on the rue Quelle Blaque. Claude thought the person might be a burglar, his outlines distorted by a sack of loot, but instead of hurrying away, the figure stood there, drinking in the neighborhood as Claude himself had done.

Since the figure was not threatening, was, in fact, compelling, Claude approached it. He was instantly glad, for it proved to be a woman, a dark, Asian woman, quite beautiful, but dressed in a seventeenth-century costume and behaving as if drunk or drugged. When the woman saw Claude, she drew her hand to her mouth and gasped. Evidently, he appeared as odd to her as she to him, yet she did not seem overly afraid.

"I thought I was back," the woman said. Her French was formal, old-fashioned. "But now I am unsure."

"What do you mean?" asked Claude.

"It is not the same as it was. My shop is full of silver wheels. There is a tower next door so tall I cannot find its top. And you, sir . . ."

She seemed actually in shock. *She must be on some drug,* Claude thought. Got loaded at a costume party, no doubt, but what was she doing in a locked bicycle shop? "Uh, how long have you been gone?" he asked.

"Only an hour or two."

He chuckled. "Well, my dear, nothing's changed in the past couple of hours, I assure you." He told himself that he should walk away, but he stayed. She was so exotic, so lost and lovely. Despite an otherworldly aloofness, she radiated an erotic heat that melted his customary caution and reason. Even should she prove to be an actress on heroin, and not the creature of marvel that she seemed, he nevertheless craved her company. His loins tingled, not merely with lust but with a kind of spiritual adventurism, almost Promethean in character, as if he might steal something from her (from her lips, her breasts, her breath) that would allow him to surpass himself. He hoped that his limo was stuck in traffic again.

"Where have you been?"

Kudra didn't hesitate. "I have been on the Other Side," she said. For the first time, she looked into his eyes.

Claude felt weak. It was a result of the eye contact, not her reply. He thought that she meant the other side of the Seine.

"And how are things on the other side?" He hoped he didn't sound flip.

"Oh, sir . . ." A tremor ran the length of her, causing her voluptuous flesh to quiver like the throat of a lovesick frog. Her bustle gown was lacy and had three-quarter-length sleeves, with which she wore neither muff nor gloves. Assuming that she was cold, Claude draped his topcoat about her shoulders.

"Actually," said Claude, "I much prefer the Right Bank. Did you really find it so unpleasant over there?"

"Oh, I would not describe the Other Side as unpleasant, sir. It is quite beyond the scope of words such as pleasant or unpleasant."

Her seriousness made him smile. "Impressed you, hey? Well, how *would* you describe it?"

Kudra neglected to answer right away. Instead, she searched the block, pivoting stiffly, like a figurine atop a music box, to stare back into the bicycle shop. She was looking for someone, although in her dazed state she may have been confused as to his precise identity.

Gradually she turned to Claude again, fixed him with a hypnotic gaze, and began a monologue so lengthy and bewildering that had it come from any mouth but hers, he would have done something rude. As it was, there was no question of interruption. She spoke softly and slowly, as if in a trance, and Claude, himself, became entranced. Her manner, her voice, her heat, her scent combined to hypnotize him, binding him with spider wire, wrapping his mind in a web of vision so thick that he could actually see the scenes she described as vividly as if he were dreaming them.

Released with a sudden puff from the electromagnetic convulsions of dematerialization, Kudra finds herself inside a covered wharf, an enormous building of damp granite and soiled marble, extending for two hundred yards or more beyond the shore of some dark sea.

Obviously a terminal, the wharf is teeming with travelers of every race, nationality, and era of time, arriving, departing, waiting.

The travelers murmur, occasionally they moan, but they do

not converse among themselves. They hustle in. They bustle
about. They stand in long lines. They go.

Although Kudra's body feels normal and intact, there is
something insubstantial, almost vaporous, about most of the
others. She is soon to learn that that is because they are
dead. They have left their bodies behind and are walking
about in mental projections, in their ideas of their earthly
bodies. They have fleshed themselves in their imaginations of
themselves, which explains why the majority of them are
rather handsome.

Only the dematerialized are housed in actual bodies, and
in all the throng, there are but two or three of these. The
dematerialized, moreover, are exempt from the rules and
regulations governing the dead. Conductors in white uni-
forms herd the dead arrivals into groups, form the groups
into lines, single-file, but Kudra is allowed to roam at will.

The conductors seldom speak, but they act with irresistible
authority. Their faces are radiant, their movements fluid and
fluttery. Kudra is reminded of snowflakes, of the fluttering
pages of books upon which poems in white ink have been
written.

Acutely aware of her own smell, for there is no trace of
odor among the dead masses, Kudra wanders throughout the
great wharf, which, though miserably crowded, is steeped in
a solitude more complete than any she has ever known.

No newspapers are for sale in the station, no sweets or
tobacco. Travelers arrive. They go. They arrive in streams,
through wide marble portals, carrying neither luggage nor
souvenirs. But where is it they go from here? To find out,
Kudra pushes to the head of a line. All lines, it turns out,
lead to the same place: the Weighing Room.

Timidly, Kudra slips into the room, where she is surprised
to find a tall, androgynous figure, half priest and half harlequin, wielding a gleaming knife.

One by one, the dead approach the harlequin priest. With
a swift, practiced stroke, he (or she) cuts out their hearts.

Upon a stone altar, there is a set of scales. The scales are
ordinary, made of brass, not gold. On the left balance, there
is a single hawk-brown feather.

The harlequin priest passes each freshly rooted heart to

his/her assistant, a young woman in a white tunic. The assistant lays the heart upon the right balance. If the heart is heavier than the feather—and time after time it is—the person is motioned to the rear of the room, where he or she joins another line, this one filing down steps that lead to the docks.

At regular intervals, ships moor at dockside. The ships are sleek and luminous. In fact, they seem fashioned entirely of light, a cold light, as staid and ordered as a Victorian drawing room. The heartless dead board the ships, which, once loaded, sail away at tremendous speeds. In a matter of seconds, they are no more than distant stars in the obsidian night of ocean.

The woman in the snowy tunic notices Kudra. She smiles. "Do you understand what is happening here?" she inquires. "We weigh their hearts. Should a person possess a heart that is as light as a feather, then that person is granted immortality."

"Indeed? Are there many?"

"Few. Precious few, I am sorry to say. One would think that people would catch on. Those who pass the test are usually rather odd. The last was a tall black fellow with bee dung caked in his hair. The ordinary rarely beat the scales."

"Where do they go, then, all those who fail?" Kudra pointed toward the water, where another ship of light was just whooshing away, leaving a milky wake.

"To the energy realms."

"Never to return?"

The woman shrugs. "As energy, perhaps. As light."

"But the ones who pass the test . . . ?"

"The immortals? They are free to take any direction they like. Free to embark on a sea voyage, to return to your world, or to some different world." She places yet another heart upon the balance, squealing with delight when it does not send the balance dish plummeting to the altar top. "Look," she says to Kudra. "Look at this one. Now here is one that comes fairly close."

This organ was ripped from the corpulent breast of a jolly-faced troubadour. He doesn't comprehend the commotion, but he is winking at Kudra, rubbing his belly, and looking as if he'd gladly trade his butchered heart for a pint of ale.

"*Had he combined his hedonism with a pinch more wisdom, had he poured slightly less into his gullet and slightly
more into his soul, he might have made it,*" says the weigher
of hearts. "*Still, he earns a pink ticket.*"

She hands the troubadour something strongly resembling a
carnation petal and motions him to a side door. Kudra fol-
lows him and learns that this door, too, leads down to the
water, but to an empty dock. From above, the woman signals
him to wait.

For quite a long time, the troubadour stands there. To
relieve his tedium, he whistles a tune, a medieval ballad of
courtly love. Suddenly, he is silenced in mid-whistle, his lips
periwinkled in a frozen pucker. A ship is pulling into view.

As it nears dockside, Kudra sees that it is a barge, of
considerable length, and canopied with pink linen, from whose
edges fringe and tassels dangle. The barge is hung with paper
lanterns, in which candles blaze gaily. Scattered about the
deck are tables and chairs, resembling those of an inn, and
here sit people eating spicy southern foods and sipping beer
and pineapple coolers. Minstrels with droopy black mus-
taches wander the deck, strumming guitars. Women in shoes
with heels like daggers dance, rattling tambourines all the
while and cooing lubricious phrases to the many parrots that
occupy crude wooden cages. From below deck, a katzenjam-
mer of libidinous voices is heard. On the side of the barge,
the name Hell has been painted.

Despite the fact that there's no odor to give magnitude to
the foods on deck or to the sex below, the passengers seem
merry. Kudra believes that she recognizes one of them. Unless she is mistaken, it is Fosco, the calligrapher from the
Samye lamasery. He is at table, in repartee with a pair of
elderly Chinamen, whom he addresses as Han Shan and Li
Po. They hurl lines of spontaneous poetry at one another,
each trying to top the last, often slapping the tabletop and
laughing wildly. Kudra waves and waves, but it is impossible
to get Fosco's attention. The dead have little interest in the
living, she surmises.

The barge scrapes against the dock with a careless rasp.
The captain, a seedy Spaniard in a comic-opera version of a
military uniform, leans over the rail and takes the trouba-

dour's pink ticket. Once the fellow is aboard, the vessel floats lazily away, bound for unknown sprays.

As the barge departs, it turns, affording a view of its starboard side. On this side, the vessel wears a different name entirely. *Heaven* is what it says.

Kudra returns to the scales. The young woman is hard at work, testing hearts, assaying the precious metals of the life well-lived. "How did you land this job?" asks Kudra.

"I was not feather-light, but I was feather-bright," she answers.

"I am not sure I understand. Yet I cannot help but notice that we strongly resemble one another, you and I."

"Indeed we do."

"Are we related? Am I an incarnation of you? Or something?"

"What makes you suppose that you would be an incarnation of me, rather than me of you?" She giggles and shakes her skunk-black curls. "It is so amusing the way that mortals misunderstand the shape, or shapes, of time."

"I am not sure I understand."

"And I cannot help you understand. In the realm of the ultimate, each person must figure out things for themselves. Remember that, when you return to Your Side. Teachers who offer you the ultimate answers do not possess the ultimate answers, for if they did, they would know that the ultimate answers cannot be given, they can only be received."

Kudra nods. She looks around her. Once one is accustomed to it, the scene on the wharf is neither dreadful nor thrilling. It is, as a matter of fact, fairly boring, an ongoing performance of bureaucratic routine. Death is as orderly as life is disorderly.

The weigher looks up from the scales. "Perhaps you ought to be going," she suggests.

"Yes. I should. But . . . how does one get out of here? Must I once more dematerialize?" As exciting as dematerialization was, Kudra was not looking forward to an immediate encore. Spiraling, ring by ring, through that zone of spin and crackle, was more exhausting than a month in a rope yard.

"That will not be necessary. There is a doorway on yonder side of the station."

Kudra stares in that direction. She is less than assured. "This place is so huge," she says. "There are so many doors."

"Do not worry. You shall find it. There is a sign above the door."

"What says the sign?"

"Erleichda."

"Pardon?"

There is a ledge on the altar, caked with dirt and blackened by blood from the dripping of the strange fruit that is weighed there. With her finger, the woman writes the word upon the ledge.

Thanking her, Kudra studies the letters until they are memorized.

"One last question, if I might," says Kudra. "Why are there no odors here?"

"Outside the portals of our station, there is a holding area, brilliantly illuminated. Had you arrived in the usual fashion, you would have been detained there until it was positively determined that you wished to be dead. The holding area teems with thousands of odors of every description; it is a vast net of odors, a clearinghouse of odors, the odors of a billion personal lifetimes, each separate and distinct. But once having accepted their demise, and having been admitted to the terminal, the dead can no longer smell nor be smelled. Otherwise it would be too difficult for them. Smell evokes memories. If smell were permitted here, the dead would still be connected to life and could not, therefore, accept their fate. As long as there is odor, there is hope of life everlasting. Because you carry odor, my lady, your presence here is potentially disruptive. Do you notice the uncomfortable manner in which the dead regard you? They cannot see you, they can only see what is dead, and they cannot really smell you, either, yet, still they sense something. Smell is like that. Did you realize that a ghost is but a dead person who has not completely lost his ability to smell? Smell is the sister of light, it is the left hand of the ultimate. It fastens the eternal to the temporal, This Side to That Side, and thus is highly sensitive; volatile, if not dangerous. So go now, dear lady, go in good scent and good fortune. It is not the last time, perhaps, that our paths shall cross."

Kudra says good-bye and rejoins the horde in the terminal, moving with some difficulty against the flow. Despite the jostling—were the travelers more physically substantial, her global breasts might have been pounded into flatcakes—she decides to have a quick peek, a sniff, outside the main entrance before searching for her escape.

She pushes through heavy traffic until she is standing in the portals, beneath the mammoth stone archway, facing an immense plaza that is without a pigeon, without an ant, without a leaf or the shadow of a leaf, yet teeming with people of every description, each and every one basking in a soft but relentless light. Some of the people are marching systematically toward the portals, others approach obliquely, hesitantly, while still others are sitting about the plaza looking as if they had been camping there for days or weeks, with no real mind to come inside.

As the weigher has promised, the plaza is smelly. It is, in fact, an ocean of scent in which the travelers are bobbing, each clinging, at first, to his or her favored aroma as if to a life preserver. Often, their final action before entering the wharf is to inhale one parting whiff of whatever it was—a child's blanket, a backyard garden, a mother's kitchen, a horse, a factory, an artist's brush, an opium pipe—that was keeping them afloat.

As one man, sniffing, enters the portals, he accidentally brushes against Kudra. He is red-nosed, rough-edged, proletarian, less than young, but creased with such a mischievous, insouciant smile that Kudra finds herself thinking that this one is a likely candidate for a pink ticket, a berth on the barge called Hell—or is it Heaven? As he takes his last sniff, he is practically pressed against Kudra, so that it is she whom he smells and not the memorable cargo of his terminated life.

Kudra is sorely embarrassed, for her jasmine perfume has long since weakened and its residue is mixed, she is certain, with grime and sweat and the body's other ardent emissions. However, the man's grin only widens at the unexpected lungful of her, and as he passes, in his hospital gown, through the

*marble gates, he heaves a sigh and mutters in a language
alien to her, "The perfect taco."*

*Puzzled by what he might have meant and ashamed that
she interposed herself between him and his farewell taste of
earthly existence, she feels that she had better be getting back
to where she belongs. She seems to recall a companion from
whom she has become separated. A bit apprehensively, she
reenters the wharf and makes her way laboriously to the
distant wall. Indeed, there are doors aplenty there, but eventually she does come upon the one to which she was directed.
It is marked neither* EXIT *nor* ENTRANCE *but*

ERLEICHDA.

And it is the right door.

So absorbed had Kudra been in the telling, Claude in the
listening, that the limousine managed to glide unnoticed to a
stop beside them. By the time the driver got out and opened
the rear door of the long black Mercedes, Kudra was finished, but the spell held them, like moths pinned to a blowing curtain. At last, the driver cleared his throat, piercing the
membrane surrounding them. Claude blinked and wiped moisture from his brow. The driver wondered how his employer
could be perspiring on such a night. "Will you join me?"
asked Claude. Even as he asked, he was assisting Kudra into
the car. What sort of weird carriage she was boarding she had
not a clue, but after the events of the past few hours, she was
prepared to accept virtually anything. The door closed. They
sat in the leather-scented darkness, thighs touching, eyes
open but unseeing, like waking dreamers, asleep yet lit by
dizzy lamps, prey to some silky fever. And in that condition
they were driven to Orly Airport, where Claude was to greet
his cousin, Marcel the Bunny, Marcel's new wife, V'lu, and a
certain friend of theirs, a man named Alobar.

THE BILL

For Darrell Bob Houston

THE BEET IS THE MOST INTENSE of vegetables.
The onion has as many pages as *War and Peace*, every one of
which is poignant enough to make a strong man weep, but
the various ivory parchments of the onion and the stinging
green bookmark of the onion are quickly charred by belly
juices and bowel bacteria. Only the beet departs the body the
same color as it went in.

Beets consumed at dinner will, come morning, stock a
toilet bowl with crimson fish, their hue attesting to beet's
chromatic immunity to the powerful digestive acids and thor-
oughgoing microbes that can turn the reddest pimento, the
orangest carrot, the yellowest squash into a single disgusting
shade of brown.

At birth we are red-faced, round, intense, pure. The crimson fire of universal consciousness burns in us. Gradually,
however, we are devoured by parents, gulped by schools,
chewed up by peers, swallowed by social institutions, wolfed
by bad habits, and gnawed by age; and by the time we have
been digested, cow style, in those six stomachs, we emerge a
single disgusting shade of brown.

The lesson of the beet, then, is this: hold on to your divine
blush, your innate rosy magic, or end up brown. Once you're

brown, you'll find that you're blue. As blue as indigo. And
you know what that means:

    Indigo.
    Indigoing.
    Indigone.

ABOUT THE AUTHOR

A former student of art and religion, TOM ROBBINS spent five years as an urban newspaperman before vanishing into the country to write fiction. Born in North Carolina and reared in Virginia, Mr. Robbins lives in northwestern Washington State.

Special Offer
Buy a Bantam Book
for only 50¢.

Now you can have Bantam's catalog filled with hundreds of titles plus take advantage of our unique and exciting bonus book offer. A special offer which gives you the opportunity to purchase a Bantam book for only 50¢. Here's how!

By ordering any five books at the regular price per order, you can also choose any other single book listed (up to a $5.95 value) for just 50¢. Some restrictions do apply, but for further details why not send for Bantam's catalog of titles today!

Just send us your name and address and we will send you a catalog!